Cold Case

KATE WILHELM

Cold
Case

MIRA®

MIRA

ISBN-13: 978-0-7783-2528-4
ISBN-10:   0-7783-2528-8

COLD CASE

www.MIRABooks.com

Printed in U.S.A.

Cold Case

1

Amy McCrutchen thought it was the first time she had ever really fallen in love. At fourteen, she had been in love before, but not for real. Billy Cook in fourth grade, then Johnny Stillman in sixth, but they didn't count, not like this. She and her best friend Greta had hovered on the outskirts of the big party that night, watching, commenting, giggling at the silliness of the celebrants, most of them in Robert's graduating class. Earlier, they had been banished from the family room, where the furniture had been pushed back against the walls for dancing. But they could still see everything, and they could help themselves to the plentiful food spread out on the dining-room table.

Earlier Amy had pointed out those she knew. "That's Chloe," she had said, indicating a girl in a red tank top and skintight white pants. "She and Robert are engaged. They're going to announce it tonight."

"She's pretty," Greta said.

Amy examined Chloe appraisingly. She had dark hair, almost

black, straight, and halfway down her back. Her pants were so tight she couldn't sit down, and she bulged a little in them. "Too fat." She spotted Jill Storey and pointed. "She's prettier."

Jill was blond and slender nearly to the point of emaciation. She wore a black sheath that clung to her torso like a sealskin and flared at the hips. Her hair was cut short and curled about her face. She was the best dancer, Amy had decided.

"Too skinny," Greta said judiciously after studying Jill, "but she is pretty. Boy, can she dance! Who's that old guy dancing? He's good, too."

"Dr. Elders. He's not a real doctor, not like my dad, just a professor. They live next door." Her father was a surgeon, and he had gone to bed an hour earlier. Amy lowered her voice to a near whisper. "Mrs. Elders has something wrong with her. Leprosy or something. Her skin peels off, and she smells bad. She doesn't come out much."

Greta grimaced. "She peels? Like a sunburn?"

"Not like that. Great big flakes of skin, with red patches. All over. Face, arms, everywhere. It's yucky."

"Gross," Greta said. "That's too gross."

"Yeah, she can't go in the sun, or where it's hot or anything. He comes over a lot, but not her. She has to be in air-conditioning all the time." Amy shuddered. "And she's real fat."

"Double gross!" Greta said. And for a time they were both silent, savoring the grossness.

They danced on the deck, helped themselves to party food and watched. And later, hot and sweaty, Amy said, "Let's sneak some beer."

Greta grinned and nodded, and they picked up glasses and made their way to the keg. Amy had half a glass and Greta was filling her own glass when Dr. Elders came out, closely followed by Amy's brother, Robert, both carrying empty glasses.

"Are you girls drinking beer?" Dr. Elders asked in a low, pained voice. "Amy, does your mother know you're drinking beer?"

Robert glared at Amy. "I told you kids to beat it, and put that beer down!" His words were a bit slurred and his voice was loud. "Get lost, brats!" Other guests had turned to look, to Amy's mortification.

Behind Robert, David Etheridge looked at her, rolled his eyes, shook his head and then winked. At that moment Amy fell in love.

Her mother walked out and said calmly, "Amy, why don't you and Greta make yourselves a sandwich and take it to your room."

Amy and Greta fled.

They had talked a long time, cursing Dr. Elders with the worst curse they could think of, that he would catch whatever it was his wife had, and that his nose would fall off. Secretly Amy wished the same fate on her brother, but she didn't say it aloud.

After Greta fell asleep, Amy was thinking dreamily of David, who had winked at her. She didn't know what color his eyes were, she realized. She had not paid attention before when she had seen him as just another one of boring Robert's stupid pals. She twisted and turned a short while, then put on a sweatshirt and jeans and cautiously made her way downstairs.

The party was a lot quieter, with piano and guitar music and a low murmur of voices the only sounds. She met no one and made her way out to the deck and beyond to a dogwood tree where she could see into the family room and hear the music but still be concealed in shadows.

There were only a few people left, gathered at the far end of the family room by the piano. The music was soft and dreamy, the spinning disco light turned off, and no one was dancing anymore. Several people were sitting on the floor; someone was sprawled on the sofa. Dr. Elders must have left, she was relieved to see. She spotted David, took a deep breath and sat down in the grass.

He would go out into the world and make a fortune, and the day she turned eighteen he would return and they would be free, run away, or maybe have a grand wedding with a diamond tiara and a ten-foot-long satin train for her, and a white tuxedo for him.

The kitchen lights dimmed, the patio door opened and her mother came out, paused a moment, then went to the far side of the deck, beyond the light from the family room and kitchen. Amy could not see her any longer, and she didn't think her mother could see her, either.

Her butt was getting cold and wet, she realized, shifting slightly, then she stopped moving. Jill Storey came out to the deck. She had a dark sweater over her shoulders. She passed the pale light to the family room and went to the railing on the side, where she became a dim figure. A lighter flared, then the glowing tip of a cigarette.

After a moment Robert followed Jill out, and Amy knew she was doomed. She was close enough for Robert to see her if he happened to glance her way. She scrunched down lower and pulled her sweatshirt up around her face.

Robert's voice, while not as loud as it had been yelling at her and Greta, was still quite audible as he drew near Jill.

"Hey, Jill baby, let's duck out of this, go up to my room for a little while."

"No way. Take Chloe," Jill said.

"Nah. You're the one, honey. We hit it off just right. Don't we?"

"I said no. Leave me alone."

"Not what you said a couple of weeks ago," Robert said.

"That was then. This is now."

"How 'bout you pay me back my twenty-five bucks, then? Take it out in trade?"

"You already took it out in trade. You got what you wanted, and so did I. Leave me alone," Jill said angrily.

Amy, freeing her eyes of the sweatshirt, watched the scene, frozen. Robert was slurring his words even more than he had been earlier, and he was swaying. He caught on to the rail near Jill. She moved back a step or two and he made a grab for her arm.

"You bitch! You just wanted the dough? Is that what you're telling me? You were in it for a lousy twenty-five? All smiles and come on, big boy, spread your legs for a lousy twenty-five. How many others? Spending money? Mad money? You liked it just fine then."

Jill's voice was furious as she said, "Liked it? Liked it! You disgust me, you and all the others. Stick it in, that's all you think of! Stick it in anything that moves. Think with your prick, that's all you know. Well, listen to me, you filthy ape. I don't need you now. I was going to be evicted, now I'm not. So beat it! Leave me alone!"

Amy drew in her breath sharply.

David had stepped out onto the deck. He crossed to stand close to Jill and Robert. "When you're ready to leave, I'll drive you home in your car," he said to Jill. "You're in no shape to drive to-night."

"So that's it," Robert cried. "You've got yourself a new patsy! I saw him pass you a key! You have the key to his apartment, don't you? You're moving in with him?" He was facing her, but his words were aimed at David as he said, "What's the deal for a key to an apartment—twenty-four-hour access? She'll keep her legs spread day and night for a whole apartment?"

"Robert, shut your mouth," David said in a low voice. "Go duck your head in cold water."

"You going to make me?"

Robert swung at David, who moved aside, deflected Robert's arm and sent him sprawling off the deck into a bush. With a cry, Jill ran to the kitchen door and entered. David watched Robert right himself and stumble to his feet, then he turned and reentered the house.

Amy realized that her mother had risen, taken a few steps toward the small group at the other end of the deck, then stopped and sunk back down onto a chaise, again out of sight. Amy pulled her sweatshirt up over her eyes again and hugged her arms around herself, shivering. It was a long time before her mother rose and went inside, and Amy didn't dare move until after that.

The next day, Sunday, the news spread like a grass fire—Jill Storey's body had been found that morning outside her apartment, partly hidden in shrubs. She had been strangled.

2

"I think the worst is over," Barbara Holloway said, standing at her office window. Shelley and Maria were at the matching window, all three watching a wind-battered tree across the street. Although it was still raining, sheets of rain were no longer racing down the street. The tree appeared safe now, but the street looked like a river, with wavelets surging up over the curb. The power had gone off half an hour earlier and, according to the radio reports, damage was extensive throughout the county.

"Another storm of the century," Shelley said. "Never mind that it's the third such in the past few years. I'm going to call Alex for a damage report."

She hurried out to her own office, with Maria following to call home, and Barbara hit the speed button for Darren's office at the rehabilitation clinic. She got voice mail, left a brief "we're okay" message, then called her father.

"I'm fine," Frank said, sounding grumpy. "The yard's an

unholy mess, and Norton's poplar tree is in the middle of the street. How are you fixed for lanterns at your place?"

"On my way to check any minute," she said. "I'll round up lanterns and candles. I imagine the clinic is using the generator, and Darren will probably be there all night. Todd went to his mother's house after school. He called a while ago. So we're all right. I guess you're marooned for a bit, aren't you?"

Across town, Chloe McCrutchen hung up her phone after speaking with Mildred Ochs. Chloe was smiling, then laughed softly. She walked through the sprawling house to her bedroom, where she found the key to the small apartment that had been built decades ago by Robert's parents, for his grandparents' use. Chloe opened the apartment door and entered, still smiling.

Over the past twenty-two years she had put on only a few pounds, and her hair was still dark and straight, but cut becomingly in a pixie style. She was in better shape physically than she had been when younger, as now she was a regular at a gym, where she worked out twice a week. She watched her diet carefully, didn't smoke or have any other habits that invited early impairment of any kind. She intended to live for a long time, and to live well.

The apartment adjoined the main house. It consisted of two rooms, with kitchen space and a sliding door to the deck and garden. After the rain stopped, she would open the windows and the sliding door, air it out, and turn on the refrigerator when the electricity was restored. Mildred would bring over a few things and she would dust and do whatever else needed doing. A tree had smashed into the apartment she had arranged for David Etheridge, she had wailed, and she had to find him a different one, but nothing was to be had in Eugene, not with the track trials coming up, and commencement, and all. He was due in on Sunday. She had one day, Saturday, to ready an apartment for him.

"Have you read his book?" Mildred had asked, and Chloe had to admit that she had not. "I'll bring you a copy and the *Times* review. It's…well, controversial, to say the least."

Chloe's smile widened. She had not read the book, but she had read about it, and about the demonstrations it had caused on campuses when David had gone on lecture tours.

"You know him, don't you?" Mildred had asked. "I believe he was in your graduating class, yours and Robert's. Apparently he's made quite a name for himself."

Chloe leaned against the door frame laughing. She could hardly wait to see Robert's face when she told him David Etheridge would be staying in their apartment during his lecture series in Eugene.

The last time they had all been in the same place at the same time had been at their graduation from the university and the subsequent parties, and now they would share the same roof. It was too bad that Robert would not be home until late. She knew he would probably use the storm as his excuse, and he would take time to conduct a little private business with a pretty staffer before leaving Salem for home. She and Robert both pretended she knew nothing about his meetings with pretty staffers; they had an arrangement they both understood and accepted. Robert was a state senator with big plans, and a party grooming him to take his part when the time came. She had a role to play in his game plan, and she played it well. But she could not suppress her smile, thinking about the news she would greet him with when he got home.

She also pretended that she had never suspected that Robert and David had fought over Jill Storey, and that Robert lost. He had come in that night with scratches and some twigs and leaves on his clothes, and had promptly vanished. She knew not exactly what had happened out on the deck but that it had something to do with Jill.

She was not surprised when Robert called an hour later to say he would not be home until the following afternoon. He said there was a big smashup on I-5 and traffic was at a standstill for miles. Her news could wait, Chloe thought, hanging up the phone. Let him have his night out first, that was fine with her.

Mildred Ochs arrived at ten the next morning, bringing a cooler chest and a bag of groceries, along with David's book and the review. Together they readied the apartment, and after Mildred left, Chloe skimmed the review of David's book. "Beguiling, with flashes of wit and humor throughout, the book deals with profound issues in language that is eloquent, simple and lucid, even lyrical at times. Etheridge argues cogently and to great effect that what he terms the delusions under which this nation was created took deep root and have grown over the centuries since the arrival of Europeans on the North American shores. He takes head-on the God myth, and goes on to the concept of empire building that is forever denied. The myth of laissez-faire comes next, and finally the sacredness of the Constitution. Anyone who is not disturbed by his arguments has not fully understood his book."

Slowly Chloe picked up the book and studied the cover. The title was *The American Myth Stakes.* She turned it over to regard David's photograph on the back. He seemed to have changed little over the years. Lean, with sharp features, an intent, nearly hungry look.

She walked to the back door, out onto the deck, thinking that possibly it had been a mistake to bring him into the apartment. Not that she could, or would, do anything about it now.

It was a beautiful day, warm with sunshine, trees and grass scrubbed clean and brilliantly green, with masses of flowers in full bloom, birdsong in the air. She felt a chill, in spite of the fine weather. Her malicious little act, she thought, could end up costing Robert dearly if it became known that he had housed David Etheridge, atheist, anticapitalist, apparently anti-American, anti-everything Robert stood for.

Robert McCrutchen was what the pundits called the perfect politician—articulate, charismatic, very good-looking, with great hair. Not quite six feet tall, just enough curl in his dark hair, just enough gray at the temples, bright blue eyes, ideal weight. He was the perfect candidate for whatever office he chose to run for. That day he was demonstrating a side his constituents had never seen.

"Are you out of your fucking mind!" Robert shouted. He threw the book across the room, his face livid. "Jesus Christ! Call Mildred back and tell her she has to find someplace else."

"Look at it this way," Chloe said. "It proves you're living up to the ideals you express. Free speech and all that. Open-minded, everyone has a right to have his own ideas. Besides, we don't have to announce it. If they demonstrate, it will be at the university, not here. Who's going to know?"

She had already used the argument that he wanted to keep the university faculty on his side, part of the base he was building as a conservative with liberal inclinations. Oregon liked its conservatives to be able to admit to at least a few liberal underpinnings.

Robert stormed out of the living room, heading for the family room and the bar. He was certain Chloe knew nothing of the encounter he and David had had that night so long ago. No one knew except David and him. He had not seen David again after that night. A lot of years had passed, he thought bitterly, and if it weren't for that goddamn book they likely would never have met again, and could even pretend that night had never happened. But an avowed atheist in his house! Chloe was right, they couldn't back out of it, not with Ochs involved. It wouldn't do to piss off the university provost. He was too ready to be pissed off, and getting him out of a spot like this meant Robert was scoring points. He would need support from the university.

Robert poured Scotch and downed it, then poured another and this time added water. He would think of a way to undo whatever damage that harebrained woman had done. He would think of something. He knew it would come out—that he had housed David Etheridge—and that it would be used against him in time. Everything came out eventually and he had kept his own record impeccable, without a blemish, anticipating full disclosure down the line. Prosecutor, then state senator, regular churchgoer, a faithful wife, good marriage, son in West Point. Perfect. Now this. He would have to think of something to undo it.

On Sundays Chloe and Robert joined a few others for a large brunch after church, and had a light supper early in the evening. They had just finished such a supper when Mildred Ochs called to say that David would be along in an hour or so. They would have dinner first and he would drive over afterward. He knew the way.

Robert glanced at his watch—six-thirty. Around seven-thirty he would wander over to Henry Elders's house, see how the old guy was doing, he said. He got no response from Chloe. It was hard to say who the aggrieved party was, he thought. By rights, it should be him, but she was acting put-upon. He shrugged, not really caring one way or the other.

An hour later, he walked around the hedge separating the two properties, then to the rear of Henry's house, along the walkway close to the hedge, the way he had gone as a kid when his mother had him carry over something or other. Strawberries, a pie or cake, something. He had hated doing that, dreading Mrs. Elders each and every time. When Amy got old enough to be the bearer of gifts, he had been relieved. It no longer presented a problem. The poor woman had finally died years earlier.

That evening he found Henry holding a sprayer, scowling at a rosebush. A harsh chemical odor hung in the air. They greeted each other, then Henry asked, "Are you satisfied with those Yard Guard people?"

Robert shook his head. "Who?"

"The landscaping company," Henry said impatiently. "Are they taking good care of your garden?"

Robert had no idea. As long as the lawn looked good, he paid no further attention.

"Never mind," Henry said. "I'll wander over next day or two and have a look. My roses have black spots. It's their job to take care of things like that, damn slackers." He motioned toward the house. "Come on in and make yourself a drink. I'm having gin and tonic. I'll wash my hands."

Then, sitting at a small table not far from the hedge, with drinks at hand, Robert told him about his predicament. "He's a radical, anti-everything apparently, and he'll live in my house for the next four weeks."

Henry thought a moment, then said, "Not in your house. In an apartment you own. He's just renting an apartment, that's all. Don't entertain him or mix socially, you're no more than a land-lord. Period. No problem."

"Lord, I hope you're right. Did you read his book?"

Henry nodded. "He's a crackpot, as you said, a radical. Re-belling against everything this country stands for. No historian takes him seriously. No doubt he and his publisher thought they had a shocker of a blockbuster, but it didn't work out like that. The masses didn't take to it, either." He made a waving gesture, dismissing the book.

They were both silent for a few minutes. Robert was listening for a car in the driveway next door. He would give David an hour or so to get there, settle in at the apartment, for Chloe to leave him and lock the door on their side.

"I always wondered," Henry said, breaking the silence, "how David got off without a real investigation after the death of that young student."

"Jill Storey," Robert said. "They said one of the vagrant dopers did it. They were thick around the campus in those days. Why wonder now?"

"They still are," Henry said. "No reason, really. Just wondered. He was romantically involved, and she was said to have been promiscuous. Was she two-timing him? Of course, she had a key to his apartment, and that alone made me wonder. I hadn't thought of that unfortunate incident for years." He lifted his glass and took a long drink. "Anyway, he got off with no more than cursory questions, I guess. Most of you young people did. Yet, they never accused a particular vagrant that I recall."

The driveway to the McCrutchen house made a sweeping curve from the street past the attached garage and front of the building, past a pull-off space for the apartment on the far side, then completed the arc back to the street. That evening, Chloe was standing at the open door to the apartment when David's car turned in. She waved him forward, motioning toward the pull-off parking space.

She was startled at how little David had changed. He still had a hungry look, still lean with hard, chiseled features, a lot of dark hair rather carelessly cut, now windblown. His picture on the book had prepared her for that, but there was something else, something harder to define. He looked a little distant, his expression seemed almost to be of amused contempt, or coolly judgmental. She remembered that his expression had made him strangely untouchable, unreachable in the past, and he had retained it from college days.

They shook hands and he said, "Mrs. Ochs explained the situation, and I saw the apartment she had intended for me. It seems it had unexpected company. A tree dropped in. It's good of you and Robert to open your door like this. Thank you."

Chloe had rather expected at least a touch of awkwardness on his part but he appeared completely at ease, amused even. He looked around the two rooms approvingly, then stood at the glass door to the rear deck for a moment. "Mrs. McCrutchen always had a lovely garden, as I recall. It's still lovely."

And it still belonged to Lucy McCrutchen, who still paid for its maintenance, Chloe thought bitterly. She and Robert were house sitters. No more, no less. She turned away and said, "That door is to the rest of the house. We keep it locked, but you're free to roam the garden, of course, and please make use of the deck. Robert's gone most of the week, but I'll be around if you need anything."

"I'm sure I won't," he said. "Thank you, Chloe."

She left by way of the deck, and if he thought it was a joke to keep the interior door to the house locked, while the deck was wide-open with sliding doors to other rooms, he did not mention it, or laugh out loud. But the glint of amusement had lit his eyes as he nodded.

3

Barbara was sitting on Frank's porch, watching the guys install an automatic watering system in his garden. Frank was not doing much more than observing and trying to keep out of the way, while Darren and Todd were doing the heavy lifting, or in this case, deep stooping and a lot of kneeling. Their gift for a belated Father's Day, Darren had said, surprising Frank with miles of coiled soaker hoses and a bag of fittings.

Frank left the garden to join her on the porch. "Fifth wheel," he said.

"I'm thinking of starting a new business installing watering systems," Barbara said. "I'd advertise heavily, stressing the experience of the crew. They did Darren's garden last week. Todd's idea."

"I'll provide a reference," Frank said. "Several."

"Can't have too many," Barbara said, laughing.

Darren and Todd both stood, and Barbara was struck again by how Todd had grown over the past year. He was as tall as his father, but only half as wide. He still had a lot of catch-up in store.

"Have you decided about going with them on their trip?" Frank asked.

"I'm not going. It's their thing. I don't think Todd will be going off on those jaunts much longer. This could be the last one, in fact. He's looking into an internship for next summer. You have to be sixteen to apply. He's into anything to do with climatology."

Todd was in advanced placement math and science classes and, after seeing the Al Gore film and reading his book on global warming, he had decided on climatology as a career. Darren had mused that he was Todd's age when he discovered he had a knack for physical therapy, and had focused on it afterward. Todd was just as focused now. They were going to spend two weeks and two days inspecting glaciers. They were allowing three weeks for the entire expedition.

Frank left her a few minutes later in order to start dinner, and she thought about the three weeks she would have alone. She was looking forward to it, she had come to realize. Sometimes she missed her privacy, and she missed her long river walks. It simply was no longer convenient; there seemed never to be a good time to get them in. She knew that Darren would never object to her going off alone for a walk, not by word, look, body language, anything, yet it didn't happen.

When she had agreed to move in with him, she'd insisted that they had to have a housekeeper, which was new for them both. Explaining that, if Darren did the cleaning, she would feel guilty, and if she had to wield a broom, she'd be as mean as a witch, she had made her case. No argument, they hired a housekeeper. Darren did most of the cooking, and Todd helped with that more often than she did, but she did a lot of the kitchen cleanup. No one complained. When she had to get off to be alone, there was the apartment over the garage, converted to an office suite for her use. Yet she was looking forward to three weeks of being alone.

For two weeks Robert McCrutchen had been accumulating every word printed about David Etheridge's appearances in Eugene. He was attracting large audiences, and an attendant unruly bunch of protesters outside Buell Hall whenever he spoke. He had given two lectures so far, two to go and then he'd be gone again. Robert was not certain he could bear to wait. The protesters might follow David home, demonstrate outside the house, have a sit-in or something, break windows... Robert brooded, hating his own reaction the times he had walked out onto his own deck at his own house, only to see David at the table at the far end. Each time, Robert had turned and retreated, with no more than a nod when David glanced his way.

He kept thinking of what Henry Elders had said, that David had gotten off easily following Jill's murder. Robert had a clear memory of seeing David join the party that night and head straight for Jill. He had passed her the key, and she had kissed his cheek. He had seen it, but he didn't think anyone else had. He asked Henry how he knew about the key and he said it had been in the newspaper accounts.

Robert had left Salem early on the second week of David's stay. He stopped to buy a box of Euphoria truffles, then went to city hall, and the police-records desk, where Bette Adkins was still working. He had known her in his prosecutor's days, and she did not question his right to copy the old file of the murder of Jill Storey. She was delighted with the truffles.

When he got home, Robert read the police reports carefully. They did not include the name of the tipster concerning the key.

Probably it had been an anonymous call. When David was asked about the key, he readily admitted that he had given it to Jill. He said she and her roommate intended to rent his apartment until September. David's roommate didn't want to let it go altogether, since good affordable apartments within walking distance of the university were scarce. The roommate would pay half the rent to hold it, but he would be in Forest Grove all summer working with his father, and planned to return to school in the fall and the women would move out. He and Jill's roommate confirmed David's story. The entire arrangement had been made late in the afternoon of the day of the party, and David had had the extra key made the same afternoon.

But, dammit, Robert thought, closing the file, someone had known about the key and tipped off the police. The newspaper accounts had been sketchy, as they always were, and he'd had no idea back then about the deal that had been made. He had believed Jill was moving in with David, as apparently others had believed from what little information had been released to the media.

Chloe appeared at his study door to say that she intended to serve a Greek salad and bread in ten minutes out on the deck and she had invited Henry to join them.

Robert started to object, and she said caustically, "It's safe. David's gone out."

Robert reflected that he had been a good prosecutor, thorough and dogged in his approach, and he had followed up on hunches until he found answers, or decided that none were to be found. He took a sheet of paper from his desk drawer and jotted down the word *Key,* then underlined it.

It nagged at him all through the light dinner on the deck, something about the damn key.

"I'm going to the Hult Center tonight, remember," Chloe said, interrupting his thoughts.

Robert nodded absently, and Henry said, "You look like a man with a thorny problem. Like perhaps a couple of really bad bills are coming that you have to vote up or down, and you're caught in the middle."

Robert laughed. "That would be simpler. No. It's Jill Storey's murder. You brought it back to mind, and it doesn't want to leave again."

"Any new thoughts on that old business?" Henry asked.

Robert shook his head. "No. And the way I see it right now there isn't going to be a way to learn anything new. Unless—" He stopped and his eyes narrowed in thought.

"For God's sake!" Chloe said, jumping up. "What are you up to? Why do you have that police file anyway? It was a nightmare twenty-two years ago. Leave it alone."

"Go on to your show," Robert said dismissively. "I'll clear this stuff when we're done."

She drained her wineglass, then left without another word.

"Unless?" Henry reminded him.

"Just thought of something. Or nothing. Are you finished here?" Robert stood, suddenly impatient to return to the police file.

Chloe drove straight to Nick Aaronson's apartment. She had not called first, but he'd better be home, she thought as she jabbed the bell.

He opened the door and stepped aside, then put his arms around her when the door was closed again. "Doll, we said not when Robert was in town. Remember?"

She pushed him away. "Well, he's in town, and there's something you should know. David Etheridge is in our apartment, on our property, and Robert is poking into Jill Storey's murder case."

Nick shook his head. "Whoa. Let's start back a step or two. Come on in."

He was her age, forty-three, six feet two, strongly built and muscular. He was a successful business-management consultant whose clientele included half-a-dozen dot coms, a few Realtors, a medical group, some developers. Privately, he consulted with a political-action group that never acknowledged his involvement. And he was Robert's chief advisor.

He led Chloe into his living room and nodded toward a gold-colored leather sofa. She sat and crossed her arms over her breasts, as if to say this was business.

"Okay," he said, sitting close by, "start back a little. Etheridge is in your apartment. Why?"

After explaining the situation, Chloe said, "But the important thing now is that old case. Jill Storey's murder. I saw the police file on Robert's desk. He's poking into it. Probably to try and hang something on David, but if it's opened, he'll be dragged in, too, even if he thinks it's a bonus if he comes on as a prosecutor and finds the killer, and it just happens to be David."

"What about that old case?" Nick said. His voice had become cold and remote. "It's history." He went to a bar across the room and poured bourbon for two, added water and ice and returned to hand her a glass as she recounted what she knew about the night of the party.

"Talk to him," she said finally. "I know they fought over her, and others might know it, too."

"Someone would have mentioned it if they'd known," Nick said.

"Tell him to leave it alone, to forget it. No one ever connected him and, as you said, it's history, unless he does something stupid."

"Robert wasn't under suspicion then. What's changed? Why would it be trouble for him now?"

"Then," she said, "we had just become engaged. You know, head over heels, all that. I had Travis six months later, and it could cause someone to ask now if the wedding was under the influence of a shotgun. I don't think it would be a secret very long that he's never stopped chasing women. He was known to have been a chaser then and had added Jill to his list. I told everyone that we went to his room together, but we didn't. After the fight on the deck, he disappeared, and Jill left in a hurry. Then, he was just the son of a loved surgeon and a well-regarded family, soon to be married, above reproach. Now he's a political figure with political enemies and a carefully created image to protect."

Getting to her feet, she regarded him for a moment. "He won't listen to me, of course, but someone needs to head him off. They'll make this his Chappaquiddick moment if he stirs it up. How much do you have invested in him?" she asked as she walked to the door. "I'm going to the theater."

At eight-thirty the next morning, Chloe was wakened by the sound of the landscape crew. She pulled a light cover over her face.

Out front, Petey started the lawn mower while Hal got to work on the foundation shrubs, and Netta took her tools around the house to the back flower border. There wasn't a lot to do this time of year, deadhead flowers, get rid of the rare weed that appeared, stir up the mulch a little.

Netta had worked her way through half of the border when she straightened and glanced at the house. She frowned and took a step or two closer, then dropped her pruner and ran to the deck.

Robert McCrutchen was sprawled half in and half out of the doorway, his head covered with ants. He lay in a pool of blood, dry and crusted. It was ringed with ants.

Netta screamed again and again.

4

"Sometimes, when I wake up, I'm afraid to move," Darren said softly that Sunday morning. "I'm afraid to open my eyes. I'm afraid it's been a dream, you'll be gone."

He stroked Barbara's hair gently, then kissed her eyelids.

"I'll pinch you every morning," she said, just as softly.

"I'll miss you terribly the coming weeks. I'll call as often as I can," he said.

Barbara could hear pots and pans clanging from the kitchen, and smiled. "I think you're being signaled."

"He used to have a police whistle. I'm glad he lost it." Reluctantly, Darren got out of bed. It was six-thirty, and Todd was more than ready to leave.

They had packed the truck the night before, leaving nothing to do that morning except have breakfast and be on their way. Very quickly it seemed, they were all walking out to the truck, which, outfitted as a camper, would be home for Darren and Todd for much of the coming three weeks.

Barbara refrained from hugging Todd. She was sure fifteen-year-old boys did not want to be hugged. Darren kissed her lightly on the lips, climbed into the truck, and they were gone.

She watched until the truck was out of sight, went back inside and said to the big tiger-striped cat, "It's you and me, pal. Get used to it." Nappy rubbed against her ankles.

Late Sunday afternoon one week later Barbara found Frank on a chaise on the back porch, with an open book on his lap. He appeared to be dozing.

Thing One and Thing Two came over to sniff her legs warily, suspicious of the alien cat smell she carried these days. She sat at the table and helped herself to iced tea.

Without opening his eyes, Frank said, "I'm not asleep."

"I thought you were reading something that instantly caused a case of dozing."

He heaved himself a little more upright and put the book aside. "Far from it. It's a book to be taken in small doses. A damn fine book."

She craned her neck to see what he had been reading. It was *The American Myth Stakes.*

"What do you think of it?" she asked, indicating the book.

"He makes his case," Frank said. "He's sharp, and he makes his case point by point. I haven't finished it yet, and maybe he'll falter, but I doubt it."

"Well, it seems that a lot of people don't share that opinion. The demonstrations have gone from ugly to uglier," Barbara said.

"A lot of people prefer to live in their own dream world," Frank said drily. "Just the idea of waking up to reality is too frightening to contemplate. And reality is what they have to face if they read the book with an iota of comprehension." He swung his legs over the side of the chair and replenished his own glass of tea. "Have you been following the Mc-Crutchen case?"

"Hard to avoid it," she said. "Anything else in the news these days? Our own homegrown saint, getting more virtuous day by day from all accounts." She glanced swiftly at the book, and the author's name. "Ah," she said, making the connection. "Etheridge. He seems to be in rather a spot, doesn't he?"

"He does. He's getting the bum's rush toward an accusation. And apparently for no reason other than what he's written and said. Ideas. Half the world's trying to kill the other half over ideas," Frank said.

In his voice there was a quiet fury that she seldom heard, and she was surprised at its intensity. "Maybe there's more evidence than what's been handed out to the media," she said.

"Maybe, but I doubt it. All we keep hearing about is what he's written, and he's damned and doubly damned for it each and every time."

Lucy McCrutchen felt adrift that afternoon. The shock of Robert's death had subsided, leaving a residue of despondency she could not shake. She felt strangely out of place in the house she had lived in for forty years, until Mac's sudden death two years before. Now she was a guest in the guest room, trying to make sense of her son's death, of what she had to do about the house, of how she felt about Chloe... She could not follow any one thought to a conclusion, but veered from one to another, back, in a hopeless loop.

She was sixty-seven, slightly built, with dark hair shot through with silver. When it all turned, she would be like a silver fox, Mac had said once. Theirs had been a good marriage, passionate for many years, and later one of comfortable companionship. But he had put in far too many hours in surgery, with patients, at the office. Little golf or vacation time had been allowed for, and it had caught up with him in the form of a fatal heart attack two years earlier. After forty-four years of marriage, it had been hard for Lucy to adjust to a new life, and she had found that she had to get out of this house, away from everything familiar for a time. She had gone to her sister in Palm Springs. Robert and Chloe had given up their town house to live here during her absence, and she had become the outsider.

She had never breathed a word about the scene she had witnessed on the deck the night of Robert's party and had managed to put it out of mind, most of the time at any rate. But he had brought it back from quiescent memory to active nightmare by having that police file in his possession when he was killed. Why? It seemed that the only explanation for having that file was connected to David's arrival.

The night of the party, had David driven that girl home, as he had offered? No one had seemed to know when anyone else left that night. Should she have told what she witnessed? The question had tormented her then, and now it was back.

The fear for her son had been overwhelming. Had Robert gone to his room, fallen asleep as he claimed? Chloe said she followed him to his room and took off his shoes. Lucy had never believed that. Chloe was not one to show that kind of consideration. But why would she have thought it necessary to lie?

Lucy was haunted by the fear that Robert had gone out after the girl, and that Chloe knew or suspected as much. Now the fear had returned with as much force and dread as before. She had accepted, *seized on,* she corrected herself, she had seized on the police conclusion that a transient, probably one on drugs, had committed the murder.

She and Mac had known Robert was promiscuous as a boy, and a womanizer as an adult, but they had never discussed it. She felt certain that Robert had been as great a disappointment to Mac as he had been to her, in spite of his successful career and his likely prospects for even greater achievements. Mac never once said as much, but Robert's public success faded in light of his private failings, in her eyes. He had become so malleable to managers, advisers, whoever was more powerful than he was, that she doubted he had believed in anything he championed. Very early she had deliberately turned her back on the positions he took publicly, refused to comment, even to talk about him in any but the most general terms, but his marriage had been too close to ignore. The marriage was a charade, a travesty, a marriage in name only, with a wife who seemed content to pretend all was well.

Lucy did not understand Chloe, and had never been able to develop any affection for her, in spite of all her good intentions. And now Chloe was a widow in Lucy's house, and she had to decide what to do about that. The loop started its paralyzing round again.

In spite of everything, she thought wearily, Robert had been the child in her womb, the infant she had adored, the son she had loved beyond all reason. In spite of everything, that was the underlying fact.

There was a soft tap on her door, and she said, "Come in. I'm not sleeping."

Amy entered. "I thought you were resting," she said, glancing at the bed, which had not been touched. "You didn't even lie down, did you?"

Lucy shook her head. "I can't seem to rest, or even sit still. It's all right. It will catch up with me and I'll sleep a week."

"Not here," Amy said. She walked to the window and stood gazing out. "You should just go back to Aunt May's place. There's nothing you have to do here now."

"But there's so much," Lucy said, thinking of Robert's clothes, papers, personal things, all to be sorted, stored, given away, something.

"Nothing *you* have to do," Amy repeated. "I'm going to my apartment to get some things, and be I'll back later tonight. I'll stay here with Chloe and help take care of things. I can do my work from here as well as anywhere else."

"Where is she?" Lucy asked.

"In her room." Amy's voice was without inflection. "Will you make your reservation, or should I do it for you? A flight tomorrow?"

Lucy rubbed her eyes. "God, I don't know." Amy turned to face her, a silhouette against the light. "It's a lot for you to have to cope with," Lucy said. "It's asking too much of you."

"Mother, no one asked me. It's okay. I'm fine. And," she added slowly, "someone has to stay here with Chloe. Not you."

After a moment Lucy nodded. "I'll make the reservation." It would be good to be out of this house, back in Palm Springs with her sister, May, she thought. May had kicked her husband out when he admitted to a long-standing affair with a woman twenty years younger than May, and the two sisters got along well.

Lucy crossed the room to her daughter and embraced her. Amy was a godsend, she thought, as she often had before. Tall, with broad shoulders for a woman, but slender and muscular, more like her father than like Lucy. Her hair was dark and curly, and her eyes so dark blue they sometimes looked black. "Thank God I have you," Lucy said. All these single women, she thought with a pang. Me, May, now Chloe, Amy. Amy and her live-in boyfriend had separated a year before. All these single women, those philandering men.

Amy kissed her cheek and drew back. "I'll tell Travis I'm leaving. There's plenty of food in the fridge, or you can order something in, whatever. It's probably going to be pretty late when I get back. Don't wait up. At least try to get some rest," she said.

Amy found her nephew in the family room in front of the television. She doubted that he had been paying attention to it, for the sound was muted and he was staring at the sliding door when she entered. That was the doorway where his father's body had been discovered.

She sat down in a chair near him. "Are you all right?" she asked.

"Yeah, sure," Travis said.

He was wearing jeans and an old T-shirt. His feet were bare, and suddenly he was the kid she had always known, not the strange young man in a uniform who had attended the funeral.

She told him her plan to go to Portland, collect a few things, make some arrangements there and return later. "I'll stay down here and help Chloe out for the next few weeks," she said.

He nodded. "That's good. I wish I could stay. The army makes decisions for me these days." He sounded bitter.

She stared at him, taken aback. "I thought you liked it."

"Dad made the arrangements, you know, pulled some strings, whatever it took, and then told me. I wanted to go to medical school, but I was headed for West Point."

"Can you get out of it?"

"Sure. In six more years. I talked to a lawyer, that's what he told me. They don't let go once you've signed that piece of paper." He laughed, but it sounded suspiciously like a sob. "I'm government property."

Time was doing a strange dance of speeding up incredibly fast, or stopping altogether, Amy thought, driving to Portland. This was Sunday, and a week ago, on Monday morning David Etheridge had called her and told her that Robert had been shot dead. It seemed like only hours ago, yet a lifetime ago. Simultaneously instant and distant. A disconnect in her brain. She had thrown on clothes, put a few things in a backpack and left within minutes of the call. She had returned to her own apartment for a very brief time only to pick up something suitable for a funeral, a few clothes to get her through the week.

Thank God she had not seen Robert's body, she had thought many times that week. By the time she arrived at the house, the police were there and a screen had been put up around the end of the deck. Chloe had been in a state of shock, white-faced, eyes wide with horror, and she kept mumbling about ants. Sitting at the kitchen table with coffee at hand, suddenly she had screamed and jumped up, rubbing her arms, shaking her hair, screaming that ants were all over her. Amy had put her to bed and called her doctor. It was a nightmare scenario, the shocked garden worker shaking on the deck with one of the men holding her hand, Chloe screaming in the kitchen, police everywhere.

David had called Lucy to tell her, afraid she would hear it on a newscast. He had not called Travis—he hadn't known there was a Travis—and Amy made the call when she arrived. Henry Elders had been hovering, making coffee, trying to be useful. He went to the airport to pick up Lucy later in the day, and again to pick up Travis. She had felt both grateful for his help, and at the same time a thought had persisted that he was just a nosy, interfering old man with nothing to do except get in the way.

Resolutely, she focused on what she had to do at her apartment—pick up more clothes, her laptop, the job she was working on. She would clean out the refrigerator, stop the newspaper delivery, put a hold on mail, call a friend or two.

★ ★ ★

It was after eleven when she pulled into the driveway in Eugene again. It looked as if every light in the house was on and she didn't want to talk to anyone, not right now. She had stopped for a coffee, and carried it and her purse inside with her, leaving everything else for later. She was very tired, she had realized driving back down on I-5. Emotional fatigue, she thought, dredging up the phrase from a long-ago class in psychology. As enervating as strenuous physical activity. More, she decided. She continued through the house to the deck.

She had intended to sit beyond the house lights, in the chair her mother had used the night of Robert's graduation party, but she saw light streaming from the apartment and, on the deck there, she could see David seated. Slowly she walked over to join him.

"I never did thank you for taking charge last week," she said in a low voice. "I'm grateful you were here and that you knew what to do. Thanks."

"It's been a tough week," he said. "Sit down, Amy. How are you holding up?"

"I'm okay. Mother and Travis will both leave tomorrow, Lawrence will go back to Salem, I hope, and things will quiet down. I'll hang around for a week or two."

Lawrence Tellman was chief of staff at Robert's Salem office. He had arrived on Monday evening and he and Nick Aaronson had assumed command of publicity, appointed a spokesman and, as soon as the police gave them the go-ahead, had taken charge of Robert's study, packing up official papers, doing whatever they needed to do. Lawrence had said he would take care of the Salem office and the apartment, and he had assured her that anything of a personal nature would be packed up and shipped to them.

Amy sipped her coffee. "David, do you know why Robert had that old police file? Jill Storey's murder?"

"No," he said quietly.

She waited, but he left it at that. Slowly, feeling she was on shaky ground, she said, "You know what they're saying, that because you turned up now, Robert was reminded about something he had overlooked before, something concerning you, and that he might have wanted the case reopened."

It seemed a long time before he responded. "I read the newspapers, too. I know what they're saying."

"Have you considered a lawyer? I think you need someone to intercede before this gets even worse."

David laughed. "What's your job? What do you do these days?"

"I work for a company that does computer-assisted architectural plans. I do family houses."

"Ah. You draw the lines that connect the joists and such, but sometimes the lines can lead you off the page. I had nothing to do with Jill's death, and nothing to do with Robert's," he stated.

"I hope the police will accept that," she said in a low voice.

"We'll see."

"I was talking to Travis earlier, and I realized he's just about the age you were then—you, Robert, Jill, all of you, twenty-one, twenty-two. You all seemed so grown-up to me, so sophisticated. Now, looking at Travis, I see a kid, uncertain, awkward in ways, groping for something. My point is that you could really be in trouble. Robert was about the age that Travis is now, and he could have been as confused as Travis is now. He could have seen or heard something that he misinterpreted. Or something else made him go after that file. Whatever it was, just by bringing it home when you turned up again puts you in danger."

They both remained silent as she drank her coffee. Then she rose. "I'd better go put my gear away. Good night, David."

5

It was twenty minutes before five on Monday when Barbara escorted her last client at Martin's to the door. It was time to take down her *Barbara Is In* sign, wrap things up and go for a walk. She wanted to check out the Rose Garden, which she had not visited all spring.

She patted Rosita Marcos on the shoulder and reassured her again that her landlord couldn't force her and her three children to move in ten days. "A letter is all it will take," she said. "Take your time to find another apartment, and don't worry about it."

As Rosita walked out, and before Barbara could close the door, a tall man reached past Rosita to hold it open.

"I have to talk to you," he said. "Now." His tone made it a demand, not a request, and his hold on the door was firm.

Rosita looked as if she would come to Barbara's defense if necessary, but Barbara waved her away. "It's all right," she said. "I'll be in touch with you." Then coolly she said to the man holding the door, "I don't intend to talk to you on the doorstep. Come on in." She was well aware that Martin would be keeping an eye out, the way he did every time the door opened when she was in the restaurant. She glanced at the kitchen door and, as expected, Martin was standing there. She nodded to him, and he withdrew.

She led the way to her table and motioned to a chair across from hers. "Five minutes," she said, "then I'm out of here."

The man was sharp faced with prominent bones. Dressed in faded chinos, a worn T-shirt, deck shoes without socks, he wore the almost uniform summer outfit for a lot of guys, she thought, with nothing at all distinctive about him, except for a handsome watch on his wrist that looked expensive, like the kind she had seen advertised in *The New Yorker* magazine. His hair was thick and dark and he could use a haircut, she thought.

"I don't need more than five minutes," he said in the same clipped tone he had used before. "One question. Is that legitimate? Can they do that?" He pulled a folded paper from his pocket, flattened it and tossed it down in front of her.

She picked it up. It was a court order. He was enjoined not to leave the immediate area pending a police investigation. "Mr. Etheridge? You're David Etheridge?"

"Yes. Can they do that?"

She nodded. "They can, and they have done it. Mr. Etheridge, I suggest that we have a little talk back in my office. We have to clear out of here by five, and I think you may need more than five minutes to consider your options."

He looked murderous, furious. A pulse was throbbing in his temple and his lips had become a tight line. "One more question before we go anywhere. What happens if I just ignore that?"

She closed her laptop and picked up her purse, fished out her keys, then said, "Probably a bench warrant, arrest, jail time. Do you want to call it quits here and now, or follow me to my office?" She stood, and he jumped to his feet and snatched up the court order.

He swore in a low savage voice. "Let's go. I'll follow you."

David Etheridge was at her heels when she unlocked the outer office door and entered, motioning for him to follow. The office was empty, as Barbara had known it would be. She had told Maria she would not be back after she finished at Martin's, and Shelley was either still in court, or on her way home.

Inside her own office, she took her seat behind her desk, and he sat opposite her, still tight faced but no longer appearing ready to erupt.

"Sorry I snapped like that," he said. "The situation is that I'm due in San Francisco next weekend. I leave here on Saturday to give a talk Sunday afternoon at a conference, and I intend to make that conference. The following week, Wednesday, I have a reservation to fly to Britain, but they demanded that I surrender my passport."

"How long are you planning to be in Britain?" Barbara asked.

His answer was in the same clipped manner as before when he said, "I have a one-year appointment as a teaching fellow at Oxford."

Barbara leaned back in her chair. "It's possible that I might get a temporary stay for a trip to San Francisco of a limited duration. You might have to post a bond, however." She regarded him for a moment, then said, "Mr. Etheridge, I think we might as well discuss the murder of Robert McCrutchen, and the reason why they are focusing on you, as apparently they are doing."

"There is no reason," he said. "The night he was shot, I had dinner with two acquaintances who were passing through town, and returned to my apartment after ten. Robert was the last person in the world on my mind that night. I had no quarrel with him, no words of any kind with him, and absolutely no cause to want him dead or alive. Ms. Holloway, he was insignificant, a nothing in my world, a two-bit small-town politician whose life or death meant nothing to me. The last time I saw him before this trip was twenty-two years ago, and in the intervening years I never heard a word from him. Since I've been back this time, I never spoke a word to him, and he never spoke a word to me. There is no reason."

"Isn't it a bit strange that you were in his house for weeks without exchanging a word with him?" Barbara asked.

"I think he decided it was politically expedient for him to keep his distance from me," he said after a moment. "And the apartment is not part of his house in the way you suggest. It is a totally separate unit, self-contained. I ended up in it as the result of a storm that wiped out the one I was supposed to have occupied."

"Okay," she said. "Let's back up a little. You knew him twenty-two years ago. Mr. Etheridge, I've been reading about this case in the newspapers, and there are hints that you and he were on bad terms years ago. Was there an unresolved quarrel, an ongoing argument?"

When he hesitated, she said impatiently, "I can't argue your case for a stay unless I know why the police thought it necessary to get that court order."

He told her about Jill Storey and her friend taking over his half of the apartment years before. "I was going to leave on Monday morning. Jill and her roommate planned to move into the apartment on Tuesday. Robert had been making a play for Jill and he thought she was moving in with me and got sore. He was drinking that night, and Jill told him to get lost. She left the party soon after that, and the next morning she was found dead. Strangled. The case was never solved. I have no idea why he had that old police file."

It all depends on how you slant it, Barbara thought, but she didn't press him about the past. Instead she asked him to tell her something about the trip he had planned for the coming weekend.

An international historical society conference, he said, was attended by historians from around the world, an annual event. "It goes on for a week. We give papers, talk, debate, argue, and quite possibly we take home a new perspective. In the eyes of the world at large, it's unimportant, of course, but these are the people who write the history books."

"I assume it's considered an honor to be invited to speak at the conference. Is that correct?"

"Yes. The fellowship is also an honor."

She nodded. "Of course. Mr. Etheridge, tell me exactly what you are asking me to do."

"Get that damn court order rescinded," he said coldly. "I thought I had made that plain."

"What I can agree to do at this time is try to get a temporary stay on the order, long enough for you to participate at the conference. When do you have to be in England?"

"Early September. But I want to go in time to find an apartment, to meet people there, and to have a little vacation time," he said.

"I advise you to cancel that flight for now. I don't believe a stay that far in advance is possible. By late August, if not sooner, the case of McCrutchen's murder may well have been closed, and the matter will become moot and you can reschedule your trip," Barbara said.

"Are you going to argue it, as well as next week's plan?"

"No. I believe I would lose both arguments if I overreached, as that would be doing."

A muscle in his jaw was working, and the temple vein was throbbing again. His voice was steady and tightly controlled, like an icicle dripping, when he said, "I'll write a check for your expenses." He took his checkbook and wallet from his pocket, and handed her two cards. "My cell phone number. The address is my New York apartment, but I've sublet it. This is a mail-forwarding service I'll be using. I don't have an address for the moment." He wrote a check and passed it across the desk to her, then stood. "If it isn't enough, I'll send you another check. If there's a refund, send it to my mail-service address. Call me when you know something. I have two more seminars, Tuesday and Thursday, seven until nine, but they run later than that. And one more public address for Friday night. Saturday morning I'll be out of the McCrutchen apartment and on my way to San Francisco, one way or the other." With that he turned and went to the door. "I need to hear something as soon as you can arrange it."

Barbara left her desk and followed him, but he was already closing the outside door by the time she reached Maria's desk.

On Tuesday Barbara got in the walk she had put off the previous day. It felt good to walk a long, long time, she was thinking as she headed back to her car. She had driven over from the office and, hot and sweaty from her walk, decided to head for Frank's house, just a few blocks away. He was following the Etheridge story, and he would find this new development interesting, she suspected. Also, he might invite her to dinner.

Frank had been working in the garden and was just out of the shower when she arrived. "Iced tea on the porch, or help yourself to wine," he said by way of greeting. "That watering system is great, by the way. Exactly right."

She took wine, and he took a glass of tea, and they sat on the back porch. The two cats eyed them, but apparently were too comfortable in the shade of a rosebush to do more than acknowledge their presence.

"You'll never guess who tracked me down at Martin's yesterday," Barbara said.

"So I won't try. Who?"

She told him about the visit and the follow-up research she had done. "That's a pretty impressive bunch, the historical society. People like Barbara Tuchman and Arnold Toynbee were regulars, and now Jared Diamond, and others like that. Big names, Pulitzer prize winners. I never heard of most of them."

"So, you going to get to what the judge said, or sit and tease awhile?" Frank asked.

She laughed. "He'll have a decision tomorrow. I left a message on Etheridge's machine to that effect. I'm glad he didn't take the call. He tends to seethe and drip ice. He called McCrutchen a two-bit small-town politician, and no doubt, in his eyes, I'm a two-bit small-town shyster ambulance chaser, and he can't wait to shake the dust of this berg."

"It's fifty-fifty whether they'll let him go for even a few days," Frank said. "And out of the country? Not by a long shot, unless they have the case sewed up tight and he isn't it."

"If I have to tell him that, maybe I'll get lucky and just leave another message," she said. "And if my luck really holds out, I'll never have another face-to-face meeting with him. I'm afraid he could be in for a bad time. The D.A.'s assistant, Allen Durand, called him a person of interest in the McCrutchen murder investigation."

Frank nodded, apparently not surprised. "If the judge rejects his plea, and he goes anyway, they'll arrest him and he'll be in jail, and if they then charge him with murder, bail will be out of the question. He'll sit in jail until a trial. You may not be out of it altogether yet."

"He doesn't know me from a Sunday-school teacher. I'd bet that he was going down a list hunting for someone who would see him yesterday and he came across me, holding open house at Martin's and accessible. Simple as that."

"Maybe," Frank said. "I'm going to his talk on Friday night. Want to come along?"

She looked at him in surprise. "You really have taken to his writing, haven't you?"

He nodded. "Brilliant work. I want to hear him expound on it. If that's what he does in these talks. I finished his book, and I recommend it highly. Friday night?"

"Can't," she said. "I have a date with a couple of friends for dinner and then a movie, or maybe dancing."

She thought of the newscasts she had seen in the past weeks and said, "Dad, you realize that those demonstrations have gotten worse and worse? Near riots, in fact."

"I'll wear armor," he said.

On Wednesday Barbara called David Etheridge and was sorry when he picked up. Crisply she said, "You have a limited leave of absence from the court order, beginning on Saturday. On Tuesday morning you are to check in personally to Judge Carlyle's clerk no later than 10:00 a.m. It was the best I could do."

There was a prolonged silence, then he said, "Ms. Holloway, I'd like to stop by for a minute or two. Is there a time I could do that?"

"Of course," she said. "I'll be in the office from three until five."

That afternoon, she braced herself when David Etheridge arrived.

He had dressed up for the occasion, she thought. He had put on socks.

Etheridge sat down and regarded her steadily. "I want to apologize. I was too infuriated to think clearly and I was rude. I'm sorry," he said.

He did not look or sound sorry, she thought, and simply nodded.

"Monday evening I stopped to consider the implications of that court order," he continued. "I have no legal training, but it seems to me that they intend to charge me with Robert's murder, and quite possibly with Jill Storey's murder, as well. They don't have any evidence, but they want to keep me available while they search for some. Is that near the mark?"

"Perhaps," Barbara admitted.

"I told Chloe McCrutchen that I'd be out of the apartment altogether Saturday morning. I'll fly to San Francisco and come back Monday night in order to check in on Tuesday morning. And I'll find a motel or hotel, possibly another apartment. I'll let you know where it is, where I am. Is that satisfactory?"

"It is. But why let me know, Mr. Etheridge? Are you leaving out one of the steps here?"

Suddenly he grinned. From stern as a hanging judge to a good-natured fun-loving guy in a flash. That was the transformation the grin made. "Yes," he said. "The missing step. If I'm charged, will you be my defense attorney?"

"If it happens, putting a defense together requires a great deal of time and complete cooperation. Will you agree to that?" Barbara asked.

"Of course. When I get back, I'm done with the seminars, no more public talks and finished with my part of the conference. I'll have as much time as it takes. I said just a few minutes today, and I meant it. I'll call on Tuesday."

Saturday morning Barbara was roused from sleep by her cell phone. The night before she had gone out for dinner with her two best friends, then to a movie, and afterward Janey had said, "Let's go dancing!" They had done that, too. It had been a late night, and that morning the last thing she wanted to hear was a phone ringing.

She groped for it on the nightstand and mumbled her name, then was jolted wide-awake by Frank's voice, "Bobby, last night David Etheridge was attacked, savagely beaten. He's in surgery, critical condition. He may not make it."

6

There hours after her morning call, Barbara drove to Frank's house. She would have been better off staying in bed, she thought grumpily, for all the good she had accomplished. At Frank's enquiring look, she said, "Nothing, nowhere. I got as high as an assistant to an assistant to the administrator of patient affairs, and that pipsqueak quoted rules explaining why he couldn't tell me anything beyond what was reported in the media. Etheridge is out of surgery and in intensive care, critical condition. His parents have been notified and are on their way. I did get him to accept my card and a message for them that I've been retained as Etheridge's attorney, and I welcome a call from them. He may or may not remember to pass the word."

The police had been as fruitless. Assault, attempted murder. Investigating. Period.

"I can't do a thing about it," she said. "We didn't get to a contract, so officially I'm not even his attorney in the eyes of the law."

There were times when Frank would have been justified in saying I told you so, but he had refrained in the past, and he did so again when she lapsed into a moody silence. "Well, you tried the aboveboard approach, let's see if Bailey has any better luck at the back door," he said.

While she was on her own search for information, Frank had called Bailey Novell, their investigator, who had a reliable contact at city hall. Getting a tip would depend on whether the man was working that Saturday or, if not, if Bailey had an in with someone else who was.

After Barbara left, Frank picked up the thoughts he had been entertaining upon her arrival. The show David Etheridge had put on the night before had been impressive.

When he came onstage, a large screen at one side of a podium had been lit to display a map of the world with the North American continent centered. He used graphics to show the rise and growth of a great nation. With devastating exactitude he had discussed the landing of the first ships from Europe, the first colonies and then the expansion, with acquisitions purchased or taken by force. He talked about the native inhabitants, bought, conquered, vanquished, resettled. He called it ethnic cleansing.

The expansion extended far beyond the shores, out into the Pacific Ocean.

It was show-and-tell, Frank thought, but effective show-and-tell in a way that words on a page didn't convey. As David talked, dates had appeared in a column down the side of the big map, and on the other side, a chart with a line tipped with an arrow, indicating an inexorable upward path, pointing toward what appeared to be a Roman emperor draped in an American flag instead of the familiar white toga and cape. The point of the arrow had come disturbingly close to the figure.

Frank was distracted from his recall by his house phone ringing. Bailey was checking in.

"They say it was a hate crime," he said. "Some kind of club or loaded pipe was used. Fractured skull, broken ribs, punctured lung, other injuries. A paper with the word *Antichrist* was under him. It's touch and go if he'll make it. My pal said the word is that if he kicks, the McCrutchen case will be closed." He added what little detail he had been able to learn, and said he'd be around until dinnertime if needed.

After passing the report on to Barbara, Frank sat on the back porch and thought about the events following the presentation the night before. Earlier in the evening he had glimpsed an old friend, Kirby Herlihew, and he had seen him again as the audience began to leave. Kirby had waved him over to the side of the stream of people on the way out.

"Don't go out that way," he had said, motioning toward the main exits. "Come on, a bunch of us are leaving by a side door. They'll use it for Etheridge in a little while. He walks over so there's no car to destroy."

Kirby taught European history, a round little man with a startling mop of white hair that forever looked windblown. He hurried, and he and Frank joined several others near the stage. "Rumor is that it's going to be uglier than ever tonight," Herlihew said in a tight voice.

Well, Frank thought, the rumor had been dead-on. Cars smashed, windows broken, fights, police making arrests right and left, the riot squad deployed. It had been bedlam for several blocks around the university. He had escaped it by going out the little-used side door, down a dark alley and taking a detour of several side streets. Sirens, screams, whistles and raucous music ebbed and swelled a few blocks away. Later he watched the near-riot on television.

A few minutes after four Barbara got a call from Lucien Etheridge, David's father. "Ms. Holloway, we—my wife and I—
would like to talk to you. Why did David hire you? To do
what?"

"Where are you?" she asked. "I want very much to talk to
you, also."

"At the hospital. In the waiting room at intensive care."

"I'll be there in a few minutes," she said.

Barbara spotted Lucien Etheridge as soon as she entered
the waiting room. The resemblance to David was striking, the
same sharp bone structure, lean and muscular body, and,
although the father had gray hair, even that was very like
David's. Thick and a little too long. He was holding a bulging
manila clasp envelope.

She approached him. "Mr. Etheridge, Barbara Holloway."

He stood and held out his hand. It was a big hand with prominent veins and enlarged knuckles. He indicated a seated woman
and said, "My wife, Dora." She nodded without speaking. Her
eyes were reddened and teary. They both appeared to be in their
sixties, and she did not look well. Whether it was shock and fear,
or illness, was impossible to tell. Dressed in a blue-and-white knit
turtleneck with a wine-colored, stretched-out cardigan over it,
gray pants and sneakers, she looked as if she had dressed hurriedly, with no thought of appearance or season. Her hair was
also gray, cut short and combed back. She wore no makeup.

"There must be someplace we can talk privately," Barbara said.
"I'll ask at the desk."

"There's a consultation room. We talked to a doctor there,"
Etheridge said.

Barbara spoke to a nurse at a desk near the door, and presently they entered the consultation room. She imagined this was where terrified parents got word about a child, a lover learned the fate of a beloved one. She shuddered.

The room was furnished with a round table with four chairs, two more against the wall, and nothing else. They sat at the table and Etheridge leaned forward. He appeared to be so tightly wound that a touch might send him flying apart. "Why did David need an attorney? You're a defense lawyer, aren't you? We've read about you, some of the cases you've defended. Why did David hire you?"

"You know about Robert McCrutchen's murder? That David was renting an apartment on the McCrutchen property?"

He nodded impatiently. "What's that got to do with David?"

"Maybe nothing," she said, and told them about the court order. "I don't know what their reason was."

Dora Etheridge drew herself up and cried, "He had nothing to do with it! Nothing! That's crazy!"

"He was on the scene, on the property," Barbara said, "and as far as I know that's the only direct connection. For now, of course, it's all on hold." Then choosing her words with care, she added, "He retained me first to get the stay on the court order and, after that was done, to agree that if it came to an accusation, I would represent him. I agreed to do so."

Dora was nearly incoherent as she protested that they couldn't accuse him of anything, and Lucien Etheridge exclaimed in a disbelieving way, "They're out of their minds!"

Barbara waited a moment, then said, "If I continue to represent his interests in whatever develops, since he is not capable of signing an agreement authorizing me to do so, I'll have to ask you, Mr. Etheridge, to sign for him."

"How much?" he asked.

Dora turned on him furiously. "What difference does it make?

Who cares how much? They might put him in jail. They could kill him. I'll sign it, Ms. Holloway."

"No charge to you," Barbara said. "David already gave me a retainer. He didn't have time to wait for the agreement to be drawn up, and we had an appointment to take care of it on his return from California on Tuesday."

Mr. Etheridge rubbed his eyes. "Sorry. I didn't mean that the way it sounded. What can you do? I won't give you the right to make life-and-death decisions."

Barbara shook her head. "No, and you must not give that right to anyone." She looked from him to his wife. "But there are other things that should be done. He has a leased car that should be returned to the company, and the apartment should be closed, his personal belongings stored for safekeeping. The conference organizers should be notified and airline tickets canceled. When he is removed from intensive care, he should be in a private room. When he's released from the hospital, he'll need a safe place for his convalescence, with adequate help until he's able to care for himself again. With your authorization I can arrange all of it, and I'll be able to get information about his attack, and keep up-to-date with his progress here. I can appoint a family spokesman to deal with the media, and I advise you to avoid them and, if cornered, say simply that you have no comment."

Dora's expression had changed when Barbara spoke of David's recovery. From despair and dread, it had changed to a look of hope. She nodded. "He'll need all of that done for him. I want it done for him."

Her husband took her hand. "We'll both sign it."

Barbara took the document from her purse and waited for Mr. Etheridge to read and sign it, then pass it to Dora. She didn't read it, just added her signature.

"I'll need his keys to the apartment and the car," Barbara said.

Silently Mr. Etheridge undid the clasped envelope and emptied the contents onto the table—a cell phone, digital camera, keys, a ring, his watch, wallet, a few papers. Dora Etheridge swallowed hard and turned her head away and her husband picked up the keys and handed them to Barbara.

"Take what you need," he said heavily. "In fact, take it all and put it with the rest of his things. He'll want it all when he gets out of here."

He pushed everything back into the envelope and handed it to Barbara. She met his gaze then and realized with great sympathy that he had not found the same hope in her previous words that Dora had. He did not expect his son to live. He looked away as she reclasped the envelope.

"Do you have a place to stay yet?" she asked.

They said they hadn't thought that far ahead.

"If you'd like, I can get you a motel not far from here, or a hotel room downtown, whichever you prefer."

They wanted something as close as possible to the hospital, and she said she would arrange for a room, secure it with her credit card, and they could present theirs when they checked in. Dora gave her a cell phone number, and very soon afterward Barbara left, and Lucien and Dora Etheridge returned to the waiting room to resume their vigil.

At a little after six Barbara called Frank. She told him what she had been up to, then said, "I'm going to the apartment to collect David's belongings before someone decides to ransack the place or the cops move in. I left a message for Bailey to pick up someone and meet me there so they can move the car. When you talked to him, did he say if he'd be around?"

"They could be out to dinner," Frank said. "Come by the house and pick me up. I'll drive the car back. I'll leave another message for Bailey." He fully understood that if David died, the police would seize his belongings, if they decided he was guilty of McCrutchen's murder. If everything was in Barbara's hands, she would have a little leverage to get some information. She said she would be there in fifteen minutes.

She was prompt, and he was ready to leave with her. "I got his parents a room," she said, on their way to the apartment. "But I bet they won't use it tonight. They'll stay right there at the hospital."

He nodded. It was exactly what he would do if it were Barbara in that bed in intensive care. He told her about the alley he had used after leaving Buell Hall. "Pretty dark, led to a quiet side street that had few lights and no rowdy troublemakers. They were all out front. It's hard to imagine anyone unfamiliar with that side door following Etheridge without his noticing."

"Not a crime of impulse, but a calculated ambush?" Barbara asked.

"Maybe," he said.

She drove along Franklin, past the university, past a strip of commercial properties, fast food, gas station, grocery, then turned off to the right, two more blocks, another right turn. This was a quiet, old neighborhood, six or seven blocks from the university, an easy, pleasant walk most of the time on shaded side streets. There were old-growth trees, a lot of shrubbery, deep shadows that evening, houses set far back on wide lots.

"If I had ambush in mind," Barbara said, "I'd pick a neighborhood like this to carry it out."

Frank made a grunting sound.

Barbara spotted the house number over the garage, pulled in and parked at the front entrance. They both went to the door. A very attractive, dark-haired young woman opened the door.

Barbara introduced herself and Frank, then said, "We are both attorneys, retained by Mr. and Mrs. Etheridge to collect their son's belongings and the automobile under lease. I didn't want to alarm Mrs. McCrutchen by entering the apartment without notifying her first."

"Oh. I'm Amy McCrutchen. The apartment is over there." She pointed to the side of the house. "May I see your identification first?"

"Of course." Barbara handed her the signed authorization, and showed her driver's license.

When Frank offered his own license, Amy blushed faintly and shook her head. "That's all right. Shall I open the door for you?"

"We have the key," Barbara said. "You're Robert Mc-Crutchen's sister, aren't you? My deepest sympathy for your loss."

"Thank you," Amy said. "You can park over there closer to the door. Would you like a hand with it all?"

Before Barbara could respond, Frank said, "That would be helpful, Ms. McCrutchen." He glanced at Barbara. "You want to move the car? I'll just walk on over."

Good, Barbara thought as she nodded. She would be the dutiful daughter taking her time packing, and he would grill Amy McCrutchen without her ever suspecting she had been done to a turn. He had a way of getting a stone to give up its secrets.

Amy stepped outside and pulled the door closed after her. "I'll walk over with you," she said to Frank. "Do you know David's condition? They won't tell you anything if you call, as I found out."

"Nothing more than they're releasing at this time. You're a friend of David's?" Frank asked.

"Not really, but I knew him. I was pretty young when he left here, and only met him again this week."

"I suppose he was your brother's friend," Frank said.

"I don't think they were really friends," she said after a moment, "just in the same graduating class. Dr. Elders had some of his students over here for evening seminars, and David and Robert were both in his class. That's when I met David." She thought that needed a bit of explaining, and added, "Dr. Elders couldn't do it at his house because his wife was ill."

"He's a family friend?" Frank asked.

Amy felt confused, not really sure how this whole line of explanation had come about, but she continued. "He lives next door and was here a lot. He still comes over frequently. He had the students come here, had caterers bring in something, and had discussions. He's retired now. Mother and Dad were happy to have the sessions here," she added. She had not given it much thought before but, saying it, she realized how peculiar it must sound for a professor to meet with his students in a neighbor's house.

Barbara parked behind David's car and entered the apartment. She walked straight through to the sliding door and opened a drape, then looked around. David had already packed most things apparently. A large suitcase was closed, and a smaller one nearly filled. Of course, she thought, he had originally planned to be in San Francisco for ten days at least, and then fly to Britain. He would have needed a lot of things. The apartment was very clean and neat, the bed made, nothing on the floor. It would be hard for her to even pretend to be busy for very long.

"This is very nice," Frank said, on entering and glancing about the apartment. He went to the sliding door and said softly, "That's a beautiful garden. Mind if I have a look?"

Amy glanced at Barbara, who shrugged and nodded.

"I'll show you," Amy said. "It's my mother's garden."

They walked out to the deck, and Barbara began looking into the dresser drawers. She found little to add to the suitcase, clean clothes for one day, today. His shaving gear in the bathroom, other toiletries there. A robe hanging on the door. It didn't take long to gather everything and pack it. A laptop computer was on the table, the carrying case on a chair near it, with a notebook and some papers. Later she would look through them all for addresses and whatever else might be helpful, but for now she simply packed the papers and notebook in the computer case and added the laptop. After finishing with the suitcases, she took them to her car and stowed them in the trunk. David had left little for anyone to clean up after he was gone. Empty refrigerator, no dirty dishes, a little coffee, enough for one pot, and nothing else. He was a considerate tenant, a neat person. Too neat? Compulsive about it? Hard to say, she decided. But certainly considerate. Leaving the laptop to take out later, she stepped onto the deck. To her surprise, Frank was seated with Amy, another woman and an older man at the far end of the deck. They were having a drink together, chatting.

"Middle America on a lazy summer evening, sharing a little good cheer," she muttered under her breath, and walked over to join them.

7

As Barbara approached the small group at the table, Frank and the other man rose. Frank introduced her to Chloe McCrutchen and Dr. Elders. Chloe nodded without speaking, then nodded again when Barbara repeated her condolences. Chloe appeared absorbed in the contents of her glass, uninterested in guests. With her black glossy hair, olive complexion and dark eyes, she was very attractive, but she also looked pinched and pale. Shadows made her eyes appear almost sunken, as if sleep was elusive.

"Would you like a gin and tonic?" Dr. Elders asked. "Your father opted for water, but I'd be happy to mix you a drink."

He looked ready to audition for a role as prissy headmaster for a movie about a boy's misadventures in a British school, Barbara thought. He said he would be happy to mix a drink, and apparently meant it. He seemed ready to leap to his feet to go do it. His hair, thin and gray, was combed precisely, with a razor-sharp part, and he was wearing a long-sleeved, starched shirt. His black trousers had a well-defined crease. Black socks, probably knee-high, she thought, and shoes completed the picture.

"Thanks, but no," she said to the offer of a drink.

"I was admiring the garden," Frank said. "It's truly beautiful. The master gardener had an unerring eye for textures, shades of green, perfect blends of blooms."

"Lucy's work," Dr. Elders said. "Lucy McCrutchen, Robert and Amy's mother. She's been away since her husband passed away." He pointed. "Over there, on the far side, the weeping cherry, that was Robert's tree, planted when they moved in soon after he was born. She planted the dogwood at this end after Amy was born. She called them her garden angels at that time. To her the garden is a living, whole organism, each plant with a special meaning—"

Abruptly Chloe rose. "If you'll excuse me," she said. Taking her drink with her, she left.

Dr. Elders looked crestfallen. "She's still in shock, and here I am being a fool, going on and on about irrelevant matters." He took a long drink. "She saw him, you know. Horrifying sight. Horrifying."

"You saw him?" Frank asked.

"Oh, yes. I heard the gardener screaming and I came right over. I saw him." He pointed to the sliding door to the family room. The room extended eight or nine feet onto the deck, with the door taking up much of the extension. "He had fallen halfway out. Ants had gotten to him, covered his face and head…"

Amy had grown more and more tense as Dr. Elders spoke, and now she stood and said stiffly, "Ms. Holloway, if you're through, I really should be finishing dinner. I'll lock up the apartment when you leave."

An unmistakable invitation to beat it, Barbara knew. "Of

course," she said. "I'm sorry to have intruded at this time. I'm grateful that you permitted us to gather the things today."

Frank shook hands with Dr. Elders. "Perhaps we can talk another time?"

"Yes. Yes, indeed. I'm in the book. Call anytime."

Barbara and Amy walked on ahead and, inside the apartment, Amy said in a low voice, "Since you're David's attorney, they probably will tell you how he is, won't they?"

"They'd better," Barbara replied.

"Would it be all right if I call you to find out? They won't tell anyone else anything, apparently."

"Give me your number," Barbara said. "I'll let you know when I learn anything."

Amy looked around, as if searching for something to write on and Barbara got out a notebook and handed it and a pen to her. Without looking at Barbara, Amy said, in the same low voice, "I had a terrible crush on David when I was a kid. Over it now, of course, but I'd like to hear. As a new friend."

"I'll be sure to call you," Barbara said. "And again, thanks for today. Here's the key back. I'll be in touch."

Frank had stopped at the door, again taking in the garden, and now came into the apartment. "I'm ready," Barbara said, picking up her purse and the laptop case, and she and Frank left.

Driving away, Barbara asked, "What did you make of them?"

"Since Chloe McCrutchen didn't really say a word, it's a little hard to tell much about her. Elders is itching to talk to someone about the murder. I'll be a good audience. Monday probably," Frank said.

"I think Chloe is jealous of Lucy McCrutchen or else just doesn't like her," Barbara said slowly, "and that Elders may be in love with Lucy."

"Back up just a little for an old blind fool. Signs?"

"Their expressions when he began to talk about Lucy and her garden—his was almost reverent. Chloe had been withdrawn, remote, but she heard him and she took on a frozen look. I thought she might break her glass, the way her hand tightened on it. Is he as oblivious as he appeared? As insensitive? Anyway, it's going to make whatever he says about that family fairly suspect. Consciously or unconsciously, he'll protect them."

"We'll need a spokesman," Frank said. "I'll get someone at the office. Keep your name out of it for now."

"Good. Amy wants to talk, too," Barbara said. "I don't think she's entirely over her adolescent crush on David. I assume you heard every word."

"I did," he said. "So you get her, and I get Elders."

"Do you want to keep the suitcases in your study for now?" she asked. "Depending on how David does, we might want to have a look at what's in them both." At his nod, she continued, "I'll keep the laptop. I want to see what's on it, what all those papers are about. There are a lot of people to be notified that he won't be keeping his commitments." She was thinking of the look of hopelessness on Lucien Etheridge's face.

"If David dies, I'll fight them before I let them close the McCrutchen murder with the implicit assumption that David Etheridge is the killer without having to prove it," Frank said, indicating his thought processes matched hers.

She was again startled at the vehemence in his tone. "*We'll* fight them, Dad. *We.*"

That night in a house that seemed emptier day by day, Barbara gazed at a wall map Todd had prepared, marking their trip. The Tetons, over to SeaTac and a flight to Alaska, a small plane into the back north country, another plane to a point very close to the Arctic Circle, back to SeaTac, then by camper up Mount

Rainier, to Mount Olympia, then home. Ambitious, and out of touch much of the time. She had missed a call from Darren that day. His message said he would try again on Sunday afternoon. She bit her lip in vexation at missing the call and promised herself to be available with her cell phone turned on for a call the following day.

She looked around for a good place to plug in David's computer, sort through the papers in the carrying case, send a few e-mails. Her first thought was her office over the garage. She shook her head. When Darren and Todd were home, she needed her office, but with the house empty she could go anywhere. She settled for the kitchen table.

First the laptop, she decided. She searched for an e-mail to the conference people—the coordinator, director or someone. She found exchanges between David and someone named Len, and sent her own message. Then she searched for the hotel reservation and canceled that. His flight to England was next. She stopped when she found it. One tourist-class ticket for David, one way, and two round-trip first-class tickets for Lucien and Dora Etheridge. They were for two weeks later than his. He had planned to treat them to a month-long trip to England, she realized with a pang. She hesitated over canceling the flights. If he died, she thought, a trip to England might be exactly what his parents would need. Change of scene, time out.

Apparently Lucy McCrutchen had needed to get away after her husband died, and Frank had left town when Barbara's mother died. She had left, too. Change of scene. As if someplace new and different would help. She got up and crossed the kitchen for a glass of water. When she returned to the table, she canceled David's flight and left the reservations for his parents.

It kept coming back to *if* he died. That would make three violent deaths, separated in time by twenty-two years, but the same cast of characters. Disquieted by the thought, she began to look over the dozen or so papers she had put in the laptop case. Notes, conference agenda, seminar notes apparently. And one that made no sense. She examined a sheet of paper with a cluster of *x*'s near the top, and three more near the bottom, and a single word on top—*Key*. She turned it over, but nothing else was written on it. A game plan? It was a printout. Did he play computer games? She wouldn't have thought so, and there were no other indications that he did.

She returned to the laptop and scanned it for his programs, the sites he had visited. She discovered chat rooms and forums on history, religion, government but no games.

She opened a picture gallery, shots he had taken and downloaded onto his computer. Clicking through them quickly, she found nothing of interest. Landscapes, faces, buildings. Then she drew in a sharp breath.

He had taken pictures of Robert McCrutchen's body.

There were several full-body shots, half in and half out the doorway. Close-ups of his upper body, his head with the ants all over it, one hand, more ants, blood ringed by ants. Looking at them, she shuddered. It was bad enough in a picture, it must have been truly horrifying in real life. Or death. There was a sheet of paper with one corner under his hand. Apparently he had manipulated the image, or had taken close-ups of the paper alone, for the next image it was a full screen, and on it the paper with the same *x*'s. That was what he had printed.

She picked up the paper again, comparing the two; one on screen, one in her hand.

Leaning back in her chair, she regarded the photos on the screen for several minutes. Chloe had cause to be in shock. Had Amy seen that body? Probably not. She had been in Portland, and by the time she got there, the investigators would have been on the scene, keeping everyone well away. David had seen it, photographed it, evidently before the police arrived. Why?

The images could be damning in the eyes of the law, Barbara knew. Murderer gloating over his victim? Obsessed with the crime? A warped voyeuristic impulse? Ghoulish curiosity? The ants made it especially grotesque.

What now? she asked herself. If he died—that damn phrase again—his belongings would be turned over to his parents and sooner or later they would come across the pictures. If he lived and was charged with murder, the police might seize the computer. Neither was a good option.

She found the digital camera in the manila envelope and examined it. David had deleted the pictures from the memory.

She closed the program on his laptop. The first step, she decided, would be to print out the pictures and decide what to do about them later. Staring at the page with the x's, she shook her head. If Robert McCrutchen had drawn them, she might never know why, or what it meant. And it was quite possible that it meant nothing relevant, something to do with politics, or a game plan.

8

"It looks as if the killer must have been in the house with him," Barbara said Sunday afternoon, drawing back from the table where she had spread the printouts from David's computer.

Frank nodded. The body was facedown, one cheek on the deck, and the top side so covered with blood and ants that nothing else was discernible. "I think you're right. From the back more than likely, making him pitch forward."

"I can't make it work," she said. "Half in the doorway like that doesn't make sense, unless the door and the screen door were already open and he was walking out. Two people? One outside, one behind him?"

"Or someone had come inside and left the doors open, and he went to investigate? Or something else." Frank resumed his study of the sheet of paper with x's, then shrugged. "That needs footnotes."

"I talked to David's doctor this morning. The swelling of his brain is going down, and they'll downgrade his condition from critical to serious and move him out of intensive care tomorrow if he continues to show progress. I want to pack his carry-on bag with things he'll need in the hospital. I arranged for a private room, and I hope I talked his parents into taking turns keeping watch in order to get a little rest away from the hospital."

"I expect one or both parents will stay right there in his room with him," Frank said, knowing that's what he would do.

"Well, I told Amy I'd call to let her know how David's doing." Barbara placed the call.

When Amy hung up, she leaned back in her chair with a sigh of relief. She had been so afraid for him, she thought, for no real reason. People, strangers, died all the time, and it was an abstract. You could feel pity or regret or any number of things, but it wasn't personal, not as if… She shook her head. He meant little or nothing to her, she told herself. Really not much different than any other stranger. Nothing personal. Still, she was relieved.

She had been on her way to have a talk with Chloe when the call came, she reminded herself, and continued through the house to the deck. Chloe was under a shade umbrella, with sunglasses on, the newspaper on the table nearby, one section on her lap, but she was not reading.

Amy sat across the table from her. "Chloe," she said softly, "I'd like to talk to you a minute. Okay?"

"Sure." Chloe didn't shift in her chair or remove the sunglasses.

"I'd like to start sorting Robert's clothes. You know, pack up things and donate them to the church for them to distribute. Something like that. Is it all right with you?"

For a long time Chloe did not respond or move. Finally she said, "Do what you want. I can't deal with it right now."

"No. I don't want you to help. Why don't you go to the coast for a few days, walk on the beach, relax. The change of scene would be good for you."

There was another long pause before Chloe said, "I'll think about it. Maybe tomorrow."

It was disconcerting, Amy thought, leaving her, the way Chloe seemed absent, not processing anything in normal time. She had been like that for days, probably still in shock. The trauma of murder, the sight of Robert's body, the ants… It might haunt her for years to come.

Amy went upstairs to the room she had used as a girl. It had long since been redecorated, no silly posters on the walls, no shelf of dolls and stuffed animals, but in spite of the changes, it was still her room, with the same twin beds, the desk and chair, even the same desk lamp. Now the desk was crowded with her computer, the house plans she was working on, reference books, a coffee mug bristling with pencils and pens like a porcupine with its back up. She had not been able to concentrate on work all that week and she still couldn't concentrate when she sat at the desk and called up the program with a basic floor plan outlined and nothing else.

Perhaps she was in shock also, she thought, gazing at the screen. She had not yet sorted out how Robert's death had affected her. Although he had been her only sibling, her brother, they had never been close. The age spread had made that impossible. At best he had been tolerant of her, most of the time indifferent, and at times he had been cruel. He had left home for law school when she was fourteen and, she had to admit, she had never missed him after that.

She had not been able to do a thing at her computer, and still couldn't. Perhaps she wouldn't be able to get back to work until she cleared out Robert's belongings. She hated how callous the thought was. *Clear him out.* But that's what it amounted to. His presence would linger as long as his clothes hung in the closets, his raincoat hung in the downstairs closet, all his things remained in place as if awaiting his return. She suspected that Chloe would not be able to consider her own plans, her future, any more than Amy could work as long as it seemed the house was waiting for Robert to return.

She was still sitting there without doing a thing when her phone rang, and in relief, she answered it. Her mother was on the line.

"How is everything?" Lucy asked.

"Not very different," Amy said. "The police aren't telling us a thing, and Chloe is still like a zombie. About the same."

"Amy, I just read an article in the newspaper here saying that David Etheridge had been attacked. When? How badly is he hurt? Do they know who did it? Why?"

Amy told her what little she knew. "It doesn't seem to be connected to Robert's death. They're calling it a hate crime."

"Dear, I'm coming home. I've boxed up some things to ship, and I'll bring the rest with me. It's time. More than time."

Amy protested, but not vigorously. "If you can relax down there, that's the best thing for you. You know you couldn't sleep here."

"Nor here," Lucy said. "No. I realized I belong there, in my own home. This has been like a time-out, an interlude, but it's past time for me to settle a few things, make a few decisions. Besides, I realized when I got back here that I want to come home."

That evening when Amy told Chloe that Lucy was coming home the following day, after a long pause, Chloe said stiffly, "That's good for you, isn't it? I'll call Lori Buchman and see if I can use her cottage over at Yachats. You and Lucy can figure out what to do with everything and I won't be in the way. Lucy will want to decide about the house now."

She didn't look at Amy as she spoke, and didn't wait for a response, but walked from the room toward her own bedroom. It had been the master bedroom, Amy's parents' room. Amy watched Chloe's back as she walked away and thought again, zombie. As stiff and unnatural as a zombie.

Chloe left the following morning, saying only that she would be at Lori Buchman's cottage for a few days. Minutes later, Amy entered Robert's room and looked inside the closet. She didn't know how long Robert had been using his boyhood room, but she realized she had known. No one had ever mentioned it. Chloe in the master bedroom, Robert in his old room or in Salem.

She started with the suits, sport coats and slacks, jeans. She emptied the pockets of a few coins, ticket stubs, parking receipts. At first she had thought she would have someone from his church go through everything in the bedroom, but she reconsidered. No point in raising rumors and suspicions now, she decided. She found two boxes in the garage and took them back up with her and started emptying drawers. Laundered shirts, pajamas, a summer robe, miscellaneous items. One drawer seemed full of matched socks, and she simply pulled the whole drawer out and dumped the contents into one of the boxes. Then she stopped.

Taped to the bottom of the drawer was a manila envelope. She pulled it free and replaced the drawer. Sitting on the side of the bed, she opened the envelope and brought out a smaller one. Inside it were five pictures of Chloe and a man. Amy gasped. Nick Aaronson. Chloe and Nick Aaronson. They were in bed, Chloe naked with a sheet around her lower legs, and Nick just as naked partly under the sheet in one, out from it in others.

Amy walked across the hall to her own room and closed the

door behind her. She sank onto her bed clutching the pictures, shaking as if with a deep chill.

She sat for a long time while questions chased one another through her head. Why? Who took them? When? Why was Robert keeping them? Did Chloe know he had them? Did Nick Aaronson? She was jerked out of her immobility by the ring of her cell phone.

Barbara Holloway was calling. She snatched up her phone as if it were a life jacket to rescue her from the sea of confusion she had fallen into.

"Ms. McCrutchen, another progress report," Barbara said. "I just got back from the hospital and they're moving David to a private room later today. His condition is still serious, but no longer critical. I knew you'd want to be told."

Amy had to moisten her lips before she could respond. "I'm grateful. Thank you. Will he be allowed visitors?" Her voice sounded forced, hollow.

"Not now. Perhaps in a day or two, and only those approved in advance. I'll make certain that your name is on the approved list." She laughed lightly and added, "Unless, of course, David says no. I don't think that will be the case." Then, before Amy expressed her gratitude again, Barbara said, "I wonder if it would be possible for me to come out to the house one day soon and have a look around."

"Why?" Amy asked.

"I told you that David's parents asked me to collect his belongings, but before that, before he was attacked, David had also asked me to represent him in the event that he became a suspect in the murder of your brother. I know this puts you in an awkward position, but since David can't do anything about his own defense, I'd like a chance to see where it happened before anything undergoes any drastic change."

"I understand," Amy said. She realized that her attention was still on the picture of Chloe and Nick Aaronson, and she closed her eyes. "Tomorrow," she said. "Around one or two? Would that be convenient for you?"

Barbara said yes and thanked her.

After disconnecting, Amy picked up the smaller envelope and slid the pictures back inside without looking at them again. Where to put it? She looked about the familiar room and shook her head. She had kept her diary under her pillow, she recalled, and thought that those pictures anywhere near her as she slept would induce nightmares. Finally she put the envelope of pictures in one of her reference books, and put it under three others. For now, she told herself. Just for now. Later she would decide what to do with them. Now she simply wanted to finish clearing out all of Robert's belongings, every scrap, everything. Get everything that had been his out of this house before her mother arrived that evening. First, she had to wash her hands.

That morning Barbara had brought Shelley and Bailey up to date before she went to the hospital. "So," she had concluded, "what we're going to want is as much info as we can dig out about that old case from twenty-two years ago. A student named Jill Storey, strangled after attending a party at the McCrutchen house."

"I'll do that," Shelley said. "Newspapers first, see how many people are still around, things like that. What else?"

"I'll keep tabs on David's condition and the investigation into his attack. I want to talk to Amy McCrutchen, and have a look at the room where it happened. Dad will go with me. We'll want the usual background material on all of them," she said to Bailey, and gave him a short list of names. "Also, whatever your pal at city hall can come up with about McCrutchen's murder. Time of death? Suspects. Deadly enemies in Salem? Was he into games? What does that sketch mean, if anything? You know the drill." She had handed him a copy of the printout with x's on it.

When the briefing was finished, she took the overnight bag to the hospital, where Lucien Etheridge was alone in the waiting room. His wife, he told her, was ready to fall over and he had left her in the motel to try to sleep. Barbara thought he looked ready to keel over, as well.

"David opened his eyes and saw us this morning," he said. "He said hi to us. They've been keeping him doped, but he opened his eyes and spoke. He's going to make it, Ms. Holloway." This last was in a whisper, as if saying it in a normal voice might somehow undo the healing process.

"I know," she said. "I talked to his doctor. They're optimistic. After they move him to a private room, we'll get a cot to go in his room and you can get some rest there. Anything's going to be better than this waiting room. Are you okay?"

He nodded. "We're fine, fine. Thank God, he's going to make it." He looked ready to weep.

9

Amy entered the study reluctantly on Tuesday, uncertain how much of Robert's personal correspondence she might find, and what she would or should do with it if there was any. She glanced over the bookshelves. The books belonged here. Her mother's gardening books, medical books, science books, fiction. She spotted Robert's university yearbook, and pulled it from the shelf, then sat down to look through the graduating class pictures. She realized she was looking for David's picture and grimaced, but kept turning pages. A sheet of paper slipped from the book. She caught it, but before returning it, she saw that it was titled *Party,* with a list of names. She put it back, and looked for David's photograph. When she found it, she thought again how little he had changed over the years. Aquiline nose, sharp cheekbones, a lot of hair. She remembered the night he had winked at her and then, with a decisive motion, closed the book hard and put it back on the shelf.

Turning, she regarded the desk with Robert's computer. She

knew that Lawrence Tellman and Nick Aaronson had made copies of material on the computer and no doubt then deleted the files, but personal things, not connected with his political affairs? She was almost afraid to approach the computer. If Nick had already sifted through the files, she told herself, there wouldn't be anything left that was incriminating or embarrassing. The question of whether he knew about the pictures kept recurring. If Chloe knew, it didn't seem reasonable for her to have gone away without first finding them, or at least trying to find them. There had been no sign of a search on her part.

Amy was looking through the computer files when the doorbell rang, and she realized that it was five minutes after one. Barbara Holloway and her father were due. Grateful for the interruption, she hurried to open the door. When she did, she felt frozen for a second, then almost reflexively took a step back. Nick Aaronson was there.

"Ms. McCrutchen, please tell Chloe I'm here."

She shook her head. "She isn't here."

His voice sharpened. "Is that her message, or is she really not here?"

"She's gone away for a few days," Amy said stiffly.

"Where did she go?"

"Mr. Aaronson, all I can do for you is give you her cell phone number. Or do you already have it?"

He studied her for a moment, then said, "I have it. If she gets in touch, please tell her that certain business matters should be attended to. You know, don't you, that Robert and I were associates? There is a great deal of unfinished business that has to be seen to. Will you give her that message?"

"I'll tell her," Amy said. She started to close the door, and he turned and walked away.

Another car was turning in at the driveway as Nick Aaronson

drove out, and Amy waited. This time it was Barbara Holloway and her father.

Amy wished they had delayed a little, at least long enough for her to wash her hands, but even as she thought that, she knew she had not touched him, that her hands didn't need washing. Still, she wished they had delayed a little.

"Hello," Barbara said, coming to the door. "Thanks for giving us this time."

"You're welcome," Amy said. Her voice was still strange to her ears, and she tried to relax her stomach muscles, which had drawn tight. "Please, come in."

Her mother walked into the hall then and said, "Who was here? I heard cars coming and going."

"Nick Aaronson was here, looking for Chloe. He's gone. Mother, this is Barbara Holloway and Mr. Holloway. My mother."

Lucy was dressed in jeans, a T-shirt and old sneakers; she was carrying a wide-brimmed hat, and her face was moist with sweat. She nodded to Barbara and Frank and said, "I mustn't touch you. I've been working in the garden, and my hands are dirty. Amy told me you asked permission to look around. Please, feel free to do so. I'll just go wash up a bit. Excuse me."

"Over there is the living room," Amy said, pointing, "and Robert's study in there." She led the way through a wide hall to hallways off to both sides, and then the kitchen. She indicated one direction. "Pantry," she said, "a lavatory, and that door opens to the garage and utility room." Then she motioned for them to enter an open door at the end. "Family room," she said. "This is where…where it happened."

It was a very large room, as wide as the double garage, about twenty feet, and six or eight feet longer. The long side wall had many high windows, and the end facing the garden was nearly all glass. A piano and several chairs were at the garage end, a long sofa along the side wall under the high windows, with more easy chairs, a television, a dining table and chairs nearly centered, a game table farther down, and at the far end another grouping of smaller chairs and end tables.

They had taken only a few steps into the room, and Amy had stopped at the doorway when she spoke again. "You know where he was?" she asked in a low voice.

"We do," Frank said gently. "We'll just be a few minutes."

"I'll make some iced tea," Amy said. "Take as long as you need." She turned and left them alone in the family room.

The floors in the other part of the house were very fine mahogany, but in here the flooring was pale golden-sand-colored vinyl, a bit scuffed in places and more worn near the windowed south wall, as if the room had been well used over the years. Slowly Barbara and Frank walked toward the other end and the sliding door that led to the deck. The door was wide-open, the screen door closed. Frank stopped about three feet away from it.

"Here," he said in a low voice, "or a little closer. Do you know how tall he was?"

Barbara shook her head. Frank turned to survey the room from where he was standing. It didn't seem likely that anyone could have sneaked up on Robert without notice.

"We also don't know how close the shooter was to him," Barbara said, trying to visualize how it could have happened. A head shot seemed to indicate close range, or else a lucky hit. There were no bullet holes in the wall, and the glass door had not been broken. "I assume this is pretty much how the room was that night," she murmured, studying the grouping of chairs by the floor-to-ceiling windows. Lightweight, padded but not bulky, not anything a person could hide behind. There was nowhere in the room a person could have hidden. The sofa was against the wall; the few easy chairs near it would afford no real concealment.

Frank turned again toward the sliding door, a six-foot-wide door, the opening nearly three feet wide. Plenty of space for a body to fall through, but why? Why had the screen door been open? Why shoot him right there? Why not sooner, or later? He shook his head.

He saw Lucy McCrutchen walk out onto the deck and sit under an umbrella. Amy followed with a tray that held a pitcher and glasses. He took a step toward the door and pushed the screen door open. It slid easily and smoothly without a sound. Had anyone heard the shot? With the open door, if other doors to the deck had been open, it seemed incredible that no one had heard a shot.

"Are you done in here?" he asked Barbara. "Let's join them on the deck if you are."

"More than ready," she said. They walked out and Frank closed the screen door.

At the table where Lucy and Amy were seated, Frank said, "Mrs. McCrutchen, you have my deepest sympathy for your loss."

"And mine, as well," Barbara said.

Lucy bowed her head slightly and thanked them. "Please, sit down. We know you must have many questions, and while I doubt that we can help, Amy and I have talked about this affair, and we understand that David Etheridge has come under suspicion. If we can assist you, we will."

"You don't believe he is guilty?" Barbara asked.

Lucy shook her head. "I don't believe a rational person commits a murder for no reason, and David had no reason to do so."

As she spoke, Amy filled two glasses with iced tea, and passed one to Barbara, another to Frank.

"Thank you," Barbara said. She asked Lucy, "Do you know why your son became interested in Jill Storey's murder after all these years? That interest, the fact that he copied the file and brought it home with him, is why the attention has turned to David. The assumption is that David's appearance accounted for the renewed interest in the case."

Lucy shook her head. "It was a major concern when it happened, of course. The investigators finally decided that the one who did it must have been a transient or someone like that, probably someone on drugs. The fact that she attended a party here earlier that night, along with about thirty others, made them ask a lot of questions about any possible connection with anyone who attended. It led nowhere, as far as I know."

"Do you know if anything happened that night that could have brought on bad feelings between your son and David?" Barbara asked.

Lucy looked out over her garden, as if to distance herself from memories of that night. "No. They were not close friends ever, just classmates, no doubt with quite different interests and after-school pursuits. The night of the party, all the young people were stressed-out with the end of the school year, finals, last-minute papers to write, then a string of parties, graduation. They were manic with relief finally, boisterous and ravenous. They started arriving at six-thirty, and by midnight many of them were gone, too exhausted to keep partying, and those who remained got much quieter, quietly talking, and no more loud music. I believe someone was playing a guitar, and I know someone was at the piano, but it was subdued. By one, it was all over."

Frank stood then and said, "I'd better be going on over to chat with Dr. Elders, but first, Mrs. McCrutchen, I have to tell you how much I admire your garden. It's very beautiful, and you have a few plants I'm not familiar with but want in my own garden now."

"Thank you," she said. She stood also and reached for her hat on a nearby chair. She picked up gardening gloves, as well. "Time to get back to a few things," she said. "Why don't you show me the ones you don't know, and if I remember what they are, you can make a note."

"Gardeners," Amy said, as they walked away.

"Obsessed," Barbara said. She drank a little tea, watching Frank and Lucy until they were out of hearing range. "Ms. Mc-Crutchen, can you talk about that morning, when David called you home? What was being done, being said. We know so little about the actual murder and the investigators aren't telling me a thing."

"It was pretty chaotic," Amy said slowly. "Police were here by then, David was still here and Dr. Elders. Chloe was in shock, and the woman gardener was in shock out here on the deck. I called my nephew, Chloe and Robert's son." She stopped and picked up her glass, but more as if to do something than because she wanted to drink from it. She swirled ice around and put the glass down again.

"Chloe said she came home close to eleven, she wasn't sure of the exact time. She parked in the garage and came in through the garage door. She glanced inside the room, saw that Robert wasn't watching television, and assumed he was in the study working. She went straight to her room and got ready for bed and went to sleep. They had separate rooms, so she wouldn't have known that he never went to bed." Her voice quivered and she looked away from Barbara, appeared to be watching her mother and Frank. He was jotting something in his notebook.

"Do you know if they found a gun?"

"Yes. It was Robert's handgun. He kept one in his desk drawer in the study. Chloe told them. She couldn't identify it, but they seemed to think it was his gun. I don't know where they found it."

"What was Dr. Elders doing over here in the morning?" Barbara asked.

Amy shrugged. "He's over here a lot. Mother says he's just a lonely old man, but he's always been in and out of our house a lot, ever since I can remember. He heard the gardener scream-ing, he said, and came hurrying over and just hung around. If your father plans to chat with him, he'd better be prepared to stay awhile."

Barbara smiled. "In time I'll go drag Dad away."

"*Rescue* him," Amy said.

Frank and Lucy had gone to the far side of the deck, and a moment later she returned alone and went back to the flower border.

"She showed him the way we always went next door," Amy said.

Barbara glanced at her watch. "I'll give them half an hour or so," she said. "If I can impose on you that long."

"Not a problem," Amy said. She glanced at Barbara and away swiftly, and asked, "Do they have any evidence or anything against David? Do you know?"

"I wish I knew what they have, but I don't. David told me there was nothing. We haven't had time for a real talk yet, and heaven knows how long it will be before he's up to a real con-versation, an interrogation. I wish I knew more about that party, who attended, if something happened that night between them, or between anyone and Jill Storey."

"I can show you Robert's yearbook, with a party list," Amy said after a moment. "There's a copier. You could make a copy of the list if you want."

"I want to very much," Barbara said.

Amy took Barbara back through the house to the study, re-moved the book and handed the sheet of paper to her. She pointed to the copier. "Help yourself."

Barbara made the copy and gave the original back to Amy. "Mind if I have a look at the photographs?" she asked. "Is Jill Storey's picture in it?"

"I guess so. She graduated that same year."

They found Jill Storey's picture and, as Barbara studied it, her reality shifted. Jill was fresh faced, vibrant looking, very pretty. What had been a distant murder of an unknown, faceless young woman became real in a way it hadn't been before. Jill had been laughing, dancing, partying, manic along with the others, and then she was dead. Hardly more than a girl, on the verge of adulthood with her future waiting to unfold, dead at the hands of a killer.

She touched the smiling face gently, and in her head the words formed, *I'm sorry.*

Dr. Elders greeted Frank effusively that afternoon. "Come in, come in. I just put on coffee. Will you share a coffee with me?"

"That would be good," Frank said, looking around the room they had entered. It was handsomely, but overly, furnished with antiques, a beautiful Oriental rug in a royal-blue-and-gold design, heavy, framed portraits on the walls, Tiffany lamps. The room looked as if no one had used it in a lifetime. And even as the thought occurred to him, Dr. Elders motioned for him to come along.

"My study is down this way. More to my liking. I always feel as if I've stumbled into a museum in here." He laughed and motioned Frank into a smaller room with dark leather-covered chairs, a television, a desk messy with papers, books on tables, overfilled shelves. "Have a seat. I'll bring the coffee. Won't take a minute."

Frank sat in one of the well-worn chairs and agreed that this was more comfortable, his kind of room. Soon Dr. Elders returned with a tray, and then with coffee in hand, they regarded each other for a moment.

"I guess you want to fill in some details about that morning," Dr. Elders said. "And I'd like to talk about it. Can't talk really to the family. Too painful for them."

"Well, we have been trying to get some facts. The investigators have been keeping what they know pretty close to their vests."

"Yes, they seem to do that, don't they? I was in the kitchen that morning, and I heard the gardener screaming. I hurried over, of course. Chloe had come out to the deck, and she was shaking, almost as if she was paralyzed, except for the tremors. It was a gruesome sight. Robert sprawled halfway out the door, blood, ants all over his head. Streams of ants coming and going. Racing back and forth, frenzied. Revolting and fascinating at the same time. The lady gardener threw up, and she was weeping, wailing really.

"David was already there, using his cell phone. He asked, no, actually he ordered me to take Chloe inside, and he demanded to know where the phone book was. He acted like a master sergeant or ranking officer, barking orders. After he called the police, he called Amy and Lucy. And he told me to snap out of it and make some coffee and to keep out of the family room. As if I had any intention of entering it. He went out to the deck while he was on the phone. Chloe was going on about ants. By then the other two garden workers were there, trying to help the woman who first saw Robert. David went to his own apartment and got a glass of water for the woman. When the police arrived, they told David to get inside and stay there. We all sat down in the kitchen and waited for the homicide investigators."

"Did you see a gun?" Frank asked.

"Not then. Later, they showed Chloe and me a handgun. It was Robert's, from his desk drawer. He got it when he was a prosecutor and never gave it up. You know he was a prosecutor a few years back?"

"I knew that," Frank said.

"He was a good one," Dr. Elders said. "He was a good man, with a brilliant career ahead. A good man. Solid. Good values. He will be missed."

"You must have known him all his life," Frank said.

"Oh, yes. We, my wife and I, were already in this house when Mac and Lucy moved in next door. And they turned out to be the kind of neighbors one can only dream of having. Lucy is the most nurturing, caring woman God ever saw fit to put on earth. If there was ever a living saint, she is one." He drank what coffee was left in his cup and refilled it. "Help yourself," he said.

Frank was sipping his own from time to time, but it was not very good, and he had no desire to add to it. "You were mentor to some of those young people in the past, weren't you?" he asked.

"Many of them," Dr. Elders said, nodding. "Robert, Chloe, David, they were all my students at one time."

"Do you recall the student Jill Storey?"

"Vaguely. It was a long time ago, and she must not have done much to stand out or make an impression. Teaching for many years, as I did, I found that quite often a few students were remarkable for one reason or another, and I remember them, but the vast majority tend to blur together, no more than a number of bodies, papers to grade, tests to give. Of course, when she was murdered, we were all shocked, and I remember that time pretty well. I was at the party that night, Robert's graduation party, the night he and Chloe announced their engagement. Her murder following within hours of the party made me revisit every tidbit I could recall that involved her in any way. Accordingly, my memory of her is confined to that one night."

"Can you recall whether there appeared to be friction between David and Robert?"

Dr. Elders shook his head. "I never gave that much thought, frankly, but I'd say no. I didn't stay for the entire party, you must understand. I liked to dance in those days, and I enjoyed that part, but when they started talking and someone started playing a guitar, I left. I couldn't say what time it was. And I couldn't say what might have developed after that. But while I was there, I didn't observe any interaction between them at all, with friction or otherwise."

He shook his head. "I don't believe they were ever friends. In those days Robert was as open and friendly as a pup, playful, and David was...*opaque* might be the correct word. He's one of the students that I remember, you see. Extremely bright, well-read and a rather gifted writer. One never knew exactly what he was thinking. In class and at the seminars he would listen with a skeptical attitude, not expressed exactly, not really hostile, but rather sardonic, almost a mocking attitude, and he argued for in-arguably false positions. His written arguments were cogent, well researched and documented, but usually quite wrong, based on false premises. In one that young, it was an untenable position." He smiled ruefully. "The young tend to be very judgmental, with an unshakable belief in their own judgment, don't they?"

"Often," Frank said, thinking of how often their judgment proved the correct one.

"That night, the night of the party, I remember that I was struck by his possessive attitude toward Jill. You know how a man can behave when he believes a woman is committed to him, and then suspects that he has been deceived. Possessive, watchful, waiting for proof. Of course, he was involved with Jill Storey. She had a key to his apartment, after all. At a party like that, everyone's flirting with everyone else, not seriously, of course, but rather in youthful high spirits. Robert was flirting with all the young women, and it didn't mean a thing. Especially since

he and Chloe had become engaged, and she certainly understood how harmless it was and was not disturbed by it. I'm not
at all certain David had the same understanding."

He was gazing at a shelf of books, but it was as if he were looking
into the past, thinking. "I've always wondered if David had just
learned that Jill was rumored to have been promiscuous, if he was
watching for a sign that it might have been true. For a serious
young man, that kind of truth can be devastating, I believe."

Frank agreed. Learning an unwelcome truth could be devastating for many people. "Did Robert mention why he had that
police file, the investigation of Jill Storey's murder?"

Dr. Elders appeared surprised by the question. "It's obvious,
isn't it? David reappeared and Robert, with some years of prose-
cutorial experience behind him, had cause to rethink something
that had seemed trivial but suddenly took on importance. He
was on to something. He said as much the evening of his death.
I was over there, invited to dinner with him and Chloe, and
Robert was talking about the case in general terms, and then he
said something like, *oh, that's it,* something to that effect. I don't
recall his exact words, but I had the impression that something
had occurred to him that he had overlooked before."

"He didn't add anything to that?" Frank asked.

"No. Chloe left for the theater, and he was eager to clear the
table and do something. I helped him take things inside, and came
home."

"Did you hear a shot, anything that might have been a shot?"

"No. Most likely I was in here, possibly watching the news,
or with the television turned on and waiting for the news."

"He might have made enemies as a prosecutor. Everyone
connected with the law makes enemies," Frank said. "And these
days it seems that many in politics also make fierce enemies. Did
he ever speak of any to you?"

"No. He was a conservative, of course, but not a flaming fire-brand. Reasoned, reasonable, as tolerant as anyone can be concerning distinctly opposing positions. Not like some in Washington. You know, people who seem to go out of their way to arouse animosity. He was to the right of me, I admit, but I consider myself more of a Goldwater Republican than one of the new breed. Of course," he added after a brief pause, as if he had only then thought of something, "it could be that he convicted someone who went to prison and just recently was released and wanted revenge."

The idea appeared to please him. He nodded and repeated it. "Someone who wanted revenge. Another variety of a crime of passion. Generally we think of love, lust, jealousy when we think of crimes of passion, but revenge qualifies, I should think. Since Robert's murder, you see, I've been thinking a good deal about why people kill other people, something that was always abstract until now."

He settled farther back into his chair, as if preparing for a long conversation. Frank glanced at his watch and said, "Dr. Elders, I've overstayed my time, I'm afraid. Thank you for your comments concerning this business. You've been very helpful, but I really should be on my way." He put his cup down and stood.

Dr. Elders got up also. "Another time. I'd like to discuss, in a philosophical way, the crime of murder, the question—has the killer ever lost anyone near and dear? Does a killer understand the impact on the survivors? Does he care? Even think about them? If he isn't a psychopath, isn't there a burden of terrible guilt? Dostoyevsky explored the subject, of course, but in a modern context would it be the same? Is it possible that we've become so inured—?"

Frank was walking toward the door as Dr. Elders continued to talk. At the outside door, Frank interrupted to say, "Again, thank you for your time."

"Sorry," Dr. Elders said almost sheepishly. "I can understand that you prefer not to talk shop, a sentiment I share when it comes to history, I suppose. Murder is a subject I had never given much thought to, and now I find fascinating. Please, if there is anything I can help with, be of any assistance at all, I am at your service."

He opened the door. They shook hands, and Frank walked out, feeling that he had escaped just in time. Barbara's car was turning in at the driveway.

Minutes later, in Mekela's Thai restaurant, over steaming green curry, they exchanged information. "We have a new name for Bailey," Barbara said. "Nick Aaronson. Chloe is gone for a few days, over to Yachats. Aaronson's looking for her, and Amy was as stiff as a board when we got there and he was on the way out. She doesn't care much for Chloe."

Surprised, Frank asked, "She told you that?"

"Of course not. She's extremely careful how she speaks of Chloe, and that was enough. Also, she was never very close to Robert, and is as far to the left as he was to the right." She added, "Amy can't believe that Robert had real enemies. She said he was too bland to make enemies."

There were a few more bits and it was Frank's turn. "You did better than I did. Elders wants to have a philosophical dialogue about murder. He apparently believes that David killed Robert. And it was Robert's own gun, kept in his desk drawer. That raises interesting questions."

"Boy, does it ever. How many people knew that?"

"Elders said that at dinner that night, Robert seemed to suddenly think of something that was meaningful about Storey's murder. They had been talking about it in general terms, and Robert said something to the effect, *oh, that's it.*"

"What did you make of Elders?" Barbara asked.

"Hard to say. Lonesome, no doubt. Nosy, talkative. I didn't see much of the house, but the living room is like a museum display, heavy and dark, expensive. I think he hates it, but for some reason doesn't change it."

"His wife had ichthyosis, a bad case," Barbara said. "She kept the house like a refrigerator, unable to stand any heat. And she hardly ever went outside. She was badly disfigured by her disease and she died about twelve or thirteen years ago. Elders was in the McCrutchen house a lot, more like a relative than a visitor. If there are skeletons, he probably knows which closet to look into and what's in it. But," she added, "he isn't likely to tell *us*."

10

That afternoon Barbara went to city hall, where she called on Lieutenant Floyd Dressler, an investigator in Assaults, who was in charge of the attempted murder of David Etheridge. His desk was on the side of a large, overcrowded, noisy room. Too many separate conversations made a background level of sound that waxed and waned but never ceased, and was punctuated with the ringing of telephones.

In his fifties, a stocky man who had five sons, and talked about them at every opportunity, Dressler had seemed to become sadder year by year, as if he had seen too much and was having trouble keeping himself distanced from it. Earlier he had not been willing to talk about Etheridge's assault, but now that Barbara was David's attorney of record, he was cooperative.

"Dr. Lester Colfax will be his primary care physician," Barbara said. "All decisions about questioning Mr. Etheridge will be made by him, and depend entirely on Mr. Etheridge's condition. Of course, no questions unless I'm present."

"Okay," Dressler said. "Our main concern is whether he saw anyone, or if he'd had real threats. You know what I mean, not just letters to the editor, but in person, e-mail, phone."

"I'll let you know as soon as he's up to answering questions," she said. "Probably in a few days. How much do you know at this stage about the attack itself?"

"Not a lot. He left the lecture at Buell Hall with a few others at about nine forty-five or a little after, possibly as late as ten. They went out a side door to an alley with little street lighting. They separated at the corner, and he headed for his apartment, probably got in the neighborhood ten or fifteen minutes later. A resident was walking his dog at eleven-fifteen, spotted him and called nine-one-one."

He shook his head. "The primary weapon was an oak rod of some sort, maybe a heavy cane, something like that. Caught him in the back of the head, skull fracture, out cold instantly. The rest of the damage was by kicks in the side, arms, ribs."

Barbara shuddered at the image it brought to mind. "Hard shoes? Boots? Fibers?"

"In the lab. We'll get a report in a few days. It looks like leather shoes. That's all I can tell you about them."

"Any idea about how many were involved?" Barbara asked.

"I think just one."

She didn't press him for reasons. He was good, with a lot of experience in assaults, and if he thought one, he was more than likely right. One extremely vicious, cruel attacker.

After a few more minutes, and when Dressler began to talk about his youngest, Joey, and his prowess in softball, Barbara thanked him and left, to return to her own office.

She sat at her desk for a long time, trying to think of possible ways the three points of a triangle might be connected, even if separated by more than twenty years. Three murderous attacks, two successful, one nearly successful in the same small sample of humanity. Too coincidental, she argued with herself, but there didn't seem to be a way to make all three hold together. The methods were too different. Killers tended to use whatever method worked the first time. But it would be difficult to strangle a grown man, and Robert's gun had been left behind and was not available for David's attack. On to method three. She shook her head as once more the triangle collapsed into three separate lines. David's attack was especially brutal in a way the other two had not been. Kicking an unconscious man, breaking ribs, puncturing a lung was too different. If the attacker had thought David was already dead, kicking him was somehow even more horrendous, maniacal even. In her mind the sides of the collapsed triangle became heavy oak staves. If the first two deaths proved to be connected, it was credible that the attack against David was what the police had decided—a hate crime.

That afternoon, Shelley tapped on Barbara's door, opened it a crack, and said, "Got a few minutes?"

Barbara waved her in. "All I have is time right now. What do you have?"

"Not a lot, but a few things. I have copies of every newspaper article I could dig out, and I tracked down Jill's roommate."

"Great," Barbara said.

Then, sitting in the comfortable chairs at the lovely inlaid table, Shelley pointed to a folder she had put on the table. "Copies of the articles," she said. "Apparently the night Jill was killed her roommate was working a six-to-midnight restaurant shift. Jill was taking a nap when she went to work, and when she got home by twelve-thirty, Jill was not there, and she went straight to bed, thinking that Jill was still at the party. And that's all she knew about it. At the party, no one knew when Jill left.

The few remaining at the party cleared out by one. No one saw any kind of trouble brewing, heard anything to indicate hard feelings of any sort, and so on. Just a fun party and a good time had by all."

Shelley spread her hands. "As you might guess, the investigators weren't telling anything worth listening to. A newspaper account, unconfirmed, said they found a loose key in Jill's pocket and it was to David Etheridge's apartment. Jill was strangled, death between midnight and three in the morning. Of course, no one saw or heard anything. And that's about all, with variations and repetitions."

"God, I wish I had that police file," Barbara muttered. "Okay, anything else? What about the roommate?"

Shelley nodded. "Olga Trenval Maas. She's a teacher in Richland, Washington, originally from Medford, where her father is a Baptist preacher. She was married some years ago and there's a thirteen-year-old daughter."

"Was married? No longer?"

"No. Divorced. She's a single mom now. She kept her married name, Maas, probably because of the daughter. Less complicated that way."

"Okay," Barbara said. Grinning, she added, "I wonder how hard it would be to commit a little theft at city hall? Pinch that old police file."

Solemnly Shelley said, "Ski masks, trench coats, black gloves, a getaway car with the motor on, a submachine gun or something. Probably not all that hard."

Barbara laughed and picked up the folder. "Beat it before I start plotting. Accessory before the fact can be a serious charge."

Barbara scanned the various articles, but Shelley's report had touched on what few details the investigators had released, and the rest was speculation, opinion pieces, demands to clean up the university area of the homeless, the transients, the panhandlers. She gazed at the name Olga Maas, her address in Richland, Washington, and her phone number.

She called the number. When the phone was picked up, a blast of music and giggles all but drowned out the voice at the other end.

"Ms. Maas? My name is Barbara Holloway, and I'm an attorney in Eugene. Do you have a few minutes?"

"Hold on a second," the woman said. The background noise became fainter, and she said, "Who are you?"

Barbara repeated her introduction. "If you have a few minutes I'd like to ask a couple of questions."

"I'm sorry. I have a houseful of girls wanting to start a cookout. I can't talk now."

"It's about Jill Storey," Barbara said. "Is there a good time to call you back?"

"What about Jill? Why are you asking about her?" Her voice sharpened, became noticeably colder. The background sounds became even fainter, as evidently Olga Maas was moving farther from the girls.

"I represent David Etheridge, and there is possible renewed interest in that case," Barbara said.

"I don't understand any of this," Olga said. "But I can't talk now. And I won't answer questions asked by a stranger over the telephone, in any event."

A girl's voice yelled, "Mother! Can we start?"

"Oh, God," Olga said. "I have to go."

"I can drive up there," Barbara said quickly. "Can we make an appointment?"

"No!" With her hand over the mouthpiece, she called, "I'll be there in a minute." Then, speaking to Barbara she said, "Look, I'll pass through Eugene on Sunday on my way to Medford with my daughter and a friend. They want to stop in the Portland mall, but it can just as well be the one in Eugene. I can see you then for a few minutes."

"Fine. I'll make a reservation at the SweetWaters Restaurant, right by the mall. What time do you think you'll be here?"

"I don't know. Not before three." The girl called again, and Olga called back, "Gillian, I said I'll be there in a minute! Ms. Holloway, I have to go. Around three on Sunday at the restaurant." She hung up.

Barbara wrote the name, Gillian Maas. Olga Maas evidently had named her daughter after her roommate, who had died nine years before her birth.

"Not a lot," Bailey said on Tuesday morning, "and most of it's pretty mundane stuff. Aaronson's the most interesting dude in the bunch. He has a consulting business, three employees and a lot of deals under his belt. Advises about where to build a casino, where to get a tax waiver to site a new plant, things like that. McCrutchen was in on some of the deals, apparently, but the trail is hidden under layers of legalisms. Seems Aaronson has a knack of learning where commissioners are agreeable to zoning changes, and it just happens that McCrutchen served on committees that oversaw zoning rules and regulations. It would take a flock of legal experts to unravel it." His morose expression indicated that he had gone as far as he intended in that direction.

Barbara nodded. "Anything about Storey? Her murder?"

"I know the lead investigator who handled it," he said. "Guy named Barton. Retired ten or eleven years ago. We had a chat. Guy who did it wore cotton gloves, no prints. She wasn't robbed, and she wasn't sexually molested. She was grabbed from behind and had cotton fibers under her nails, but probably didn't put up much of a struggle. She was legally drunk. He figures the killer was interrupted, or thought he was being interrupted, and ran before he got to the money in her purse, eleven bucks. But a dopehead would have cleaned it out, or he would have taken it with him. That's as far as it got, and he doesn't remember much more about it."

"Just one of those things," Barbara said bitterly.

Bailey shrugged.

"Okay," Barbara said. "I'm going to the hospital to check on Etheridge's room. But until the police make their next move, we're on hold. I have a list of the partygoers that night. About thirty of them. Maybe just a quick scan to see if anyone is worth real attention. Then nothing more for now."

She gave the list to Bailey. He pulled himself up, picked up his duffel bag, saluted and walked out in no particular hurry.

"Anything for me?" Shelley asked.

"Nope. Back to routine for now."

Shelley went to the door, paused and said, as bitterly as Barbara had done, "Just one of those things. Right."

At the hospital Barbara was relieved when she was stopped at the nurse's station and asked for ID. The nurse on duty consulted a computer screen and waved her on. It was very quiet in this wing with gravely ill patients. She found the room and tapped lightly on the door before entering. Lucien Etheridge was in a chair by the bed, and rose swiftly when he saw her.

"He's really doing fine," he said, motioning toward David, who looked terrible.

One side of his face was bandaged, as well as his head, and he was very pale, his eyes sunken.

"They made him get out of bed a while ago," Lucien said. "And he did it. Stood right up."

Lucien didn't look a whole lot better than his son. A cot had been provided, overcrowding the room, but at least Lucien or his wife could try to get some rest now.

"I think they always make the patient get on his feet as soon as possible. They say it helps the healing process." She turned to David. "Hi. Your doctor said five minutes and no questions yet. Just a quick hello."

Weakly he said, "Didn't think the next time we met, I'd be in bed, dressed in a gown."

Barbara laughed. "I think this puts us on first-name terms, David. I really won't stay this time, but I'll be back. If there's anything I can bring, tell your dad to let me know."

"Some videos," Lucien said. "Maybe Charlie Chaplin, or Harold Lloyd, Marx Brothers, things like that."

"Sure," she said. "I'll drop some off later today, and come for a real visit tomorrow. See you later, David."

The Buchman cottage was situated in Yachats on a high cliff overlooking the ocean. Late that Tuesday afternoon, sitting on a deck enclosed on both sides, making an effective windbreak, with only the ocean side open, Chloe had to admit that this change had been good for her. She had been nearly catatonic, haunted by nightmares about ants no matter how many sleeping pills she took. They had left her stuporous the next day, unable to think. The change had broken the pattern.

She had gone over the same figures again and again, and regardless of how she manipulated them, the results were always the same, or so nearly the same as not to matter. With the insurance she would have little more than two hundred thousand dollars. Selling off a few stocks, the Lexus, everything she could think of, would bring in more, but not enough. How long it would last she had no firm idea, but she suspected it would not be very long.

All her dreams, her patience, her plans, her acceptance of Robert's fooling around, all of it wasted. And now what? She had no answer. A job? Doing what? She had no skills, no training, a bachelor's degree in nothing much. Not enough to get her a decent job, but enough to make a good governor's wife, or a senator's wife living in a Watergate apartment, until something better came along.

She would have to drop her season tickets to the Hult, to the Shakespeare Festival, her shopping trips to San Francisco, the country club.

She was startled and nearly fell from her chair when she heard a voice behind her.

"Why the hell haven't you answered my calls?" Nick Aaronson demanded.

She jumped up, keeping the chair between them. "What are you doing here? How did you get in?"

"You left the door unlocked, doll. We have to talk."

"Get out! Get out or I'll call the police!"

He laughed. "Get your ass in here so we can talk."

"I have nothing to say to you."

"I have plenty to say. Get in here!" He took a step toward her, and she edged back a little. "Careful, sweetheart. It's a long drop. What's the matter with you? You're afraid of me? Why?"

Warily she moved around the chair and he stepped back inside, crossed to the middle of the room, where he stopped, watching her. "You are, aren't you? Why?"

"Did you kill him? Did you?" Her voice rose and she swallowed hard.

"You're out of your fucking mind! Jesus Christ! Come in and sit down. No, I didn't shoot lover boy. Jesus."

Still moving carefully, she went inside, to the table in the kitchen, and sat on the edge of a chair. He didn't move until she was seated, then took a chair opposite her.

"Is that what you've been thinking? Why you didn't pick up your phone or call back? Are you really crazy?" He rubbed his eyes. "Do you have anything to drink here?"

She pointed toward a cabinet and watched him go to it, take out a bottle of Jack Daniels and pour some into two glasses. He added water and returned to the table, handed a glass to her and sat down again opposite her.

He took a long drink, then said slowly, "You know Robert and I worked a few deals together. They paid off for him. Six hundred thousand."

She shook her head. "I don't know anything about that, and he didn't have that kind of money."

"Tellman has it," Nick said. "Robert passed it on to him. They were building a war chest for when Robert ran for governor."

"How can I get it?"

"You can't. Forget it. Tellman will find a new boy to back. That's seed money. But, Chloe, baby, there are a couple of pending deals that Robert would have collected on, and Tellman will never see a cent of it. That will be yours."

She narrowed her eyes and picked up her own glass, took a sip, put it down. "What's the catch?"

"There could be a problem," he said. "Robert hired a detective three years ago, and he ended up with some pictures that really should not be released to the public. He showed them to me. Good likenesses of you and me. Very good likenesses."

She felt her lips go stiff and her mouth go dry. Three years ago was when she and Nick began meeting. A weekend now and then, a shorter stay in a motel somewhere, afternoons in his apartment.

Abruptly, she got up and went to the door, where she stood looking out. "Why? Why show something like that to you? Where are the pictures? Why are you telling me now?"

"You're involved," he said coldly. "I'm building a good business, bigger all the time, and those pictures would ruin it. Four deals in the works would vanish overnight. And, Chloe, they could cause a real investigation, make people ask hard questions about a few past deals and drag Robert right to the center of it. He covered his tracks pretty well, but a real investigation would uncover them. Are you prepared to defend a possible lawsuit? You know how much it could cost you? If you didn't defend it, the estate could be nicked for everything in it. And you'd miss out on Robert's share of the pending deals. That's why I'm telling you."

She swung around. "You don't have the pictures, do you?" Her voice was shrill. She returned to the table and took another sip of her drink, then a bigger one. "He showed you the pictures and kept them, didn't he? Where are they now?"

"That's the problem," Nick said. "Where are they?"

She sank back down into her chair and for a few seconds they were silent, regarding each other warily. His expression was as remote and as cold as a stranger's, she realized.

He spoke first. "You have to go back and find them. They weren't in his desk. I don't think he would have left them in Salem. Too many people might have come across them. Did you open the safe-deposit box, look over the stuff in it?"

"I looked. I didn't see any pictures," Chloe said.

"They'd be in an envelope or something, not loose," he said impatiently. "Look again, open everything in that box. He could have put them in with other papers. If they aren't in the safe-deposit box, they're in the house, in his things."

She moistened her lips. "Amy wanted me to leave so she could pack up his things, give them to the church."

He cursed savagely, drained his glass, stood and went to the counter to pour another drink. "Get back there now, tonight, and start looking. If she found them, what would she be likely to do with them?"

Chloe shook her head. "God, I don't know. Hide them again probably. Burn them. I don't know."

"You'll have to search her room, too. I'll follow your car back to town. Get your stuff together."

She finished her own drink and got up. At the door to the bedroom she looked back and asked, "Why did he show them to you?"

"He was cutting himself a piece of the pie. It's the American way."

Blackmail, she thought dully. Robert was blackmailing him. She felt her fear of Nick rebound. What better reason to kill someone than blackmail? If she found the pictures, she thought then, she would have the same ammunition that Robert had had, but she would be forewarned of the danger.

11

On Friday Barbara dropped in on Frank. "Nothing," she said glumly. "Dressler was in to ask questions today. David didn't see anyone, or hear anyone following him, so we have to assume a real ambush. No e-mail threats recently. He has a filter on his e-mail, only preapproved people can send to him. So that's a wash, too."

She was no less glum when she continued. "The doctor wants to release David on Monday or Tuesday and put him in a convalescent home for the next two weeks at least. I told him no. To the convalescent home idea, that is. No security. David's ready to make a jail break, except he's still too weak to do much more than crawl out."

"Crawling out in a hospital gown might draw someone's attention," Frank said. "Let's think about where to put him. Not a hotel or motel."

"Dr. Colfax said he'll need nursing care for a week or two, and he'll start some therapy. Apparently he had significant nerve damage in his arm. He'll be sore and hurting for weeks. Broken ribs take a long time to heal, and opening his chest the way they did to repair his lung guarantees that he won't be self-sufficient for quite a while."

Frank nodded. "I'm going to pick some beans. I wonder if the rehab clinic would take him in?" He didn't wait for an answer, but went inside to get his colander.

If they had an empty bed, she thought, why not? He would need therapy, which they could provide. They had a nursing staff, and they enforced strict rules about who could enter and when. Dr. Colfax would have to order it, get authorization from David's insurance company.

But first she should bring it up with Darren when he got back, make sure they had an empty bed. She bit her lip. Darren had called every day during the past week, and he and Todd would return on Sunday afternoon, while she was talking to Olga Maas. She had not yet told Darren that she would be tied up when he got home. He was too eager to get back. She had not been able to bring herself to put a damper on his anticipation.

Earlier that week Amy had been dismayed when Chloe returned after only two days. Those damned pictures, she kept thinking. She had to do something about those damned pictures. When it became apparent that Chloe was searching, she had mailed them to herself in Portland, to be put on hold with the rest of her mail.

That Friday she went to Portland for an office meeting, and rented a post-office box. She would check her mail every Friday when she drove up for the office meetings. And that one envelope could stay in the P.O. box.

Back in Eugene on Friday night, while she and her mother were on the deck having coffee, she said, "There's no problem having me work at home, as long as I can get to the Friday meetings."

"Have you and Chloe had words?" Lucy asked.

"Of course not. Why do you ask?"

"I'm not sure. Her attitude, yours. You're both so watchful, so careful what you say, exactly the way people are if they have quarreled. She wanted to know if you found anything in Robert's pockets. I told her I had no idea. By the time I got here, all his clothes were gone."

"I'll tell her," Amy said. "I left all his personal things, the BlackBerry, his wallet, watch, keys, things like that, on his bureau. She must have found them."

"I don't want any quarrel to erupt," Lucy said in a low voice. "Chloe has a difficult decision to make, and I want to leave her alone to make it."

"But she does have to make it," Amy said. "Obviously you're not going to let her keep living here, in your room."

"Just leave it alone," Lucy said. "Don't you bring it up, or even hint at it."

"Right," Amy said. "Barbara Holloway said I can visit David tomorrow. Remember when I was sixteen and had appendicitis, you brought in *Candide* and read to me? I was too tired to hold a book, and that was so nice, just lying there listening, maybe dozing a little. I'll never forget how nice it was. I'm going to take *Candide* and read to David, if he'll let me."

"You hardly even know him," Lucy said, surprised.

"I feel as if I know him pretty well," Amy said.

Later that night Amy wandered into the study to get the old copy of *Candide,* and before leaving she pulled the yearbook from the shelf. She opened it to the photos of the graduation class and studied David's picture again. He looked very young, and while not handsome, the hard lines and planes of his face were more appealing than the pretty-boy faces of any Hollywood star she could think of. She closed the book and started to replace it, then realized that the paper she had left sticking out a little was missing. She opened the book again and turned it upside down, fanning the pages. The party list was gone.

Why? she wondered, back in her room. What possible significance could that have for Chloe? She had no doubt that Chloe had gone through the books searching for the pictures. But a party list? Why that? She examined her own room. Two framed pictures of sleek horses, left over from her adolescent love for horses, were slightly askew, her underwear slightly disarrayed, the reference books not in the order she had left them.

On Saturday when Barbara went to the hospital, Lucien and Dora Etheridge were in David's room, and they both looked exhausted.

"We'll go down to the cafeteria for some lunch and leave you to talk," Lucien Etheridge said. "We'll be back in about an hour, son."

Barbara waited until they were gone, then sat in the chair Dora had vacated. "How's it going?" she asked.

That day David's bed was cranked up to nearly sitting position. He looked better day by day, the tubes were all gone now and the IV out of his arm. His face was no longer bandaged, and while bruises were still undergoing interesting color changes, the abrasions were healing well.

"I'm ready to fly the coop," he said. "Good answer?"

"Pretty good. We're arranging the transfer, probably to a rehab clinic where you can get the therapy you'll need."

"Do me a favor, Barbara," he said. "Tell my parents that they won't be able to keep me company after I'm out of here. They should go home, give us all a little rest."

"Good," she said. "It's something I wanted to bring up because where you'll be going the staff wouldn't allow it anyway. They go by the rules and have good security. They'll keep you busy with therapy and out walking in gardens. No more lolling about in bed."

"Music to my ears," he said.

"This is going to be your call," she said. "When you feel up to it, we have to have a long talk. You know, inquisition time. But only when you're up to it."

"Back to the real world," he said.

She nodded, then looked toward the door when there was a soft tap. She went to the door and was surprised to see Amy McCrutchen.

"Okay if I come in?" Amy asked, looking beyond Barbara at David.

"Come in," he said. "Forgive me if I don't get up to greet you properly. Next time."

"I thought, if you like, I'd read to you for a little while," Amy said hesitantly.

"Good idea," Barbara said. She turned to David. "I'll have a chat with your parents. See you tomorrow."

She found his parents in the cafeteria, where Dora's salad looked untouched and she was leaning back in her chair with her eyes closed.

Barbara told them about the plan to move David to the rehab clinic. "They'll probably take him over on Monday," she said. "But I have to tell you that you won't be able to spend much time with him there. Just regular visiting hours, about an hour a day is all."

Lucien looked ready to protest, and she said gently, "He's concerned about you and his mother, Mr. Etheridge. He can see how hard this has been on you, and it's not good for him to have anything else to worry about at this time. It would be far better for all of you if you go back home now. He'll be safe at the clinic, and they'll keep him busy with therapy. He'll be very relieved to know you're home getting some rest."

"It's been hard," Lucien said after a moment. "Not doing anything but sitting around is hard, Ms. Holloway. We're working people. It's been hard."

"David knows that," she said. "He can see it in your faces."

Dora looked torn between wanting to go home, and wanting to stay with her son.

"You have to consider what's best for him," Barbara said. "He needs all his strength and willpower to continue healing, and worrying about you saps both."

"She's right," Lucien said after another pause. "The weeds are probably overrunning the garden, and things will want watering. We should go home. We can come back for visits and talk to him on the phone." He looked at Barbara. "He'll have a phone, won't he?"

"Of course, and he has his cell phone. That's not a problem." She stood and said, "Take your time with lunch, go for a walk or a drive. It's a lovely day, and the fresh air will be good for you. David has a visitor reading to him, and I imagine he'll have a nap afterward. There's no need for you to rush back."

Mission accomplished, she thought when she left them. Dora was eating her lunch, and Lucien wanted to go home. And now, she added to herself, there was absolutely nothing she had to do until Sunday afternoon. She'd take a walk, shop for a few groceries, change the sheets on the bed. Make sure the house was straightened up a bit, no dirty dishes in the sink. Maybe polish her fingernails. She glanced at her hands and tried to remember the last time she had polished her nails. Her memory failed.

★ ★ ★

She arrived at the SweetWaters Restaurant at ten minutes before three on Sunday. It was nearly empty at that time of day, as she had suspected it would be. The brunch crowd had left, and it was too early for happy hour. She had reserved a table by a window, and, seated at it, she told the waiter that she would have an iced coffee while she waited for a friend. She had brought a book to read, but she sat gazing out the window at the flashing river instead.

Olga Maas arrived at three-twenty. She was a tall, strong-looking woman, large boned and muscular. Her hair was light brown, straight, shoulder length. Her eyes were brown and deep set, and she had the high, fine cheekbones Barbara associated with Slavic women.

"Ms. Maas?" Barbara said, rising. "I'm Barbara Holloway. Thanks for agreeing to see me. Please, sit down. Would you like to order something to drink, a sandwich? Lunch?"

Olga Maas shook her head. "Just iced tea," she said.

Barbara had taken out her driver's license to show and Olga waved it away. "After we talked on the phone, I looked you up on the Internet. I know who you are." The waiter reappeared and she ordered her drink. "You said you wanted to ask about Jill Storey. I still don't know why."

"You know that Robert McCrutchen was shot dead several weeks ago?" Barbara asked.

"Yes. I read about it. What does it have to do with Jill? Or with me?"

Quickly, touching just the highlights, Barbara explained. "So the fact that he had that file, and that David was renting an apartment in the house, has turned the attention of the investigators toward David. They seem to assume that somehow it's linked to Jill Storey's murder."

Olga looked mystified. "I don't know why. They were the best of friends."

"Some people are hinting that he was romantically involved with her, and jealousy might have played a part."

"For heaven's sake! That's crazy. They were good friends, period. Childhood friends. The girl-next-door, boy-next-door kind of friendship. They made mud pies together. She taught him how to dance. You don't turn that kind of friendship into romance."

The waiter brought her iced tea and she took a long drink.

"Will you tell me about the key to his apartment?" Barbara asked.

"Sure. Jill was a brain, going after an MBA on scholarships, and she was doing just fine until that spring. She got mono. We were both working at the same restaurant, part-time, just making it, but making it, until she got sick. She couldn't keep working and fell behind in her class work. She had to keep her grades up for the scholarship and she was pretty desperate. She talked to her instructors, pleaded with them, and managed to get extra time to finish things. So she was managing that, but the money was a crisis. We weren't going to be able to pay our rent *and* buy food. We were both from poor families who couldn't really help, or wouldn't." She sipped her drink and looked out the window, then continued.

"We were sitting at an outdoor café, sharing a Coke," she said. "David came by and joined us, and we ended up telling him our tale of woe." She kept her focus out the window. "Anyway, David said he would be leaving on Monday, and he said his roomie, Ted, wanted to keep the apartment for the fall term. He suggested that it might be possible for us to move in, split the rent with Ted, cut our expenses that way. He said he'd call Ted and clear it with him and get back to us later about it." She picked up her tea and swished it around in her glass. Her voice dropped then as she said, "David called the waitress and he picked up the check. He used a twenty to pay for it and gave Jill the change.

"He called later on, just before I went to work, and said it was all set. He'd had another key made, and he'd give it to Jill at the party. She lay down to nap. She said she wanted to rest so she could get stinking drunk at the party and dance her feet off."

Olga looked at Barbara then and said, "That's the story about the key. That's what I told the police. They have no reason to be suspicious of David."

Barbara motioned to the waiter and ordered antipasto. "Something to nibble on," she said. "How did Jill get to the party that night? Did someone take her?"

"No. I had a car. She took it. The restaurant was by the Bijou, just around the corner from our apartment. I always walked over. We both did before she got too sick to work."

"Was she likely to have picked up a hitchhiker that late at night?"

Olga shook her head emphatically. "No way. Not at any time of night."

"Were you in the graduating class with her?" Barbara asked after a moment.

Olga had returned to river gazing. "No. I was a year behind her. I went back home a week after... I went home and stayed down there, got my degree at Southern Oregon in Ashland the next year. I didn't think I could stand going back to Eugene, back to the U of O."

The waiter brought the antipasto and a basket of bread and crackers. Barbara helped herself to a slice of salami. "I know this is painful for you, but can you tell me a little about Jill's background, home life, anything that might shed a little light on her death?"

Olga hesitated, then said in a nearly toneless voice, "She had two older sisters, five or six years older or a little more, and they had very little to do with her. Her father was disappointed, even angry, to have a third girl and no son. I think her home life was pretty bad, lonely for her, and there was very little money. I don't think she was abused, unless you count being ignored and belittled. Her father had a truck, hauled trash for people, moved appliances, things like that, when he could get the jobs. David lived next door, literally next door, and they were pals from a very early age. His dad was in construction, seasonal work, and they had little money, but his parents seem to have adored him, and they were good to Jill. They made up for a lot, I think."

She began to pick up tidbits from the platter, almost absently it appeared, simply because the food was there. And slowly the picture of Jill's childhood and adolescence through high school emerged. Emotionally neglected, hungry for attention, recognition, which she never got at home, despite her intelligence, despite winning a coveted scholarship, her continuing success in college.

"Did she have boyfriends in college, seem interested in any particular guy? Could there have been some jealousy involved?" Barbara asked.

Olga shook her head. "No time for any of that. School, three-point-eight grade average, work as many hours as possible and no time for guys. That was her life. She took classes that made my head spin just looking at her textbooks. Statistics! Math. Economic theory from the days of the Ark to present."

"History, apparently," Barbara said. "She was Dr. Elders's student that last term."

"Undergrad requirement," Olga said. "She had to take a history class and that was the only one she could fit into her schedule."

Possibly her lack of interest accounted for Elders's scant memory of her, Barbara thought. "It seems strange that if she was still suffering fatigue from mono, that she would have been one of the last to leave the party that night."

"Maybe not," Olga said after a moment. "You can't believe the relief we both felt at the thought of cutting our expenses for rent by more than half. We did the numbers after David left us that afternoon. It meant she could fully recover, and in the fall she would have been a T.A., no more heavy trays to carry or crazy hours, a completely different life. And her real fear of losing the scholarship was gone. You have no idea how desperate an intelligent girl like Jill can be to change her life, to escape. I think she was experiencing an almost hysterical reaction to fear and dread of being forced back home, to a go-nowhere job, to her mother's kind of existence. I imagine she did nearly dance her feet off, and ate and drank far too much."

She had begun speaking with an intensity that she had not shown before and Barbara wondered how much of Jill's life reflected Olga's own desperation to escape a dreary home life.

Olga glanced at her watch, finished her tea, and said, "I have to go get the girls. It's a long drive to Medford and I want to get there before dark."

Barbara got out her credit card. "Let's get a box and let you take the snacks along. The girls will eat it, won't they?"

"They'll eat anything not moving," Olga said.

The waiter came, left for a box and returned promptly. Taking the credit card with him, he left again. Olga emptied the platter and stood. "Thanks for the snacks," she said.

"No, I'm the one to give thanks. You've been very helpful in filling in a cloudy picture in my mind. I appreciate it," Barbara said.

Waiting to pay the tab, she thought about the passion that had come to Olga's voice as she described Jill's state of mind the last night of her life. She remembered that lovely young face in the yearbook and felt her pity for Jill swell anew.

No one that young, that determined and so full of promise should have her life choked out.

Darren's truck was in the driveway when Barbara arrived home. She hurried into the house, on to the bedroom, where she could hear the shower running. She stripped off her clothes and tossed them toward the bed, and seconds later she opened the shower door and stepped inside.

"Welcome home," she said softly.

12

Monday morning when Frank joined Barbara and Shelley, he said, "I talked to Lester Colfax a while ago. David's doctor," he added to Shelley. "Lester agreed that the rehab clinic would be suitable for David. The transfer will be made this afternoon, depending on the results of a new MRI scan. He has a list of names of visitors to be allowed and he'll speak to Darren about treatment."

"Good," Barbara said. She told them what little she had learned from Olga Maas, then spread her hands. "So now we wait to see what the cops do next. Interesting, though, isn't it, that three women seem to accept that David had nothing to do with Jill Storey's murder and for that reason, the lack of motive, nothing to do with Robert's murder. The victim's mother, his sister and a friend's roommate from two decades ago."

"What's strange about that?" Shelley asked, frowning.

"Amy was a kid when David left these parts, and didn't meet him again until after her brother was shot to death. Mrs. Mc-

Crutchen had seen him only as another student among many years ago and Jill's roommate hardly knew him at all. Just interesting."

Frank nodded in agreement, and Shelley said, "Well, maybe they know something about him, or about one or the other death, that makes them sure."

"Exactly," Barbara said. "Well, I'll have a long talk with David later this week and until then, there's not much we can do."

The weather took a turn that week, and by Thursday, when Barbara and Frank arrived at the rehab clinic, the temperature was in the high nineties and climbing. After leaving the cool car to enter the bake-oven heat outdoors, the clinic felt almost too cool.

Annie McIvey met them and greeted them both as old friends. She was one of the trustees in the nonprofit clinic and nominally in charge, but that was known to be a mischaracterization. Darren really ran the clinic.

"He's with a patient," Annie said, "but he said to show you to his office, and David will be down in a minute." She preceded them to the office and opened the door.

Darren's office was scrupulously neat. His desk held several folders with nothing loose scattered about, pens and pencils in a mug, a vertical blind closed most of the way.

Three chairs were arranged by a table with a sweating pitcher of ice water and glasses. Barbara and Frank were still chatting with Annie when there was a tap on the door; one of the interns opened it and David walked in.

Although he moved carefully, his color was better than it had been before, and he was steady on his feet. He was wearing chinos, a short-sleeved cotton shirt not tucked in, and Birkenstocks. His right arm was still discolored with bruises.

Annie excused herself and left them as Barbara introduced her father to David. "Dad is my colleague," she said as they all seated themselves. "He keeps me on the straight and narrow as much as he can."

David nodded, then said gravely, "He must be good at it. People around here seem to regard you as a modern-day Saint Joan."

She waved it away. "Rumors, nothing but rumors. David, I'd like to start back at the beginning. Back twenty-two years or more. Okay with you?"

"Sure," he said. "Back to my childhood, back to Jill's childhood. I assume that's what you mean."

"It is. Whatever you want to tell us, and if we have questions, they'll come later."

"We lived on the outskirts of Gresham," he said. "Fields around and some woods, not quite rural, but close. It's all built-up now, of course. They lived next door to us, with no other kids our age in sight. Jill and I were playmates from my earliest memories of playing outside. We were explorers, astronauts, Indians, whatever came up, made-up games for poor kids with few toys and no planned activities."

As he spoke the picture he painted was a repetition of the one Olga had related. Jill's two older sisters, aloof, disdainful; a father who rejected his youngest daughter from the day of her birth; a mother unable to cope with an extremely bright child.

"Her parents didn't want her to go to college, even though she had that scholarship. They wanted her to get a job, get married, settle down. We came down here together, and she was never really back home again, except for infrequent, short visits. She worked summers, after classes, whenever she could. They never gave her a cent. I saw her now and then, but not a lot. Different classes, different tracks. She was in business, I was in humanities, and we both worked part-time."

Barbara poured ice water and handed him a glass and another to Frank. "So neither of you lived in the dorms."

"No. We were both what they call geeks now, serious about school, and no interest in or time for dorm games, sororities or fraternities and no money for them in any event. Okay, getting up to the last year. That spring was the first time we were ever in the same class, Elders's history seminars. It shocked me to see how worn-out she was. Pale and thin as a rail. She told me she'd had mono, and was trying to get through in spite of it. She was afraid she wasn't going to catch up and that she would lose out on the scholarship and the MBA she was determined to get. I told her to talk to each instructor and try to make deals to allow some extra time. A week or so later she told me she'd done that, and it was going to be all right. Then I saw her and Olga on the day of the party."

He drank his water and shook his head at Barbara's offer to refill his glass. "I was going to leave on Monday," he said slowly. "My roommate, Ted Folsom, had already left for the summer, but he wanted to keep the apartment, and it occurred to me that Jill and Olga could help. They jumped at the chance, sure that they could get half the rent between them. I called Ted as soon as I left them, okayed it with him and I had an extra key made. Since I'd be in and out until Monday morning, I didn't want to give them mine, and I knew I wouldn't see them early on Monday. Later I walked over to the McCrutchen house. Jill was already there, and I gave her the key."

"Did you and Jill ever date? As in romantic dating?" Barbara asked.

"Never," he said.

"Did you give her money?"

"That spring I did. Ten bucks one time, fifteen another time. If I'd had more, I would have given them more. You have to realize they were dead broke. Olga couldn't carry both of them on her part-time job, and Jill wasn't able to work for months that spring."

"Okay. At the party, did you and Robert have an argument?" Barbara asked.

He hesitated, then said, "He was pestering her, and I told him to bug off. No big deal."

"Pestering her how?"

"Look, Robert was a chaser all through school. But he and Chloe had just become engaged. They announced it that night, and he had no business trying to hustle Jill. She told him to get lost and so did I. End of the little melodrama. The whole thing lasted less than five minutes, and no one else was on the deck."

"How did Robert behave after that little episode?"

"I didn't see him again that night."

"What about Jill? How was she afterward?"

He shook his head. "I didn't see her, either. I think she left immediately after that."

"How much longer did you stay at the party?"

"Ten, fifteen minutes. There weren't many of us left by then, and when people realized that Robert had left, everyone decided it was time to call it quits. I walked back home," he said, before she could ask. "I walked over, and I walked back to my apartment."

"Back up a little. Did you have other classes with Robert?"

"A couple early on. But we weren't friends, or anything like friends. I never even saw him out of class except at the seminars. Why?"

"Well, you said you hadn't seen him for more than twenty years, and more or less implied that he wasn't the brightest bulb on the tree, a two-bit politician, a nothing in your universe. What was that based on?"

"The little I saw of him left the impression that he was a mediocre student, a shallow thinker, with no interest in anything except fun and games, A frat boy. Of course," he added after a pause, "he could have changed, matured, and since he passed the bar exam, it stands to reason that he did apply himself to some extent."

For the first time, Frank spoke. "Let's have a little break. David, do you want some coffee? Maybe we could have some about now. We don't want to tire you, and if you want to knock off at any time, just give the word."

"I'm okay," David said. "Coffee would be good. They make pretty decent coffee here, by the way."

"I'll go rustle up some," Barbara said.

"I read your book, *The American Myth Stakes*," Frank said. "Damn fine book. Congratulations."

Barbara left while Frank was speaking. Outside the door, she turned toward the reception desk, and met Darren coming from one of the treatment rooms. He grinned broadly when he saw her, pulled the door closed, then embraced her. "What I'd like to see every time I leave one room for another," he murmured into her hair.

"You'll scandalize the staff," she said with a laugh. "What do you think of your new patient, David Etheridge?"

Darren gave her a squeeze, kissed her lightly on the lips and drew back. "Good guy. A trouper. Working hard and making progress. Enough?"

She laughed again. "What a pro! I'm on a coffee search. Any reason we should be careful with him?"

"If he decides he's had enough, he'll tell you," Darren said. "Come on, we'll order coffee. Then I'm back to the salt mines."

"Let's take Dad for a meal somewhere with air-conditioning later." Todd was at his mother's house for his usual summer visit, and Darren was working long hours, catch-up week, he had said, dismissing it. She had no intention of preparing a meal or expecting Frank to make dinner in the heat.

"You're on. I'll be late," Darren said.

They had reached the reception desk. "I'll wait at Dad's. We have things to discuss, and it's no hotter there than at home. See you later." She asked Molly, at the reception desk, if she'd call the kitchen for coffee, then returned to the office where Frank and David were still talking about his book.

"I condensed some lectures," David was saying. "Tied them together with the theme of myth making, and it seemed to work okay."

"Not just okay. Brilliantly," Frank said.

"Coffee's on the way," Barbara told them, taking her seat again. "I saw Darren and he assured me that if you decided you'd had enough interrogation, you'd be forthright about telling us. I assume that he spoke from personal experience."

David shrugged. "I may have a tendency to forget diplomacy from time to time."

A few minutes later Molly brought in a tray with the coffee service, smiled at David and left again. Barbara examined David, looking for whatever it was about him that made pretty young women look at him that way.

"I don't want to belabor this much longer," she said, after pouring and passing the cups around. "Just briefly for now, fill us in on that Sunday night, and Monday morning. The night Robert was shot."

"Okay. I had dinner with Randolf Gergen and his wife. He's another historian, and they were on their way to San Francisco, making a minitour of the northwest on the way. We talked a long time and I got home before eleven, but I can't say exactly when. I turned on the news at eleven, so that part's firm. I didn't hear a shot, and I didn't go out on the deck. I was making a few notes to add to my prepared text for my talk."

He sipped the coffee and nodded. "Good. Monday morning.

I heard the woman screaming and ran out. She began throwing up, out on the lawn, and I saw Robert's body by the door at the other end. I ran over, but no point to that. He was dead. You know about the ants. Chloe seemed to be in shock and almost instantly Elders appeared. I told him to get Chloe inside, and I ran back to my place for my cell phone, and I picked up the camera and put it in my pocket. I took water and a box of tissues out for the gardener. I called nine-one-one, and asked Elders where a phone book was and told him to make some coffee. I found an address book on a little desk in the kitchen. I took it out to the deck. I wanted to call Robert's mother before she heard it on the news. I saw Amy's name in the book and called her first, then I called Mrs. McCrutchen. I was standing in front of Robert's body, maybe trying to screen it from view of the woman. And I took pictures of the body. I'm not sure why, but I did. I thought maybe there was a paper by his hand. I couldn't make out what was on it. Anyway, I took pictures, and put the camera back in my pocket, and by then the police had arrived. They ordered me back into the kitchen and I went in and sat down. I was still there when Amy arrived and Chloe started screaming. Amy took her and put her to bed. Elders was fussing around, doing coffee, getting in the way, and the police made him sit down and stay down. And that's about it. Of course, they began asking questions, but we went to my apartment for that."

"Why did you take the camera out when you went for the cell phone?"

"They were together. I just grabbed them both and stuck them in my pocket. From the outside, they look pretty much alike. I needed both hands for the water and tissues. I didn't stop to think about it."

"And you think the paper you saw made you decide to take pictures?"

"Maybe," he said. "It looked strange. No writing, just some marks that I couldn't make out."

"I have a copy," Barbara said. She told him about looking over the camera and his computer file of pictures. "When I was canceling various things, I came across them. I made a copy. Have you looked at it again, that paper?"

"Sure. And I still don't know what it signifies."

"Me, neither," Barbara said. "Did you see the gun?"

He said no. At her questions, he said he had not gone into the house at all since coming back to Eugene, not beyond the desk in the kitchen, and then the kitchen table when the investigators told him to go inside.

"So they won't find your fingerprints anywhere in the house. Is that right?"

"Yes. Just where I told you. Unless they're left over from twenty-two years ago."

A new sharpness in his voice made Barbara suspect that he was tiring, and she finished her coffee, then said, "Let's leave it at that for now. We'll come back to it later if we think of anything we'd like to clarify."

She stood and watched David closely as he got up. He seemed much stiffer than when he came in, and for a second or two, he remained hunched over slightly, holding on to his chair back before he straightened all the way. No one commented, but she suspected they had stayed longer than was good for him. She was aware that Frank had moved a step or two closer to him.

They separated in the wide hallway outside the door, with David heading for the elevator, and she and Frank for the outside door. They walked out into blazing heat.

The air conditioner in Barbara's car had made little difference on the short drive to Frank's house, and she was drenched with sweat by the time they arrived. She headed for his back porch and deep shade. He turned on a ceiling fan, and a floor model, and they sat in silence for a time. To all appearances there were two very large, dead, gold cats stretched to what seemed an impossible length, in the shade of a rosebush. Neither one even twitched at their arrival.

"If his story and Olga's hold up, it's hard to see how a case can be made for Jill's murder, and without that as motive, harder to see them making a case for Robert's," she said finally.

"I hope to God they don't try," Frank said. "He's transparently honest, when he isn't dodging. And it's too obvious when he's dodging."

"Yeah, there is that. Not enough practice lying. Also, he comes across as a little too arrogant, too dismissive of anyone not quite as smart as he is, and that includes most people, apparently. It would include a possible jury panel, and they tend not to cuddle up to that kind of personality. Plus, he'd have to curb his contempt for Robert. I bet he doesn't even know how much he reveals it." But, she added silently, he had something that made pretty young women smile at him in a certain way. A jury panel made up of pretty young women? In your dreams, she thought derisively.

13

By the time Nick arrived that Friday morning, Chloe was already sweaty. Her hair was plastered to her head, her bare legs glistened with moisture, and her tank top was wet where it touched her. She glared at Nick.

"I told you they aren't here! I searched her room, her purse, everything. I know she didn't take them to Portland. The only thing she had with her was her laptop and the purse, and I had already looked inside."

"If she didn't take them, they're still in the house," he said.

"Well, have fun. I'm packing up my things to get out of here. I have a nice cool apartment with a swimming pool waiting for me."

She turned her back on him, but he caught her arm and swung her around. "Don't take that tone with me, doll. Keep in mind I'm not alone in those pictures. You're there, wearing a hell of a lot less than you are right now. You're going to help me look. When do you expect them back?"

"Lucy said it would be late," she said sullenly, rubbing her arm where he had grabbed her. "Amy's meeting is for one o'clock. They won't get out of Portland before four, and if traffic is heavy, they'll wait and come after dinner."

"So we have four or five hours. Let's get at it. The study first," he said.

"I already looked there."

"We'll look again." He reached for her, and she stepped back, then walked around him to the study. "Take the books," he said, right behind her. "Each one. Like this." He pulled a book from the bottom shelf, held it by the spine and riffled through the pages, then put it back and drew out the next one.

Chloe eyed the shelves, about eight feet of shelving, nearly floor to ceiling. After a moment she began taking out one book after another. Nick moved on to the desk where he opened a drawer, examined everything in it, then pulled it out to look at the bottom.

He looked under the desk, turned over the chair to examine the bottom, went on to a table where he repeated this, then upended an easy chair, a standing lamp to look at the undersides. When there was nothing left but the top two rows of books, he began to look through them alongside Chloe.

Neither spoke again until every book had been removed and returned to the shelf.

"Her room," he said curtly.

Chloe led the way upstairs to Amy's room, where it was obvious at a glance there were few places to hide anything. Nick stood near the bed, looking around, then said, "Help me lift the mattress. We'll do it in here, then in Robert's room, and I'll finish up. You can get on with your packing."

She helped lift the mattress and watched him look it over. They replaced it, went to Robert's room, where there was even less to search. The room and closet had been stripped, a bedspread was on the bed, but other bedding had been removed.

She left him in Robert's room, returned to her own room downstairs and sat on the side of the bed, thinking. If Amy had found the pictures, she could have burned them. Or she had hidden them again in order to make use of them later. But how? Not blackmail. She felt certain of that much. But Amy had become interested in David Etheridge, and David seemed to be the one the police were interested in, not Nick, or anyone else. Chloe's eyes narrowed. If Amy had the pictures, she might turn them over to David or to Barbara Holloway. They might try to implicate her, or her and Nick together, in Robert's murder. She had thought earlier that blackmail was sufficient motive for murder, but couldn't that be applied to her, as well as to Nick?

She got up and went back upstairs, where Nick was still in Robert's room. He had rolled up much of the rug and was unrolling it when she entered.

"Nick, when we moved here, we put a lot of stuff in storage. That was two years ago. What if he never brought those pictures to this house in the first place?"

He cursed as he finished flattening the rug. He looked as hot as she was, with great wet patches on his shirt. Like her, he was wearing shorts and his legs were shiny and moist. "Let's get something to drink," he said, and pushed past her and down the stairs.

In the kitchen he washed his hands and splashed water on his face, then drank a glass of water before saying anything. "Okay, maybe you're right. He knew they'd be safe in storage and just left them there. He showed them to me three years ago, while you were living in the town house. So either they're in that stuff, or little sister Amy found them and has put them somewhere. We have to know which."

She nodded. "I know we do. There's nowhere else in this house where Robert would have hidden them, or where Amy would have if she found them."

He drew another glass of water, crossed to the table and sat down, regarding her with suspicion. "So why are you so cooperative all at once?"

She sat opposite him. "Amy's getting involved with David Etheridge. God knows why, but she is. She visits him every day. And the police suspect him of killing Robert. Those pictures could make them change their prime suspect to us. It's that simple."

"What's his motive?" Nick asked. "Opportunity doesn't quite make it."

"Jill Storey's murder," she said. "They fought over her on the night of the party here. The night she was killed. David won. Protecting his own, something like that."

Nick shook his head. "They cleared him years ago, if he even was suspected to begin with."

"Maybe they'll unclear him," she said slowly. "I never mentioned that fight. You didn't, either, did you?"

"I wasn't even—" He stared at her, raised his glass and drank again, then said, "No, I never did."

They were still sitting at the table a few minutes later when Henry Elders tapped on the screen door. "Hi," he said. "Is that Nick Aaronson? I haven't seen you in years. How've you been?" Without waiting for an invitation, he entered the kitchen.

"Nick's helping me move," Chloe said. "Hot work."

"You're moving out? Is Lucy home to stay? Is that the plan?"

"Something like that," Chloe said. "She isn't home. She went to Portland with Amy."

"But she's come back to stay. That's very good news." He smiled broadly. "I've missed her. Is Amy planning on moving back, too?"

"I don't know what she's planning," Chloe said. "We were just talking about that. It seems she's become fixated on David Etheridge, and I think he's bad news for her."

Henry's pleased expression changed to one of dismay. "Oh, my, that certainly is bad news. How could she? Doesn't she realize that he most likely killed her brother?"

"Why would he have done that?" Nick asked. He lifted his glass and peered at Elders over the rim as he sipped.

"Because Robert was on to something to do with Jill Storey's death years ago. Something that was very threatening to David, of course. You know he was quite involved with Jill, don't you? And she was trying to shake him or something."

"I've heard that's the case," Nick said. "I didn't realize you knew about it."

Elders shrugged. "I thought most people knew. Well, I'm happy that Lucy's home to stay. I'll let you get on with your packing." He went back out the way he had come, through the back door.

"Nosy old bastard," Chloe said in a low voice. "I bet he saw your car and couldn't stand not knowing who was here. God, I'll be glad to get out of here. I'm going to finish my packing."

"I'll help," Nick said. "Then, let's go get some boxes out of storage."

At eight that night, Chloe sat at her table across from Nick, the remains of a take-out dinner between them. Her apartment was strewn with boxes and piles of bedding, linens, kitchenware, odds and ends. She regarded Nick with hatred. "Now what?"

"She has them," he said flatly.

"So we ask her to please hand them over," Chloe said bitterly. "Or do you propose to string her up by her thumbs until she tells you where they are? Or just pray for a highway accident that wipes her out?"

"Shut up," he said, in an absent way, as if he were not really paying any attention to her words. "Where's Etheridge?"

"I don't know. In a convalescent home or something."

"He's going to recover?"

"So they say. She doesn't tell me anything more than what a spokesman puts out."

"Where's her apartment?"

"Portland."

"I know Portland," he snapped. "Street address."

"I don't know," she said angrily. "Stop taking that kind of voice to me. She's not my girlfriend, she doesn't tell me a thing and I never asked. It's in the address book at the house. That's all I know."

He rubbed his eyes. "We have to go get it tonight," he said. "Now. If they stayed in Portland for dinner probably they aren't home yet, but if they are, you can say you're just checking to make sure you didn't leave anything. I want that address."

"Nick, I'm beat. I'll get it tomorrow, or Sunday."

"Now," he said, getting up from the table. "I'll drive."

"Look, even if she hands them to the police, she can't prove Robert ever had them."

"His prints are all over them," he said. "Mine are, too." His voice was as cold as ice then when he said, "If I don't find them in her apartment, Etheridge might have to have a little setback."

Chloe felt a chill as his words penetrated deep within her, and she rose slowly. "No," she whispered. His expression was bleak, his stranger's face implacable, and she knew he meant it. She recalled something Henry had said after David's attack—if he died, they'd close the books on Robert's murder. Obviously if David was the murderer, there was no point in keeping the case open. But if he was going to live, and if Amy gave him the pictures, it could mean a thorough investigation including the deals Nick and Robert had perpetrated, meaning possible criminal charges, the possibility of being investigated as a suspected murderer. Nick clearly did not intend to let any of it happen.

She had felt many different emotions concerning him, lust, even love for a brief period, hatred, contempt, but never before had she feared him, not until after Robert's murder. That fear surged again.

"Dad got his copyedited manuscript," Barbara told Shelley on Monday. "We might not see much of him for weeks." Frank's second book, this one on case law, was due for publication in the fall. "And Bailey's still checking out all those party attendees. We're at a standstill for now."

They discussed the coming week with little enthusiasm. The heat was not letting up, business at Martin's restaurant was slack, and they'd both had court dates postponed for various reasons. Barbara suspected that judges, prosecutors, defendants, claimants all were cooling off at the coast.

"So, surf the Internet, do your nails, go home, whatever you want," Barbara said, leaning back in the easy chair. "It's too damn hot at home to go there, and the park isn't any better. I'm going to hang out right here."

"I'll finish up a couple of things and head for home and the pool," Shelley said.

Barbara waved her out. It was maddening being at a standstill. Two murders and one attempted murder, to all appearances totally disconnected, but with David at the center each time. David surrounded by a small circle of others. It felt like knowing about a closed party for which she did not have a password, and was denied admittance.

She was relieved when her phone buzzed and Maria said Lieutenant Hoggarth was on the line.

"What can I do for you, Lieutenant?" she asked pleasantly.

He sounded brusque, annoyed, or perhaps even angry, and not at all pleasant. "I want to know when we can talk to David Etheridge," he said. "Where did you stash him?"

"Oh, dear. Lieutenant Dressler already talked to him," she said sweetly. "Didn't he tell you?"

"You know damn well that isn't what I want to talk to him about. Look, Holloway, I don't want to play games with you. It's hot as hell, and I'm sore. I didn't want this case, but I've got it, and I need to talk to him."

"His doctor will make the decision," she said, assuming a patient teacher-to-recalcitrant-student voice. "David is recovering from life-threatening injuries and he's in no shape for the rubber hose and bright lights. As soon as I hear, I'll let you know."

He muttered something inaudible that very likely was a curse, then said, "That court order's still in effect. Keep that in mind, and tell him to keep it in mind."

"Cross my heart," she said. He hung up with a crash, and she grinned and hung up her own phone. Poor Hoggarth, she mused. It seemed that whenever she was involved in the defense of a capital case, he automatically was put in charge. Bad karma, no doubt.

She resumed her musing. Password, she thought again. She needed a password, a key. She opened the Etheridge file on her desk and found the printout David had made of the paper with *x*'s on it, and the one word, *Key.* A key to the puzzle? Key to Jill's murder? A matter completely separate? The cluster of *x*'s near the top of the sheet of paper, each one carefully drawn, neat, as if each had been separately considered, then added. Three near the bottom drawn with the same neatness, the same appearance of careful positioning, meaning something. She stared at the *x*'s. The paper told her nothing. She replaced it in the folder and eyed some mail she should be answering.

She put off the mail to go on the Internet instead to look up Robert McCrutchen's voting record as a senator, the bills he had sponsored or supported, those he opposed. She learned specifics, but nothing substantial to add to what she already knew about him. Rock-hard conservative, moderating his language about a few social issues, pleasant and affable most of the time, accommodating...

"Politician," she muttered under her breath, and looked up David again. Three published books, each one modestly successful, good critical notices and reviews and some harsh criticism. His appointment as an Oxford lecturer apparently was a real plum, more than she had realized before.

Maria buzzed her to say Amy McCrutchen was on the line.

She took the call. "I really need to see you," Amy said. "Is it all right if I come over? I just left the clinic."

"Sure. Is it about David? Is he okay?"

"Yes, much better. It will take me ten minutes. I'll come right over."

She wore a sleeveless, pale blue cotton dress that seemed to touch her at the shoulders and nowhere else, but there was no garment that helped with the temperature at one hundred degrees.

"Sit down and cool off," Barbara said. "I'm having iced coffee. Do you want that, a Coke, ice water?"

Amy shook her head. "I'm all right. Today, someone followed me to the clinic."

"Tell me about it," Barbara said. She indicated the chairs by the round table, then went to the little bar for ice cubes and water. She put the filled glass in front of Amy, who was sitting on the edge of her chair.

"I had to go to the post office, and then I went to the clinic.

I saw the car on my street first, then again when I drove around looking for a parking space by the post office. You know, there's nowhere handy there. I parked a block away, and the same car drove right by. I saw it again when I turned in at the clinic. It kept going. But he knows where I went."

She said it in a rush, and then picked up the water and drank deeply, but continued to sit upright, almost rigidly on the edge of her chair.

Barbara waited until she put the glass down. "Take it more slowly," she said. "Are you sure it was the same car? A lot of them look alike, you know."

"We don't have much traffic on our street," Amy said. "That's what made me notice. It was parked up the street and it started when I left the driveway. Black, two door. I don't know what make it was, maybe a Honda. I drove on Franklin, then Sixth to go to the post office and it did, too. I know it was the same car. That time of day traffic's light. I had to drive past the post office to find parking, down toward the train station. And it kept going, but that's all that's down there, just the train station. There was more traffic on the bridge, but after I turned off and got on Country Club Road, I saw it again. We were the only two cars in sight going in that direction. I know it was the same."

Barbara nodded. "Could you see the driver?"

Amy shook her head. "A man, that's all I could tell. When I was putting coins in the parking meter by the post office, I didn't notice the car until he was already past me. Just a man."

"What about over the weekend? Did anyone follow you then?"

"I didn't leave the house Saturday or Sunday," she said. "I spent the weekend working. Besides, David's parents visited him over the weekend, and I didn't want to intrude."

"Hold it a minute," Barbara said. "I'll call Darren and alert him."

He was with a patient, Molly said on the phone. Barbara asked her to relay her message for Darren to call as soon as he had a minute. She returned to her chair. "Are you sure you don't want iced coffee or something else to drink?"

"Maybe iced coffee," Amy said. She finally shifted her position on the chair and looked less likely to bolt and run.

Barbara prepared the coffee, then said, "You said David's much better. That's good to hear."

"I hadn't seen him for three days and the change is really marked. He's walking a lot more, he said. But early, before it gets so hot. He's getting his strength back and he's pushing himself."

"I'm sure Darren won't let him overdo it," Barbara said. Her phone rang and she crossed over to her desk to take the call. It was Darren. She told him what Amy had said, then added, "Absolutely no visitors except family, Amy, his doctor or one of my crew. And please make certain that back gate is kept locked. Okay?"

"You know it," he said. "Look, there are four husky interns on duty these days, and a receptionist with a brain and a good voice. He'll be all right. See you later. Love you."

Four interns? Usually he trained two at a time. That probably helped account for the long hours he was putting in. The thought raced through her mind as she hung up and returned to her chair.

"They'll keep an eye out," she said. "Did you mention this to David?"

"No. I didn't want to alarm him while he's so helpless. He really is, you know. Helpless, I mean. He knew something was wrong, and I said it was the heat."

Barbara nodded. "It was good thinking not to tell him, and also good to give me the word." She paused, then said, "Can you stay a few minutes? I'd like very much to ask a few questions."

Amy nodded. "Sure."

"Do you have any memory of the graduation party your parents gave for Robert and his class?"

"Some," Amy said. "Remember, I was just fourteen, and not allowed in the family room where they were dancing. Why?"

"I'm trying to get a handle on that graduating group, and they keep slipping away. Conflicting memories. Not unusual, of course, but hard to sort out. Can you think back to the party and talk about it, what you remember? If there were tensions, quarrels, anything more than fun and games. Whatever comes to mind."

"I remember some things pretty well," Amy said after a moment. "Robert and Chloe announced their engagement, for one thing. And there were champagne toasts. We, my friend Greta, and I, didn't get any." She grinned. "That's the sort of thing we remember, isn't it?"

Smiling, Barbara agreed.

"There was a lot of food," Amy said. "We ate a lot, and so did most of the others. I remember that Jill ate a lot, and she was so thin. It didn't seem fair that she could eat like that and stay thin."

"You knew her?" Barbara asked.

"No, not really. I had just turned fourteen, and they were all twenty-one, twenty-two, even a little older. It's hard to bridge that kind of gap. I doubt any of them paid attention to me at any time, and I certainly had not paid attention to them the times they'd been to the house for the seminars. But she was very pretty and, as I said, thin. That made me remember her, I guess. Then, her murder seemed to fix her in my mind. Also, she was a really good dancer." She shook her head. "I didn't know then that she had been ill, and she was poor. Maybe that was the first time in ages that she'd had more food than she could eat. At fourteen, we don't think of such things, I guess. I know I was really callous about poor Mrs. Elders." She glanced quickly at Barbara, then away. "I just thought how gross she was," she said in a low voice. "Peeling skin, fat, smelled bad, whiny. Severe ichthyosis, but I just saw the effects and hated them. Their house was like a refrigerator, and Dr. Elders would be outside grading papers or reading because he would freeze inside, and she couldn't stand to be out." She paused again, then said, "I think kids that age are extremely judgmental. I know I was, and most of the girls I knew were. We judged without knowing anything."

"Did you like Dr. Elders?"

Amy shrugged. "I didn't like or dislike him for years. He just was there, Robert's teacher, my parents' friend, and he was nothing to me, just another boring adult. Once in a while, he'd notice me and put on that kind of condescending smile some adults inflict on the young because they don't have anything to say to them. After the party that night, I decided I definitely did not like him."

"What happened that night?" Barbara asked.

Amy told her about trying to sneak beer. "Neither of us had ever had any, and we just wanted to try it. But he acted as if I had committed high treason. He got all sad and soulful, as if he feared hellfire and damnation awaited us. You know, more in pity and deep sorrow than anger. He'd been dancing a lot, and he and Robert were hot and sweaty, on their way to get some beer, but for us to do the same was cause for mourning."

Barbara laughed. "Do as I say, not as I do. Kids find that really offensive, don't they?"

"You bet they do! I decided on the spot that he was a sanctimonious hypocrite. Anyway, Mother came out and told us to get a sandwich or something and take it to my room, and that was that."

But, she added to herself, that was when she had fallen in love for the first time. And, she was afraid, for the only time.

"What time was that? Do you recall?" Barbara asked.

"After eleven. A quarter after, something like that. Greta and I took stuff to eat to my room and talked and got ready for bed." Her focus shifted away, and she sipped her coffee.

"Was the party still in full swing when you went up?" Barbara felt that there was a new tension in Amy, perhaps even an evasiveness that had been absent earlier.

"Some people had left by then, and hardly anyone was still dancing. For a little while I could hear the music, but then the loud music stopped, and someone was playing the piano and one of the guys played an acoustic guitar."

"Did you hear Robert go to his room?" Barbara watched Amy as she asked, curious whether she would rise to the defense of her brother.

"No," Amy said, not at all easing the new sense of tension in the air. She appeared unaware of it. Before, it had been apparent that her responses were spontaneous, not guarded, but now she was being careful, measuring each word. "We had music on in my room, and we were talking. I didn't hear him at all that night."

"Amy," Barbara said slowly, "I've heard from others, including David, by the way, that he and Robert had some kind of confrontation over Jill. Apparently it was after you and your friend went upstairs. Did you see anything that might have led to words or worse between them?"

Amy shook her head and drank more coffee, emptying her glass. "Robert might have watched them dancing earlier," she said after a moment. "David told me that Jill taught him how to dance, and they practiced together when they were in high school. They danced well together. Several people noticed. Greta and I did." Again she was avoiding Barbara's gaze, watching a dwindling ice cube as she tilted her glass one way then the other.

Frustrated, Barbara wanted to shake her. Not yet, she thought. It could come to that, but not yet. "Okay," she said. "I'll have to leave it for now. Are you planning on staying here in Eugene very long?"

"I don't know how long," Amy said. "Chloe moved out, and I can work from the house as well as anywhere else, as long as I go up on Fridays. I'll hang around and keep Mother company for now. She went to Portland with me on Friday, in order to go to a nursery that specializes in tropical plants. She wants to restore the family room to a sort of conservatory, the way it used to be. They'll deliver a lot of stuff on Thursday and she'll need help." She was back to speaking in the fast flow of easy words, visibly more relaxed. Lucy had decided to have the master bedroom and bath redecorated before she moved downstairs, Amy continued.

As she talked on, Barbara knew that it was time for the discussion to come to an end. Amy would evade for now anything she had already decided not to discuss. After another minute or two, Barbara stood. "I've kept you long enough," she said. "Thanks for answering my questions."

As soon as Amy was gone, Barbara called Bailey. "Council of war first thing in the morning," she said. "Can do?"

"Righto. I'll have most of that rundown by then. Anything else?"

"No doubt, I'll have more in the morning. See you then."

She called Frank's cell phone, not certain if he was at the office or at home. He answered after many rings. She hoped it was not because he had been working in the garden. He had no business doing anything in the heat of the afternoon. He said he was at the office, surrounded by papers. He sounded annoyed.

Quickly she summarized Amy's visit. "Bailey's coming in the morning. You want to sit in?"

"I'll be there," he said.

"What's wrong?" she asked then. "You sound pretty pissed off."

"That's too mild. I have every right to sound as mad as hell. I have a damn fool copy editor who wants to be my collaborator! Damn fool!"

"You're way out of my field," she said. "Stay out of the sun, and I'll see you in the morning."

Leaning back in her chair, she thought a long time about Amy. She obviously had seen or heard something she had no intention of talking about. When had she had time to fall in love with David? As a kid? Did that count? She was thirty-six, still single. No lover in her life? No affairs? That was hard to believe. Extremely good-looking, intelligent, well educated, she would have had guys after her for years. She had just turned fourteen when David went off to grad school, and he had been out of her life for the next twenty-two years. Most likely she had thought him as out of her life forever.

She made a few notes about the conversation, but there was little information after the salient fact that someone knew now where David was convalescing. All the rest was nuance, implication, a kid's memory of a long-ago party. A kid's verdict on who was a good dancer.

She gave it up as futile. Eventually she would have to find the right lever to use on Amy, to pry out of her what she was hiding, but later. She tidied up her desk, told Maria to beat it, and left for a deli and a cold dinner to take home.

That night Darren told her that Dr. Colfax was planning to release David on Friday. He could continue healing at home. The council of war she had mentioned to Bailey took on a new meaning.

14

"The problem is where to hide him and still have him accessible," Barbara said to her team.

"How much money does he have?" Bailey asked. "He makes a good salary as a tenured professor, but he's on sabbatical, taking a pay cut. The England deal is off. The books have made pretty good money, but good enough for a round-the-clock bodyguard?"

"I don't think he's loaded," Barbara said. "I'll ask him money questions as soon as he's up to it. And we know there's no rich uncle in the wings."

Bailey looked gloomier than ever. He knew how much a murder investigation could cost, and how much a private hideout and bodyguard could cost, and it was obvious he knew David would not be able to cover it.

"We'll see to it that the bills get paid," Frank said, as if to reassure Bailey that he was still part of the defense, no doubt cheering him up, although his expression didn't reflect much cheer.

"I have to make a phone call," Shelley said. "I'll be right back." She hurried from the office.

"Okay," Barbara said. "Moving on. We'll deal with the financial situation one way or the other. The question is where, and whom to bring in to stay with him. Keep in mind that we don't know for how long. A few weeks, months? Until he's able to take care of himself? That nerve damage to his arm makes a huge difference, one hand is almost useless for now."

"Chest surgery such as his takes months," Frank said. Resigned, he asked Bailey, "Do you know if Herbert is free to do a job?"

Bailey, in Frank's opinion, was the best private investigator to be found, and he knew that in Bailey's opinion Herbert was the best bodyguard to be had. Accordingly, neither of them worked cheap.

"I can find out," Bailey said. He never questioned Frank's requests or brought up the question of money with him. He felt free to do both with Barbara, to her annoyance.

Shelley returned and resumed her place on the sofa. "I just talked to Alex," she said. "We'd like to invite David to be our houseguest for the next few months, if he's willing." High color flooded her face, and she looked very happy. "Alex loves the idea," she said, "and Dr. Minnick thinks it's a fine idea. We talked about his book over the weekend, we even argued over parts of it, and Alex is dying to meet him."

Alex, grotesquely disfigured by a congenital birth defect, was a highly successful cartoonist, producing both a wildly popular daily comic strip, and periodic cartoons for national magazines, all anonymously. He was the mysterious X whose political cartoons were reproduced extensively. He had made a great deal of money doing his work, and Shelley was even wealthier with a hefty trust fund. Her father built yachts. David certainly would not be a financial burden to them.

"You know we have room," Shelley said, talking fast, as if to forestall an argument that no one had voiced. "And we're isolated, with a dog that won't let any stranger on the property without setting off alarms or even attacking. When his doctor says it's all right, he could swim. There's a lot of room outside for him to walk, and when he's strong enough, there are the hills behind us."

Their rambling house was set in the foothills of the Coast Range, with no close neighbors. Alex, not quite as reclusive as he had been a few years earlier, still tended to avoid encounters with strangers. Barbara held up her hand as Shelley seemed prepared to keep arguing her case.

"We don't have to decide this moment," Barbara said. "You'll need time to think about it, and could change your minds. It would be a stranger in the house for an indeterminate length of time. And we have to consider the complications that would come up. Checkups by his doctor, interrogations by Hoggarth, visits by his parents and Amy. I'll need to see him a lot."

Shelley beamed, showing every dimple a benign fairy godmother had bestowed on her. "We can handle all of that," she said. "We've dealt with worse problems." It was apparent that in her mind it was settled.

After the others left, Barbara looked over the report Bailey had provided concerning the graduation-party participants. He had warned her that most of the guests had dispersed all over the country. Only eight were still in the state, five in Eugene, two in Portland, one in Roseburg. She concentrated on those.

Chloe, Nick Aaronson, a woman now married to a veterinarian, a man with no visible means of support and a man in real estate all lived in Eugene. A Portland man owned a winery nearby and the other one was a doctor. The Roseburg man managed an office building.

And Dr. Elders, she added, and put his name down to make it as complete as possible. His name was not on the list of invited guests. Had he crashed the party? An informal invitation? Amy might know, and her mother more than likely knew for certain.

Of those remaining in the area only Chloe and Nick Aaronson seemed to have had any connection with Robert. The list was a starting place, she decided. What she really wanted to know was which of the attendees had still been at the party as it was winding down and whatever happened between David and Robert occurred. Someone, besides Amy, could well have seen something significant and failed to mention it. She made a copy and put it in her briefcase. The original went into the Etheridge folder, which was still distressingly thin.

From his appearance on Thursday, David was well, restored to health, but Barbara knew that was deceptive. He needed a few more weeks, Dr. Colfax had told her. David was poring over the list of partygoers.

"Gil Hyneman," he said, "playing the piano. And Chris Wooten at the guitar. I know they were still there. Gigi…" He shook his head in exasperation, ran his finger down the list and found her whole name. "Gigi Symes. And you know Robert, Chloe, Jill and I were still there. Someone, I don't know who, was asleep on the sofa. His back was turned. A couple of others…" He looked over the list again. "Lisa Brodmore. I'm sure there were more, a couple maybe. No names or faces, just a sense that there were a couple of others. Sorry."

"You've done great," Barbara said, taking the list. She circled the names he had mentioned, returned the list to her briefcase. They were in Darren's office again. She leaned back in her chair and said, "We have to talk about a few things, David. Are you up to it?"

"As long as I don't have to punch my way out of a paper bag, I'm good for anything." His expression did not match his lightly spoken words. He looked grim.

"Okay. First, your doctor is sending you on your way tomorrow, as you know. I want to keep you under wraps for a few more weeks, until you're ready for that punching match. We have a good place lined up, secluded, secure and very, very nice."

He held up his hand. "Hold it. Let's cut to the main topic. Are they going to bring charges?"

"I think so. Scuttlebutt had it that if you had been killed in that attack, they would have closed the McCrutchen case as no longer pertinent to pursue since the prime suspect was no longer with us."

"So I'll need a defense counsel for months. Right?" he asked. She nodded.

"Barbara, I can't afford to go to a very, very nice place where I'll be secure and secluded. My insurance will pick up about sixty percent of my hospital bill, this clinic, doctors and so on. It won't pick up anything for a hotel. Do you have any idea how much it costs to loll about a couple of weeks in a private room in a hospital, two more here, the kind of surgery I had, various tests and specialists, etcetera, etcetera? Top it with a defense team for months. It's going to break me. Back to undergraduate days of penny-pinching and a loan, that's my immediate future."

He smiled, but it was a parody of humor. "Can anyone accused of murder even get a loan? I'll let you know. I was being clever, paying off student loans as fast as I could, not saving a lot. My folks didn't believe in paying interest on loans, and I guess I don't, either. Pay them off, be done with them." He waved his hand, as if to brush it all away. "Now, let's move on to Plan B."

"No Plan B. David, whoever attacked you was there waiting for you. It was not a random crime. You were ambushed. I intend to keep you out of his hands, or feet, as the case may be. And when we find out who he is, not only will he be charged with attempted murder, we'll bring a suit against the bastard, and you'll collect enough in damages to pay your bills and then some." Unless, she thought but did not voice, the bastard didn't have any money. She continued aloud, "For the next several weeks my colleague Shelley and her husband are inviting you to be their houseguest. They are both quite wealthy, believe me."

"Why do you say ambush?" he asked.

"You didn't hear him following you. And someone followed Amy here on Monday. What random crazy person would know to follow her to locate you?"

"She didn't mention that," he said, tight-lipped and angry.

"Not to you. She told me."

"Tell her to keep away from me," he said.

"Don't be ridiculous. I'm not a messenger girl. I don't intend to tell anyone where you'll be. It's up to you if you tell her. What I will tell her is that the only visits from now on will be if she's escorted by one of us, and only if you agree to such. Now let's talk about the coming weeks. I'll want to bring Dad out for a talk on Sunday, and next week a police lieutenant named Hoggarth will interview you. I can't put him off any longer. We'll arrange for that to happen in the office. We'll get you there and back. Hoggarth doesn't have to know where you'll be staying, as long as we produce you on demand." She had a few more things to add, then closed her notebook and put it in her brief-case. "Okay with all that?"

He nodded, but then said, "It doesn't make sense, Barbara, killing Robert, attacking me. Lots of people would like to see me six feet under, but not the same people who might have wanted the same for Robert. Neither friends nor foes overlapped where we were concerned. They must be two separate incidents."

"Makes it interesting, doesn't it?" she murmured, rising. "So Bailey will pick you up tomorrow, and I'll see you on Sunday."

Two cars were pulling into the parking lot as she left. Visiting hour had started. Amy, no doubt, would be there sooner or later, and either David would tell her where he was going, or not.

Amy called in the afternoon. "You told David, didn't you?" she said.

"Yes. I had to make him accept that he is in danger," Barbara said.

"Right. He doesn't want to see me anymore. Thanks a lot."

"Amy, has it occurred to you that he could think you're in danger, too?"

"Why did you say that? In danger how?" Amy asked.

"I don't know how. But someone has linked you to him, and that someone could be the same one who attacked him and could pose a danger for both of you. I think David's aware of that possibility."

"I'm dangerous for David, aren't I?" Amy said in a whisper.

"No. Not you personally. Just whoever followed you. Perhaps he would do a better job at keeping out of sight and follow you again. We'll arrange for visits later."

After a moment, Amy said, "I don't even know where he's going."

"His parents won't know, either," Barbara said. "He'll keep in touch by phone. Do you have his number?"

"Yes," Amy said. "He gave it to me. I'll keep in touch with him."

"Good. If you think you're being followed, or anything else suspicious happens, give me a call, will you? Or call the police. You can always say you suspect a stalker. That gets their attention."

"I'll call you and the police," Amy said. "And try to get a license number or something. I was so dumb not to get it before."

"We're not usually prepared to act when it's something so far out of our sphere," Barbara said. "I'll talk to you later."

After disconnecting, Amy regarded her bed, and an intense memory played in her head. As a kid, whenever she had felt mortally wounded, she had flung herself on the bed, buried her face in her pillow sobbing, and pounded her fists furiously, her legs flailing. An incongruous picture, she thought, but she now wanted to fling herself down and bury sobs in her pillow.

"Cut it out!" she told herself sharply. She had not seen David for over twenty years and, in truth, had not thought of him many times over those years. She could live through the next weeks. But she still wanted to fling herself down on the bed and sob.

Amy's Portland apartment was one of two upstairs units in a lovely large house that had been remodeled years before. The owners lived on the first floor and spent as much time on the coast during the summer months as they did in town. Another couple lived in the other upper apartment, worked full-time and were seldom home through the day. Amy rarely saw any of them. No one was in sight on Friday when she let herself into her apartment. And she knew instantly that it had been searched.

Books had been moved, not replaced where she had left them; sofa cushions were untidy, as if they had been lifted and dropped back however they happened to fall. She walked through to her bedroom and opened a drawer. Her underwear was a jumble. He didn't care that she knew he had been there, she thought dully. Maybe he wanted her to know, frighten her, give her a warning. She sat on the side of the bed and hugged her arms about herself. Nick Aaronson, she thought. Looking for the pictures. They knew she had them.

She closed her eyes and rocked back and forth trying to think what to do. She couldn't call the police. They would want to know why someone had searched. She couldn't tell anyone, she realized. Not unless she wanted to turn over the pictures.

As she rocked back and forth, she kept seeing her mother's anguished face when her father died. She had been so frightened for her mother, who had seemed to lose all interest in living. And her renewed anguish at Robert's death. What would it do to her now to have him revealed as a blackmailer? It would be like losing him again. And Travis? She had babysat him, considered him almost a brother, more than she had ever thought of Robert as a brother to protect and care for. If Nick killed Robert, had Chloe been involved? But you don't kill a blackmailer unless you have the material he was holding over you, she reminded herself, as she had many times since finding the pictures. She rocked back and forth and her chaotic thoughts swirled.

Eventually she rose from the bed and went to the bathroom to wash her face and hands. She had to go to the office, then collect her mail. She stopped moving again. A safe-deposit box, she thought. She would get a safe-deposit box and leave the pictures in it. She should have done it before. Dumb, dumb, she told herself. Stop being so dumb!

Her thoughts kept swirling. Aaronson must have searched her apartment, but there was no reason for him to have followed her to find David. Aaronson was not a threat to her or to David, at least as long as she had the pictures in a safe place. Suddenly she was glad that she wouldn't know where David was, no matter how much she wanted to see him. She couldn't lead anyone to him again. David was right, she thought—whoever had followed her could be a threat to them both.

15

Steaks on the grill, baked potatoes, salad. Barbara decided she could manage that on Friday afternoon, heading for the super-market. Darren was putting in overtime again, and he had warned her that it could be the norm for quite a while. Four interns to train, plus the usual routine and the catch-up work required after his absence of three weeks made for a demanding schedule.

"Why four?" she asked that evening, while the potatoes were baking, the steaks marinating. Darren was having a beer and she had Fumé Blanc.

"Sort of orders," he said. "I told you about that major who came around to the board of directors meeting, didn't I?"

"No. When?"

"While I was in Alaska," he said.

"Why? The last I heard, the clinic is a nonprofit corporation, not army affiliated."

"From what I've been told, he said the magic words. Someone

might question the charitable status, maybe it wouldn't go anywhere, but it could be time-consuming with a lot of paperwork,
appearances, audits. The usual." His voice was low, ominously
low, the way it got when he was angry or upset. "We could by-
pass all that by accepting a couple of their people to train now
and then."

She stared at him. "He threatened you? The clinic?"

"Of course not," Darren said, in that same low voice. "He made
a suggestion. The army needs more trained therapists—we train
therapists. A little cooperation goes a long way. They'll pay, naturally. We seem to have a contract with the federal government
now."

"What else?" she asked sharply. "Are they enlisted men?"

He shook his head. "Private contractors. And their corporate
officers believe that a year or two is too long. Six months should
be plenty of time."

"The board accepted those terms?" She could not conceal her
own anger through softening her voice or sounding musical.
Darren always trained highly qualified and recommended interns
who had completed satisfactorily all the prerequisite courses. It
took at least a year, and quite often two, and he accepted only
two at a time. Apparently selection would be out of his hands
now and God alone knows what their qualifications would be.

"The board considered the alternative and accepted," he said,
and lifted his can. "Two for now, since I already have two, and then
four at a time of their people. Sort of an open-ended contract."

She did not miss it that he said "the board considered." He
was on the board. "Jesus! You didn't have a vote?"

"It's okay," he said mildly. "But it does mean that for a while
I'll be going in on Saturday and Sunday for a few hours."

She interpreted that to mean the new interns were not qualified. "Have they had premed?"

"No." He rose from the deck chair. "I did add a bit of a caveat. If, after six months, I don't believe they're well trained, I won't certify them."

"And the consequences if you don't?"

"Actually we didn't get into that yet. Want me to start the grill?"

"Yes. I'll check on the potatoes and toss the salad," Barbara said angrily.

In the kitchen, she jabbed a potato savagely, wishing it was a certain major she was skewering. What it meant, she thought then, was that Darren would not be able to train highly qualified and eager applicants, always far too many to accommodate. The two accepted were the cream of the crop assured of instant employment when they finished under his tutelage.

And after six months? She suspected there was not a member of the board who would hesitate to toss him overboard if it meant a choice between losing him or putting the clinic at grave risk. They would agonize over it first. She also knew that given that choice Darren would make the same decision, that he was expendable, the clinic wasn't.

Later, as they ate, Darren said, "You know that David is going to have to continue therapy? He has exercises to do on his own, and I want to see him next Friday. Is that going to be a problem?"

"I'll see that he gets to the clinic," she said. "Is that arm going to heal, get back to normal?"

"I'm sure it will, but it's going to take time. Nerve damage is slow to recover fully. He said he didn't know where you plan to take him."

"Shelley's house," she said. "No one is supposed to know that. I'd rather not tell Todd, if that's all right."

"Sure. He's coming home Sunday afternoon. I'll leave the clinic and go pick him up. Two, about then."

She told him that she and Frank had to talk to David on Sunday. "We'll go on to Dad's house after that, and you and Todd can come over for dinner."

Darren smiled. "We're going to have a rough time for quite a while, aren't we? Our first real test."

"I'm afraid so," she admitted. And that summed it up precisely, she realized. Their first real test as a couple.

On Sunday when she and Frank arrived at Shelley's house, they found David more relaxed than Barbara had ever seen him.

"The perfect hole-in-the-hill hideout," he said, almost cheerfully when he greeted them. "Even my own private psychiatrist. He's been careful not to start diagnosing me just yet."

Dr. Minnick smiled. "Argued a little, but no diagnosis. He—" he pointed to David "—holds up his end of an argument just fine. I think he likes it. I'll have to find the significance of that when I have time."

"I thought we'd have our little conference in my office," Shelley said. "Alex and Dr. Minnick can cool their heels where they want."

Alex waved them away. "Secrets, nothing but secrets."

Shelley led the way to her office, a spacious room furnished more like a living room than an office, with sofa, easy chairs, coffee table, wide windows overlooking the back of the property and her desk that was all but hidden under papers and books.

"They've made me feel like the prodigal son," David said. "I think Dr. Minnick is fixing to fatten me up some."

"A born nurturer," Barbara said. "Now, on to business. I'll need the names of your dinner companions the night of the murder and an address for them. And I know it's a drag, but I want to ask the same kind of questions I expect Lieutenant Hoggarth will be asking. Keep in mind that you don't volunteer anything, just answer his questions. Okay?"

"Shoot," David said.

"Exactly what was your relationship with Jill Storey?"

It went on for an hour. His answers were concise and to the point most of the time, and his story was what she had already heard from him with a little variation in the wording.

"You really think he'll dig into the past that much?" David asked when she leaned back, satisfied.

"He has to, or there's no motive. That file, your presence, Robert's renewed interest in Jill's murder. That's going to be his starting place. He's had several weeks now to carry on his investigation, ever since he knew that you would recover, and I have no idea how far he's gone, what he's been told. He's a good investigator, and he'll have been as thorough as possible. If they arrest you and turn over discovery, I'll have some answers, but until then we're in the dark. I doubt that he'll connect the attack on you with Robert's murder, especially if Dressler has determined to his satisfaction that it was a random hate crime."

"We'll be there," Frank said. "If Milt strays too far afield, we'll stop him. You won't be under oath, but your testimony can be used against you in the future, so you'll want to be careful not to lose your temper and to curb your tendency to let sarcasm color what you say. You realize, I hope, that you do have such a tendency."

"So I've been told," David said. "I'll work on it."

"At least try," Barbara said with resignation. She suspected that he had no idea how often he slipped over that particular edge.

David shrugged. "Try harder, you mean. I promise."

"Moving on," Frank said. "This interview will be preliminary, not the formal statement they'll demand if they decide to charge you. And if they go that far, an arrest will follow, arraignment, hearing for bail bond. We'll be with you every step of the way."

"How much bail?" David asked.

"We don't know," Barbara said. "I'm going to try to keep it low, but without it you'll be in jail awaiting trial."

He shook his head. "I hadn't put that on my list of expenses," he said after a moment.

They discussed a possible trial date, and agreed that before the end of the year would be best. "That means by the end of November," Barbara said. "Judges hate to start capital cases close to Christmas, because jurors became annoyed if their holiday shopping and other preparations are too disrupted."

David laughed.

They wrapped it up soon after that and Barbara and Frank turned down invitations to stay for a drink, snacks, dinner, anything else at all. "Stop," she said. "You haven't offered chocolates, and that's my weakness. No, we'll be on our way. Things to do. See you tomorrow," she said to Shelley. "I'll be in touch as soon as I know when Hoggarth will be around," she added to David, and she and Frank left.

"What do you think?" she asked Frank, driving to his house.

"Milt could turn mean with him," Frank said. "Depends on David's attitude."

She nodded. "He's been warned."

"What else is bothering you?" Frank asked then.

She told him about the clinic. "It takes two years if the intern has no medical background at all, just the desire. One year for someone who's done premed. And the bozos they're bringing to Darren? Who knows? Mercenaries off the street? Maybe."

He made a low throat noise, cleared his throat, then said, "We live in ugly times, Bobby. They're running roughshod, out of control wherever they can get away with it."

They were both silent for the next several minutes, then Frank said, "Turn off at Greenhill, go to Alvadore. Early

Elbertas are in. Too early, maybe, and not as good as late peaches, but I want some anyway."

Crazy weather, global warming, government out of control, Iraq... Ugly times, Barbara reflected, slowing down to turn onto Greenhill Road.

"I hate to get Bailey involved before we even know if we'll have a case to defend," Barbara said on Frank's porch a little later after they had laid out the plans for the coming weeks. "But, neither do I want to wait any longer. I've noticed that November comes charging along pretty fast."

"We shouldn't wait," Frank agreed. "We're in, and I assume a charge will come along."

"Right. Hoggarth's questions will give us an idea about what they have. There's no forensic evidence to link David with either death. No DNA, no fibers, no eyewitness, nothing."

"So they rely on opportunity and motive," Frank said. "Many cases have been won on no more than that."

"I know. But I also know it's easier to shoot down a case with no more than that. I'm counting on nothing more turning up. Maybe that's too strong. I'm hoping nothing more turns up. It sure would be fine if Robert had been the kind of guy who makes bitter enemies with murder in their hearts, but there's no sign of that. A go-along, get-along sort of guy, everyone's pal. No doubt a little corruption, some shady deals along the way, maybe influence peddling, money under the table, a bit of phi-landering. But nothing really big-time."

Frank went inside to make a peach cobbler, and she contin-ued to sit on his porch, surveying his garden. Weedless, neat, beau-tifully tended. She compared it to the garden in Darren's yard, and had to fight back a surge of guilt. She had weeded it half-heartedly a time or two during Darren's absence, but mostly she had forgotten it. A garden needed constant weeding, she had come to realize. Abruptly, she stood and went inside for a glass of wine.

That evening they had what Frank called an old-fashioned country dinner—ham, potato salad, a green salad, snap beans, sliced tomatoes and corn bread, topped with a peach cobbler. He had made an incredible amount of everything. There were plenty of leftovers for the noncooks.

As they ate Todd talked excitedly about the science project he had decided to put together. "See, it's going to be in two parts, a slide show of the glaciers and how much they've melted already, and how much the sea ice has melted. You know, polar bear habitat. With commentary. That's part one. For the other part I need two clear glass things, jars or something, with straight sides, and the same size. I'll put a brick or something like that with a block of ice on it in one, and the same size ice in the other one, not on anything. Then fill them both to the same level with salt water. One represents sea ice and the other one glaciers on land. Then let the ice melt. Sea ice won't make the water rise, but the melting glacier will. Then I'll measure the salinity again to show that it's not as salty as before, and that kills a lot of things that live in salt water. Climate-change demonstration."

He looked triumphant and obviously enjoyed the approval the others voiced for his project. "You're doing your part," Frank said. "That's a very fine project. If you need help finding your containers, give me a call. I have plenty of time to help you scout them out."

Smiling, Barbara and Darren exchanged a look. Todd had found a grandfather, and Frank was playing the role exactly the way he should, and enjoying it.

After his company left that night, Frank sat in his study with the crossword puzzle and thought about the coming weeks. He had his work to do on his book, office work with Patsy. She was checking the footnotes and index, while he was going over the text and restoring his own words and phrases that the copy editor had changed. Damn fool, he thought again, didn't know the difference between *corpus delicti* and *habeas corpus.* And then there was David's defense. He was involved in a way that he seldom was with Barbara's cases. Most often he was on the sidelines this early, and played a bigger role as the court date approached. But he had read David's book. That made the difference. David was taking a stand, and he would have supported that stand if David hadn't had a penny to contribute to his defense.

Darren was taking a stand, too. One that could cost him his position, change his life. Others came to mind. Shelley, beautiful and rich. She could have gone the way of too many celebrities, filled the tabloids with her exploits, but instead she was working hard on behalf of those who had little or nothing. Alex with his pointed political cartoons exposing corruption and deception again and again. And now Todd was standing up.

It gave him hope, he thought, and smiled. It gave him hope.

16

"Okay, gang, it's full steam ahead," Barbara said on Monday morning. "Bailey, everything about Robert McCrutchen you can dig up. His Salem contacts, women, deals involving Aaronson, debts, the whole picture. Same for Aaronson and Chloe McCrutchen. You know the drill." Bailey scowled and made a note.

Barbara turned to Shelley. "Here's a list of the ones we know stayed at the party late. Specifically, we want to know if there were others, and if any of them saw anything having to do with the confrontation between Robert and David. If any of them knew Jill well enough to shed some light. Skip Nick Aaronson and Chloe. I'm saving them for later. I'd like some names for a few friends of Jill. Again, whatever you can learn. Who saw others leaving? A play-by-play of the final hour of the party. That's for openers," she said.

"Bailey, we need to get David here by ten on Wednesday for Hoggarth to go at him. And he has to be at the clinic on Friday at two in the afternoon for a session with Darren. However you want to arrange it. Hoggarth will take an hour or more, and same for Darren. Then straight back to the hideout."

"It's going to take some time," Bailey grumbled. "Salem's closed for the summer."

"So fire up your horse and get started," Barbara said.

His scowl deepened. He drained his coffee cup, heaved himself upright and ambled to the door. "I could have been a plumber, like my old man. No chasing shadows in the summer heat." He saluted and left.

"Anything else for me?" Shelley asked, more than ready to take on whatever Barbara suggested.

"That's going to be quite enough, I imagine. How's it going at the house?"

"It's great! David and Alex were meant for each other. Talk, talk, talk. Alex has been showing David some of his drawings. You know how unusual that is? For him to show anyone?"

Barbara knew. "It's a tremendous relief that they hit it off. It could have gone either way. I'll take Martin's tomorrow, by the way. Just a couple of things I have to wrap up there, and then we'll have to go to one-a-week specials for a while."

Shelley left and Barbara went to her desk to sort out her next moves. Frank had skipped that morning meeting, but he would be there on Wednesday. Meanwhile there were several things she wanted to get to. She looked up Brice Knowlton's number and called him.

Many times when she succeeded on someone's behalf, the grateful client had all but begged for a chance to do her a favor. She rarely followed through by asking for one, but now she intended to do just that.

Not only was Brice at home, he even answered his phone. She had feared she would have to leave a message and wait for a call back. After identifying herself, she said, "I wonder if you could do something for me. I don't know if it's against university rules, though."

"If it is, we'll break them," he said cheerfully. "What is it?"

"I want transcripts of grades of a student from years ago, especially from her last year. Twenty-two years ago, in fact. Can they be had?"

"Sure. Nothing gets tossed by the university. Whose grades?" Knowlton asked.

"Jill Storey," she said. "You probably read something about her in the newspaper recently."

He whistled softly. "McCrutchen's murder. You're involved?"

"In a way," she said. "I'd really like to see Storey's grades and drain your brain with a few questions if that's all right."

"You know it is. I'll see what I can do. Twenty-two years ago? I'll call you when I have something."

She asked how his father was doing, and he was rhapsodic in his response.

Next she called Lucy McCrutchen and asked if she could drop in sometime that day. Lucy suggested one o'clock and that was done.

Routine stuff until her appointment with Lucy, she decided. Lunch after that, and a walk sometime before heading for home.

That day when Amy admitted her to the house, her first question was about David. "Is he okay? I haven't talked to him since he left the clinic."

"He's fine," Barbara said. "Haven't you called him?"

"I...I left him a message," Amy said. "He hasn't called back." She looked miserable. "Mother's on the deck. She said to bring you out when you got here. Do you want to be alone with her?"

"Not necessarily, unless Elders drops in."

Amy grimaced. "I told Mother to run him off with a stick, or turn the hose on him. Or something. He's courting her, to use a good old-fashioned phrase, one that suits him just fine." They walked through the house toward the deck as she spoke.

Barbara laughed. "Your mother struck me as a woman who can handle a situation like that."

"I think she's being too nice, too patient. He's a goddamn pest," Amy said.

They went out through the kitchen. Lucy, like Amy, was in shorts and a T-shirt. Her broad-brimmed hat and gloves were on the table. She had a nice sun glow on her face and her legs and arms were showing a tan. A sweating pitcher and glasses were on the table.

She waved Barbara toward a chair. "Lemonade," she said. "Please, help yourself."

Barbara and Amy sat down and Amy poured lemonade into two glasses, passed one to Barbara.

"You've put a lot of plants on the deck over there, haven't you?" Barbara said, motioning toward the far end where the deck extended to the end of the house.

"That's how I always kept it in the summer," Lucy said. "Plants inside for the winter, out here for the summer. They like it. The contractor thought I was crazy when I told him I wanted the deck to extend out to the end like that. He said it was wasted space, we'd never use it. And it made for more unusable space from there to the fence line, just eight feet, like an alley. He was wrong. I knew what I wanted it for. It's plenty wide for the plants, and for me to tend them. And I put heather and helle-bore in what he called the alley, with stepping stones to get through the growth. It all worked exactly how I wanted it."

Barbara nodded, less interested in what plants liked than she was in getting a question or two answered. "Mrs. McCrutchen, you know I'm representing David Etheridge. I expect him to be charged with the murder of your son, and I don't believe he did it, but it's an awkward position for both of us for me to be asking you to help. I appreciate that."

"I want to help," Lucy said. "Like you, I don't believe David did it. What can I tell you?"

"I'm trying to fill in blanks for the night of the graduation party held here. I have a list of those who were last to leave, but it isn't complete. I'm hoping you'll be able to help finish it."

Lucy looked woeful. "You have to understand that I didn't know a lot of those youngsters. Some had attended the seminars and I had met them previously, but there were many more that I'd never met before that night and their names were gone almost as fast as I heard them. Let me see the list and I'll try, but I doubt I can be of real use."

Barbara handed her the list, and watched her ponder each name, then move on.

Lucy returned the list, shaking her head. "I'm sorry, I can't add to it. There are some there that I had never met before, and I couldn't even have put their names forward. I know Jill was still here. I recall that she had been to a few of the seminars, not many, and how ill she had appeared to be. That night she seemed almost feverish, overexcited in the way that people often become after being so ill. The poor girl was so thin, I was afraid she was over-doing it."

Barbara put the list back in her purse. "Thank you for trying," she said. "In trying to complete the party list, I saw that Dr. Elders's name was missing. Was he an invited guest?"

"No, not formally invited, if that's what you mean. I invited him to come over and join us for dinner and to take a plate home for his wife. Well, he loved to dance, and he enjoyed the young people, so he returned to join in when they started dancing. He left when they stopped. He came to the living room to thank me for letting him stay, and he was drenched. Maybe he hadn't danced that much in years."

"Well, it was worth a try," Barbara said. She drank the rest of the lemonade and stood. "Thank you for letting me intrude on you again."

"I wish I could have helped," Lucy said. "If you have anything else to ask, please don't hesitate to do so."

Amy went back out with Barbara and, at the front door, she said in a low voice, "You really think they'll charge him with Robert's murder, don't you?"

"Yes, I really do."

Amy glanced behind her, then said, "I have to tell you something."

"Come to lunch," Barbara said. "We can talk."

"Wait a minute. I'll put on a skirt and tell Mother I'm leaving." She hurried away and returned very quickly, buttoning a wraparound skirt over her shorts. "Okay. There's a little place not far from here, The Grill. On Franklin."

It was a student hangout in the school season, but practically empty that afternoon. In a booth, they both ordered, and Amy toyed with her silverware and napkin while they waited for salads to be delivered.

Barbara did nothing to hurry her. Amy was too nervous to add to her anxiety. Then, with their lunches in place, Amy left hers untouched, leaned forward and said in a low, intense voice, "That night, the night of the party, I told you how Greta and I were sent up to my room. But I didn't stay. I couldn't go to sleep. Too wound up or something. I put my clothes back on and went downstairs, out to the backyard. I looked in the windows to the family room and saw everyone gathered by the piano, and then I sat in the grass by the dogwood tree. Daydreaming, making up fantasies, just thinking. Jill came out…" She told it all exactly as she remembered, leaving out only the part that included her mother.

Barbara forgot her salad as she listened. "You're sure those were her words, that they disgusted her?"

"Yes. I didn't attach any particular meaning to them then, but after I learned a little, grew up a little, I realized that I think she meant she was a lesbian. And she was disgusted by what she had done and by men in general. It wasn't just her words, it was the way she said it," Amy said.

"Good God!" Barbara said. "Have you mentioned this to anyone? Did you ever talk about it to anyone? The police investigators?"

Amy shook her head. "Never. No one ever asked me a question. You know, I was supposed to be in bed. But David must know it. Growing up close to her, he must know it. And he never told, either."

"Could anyone else have heard what happened out there?"

"I'm sure not. They were at the end of the deck. I'll show you." She groped in her purse for a pen and notebook.

Barbara brought out her list and turned the paper over. "Show me here," she said, then watched Amy draw strong, unwavering lines of the deck, the family room, kitchen. Her architectural training was evident in the sure way she depicted the area, all to scale.

"I was here, fifteen feet from the end of the deck," Amy said, and drew a wavy arc for the tree. "They stood at the end of the deck, here. The windows are stationary, thermal pane. The door to the family room opens to the main deck, and people were at the far end of the room, near the piano. The family room is twenty-six feet in length. They were all too far away, and the window wall's a sound barrier. They couldn't have heard a thing."

"Could anyone have come to the near end of the room without your noticing?"

Amy shook her head. "There were plants on the deck, low, like now, but anyone moving around in there would have been visible."

"The deck would be like a sounding board," Barbara said, studying the drawing. "And you're sure no one saw you?"

"I'm sure. I was being careful to avoid Robert after he caught us getting beer."

"Amy, why would he have been pursuing Jill on the same night that he announced his engagement to Chloe?" Barbara said.

Amy ducked her head. "Remember, I was just fourteen and no one tells you anything at that age. I think twenty-some years ago kids that age were a lot more ignorant than they are today. Anyway, they got engaged, and married in June, and in December Chloe had an eight-pound baby. I don't think Robert cared a thing about her, and I'm almost sure she never cared for him."

Barbara leaned back and let out a long breath. Two bombshells in a row. "They were married for twenty-two years! Why?"

Amy shrugged. "I don't know. We never were close. Robert was away at law school, then I was away at school, and when I was home for the summers, they were always busy. Age difference, different lives, interests. I got to know Travis, their son, a lot better than I ever got to know Chloe. After I got the job in Portland, I never saw them. Just at holidays and birthdays, never to really talk to her."

Barbara took a bite of her neglected salad and after a moment Amy began to eat hers, but she clearly was not interested in food. She leaned forward again. "But you can see that, no matter what,

David didn't have a reason to kill Robert. He knew about Jill. That night, he was like a brother, that's all. No love interest, no sexual interest, no raging jealousy, just friends. It didn't matter if Robert had that file. Nothing in it could have hurt David."

Barbara nodded. "When I was a kid, one year Dad gave me a small globe, the kind you shake and snow falls. This one was a little different. You turned it upside down and the whole scene changed while the snow was falling. You've just turned a sphere on its head. I have to think about all of it."

After dropping Amy off at her house again, Barbara drove straight to the park and started to walk. It was pleasant, but the temperature was due to go up as another heat wave hit later in the week. In and out of shade, blackberries ripening, not quite ready, flashing river, egrets, it was all comfortingly familiar, yet always subtly different, too.

How to corroborate Amy's assessment of Jill Storey, that was the question, she told herself. A prosecutor would rip it apart— Amy had been little more than a child. She had a crush on David. She had misheard, misunderstood, dreamed it, made it up out of whole cloth. Her word, her interpretation, wasn't enough.

Olga? Barbara doubted it. She had fled back home to her Baptist minister father, the very conservative area around Medford, and she had remained there for several years. Pieces of the puzzle were falling into place, however. Olga had supported Jill for months during her illness, named her daughter Gillian, stayed married only three years. Were they a couple? Would she admit to being gay? Or that she'd had a gay relationship twenty-two years ago? Barbara didn't know the eastern part of Washington State where Olga lived and taught school, but she suspected it was as conservative as the Oregon side of the river, and very likely residents there would not tolerate a gay teacher for their children.

David's corroboration, if it was forthcoming, would mean little; he had too much of a motive to make the claim. It could be seen as blaming the victim, changing the subject or simple lying.

Her thighs were starting to throb, and she headed for a bench in the shade, where she continued to worry about the problem. Kids on inner tubes sped by. A canoe or two. Bicycles on the path. Joggers with agonized expressions, pushing the wall. Had there been a gay community of support two decades earlier? Had Jill feared losing her scholarship if exposed? Probably, she decided, and it could have been a real possibility then. Perhaps it still was for some of the scholarships and grants.

She started compiling a list of her gay friends who had been in the area twenty-some years earlier. It was a short list, but at least it was a starting place. She walked back to her car and drove to the office to make a few phone calls. It was going on six-thirty when she realized the time and muttered a prayer of thanks to Frank for providing dinner for that night. Leftover potato salad and ham. She had two people lined up to talk to. A starting place.

17

Brice Knowlton caught up with Barbara at Martin's on Tuesday. He was beaming. "Here I am with the goods."

She laughed, went to the door to take down her *Barbara Is In* sign and waved toward her table. "Coffee, iced coffee, is my drink these days?"

"Sounds good," he said. "It's getting hot again. You look great, by the way."

"Thanks." She went to the kitchen door, but Martin was already on his way out. "Another iced coffee, please." He nodded, smiled at Brice and vanished back into the kitchen. Seconds later he brought it.

"No problem with the transcript," Brice said, putting an envelope on the table. "You said you had some questions?"

"Enlightenment. What happens when a good student becomes ill and can't complete her course work near the end of the year, with her graduation at hand?"

"Not a real problem," he said. "Professors, despite all rumors to the contrary, are fairly decent people. They have a good deal of leeway in how they handle it, but most often they'll just give her more time. If she can finish the work during that school year, no problem. If it takes longer, put an I for Incomplete on her record, with a year to make up the course and get a grade. Or she can withdraw without harming her grade-point average, and there's a W on the transcript, no harm done. If she fails to make up the work within a year the Incomplete becomes an F automatically, and that can be a potential problem."

"You said the professors have leeway. What else might they do?"

"Well, I know one instance where the instructor gave his student a list of books to read, and demanded a paper that would have amounted to a dissertation. The kid got the drift and withdrew."

"And if she dies before she completes the makeup work?" Barbara asked.

"After a year the Incomplete becomes an F, but in that case who would care?"

Barbara nodded and sipped her coffee. "Thanks, Brice. I'm trying to fill in gaps, populate blank spots. This has been helpful. You say your father's doing well?"

His smile widened. "A changed man! Rejuvenated!"

For the next several minutes they chatted. After he left, Barbara gathered up her things, waved to Martin and his wife, Binnie, and returned to her office.

"Go home," Barbara said to Maria. "I'll be leaving in a minute or two, and it's getting like an oven again out there."

Maria smiled and nodded, and continued doing whatever she had been doing at the computer. Barbara went into her own office and took out Brice's envelope.

Apparently Jill had made up all her overdue work. A's and two high B's. No Incomplete, no Withdraw. As both Olga Maas and David said, she had been serious about her schoolwork.

She put the transcript in the folder on her desk and took out Shelley's envelope with the newspaper accounts of Jill Storey's murder. Very little had been reported beyond the fact that she had been strangled. She had been very pretty, Barbara thought again, studying her photograph. The accounts were simply a rehash of the bare facts, glimpses of her background, her family, her scholarship. Nothing useful. The party was hardly mentioned, just the fact that she had attended a party, drove herself home, parked, and on the walk from her driveway to the front door of her apartment house, she had been killed. Frowning, Barbara replaced the newspaper stories in the envelope and returned it to the folder. She wanted that police file, she thought vehemently. She wanted to know what they had learned and had not reported.

After another minute or two, she called Bailey. When his answering machine came on, she said, "Bailey, for God's sake, pick up the phone. I know you're there."

He picked up the phone. "I'm here, and I'm eating dinner. I don't answer the telephone when I'm eating dinner."

"Sorry. Just one thing. In the morning, plan to get David here at about twenty after ten."

"Ten, twenty after, make up your mind," he growled.

"I just did. See you in the morning."

Hoggarth would be there at ten, David twenty minutes later. Of course Hoggarth would be sore, but what else was new? she though derisively, and decided she had done quite enough for one day. It was time, past time, to go pick up dinner and head for home.

Barbara swung by a bakery on Wednesday morning and bought an assortment of pastries before going to the office. Shelley was already on hand. Barbara stopped at her open door and said, "I'd like you to wait until David arrives, and come in with him. Okay?"

"Sure," Shelley said.

"There's something I want to go into with Hoggarth, and you cramp his style," Barbara said by way of explanation.

Shelley grinned and nodded. "Gotcha."

Frank arrived a few minutes later, eyed the pastries and looked at Barbara accusingly. "What are you up to now?"

"I'll offer our guest some refreshments," she said. "Can you call it buttering up someone if there's no butter?"

"Can you be charged if you cause a healthy man to have a coronary? You want to clue me in?"

"I want his cooperation, that's all," she said. "I'll be humble about it. You'll see."

Frank snorted, sat down and helped himself to coffee.

Hoggarth arrived promptly at ten, looking hot and rumpled already. His face was redder than usual from the heat, and the bald dome of his head glowed under moist skin. Eyeing the pastries, he said brusquely, "What do you want?"

Barbara waved him to one of the easy chairs. "I thought we all might like a little something while we wait for Bailey to deliver David. I believe they'll be a couple of minutes late. Coffee?" She was already pouring it, and passed the cup across the table to him. Picking up a cinnamon roll, she said, "These are from the French Horn. Still warm when I picked them up."

Hoggarth chose a Danish, and watched her without a word.

"I've been thinking," she said, "how it seems to work out that whenever I have a capital case client you get assigned to the investigation. Curious, I thought, but then I considered how your captain must regard us. We sometimes manage to wrap things up in a manner that makes your department look extremely good. Wouldn't you agree?"

He continued to maintain his stony silence.

"Your captain seems to like this combination, for whatever reason. Of course, we hit speed bumps now and then, but we've always overcome them."

Frank, watching, knew that Barbara was calling in a few chips and he suspected that Hoggarth was thinking the same thing. She had saved him some embarrassment in the past, and while it was true that he owed her, it was also very likely that he did not want to be reminded of it.

"Knock it off," Hoggarth snapped. "Just tell me what you're after this time and let's get on with things."

"I can't fool you, I guess," Barbara said, smiling faintly. "I do want something. The original file that Robert McCrutchen had in his possession when he got the bullet. It's already been copied, so no real effort is required."

"No. Where's Etheridge? Tell him to get his ass out of the closet and let's start."

She shrugged. "Or, I could go for a subpoena, but that can get messy, and there's always a bit of publicity, plus the delay. If you're building a current case based on information that's twenty-some years old, I'm almost sure a judge would agree that the defense deserves a look at that same material, if only to make certain that people say today more or less what they said then. But, more, it would mean we can't start our efforts in a truly cooperative way, but would leave the starting gate as adversaries, however friendly that adversarial posture might be."

Hoggarth ran his hand over his scalp. He did that often, possibly in disbelief that so much hair had vanished over the years.

She smiled at him. "The cinnamon roll is delicious. I recommend them."

He finished his Danish, wiped his hands, drank some coffee, then said, "I'll think about it."

Barbara didn't think he meant the pastry.

A minute later Maria buzzed to say Bailey had arrived with David, and very soon David and Shelley were seated at the round table.

Hoggarth started. He covered the past, when David and Jill had been childhood friends, neighbors, up through the night of the party. It was all general until then, when he began with specific questions.

"Did you ever give her money?" he asked.

"Yes. As kids sometimes one of us had an extra quarter when the other didn't for ice cream after school, or a soda or something."

"Did you give her money during those last six months of her life?"

David nodded. "Twice. Ten once, fifteen another time."

"You gave her twenty-five dollars. Is that right?"

"Yes, altogether it came to twenty-five."

"What was it for?"

"Nothing. Friendship. She was broke."

Hoggarth went into the episode with the key in excruciating detail, a minute-by-minute account for that afternoon up to the time David gave it to Jill at the party. He did the same with the confrontation on the deck.

"You followed them both out. Why?"

David shook his head. "No real reason. Robert had been drinking, and he could get in your face when drinking. I thought he might be harassing her. He'd been flirting with every woman at the party that night."

"The night of his engagement announcement," Hoggarth said, not quite a question.

David didn't respond.

"Then you had a fight on the deck, didn't you?"

"Absolutely not. He took a swing at me when I said to leave

her alone. I ducked and he lost his balance and took a spill into the bushes along the deck. End of it. He stepped back up on the deck and I went inside."

"Did he accuse you of being her lover, of planning to live with her?"

"He knew about the key," David said. "He saw me give it to her, and he assumed the worst. He was wrong."

"Did you take Ms. Storey in with you after that?"

"No. She left when Robert fell. I didn't see her again."

"How did you get home that night?"

"I walked."

Hoggarth belabored the next few minutes—when did Jill leave? Who saw her leave? Did he leave with her?

He moved on to the night of Robert's murder with the same kind of painstakingly thorough questions, where he and his companions had eaten, their full names and addresses, when he got there, when they separated, when he got back to the apartment, what he did then...

After another hour, Frank said, "Milt, I think David is showing signs of fatigue. Maybe we can wrap this up soon."

Although David was looking very tired, his voice remained steady and his answers concise, well thought out and to the point again and again. He had not once lapsed into the sarcastic mode Barbara had warned him about. During the past hour or so, his right hand had drawn up in a peculiar way, not quite clawlike, but not relaxed, either, and he had used his left hand exclusively when he raised his coffee cup.

Hoggarth nodded. "We're done for now." He put a notebook back in his pocket. Glancing at Barbara, he said, "I'll be in touch."

She walked out through the office with him, and at the outer door, she said, "He's going to need therapy for several months. He may never regain full use of his hand and arm."

"I noticed," Hoggarth said. He reached past her and opened the door, then said again, "I'll be in touch."

Back inside her office, Barbara said, "Relax, David. Maria had orders to call Bailey the minute the lieutenant left. Then back to the hole-in-the-wall for you. Maybe a dip in the pool, nap."

"Hard work," he said, and for the first time he sounded as tired as he looked. "I keep having to remind myself that I'm really awake, not hallucinating. It doesn't stick. They're really trying to pin it on me, aren't they? Robert's murder, and Jill's, too."

"It seems they're going that route," she admitted. "I keep having the feeling that someone is feeding them a line. When I get discovery, I'll find out who that someone is."

"What makes it interesting," David said, "is that it has to be someone with a connection to the here and now, as well as to twenty-two years ago and Jill's murder. Rather limits the cast of characters, doesn't it? No political motive. Rule out a Salem connection."

"You think the same person killed Jill and Robert?" Shelley asked.

"Not necessarily," he said. "But someone who knows enough about the past to know that if her death can be tied to me, it provides my motive for Robert's death, assuming he found something that could tie that knot. Otherwise, there isn't a motive. It raises another interesting question," he said, looking at Barbara. "Who in that small cast of characters did have a motive for killing him?"

She nodded. An interesting question, indeed.

Barbara entered the Art Colony art supply shop and gallery that afternoon to be greeted warmly by the two partners, Lou Granville and Sal Wellman. Lou, in her early fifties, had lived in Eugene all her life, Sal, several years younger, for the past fifteen years. They chatted for a minute or two about business, a coming art show, the hot weather, and then, feeling the civilities had been observed, Barbara asked the questions that had brought her to the shop.

"Have you read anything about the McCrutchen case?" They both nodded.

"Okay, then you probably know that there could be a link to a woman named Jill Storey, who was also murdered twenty-two years ago. Lou, you were around here at that time, did you know her?"

"Nope. Never met her," Lou said. "Why?"

"She wasn't part of the gay community then?"

"Honey, there wasn't much of a community in those days, but the answer's the same, no. Did she belong?"

"That's what I'm trying to find out," Barbara said. "I've heard hints, but nothing conclusive, and it could make a difference."

"Was she from here? Into art in any way?" Sal asked.

"From Gresham," Barbara said. "She was going to the U of O, majoring in business, and probably had nothing to do with the art crowd."

Sal and Lou exchanged looks, then shook their heads. "Business students weren't likely to come out, not in those days, probably not now, either," Lou said. "My field? Who gives a damn? But business?" She shook her head again.

"I was afraid that was the case," Barbara said. "Do you know if Marli is in town? I called and left a message, but she hasn't called back."

"She's in Chicago," Sal said. "Her brother's wedding. But you might as well forget her. Lou knew everyone then, and still does, unless they're hiding deep, deep in the closet." She laughed a bitter little laugh, then said angrily, "That's the real problem. If they'd all just admit who they are, it would make it easier for everyone. Folks would have to take notice if ten percent of the goddamn population all stood up together."

Lou put her hand on Sal's arm and she subsided.

"How about a partner when she was at the university?" Lou asked.

"I'm sure there was one, but she's hiding, too, I'm afraid. She teaches in Richland, in Washington State, not too far from the Walla Walla area," Barbara said.

"Probably hiding. I know a couple of people in Walla Walla," Lou replied.

"I wouldn't out her," Barbara said quickly. "If she's in hiding, there's probably a reason."

"In that part of the country?" Lou laughed, but her laughter came from real amusement. "But at least you'd know. Want to give me a name?"

Barbara hesitated only a moment. She had known Lou for many years, and she knew Lou would never do anything to hurt another lesbian. She gave her Olga's name. Even if she never used any information Lou might give her, at least she would know if she was on the right track.

18

Friday afternoon Barbara stood in the broad, bright corridor of the courthouse talking to her client, a middle-aged, gray-haired, stocky Hispanic man. His eyes were wide with bewilderment.

"When do I have to come back? How many times?" Roberto asked.

"Never," Barbara said. "The judge dismissed the case. It's over."

Roberto blinked, and spoke in rapid Spanish to his wife. She looked from him to Barbara, her eyes filled with tears. "It's true? It's over?" Her voice was little more than a whisper.

Barbara assured them both that indeed it was over, they were free to go home.

Their outpouring of gratitude made Barbara shift uncomfortably until, behind Roberto's head, she spotted Hoggarth watching with an impatient expression. She excused herself, and escaped before Roberto could embrace her and his wife do something even more embarrassing, like kiss her hand.

Hoggarth walked toward her as she extracted herself from her client. Drawing near, without preliminaries, he said, "I want a formal statement from your client on Wednesday morning. Ten. And let's start at ten this time." As if it were an afterthought, he handed her a thick manila envelope. He turned and walked back the way he had come.

She called after him, "Thank you, Lieutenant."

He did not acknowledge it.

Back to the office and blessed air-conditioning, she decided, although she had told Maria she would go home after court. It was too hot in her house to do any serious reading, and she suspected that she had some to do. She drove straight to the office.

Maria had left and Shelley was gone, had been gone much of the week, tracking down the people on the list Barbara had provided. Darren would not leave the clinic until seven and Todd was hanging out at a pal's house where there was a swimming pool. She would order Chinese food, pick it up close to seven and head for home then. She settled down to read the file.

For several hours that day Frank had been working on his edited book, now and then cursing when he came across more of the asinine comments made by a for-hire copy editor. He had called his regular editor, who shared his anger and apologized profusely. Not mollified, Frank made the necessary corrections, while Patsy struggled with the footnotes and index. At four he called it quits for the day.

"We'll both lose our minds if we don't take a nice weekend break," he said at Patsy's office door.

"Are you leaving?" Patsy asked, taking off her glasses, rubbing her eyes.

"You bet I am. Want to give me a lift home? Is your house intolerably hot?"

She shook her head. "Closed up all day, window fans at night to blow out what hot air gets in, it doesn't stay too bad."

They put everything away until Monday and left.

At seven he walked into the Ambrosia Restaurant. His house was too hot to think about cooking, he had decided, and made the reservation for himself. He was surprised to see Lucy Mc-Crutchen at the restaurant door, apparently on her way out.

"Good evening, Mr. Holloway," she said. "I hope you have a reservation. If you don't, I'm afraid you're out of luck, as I just found out."

"Please," he said. "Share my table. I did call. One, two, same table. I don't think they make tables for just one, do they?"

She hesitated a moment, then nodded. "Thank you. That would be nice. Actually I don't like eating alone in a restaurant. Do you?"

"I rarely do it," he said. "And no, I don't like it, either."

Minutes later they were seated at one of the upstairs tables. The restaurant was cool and dimly lit, enhancing the coolness, a welcome relief.

"I'm glad I ran into you," Lucy said after they ordered. "You remember those pink poppies you admired? They are finished blooming and soon they'll go dormant. I plan to divide them in mid-August, if you'd like a start."

"You don't intend to dig those roots out, do you? Do you know how long they are?" Frank asked.

Amused, she said, "Of course. It won't be the first time."

"Make a deal," Frank said. "I'll provide the labor in exchange for one."

They chatted easily and Lucy thought how nice it was to share a table with a charming man whose interests coincided with hers. If Henry had not wandered over late that afternoon, she reflected, she would be in her house eating alone and reading a book. This was better. Poor Henry. He had asked, practically begged her to have dinner with him in his house, where the central air-conditioning was on, the house cool enough for a sweater, he had said. They could listen to music, or watch a movie, order dinner in. She had long thought his house was more like a crypt than a home and she had begged off, plans with other friends, she had said vaguely.

Their conversation drifted from topic to topic effortlessly, and it seemed very soon that they had finished with coffee and were ready to leave. Frank walked to her car with her.

"Lucy, this has been one of the most pleasant evenings I've had in a long time. Thank you for joining me," he said.

"Thank you for letting me," she said. "I've enjoyed it, too. I'll call you when the poppies are ready."

He waited until she started her car and was ready to back out of the lot, then turned to retrieve his own car and drive home. She had insisted on paying for her own dinner. He didn't know why he had found that pleasing, that she insisted on paying for her meal. They had talked about Amy, Travis, gardening practices, gardens they had visited on trips, food, many things, but not about her late husband, or his dead wife. She had not mentioned Chloe, had not talked about Robert. They had not talked about murder.

At the same time that Frank was saying good-night to Lucy, Barbara was regarding Darren, who had stretched out on the futon in the basement den, just to rest a minute he had said. He was sound asleep. The den was degrees cooler than the upstairs, and she decided not to disturb him, but leave him alone to sleep there that night. He was so tired, more tired than she had ever seen him. When she asked how his new interns were doing, he had said, "If I had them in a high school class, I'd send them back to middle school. I've got them both studying Physiology 101."

She brought a light blanket down and put it within reach for later. It would cool off before morning. After turning out the lights, she went back upstairs to clear away the remains of the Chinese dinner, and finally to consider the police file she had read once and brought home for a closer reading. Knowing that her office over the garage would be even hotter than the house, she rejected it.

Her office in town, she decided at last. Cool, quiet, good light, space to spread papers. Without further thought, she jotted a note for Darren, just in case he woke up, gathered her things and went back to the office.

What Hoggarth had given her was not the same copy Robert had had, she thought later. A copy of a copy, it was not great, and in places it looked smudged; in other places it seemed that someone had covered margin notes before making a new copy. Under a strong light it was possible to tell where notes had been hidden. And the smudges, she felt certain, after examining them closely, had been highlighted on the other copy. The lines looked darker, dirtier, more smudged than other parts of the documents. She made margin arrows to indicate them, then started to read again at the beginning.

Later, Barbara leaned back in her chair, frowning. The high-lighted sections had to do with the key, and the margin notes had accompanied those passages. Probably Post-it notes had been used, leaving an outline, hiding the note itself. To all ap-pearances that key had caught Robert's attention as nothing else had, and that was understandable. Nothing else was worth no-tice. Who had known? David and Jill, Olga and David's room-mate. Robert had known. Who had called in the tip? An anonymous tip. Her frown deepened. Jill could have mentioned the key to someone, of course, but it seemed unlikely. And when? She had been napping when Olga left for work, and didn't even have the key until David arrived close to seven-thirty. By then the party was in full gear and noisy.

Who else had known? Barbara went to her desk and found the copy of the paper with x's carefully drawn in, then sorted through the folder until she found her list of the last few to leave that night. She turned it over and compared the x's to what Amy had drawn—the sketch of the family room, deck, kitchen. She had not included people, just the sites. Robert had populated the sites, she thought looking from one to the other. His x's were as nearly proportional to the distances as Amy's more-precise drawing indicated.

He must have been working on it when he was interrupted, she thought. Possibly, he had been trying to figure out who could have overheard what was said on the deck. Interrupted, he carried the paper with him on his way to being shot.

Who had called in the tip about the key in what appeared to be an obvious attempt to incriminate David? Probably none of those represented by an x. She remembered what Frank had told her of his conversation with Dr. Elders. He had assumed that David and Jill were intimate because he had seen the item in the newspaper concerning the key. Probably most people had assumed the same thing, since none of the newspaper accounts had explained why she'd had the key.

Barbara returned to the police report and this time made notes as she read. Who had gloves in the summer? Cotton fibers on Jill's neck, in her nails. Frank kept cotton gloves for light gardening. He bought two or three pairs at a time, he had said long ago, because he wore them out fast, and he kept heavy gloves for serious pruning, roses, tough jobs. She visualized Lucy's hat and gloves on the table on the deck at her house. Cotton, she was certain. Extra pairs? No garden dirt had been found on or near the wound, at least none reported, and it would have been. Clean cotton gloves. No transient lurking in the bushes at Jill's apartment house would have had clean cotton gloves. An ambush, like the attack on David? Or someone Jill had with her? Someone who had been at the party and had stolen Lucy's gloves?

The police had interviewed many of the partygoers, but only David had held their attention for any length of time, and as soon as the mystery about the key was resolved, they had turned to the alternate theory of a homeless hanger-on around the campus.

They botched it, she thought. No hard questions for those nice middle-class young people having a respectable party in the home of a much-loved local surgeon and his wife, who would not have tolerated any misbehavior. The party had not been a wild student kegger with fights breaking out, windows broken, a few cars dented, any arrests.

A few genteel questions had been asked of Lucy about the behavior of the party guests, which she'd described as above reproach, exemplary. The same kind of treatment for Dr. Elders. It was not reported that he had observed David acting possessively, jealously toward Jill. Was his recollection now a correction due to careful thought? Revisionist history? Rationalizing? If Jill had David's key, Elders probably had cause to believe he was jealous. Impossible to tell, she decided, and moved on.

Lingering a moment over Chloe's statement, Barbara wondered how much of it was true, how much a cover-up for her fiancé. She claimed he had stumbled and fallen in the shrubs and she went upstairs with him to make sure he got to bed safely. When she returned downstairs, almost everyone had left, and she drove herself home. No mention of a fight on the deck, trouble between Robert and David. Had she known, suspected?

If they'd all signed a pact, Barbara thought in disgust, they could not have done a better job at keeping the murder of Jill Storey distant, removed from the McCrutchen house and everyone who had been there that night.

There were several photographs of Jill taken from different angles. She had been dragged behind bushes, out of sight from passersby on the sidewalk. A sweater was partly under her, her keys near the walk to the apartment. These weren't the autopsy pictures, but of the crime scene, showing her facedown on grass. Her shoulders were bare. They appeared extremely bony. A small dark purse was near the keys in plain sight. It would not have been left behind by a transient. Barbara knew that much, and felt as if that much was all she knew about the death of Jill Storey.

19

"Watch," Todd said that Sunday on Frank's back porch. Earlier, he and Frank had gone out on an errand, and now he had two square glass vases on a table together side by side. He put a piece of ice in one, and a brick in the other with an identical piece of ice on top. Carefully he poured water tinted blue into both vases to come within about half an inch of the top of the brick. "Now we wait," he said.

It was twenty degrees cooler than it had been the day before, and everyone was more cheerful. Darren had come home from the clinic early. "My new boys don't work Sundays," he had said. "I think they were hungover, but they claimed religion took precedence. Fine with me. I want to get to some gardening."

Watching ice melt, Barbara thought. Fitting way to spend a lazy Sunday evening. She sipped her wine. "I have a plan for you," she said to Darren. "I figured it all out overnight. I know you can't turn the new guys loose on a patient, but why not let them work on each other? I was thinking of that contraption you use to hang people. I know, I know. You call it something else, stretching the vertebra out or something. In no time, you'd be down to one student, and cut your work in half."

Darren drank from his can of beer, then nodded. "Sounds good. Frank, any liability if they manage to do one another in like that?"

Frank laughed. "I'm out of it. Todd, you want to help out in the kitchen?"

Todd jumped up.

Later Todd was disappointed that the melting ice had not caused the water to rise high enough to cover the brick. "More water next time," he said. "Or maybe I could cut the brick in half, use less water, and make more of a point." He looked at Frank, "You think I could cut a brick in half?"

Darren laughed softly when Frank and Todd took the brick into the garage where Frank had some tools. More than once Barbara had been deeply moved by the way Frank had taken to Todd. How many times she had thought he really wanted a son. With never a hint or suggestion that such was the case, the thought had recurred over the years, and now he had skipped the middleman and gone straight to a grandson, and he reveled in it. Finally, she thought, finally maybe she had done something right.

Bailey slouched in his chair on Monday morning, after slinging his coat over the back of it. He usually carried a coat even in the summer, but it was doubtful that he had ever put it on. Barbara thought it must be showing signs of wear in strange places from being carried over his arm year after year.

"Not much yet," he said. "The McCrutchens had expensive tastes. Spent every cent that came in, and piled up hefty credit-card debt on top of it. Trips, his pricey apartment in Salem, clubs, new car every year. They take turns. She's living in an apartment with rent that starts at eighteen hundred—with maid service, two thousand. She has maid service. He played around, spent on women, piece of jewelry now and then, always the best restaurants, like that. Generally liked in Salem. A pretty good politician without any real axes to grind. Details," he said, pointing to the folder he had put on the table.

"No woman trouble in sight, just fun and games. Got thick with Aaronson about three years ago, mostly land deals from what I could find out. It's going to take audits, and a lot of digging and a lot of time to get to the bottom of it. There's a possibility that cash he got from a few deals could have gone straight to a war chest for a run for governor. Or a secret account. It went somewhere, not his bank account. It also looks as if some big boys in Washington were taking an interest in him."

He looked at Barbara shrewdly, and said, "It also looks as if Aaronson had more than enough reasons to want to keep his pal alive and helpful, not six feet under."

He helped himself to more coffee, added sugar and cream and consulted his notes.

"Aaronson rakes it in as a consultant. No money problems, good credit rating. Never married. Several lady friends, nothing serious. Condo in town, time-shares condo on the coast, three employees. No complaints from them. He gets things done for his clients, makes it happen. He seems to be a big contributor to a charity he helped organize." He looked surprised when Frank made a snorting sound.

"If Chloe McCrutchen played around, she kept it very quiet. Not a hint that I could find. Likes shows at the Hult, up in Portland, sometimes Seattle or San Francisco, Ashland. Plays golf at the country club, belongs to a fitness club. In other words, nothing. It's all in there." He pointed again to the folder, then leaned back to drink his coffee, report complete.

Zilch, Barbara thought. Dead end. She turned to Shelley.

"Apparently there's general agreement that from eight to ten people stayed at the party late. I talked to them either in person or by phone, and tried to link names when they left together, but there's a bit of confusion there, and one of them kept mixing up that party with another one he went to. No one noticed any particular attention directed by David toward Jill. And no one seems to know when she left or when he did, either. They noticed that Robert had disappeared and decided the party was over and the remaining few took off."

"Eight to ten," Barbara said. "That meshes with what David said, and with the *x*'s Robert drew. He had nine, but not one for the kid sleeping on the sofa, who made it ten. Ten little Indians, and no one saw a thing or overheard a thing. Way it goes."

She glanced at Frank, who shook his head. "Well, nothing more until a charge," she said. "The formal statement Wednesday, charge next week more than likely. I expect another flood of publicity after a charge is filed. Popular state senator, somewhat notorious writer. A lot of people will be after David's scalp and they'll be honing their hatchets."

She remembered Frank's words—half the world trying to kill the other half over ideas. It was bound to play out right here in River City.

"Anyway, the point is that it will increase the risk of having David's whereabouts revealed. Your department, Bailey. Don't let it happen."

He scowled and nodded. "Will he keep on going to the clinic?"

"Probably. I'll ask Darren."

His scowl deepened. "And he'll have to appear when they charge him, a bail-bond hearing," he said gloomily. He drained his cup. "Anything more for me?"

"One thing," Barbara said. "Listen to this." She brought out the notes she had made after her talk with Amy. "It's a bit of dialogue between Robert McCrutchen and Jill Storey the night of the party. First Jill."

She read the words. "'I said no. Leave me alone.' Robert's response, 'Not what you said a couple of weeks ago.' Jill again, 'That was then, this is now.' Robert, 'How 'bout you pay me back my twenty-five bucks, then? Take it out in trade.' Jill, 'You already took it out in trade. You got what you wanted, and so did I. Leave me alone.' I'll skip a line or two. Her last words, 'Liked it! You disgust me, you and all the others. Stick it in, that's all you can think of! Stick it in anything that moves. Think with your prick, that's all you know. Well, listen to me, you filthy ape. I don't need you now. I was going to be evicted. Now I'm not. So beat it! Leave me alone!'"

Barbara looked at Bailey. "How do you interpret it?"

He regarded her suspiciously, as if confronted with a trick question. "She's telling him to get lost."

"More," Barbara said.

He looked mildly embarrassed then said, "Sounds like she needed money, he had some, and they made a deal. He thought he was entitled to more than he got, and she didn't."

With a sigh Barbara returned the paper to her folder, and said to Shelley, "I think we may have a gender gap here." Shelley nodded.

"Tell me what I'm missing," Bailey said.

"We think that dialogue suggests that she was a lesbian."

He looked doubtful. "Maybe. You want more than that. She said something about others, not just McCrutchen. A sideline with her? Routine? Lots of things come to mind before being gay."

"That's the problem," Barbara said. "Ambiguity is the problem."

After Frank and Bailey left, Barbara and Shelley sat on the sofa and cross-referenced the names of the people who had stayed late at the party.

"Self-identified, and referenced by one other person," Barbara said. It didn't take very long. Everyone remembered at least one other person, sometimes several. "Ten altogether," Barbara said at last. "One zonked out on the couch. Three on the deck, the others by the piano."

"And none of them who recalls any kind of unusual behavior on David's part, or Jill's," Shelley added. "Back to the starting gate?"

"Back to the paddock," Barbara said ruefully. "We've just confirmed what Amy already said. Even if someone besides Robert saw David pass something to Jill, he wouldn't have known it was his key. The problem is that after the newspaper account mentioned that she had his key, recollections could shift to accommodate that, and intimacy was assumed, exactly the way Elders assumed it. That would not be helpful. Who knew about the key back then is the pertinent question. Who passed the tip to the media?"

Hoggarth and his stenographer had come and gone that Wednesday, and David was leaning back on the sofa, obviously tired, but not as weary as he had been just days ago. His strength and his better coloring were both evidence that he was making a more rapid recovery, as if an invisible hurdle had been passed. Hoggarth had been as thorough as he had been previously, covering the same material, both murders, but such an interrogation was tiring for even the healthiest suspect.

"I'd like to order some lunch in, and talk a bit," Barbara said. "Sandwiches, soup, whatever you want."

They placed their orders with Maria, and had coffee while they waited for sandwiches to be delivered.

"David, we need to talk about what to expect in the next

week or two," Frank said. "Possibly a charge, arraignment, booking, a hearing for bail bond, and so on. We'll be with you every single step. It's possible that they will charge you with both murders, try Storey's first, hoping for a conviction that will make McCrutchen's a snap. I think they are leaning in that direction from the questions Milt asked."

"I feel like a Kafka character caught in a nightmare with no waking up possible," David said. "If it weren't my own neck, it would strike me as a farce, unbelievably stupid."

"Keep that in mind, David," Barbara said. "It is your neck. And we'll need all the help we can get to keep that neck intact."

"Why?" David asked. "They can't have any real evidence. No eyewitnesses. Nothing. Why go after me?"

"I think they'll try to make a case that you and Jill were more than platonic pals, that you were jealous and possessive, and when she tried to pull loose, you struck out at her. That's the only case they can make. The rest of it is prejudice. Your book, your avowed beliefs and, maybe more important, the things you profess not to believe in. How many of our good citizens are admittedly atheists? Ten percent? Fifteen?"

"Thirteen," he said.

"I'm afraid a general belief is that atheists are inclined to take the law into their own hands, mete out their own punishment when they see fit and scorn the morality that guides everyone else on the straight and narrow path of righteousness."

David did not argue the point. "I'll be tried for what I believe," he said. "At least no one gets burned at the stake any longer. Count my blessings." He shrugged. "Okay, onward. What to expect."

Impatiently, Barbara shook her head. "Before we get into that, I have to settle something. David, was Jill a lesbian? Just give me a straight answer."

For what seemed a long time he did not move or speak. "Why do you want to know?" he said at last. "What possible difference can it make?"

"It could save your neck if she was, and if we can establish that as a fact," Barbara said. "It's a starting place for me. And God knows I need a place to start."

"Let me tell you something about our past," David said after another pause. "We were misfits, both of us. From the get-go, misfits. I was a skinny geek, a nerd, a brain, emotionally and physically immature much too long, afraid of girls because they always seemed to know things I couldn't understand. Or they were just mysterious, not like me. I hated competitive sports and wouldn't have been any good at them in any event.

"And she was, too. She was pretty, the prettiest girl in high school, but that didn't help and probably made it worse for her. Wrong clothes, no money, wrong kind of family, lived in the wrong place and too damn smart. Neither of us had any real friends except each other. We read books and talked about them, and even that made us weird."

He was speaking in a semidetached way, as if thinking out loud, with no particular emphasis on the meaning of his words. He could have been talking about strangers, Barbara thought.

"Anyway, that's the general picture. The summer we were sixteen we were down by a small creek nearby, a place where we had gone to play for most of our lives. She started to cry. Her sister's boyfriend had cornered her and kissed her, and she was frightened by her reaction—nausea, revulsion, self-hatred, hatred for him. It came out that day. She liked girls, and it was terrifying to her, the way she felt about girls. She was terrified that someone would find out. She was desperate to get out of the kind of situation she saw all around her, girls looking for boys, marrying young, babies, poverty, dead-end lives. She was desperate for an education, determined to have a decent life. She was afraid she'd be labeled a deviant, a pervert. She was afraid her father would drive her out, make her live on the streets or something. Remember, we're talking nearly thirty years ago, and she was justified in being afraid. She made me promise never to tell. We made a pact that day. We'd pretend I was her boyfriend, and we'd keep on the way we had been, but the other kids would see us as a *thing*, as the saying goes. I could avoid the girls who were terrifying to me, and she could avoid the guys. Until we hit the university here, we continued to be considered a couple."

He looked at Barbara then, the first time since he had begun speaking. "That pact saved us both," he said. "It got us through those years. We owed each other a lot from then on."

Dismayed, Barbara asked, "Didn't anyone else in Gresham know about her?"

"I don't think there was ever the least suspicion. Homosexuality wasn't talked about, not in the air. I don't think anyone I knew had ever given it a thought."

"What about at the university?"

"Midway through her freshman year, she met Olga," he said. "By summer they were living together, considered to be roommates, friends. Maybe people suspected, I don't know, but I doubt it."

Barbara stood and picked up the coffee carafe. "I'll get a refill," she said. "Our lunch should be here any minute."

What it meant, she thought, walking to the outer office, was that most likely there was no way she could establish the fact that Jill Storey had been a lesbian unless Olga admitted it. David's word would not be enough, and from Bailey's reaction to the dialogue she had read to him, neither would Amy's be good enough. The secret pact that had saved David and Jill in their turbulent adolescent years, could spell his doom now.

20

"Your Honor," Barbara argued on Friday of the following week, "because Mr. Etheridge's continuing treatments require follow-up evaluations by his surgeon and neurologist, and regular sessions at the physical therapy clinic, plus demanding at-home exercises with specialized equipment, it is necessary that he be allowed to continue his medical regimen or risk the permanent loss of function in his dominant arm and hand. Such care would not be possible if he is confined in an overcrowded jail. I have statements from each of his doctors and the physical therapist outlining their prognoses and prescribed routine for the next several months."

"Objection!" cried Roy McNulty, the assistant district attorney. "He stands charged with two vicious murders. By his own words he has demonstrated his disdain for government, his lack of respect for laws and his disbelief in the higher authority of religion to guide human behavior by a divine sense of moral and ethical conduct. There is no reason to believe that he will not flee—"

"Object!" Barbara said angrily. "This is not the Galileo court of inquisition. Mr. Etheridge has not been charged with criminal political or religious belief. He is not charged with heresy. His writings are not the matter before this court. He himself was subjected to a murderous attack that left him critically injured. The presumption of innocence must embrace his right to continuing specialized medical treatment and the opportunity for a full and complete recovery from those injuries."

"He already had tickets to leave the country!" McNulty said in a grating voice.

"Which have been canceled," Barbara snapped. "And he has surrendered his passport!"

Judge Carlyle waved them both down. "Back off. Let me see those medical reports," he said to Barbara.

An hour later it was done and they were in Bailey's SUV on their way to Frank's house. Alan McCagno and David were in the back of the van, out of sight behind the dark rear windows. Alan helped David out of his coat and slipped it on. At Frank's house, Alan, flanked by Frank and Bailey, entered the house after Barbara went ahead to open the door. Another car had pulled in at the curb and a videographer jumped out, only to be met by another of Bailey's operatives, who managed to keep between him and the group entering the house. Inside, Bailey saluted and left, and a minute later he and David were on their way back to Shelley's house in the foothills of the Coast Range.

"Like clockwork," Frank commented. "Good work in court today, Bobby."

"Thanks," she said. "Touch-and-go for a while. McNulty really wanted him in jail. I think it was a taste of what's to come."

Frank nodded. An opening salvo had been fired.

Barbara was almost relieved that the charge finally had been brought, that the standstill had ended. Now, or at least soon, she would start getting discovery, probably many hundreds of pages of statements, testimony, dead ends, but also enough to let her know the basis for the prosecution's case. Now the case was out of Hoggarth's jurisdiction. It had been turned over to the district attorney's office.

After everyone was gone, Frank checked his telephone messages and was pleased to see one from Lucy McCrutchen. The pink poppies were ready to be dug and divided. He called her back.

"How about late afternoon tomorrow," he said. "Is that a good time?"

"Fine. I'll expect you at about four," she said. She paused a moment, then said, "Is it true, David was charged with both murders?"

"Unfortunately it's true."

"I'm so sorry. It's so unjust. Amy will be devastated, I'm afraid."

Frank continued to sit at his desk while pondering the question he had posed before—why was Lucy McCrutchen convinced that David was not her son's murderer? A man she had not seen for more than twenty years, and had known only as a student among others in the past. He was very much afraid that the time would come when he would feel obliged to ask her, and he was reluctant to do so.

When he showed up at Lucy's door on Saturday afternoon, Frank was carrying a bag of tomatoes in one hand and a spade in the other. The blade was unusually long and narrow, and it was sharp. He had sharpened it that morning.

Lucy was delighted with the tomatoes. She led the way to the kitchen where she set a shallow wooden bowl on the table and put the tomatoes in it. "Brandywines!" she exclaimed. "You grow Brandywines?" She held one up and turned it around examining it. "They'll never take first place in a beauty contest, will they? But they're the best."

"To my mind they are," Frank agreed. "And that one, the dark one, I found those seeds in a seed exchange. The woman who had them said her grandmother brought the seeds over from Germany, real heritage tomatoes. She called them Black Germans, and I do, too, for want of a name recognized by horticulture. They're very good, too."

"I used to have a vegetable garden," Lucy said. "It kept shrinking as the children grew up and then left, until I had only those few things I thought we couldn't bear to do without. Tomatoes, a few Kentucky Wonder beans. Just a few things. I haven't done that since. Perhaps next summer, I'll have those few things again."

Frank nodded. He had done no gardening for three or four years following the death of his wife. He hefted the garden spade. "And this was meant to dig out taproots. Not much good for shoveling snow, but great for taproots."

They went out to the garden. "I haven't cut the foliage back yet. I thought that should wait until you have a go at them. Can you use two?" Lucy asked.

She watched him closely as he made his way through the flowers to the poppies, then, apparently reassured that he knew not to trample anything, she withdrew to the shade of the dogwood tree. "It's funny how some plants find their own level, isn't it?" she said. "Lilies will work themselves as deep as they like it. I wonder how they manage to do that. And alstroemeria! I tried to dig some out once, and had to give up. Heaven only knows how deep those roots had gone."

They both laughed as they exchanged garden stories. When

Frank had his two poppies, he filled in the narrow holes carefully and covered them with mulch.

"You'll want to wash your hands," Lucy said. "And then a glass of wine and a little snack to celebrate a successful mission."

A few minutes later they were seated in the shade on the deck. Lucy had brought out a tray with chilled pinot grigio, and an assortment of cheeses. A bowl nestled in a bed of ice held shrimp, smoked oysters and pickled mushrooms.

"This is very pleasant," Frank said. "A lovely garden to gaze at, excellent wine and good company. Thank you."

"I like this time of day," she said. "It always seemed things tended to calm down about now, no matter how hectic they had been earlier." She glanced at him, looked away and asked, "Are you still working as an attorney?"

"Sometimes, but not enough to earn my keep. Right now I'm working on a book that's been edited by a moron. Damage control is how I see what I'm doing."

"You also write books?"

"This is the second one. Legal cases. Not much of an audience for them, I'm afraid."

She started to say something, then looked past him and said, "Hello, Henry."

"Sorry," Henry said. "I didn't realize you had company. I thought we might share a glass of wine." He was carrying a bottle. "Oh, it's Mr. Holloway. How's it going? I hear that Etheridge was charged with two murders. Are you still involved in that?"

"He's our client," Frank said.

"I always wondered what it would be like to deal so closely with criminals. Is the criminal mind different? Can you tell from talking to them? It must be hard to defend someone you know committed a serious crime. I mean, how can they rationally justify it?"

"Under our laws everyone deserves a fair trial," Frank said. "It's that simple."

"But can you defend someone you know is guilty? It seems a real conflict must arise in your own mind. Or does it?"

"Henry, for heaven's sake. If you're going to join us, go get a glass and take a chair. Stop looming over us like a gargoyle," Lucy said. "And stop coming on like an avenging angel."

"Sorry," Henry said. "I never got to talk to a criminal attorney before. It's a fascinating subject. I'll get a glass."

Frank laughed and sipped his wine. "Defense attorney is the phrase."

Lucy smiled, but it was a strained expression. "He can be trying," she said when Henry went into the kitchen.

Henry returned with his glass, sat down and helped himself to wine. He leaned forward, but before he could pose another of his questions, Frank said, "We were discussing the mechanism of how bulbs, rhizomes and the like can work their way into the soil to the level they find necessary. They have no musculature to accommodate such movement. It's a fascinating topic. How much do plants know, how do they communicate? We know that a disease or harmful insect can cause one plant to signal its presence, and soon nearby plants have activated their defense systems. How does that work? Some believe it's a chemical reaction. But that doesn't explain how they can move in the soil."

"I tried to get a sea holly to grow in the border," Lucy said, "and it just wouldn't thrive. But then several came of their own accord in among the stones of the patio." There was a gleam in her eyes as she said this.

Henry picked up a shrimp.

"Volunteers are a mystery, too," Frank said. "Sometimes things I've never had in the garden, and don't believe any near neighbors did, either, suddenly appear."

"Getting back to the criminal mind," Henry said. "Are they different?"

Frank shrugged. "I'm not a psychologist. You could look on the Internet for any studies."

Henry picked up another shrimp.

After discussing the mysteries of plant life for a few more minutes, Frank glanced at his watch. "I really shouldn't stay any longer. Thank you for the poppies, Lucy. I'll give them a good home, even if not as beautiful as the one they're leaving."

"I'll see you out," Lucy said. "Be right back, Henry." Walking through the house, she said, "Poor Henry. As Amy has said many times, he can be a pest. Thank you for the tomatoes."

At the door, Frank hesitated a moment, then said, "May I call you sometime? Perhaps we could have dinner again?"

She nodded. "I'd like that very much."

In his car, driving toward his house, Frank began to chuckle. Poor Henry indeed. He had known very well that Frank was there. The son of a bitch was jealous, Frank thought, and laughed out loud.

Amy had been driving aimlessly most of the afternoon that Saturday. She had stopped somewhere and walked, had driven again, walked, driven. It was dark when she returned home. Lucy was in the family room with the television on.

"Mother, we have to talk," Amy said, entering the room.

Using the remote control, Lucy turned off the television. It had been on but she couldn't have said what had been on the screen. She nodded toward the other end of the sofa.

Amy chose a chair facing her mother instead of the sofa. "You know they arrested and charged David," she said, fighting to keep her voice under control. Lucy nodded. "You have to tell them about that night, the night of the party," Amy said.

"What happened out on the deck. I told Barbara Holloway, but it wasn't enough. You have to tell them, too."

Lucy shook her head. "I don't know what you're talking about."

"You know. Mother, I was out under the dogwood tree. I saw and heard it all. And you did, too. I saw you on the deck. You saw and heard the same things I did." Her voice was rising, and she drew in a breath. "Mother, you know David didn't kill Jill. You know why. She was a lesbian, not interested in him or any other man, and he knew that. You know it, too."

Lucy moistened her lips and shook her head again. "I was in the living room. You were in bed."

"Mother! I saw you!"

Lucy stood. "If she was a lesbian, they'll prove that without me. You're letting your imagination run away with you. I don't know why you're so interested in David. You don't even know him. If he didn't do it, they'll clear him."

"What if they don't?" Amy cried. "Why won't you admit what you know? Robert's dead and gone and doesn't need anyone covering up for him. David needs help. Why won't you admit it?"

Lucy swayed slightly and held on to the arm of the sofa. "I can't," she said in an agonized whisper. "You don't understand. I can't."

"Why not?" Amy's voice rose to a near scream, and she jumped up, shaking all over. "Why not?"

"My son. My child. I can't turn against my own son. What if they accuse him of going after her? I can't do that!"

Amy sank back into her chair. "Oh, my God. That's what you think? He did it?"

Lucy's face had become ashen. "Don't say that. Don't even think it. Just leave it alone." She closed her eyes, repeated, "Leave it alone." She walked stiffly from the room.

21

"We've done what we can," Frank said. "We'll both go mad if we keep going over it. Let's box it up and send the thing back. Make a copy first. We'll never remember all the corrections we've made." They both glared at the offending manuscript.

Patsy nodded. "I'll bring it in as soon as that's done."

"Fine. Good work, Patsy. Thanks."

At his desk, waiting for Patsy to type the letter to go with the manuscript, he thought about Lucy McCrutchen. Too soon to ask her to dinner? Deciding the answer was no, he dialed her number.

"Good afternoon," he said when she answered the phone. "I thought, since Amy is out on Fridays, perhaps it would be a good time to have dinner with me. Tonight?"

"Oh, Frank, I'm sorry. I'm all tied up. But thanks for asking," Lucy replied.

"I'm sorry, too. We'll make it another time."

They chatted for only a moment, and when he hung up, he

regarded the phone thoughtfully. She sounded different. Strained? Upset? Second thoughts about seeing him? It sounded like it.

Lucy replaced her phone and walked out to the deck. The past week had been hellish, and now this. She didn't feel as if she could face Frank. It had come as a wrenching shock to learn that Amy had seen that incident on the deck so many years ago. And a worse shock to realize that Amy knew she had been out there. During the week, the tension in the air had been nearly palpable, with a deadly silence between them. The ease she had always felt with Amy was gone, and its absence left a hollow yearning for its return, and for the comfort she had found in her beautiful daughter. She had an almost desperate fear that she had lost her, just as surely as she had lost her husband and her son.

Amy couldn't be in love with David. She didn't even really know him. It was a romantic fixation of some sort in which she saw herself saving him, his gratitude... Lucy made herself stop going over that yet again. All week the same arguments had played themselves out in her mind over and over. If Jill had been a lesbian, that should be easy enough to establish without her help. She believed just as Amy did that that had been Jill's meaning on the deck years before. Something in her tone had made her meaning clear. Men simply don't lust after childhood friends who are also lesbians, she told herself once more, and that meant that David had had no motive for killing her, or for killing Robert. Lucy bit her lip, fighting against the recurring arguments. David was a stranger to everyone here. No one owed him a thing. The authorities couldn't hold his book against him, let prejudice overcome reason. The system was fairer than that. It had to be fairer than that.

Abruptly, she rose and went inside again. The last thing she wanted these days was to have to make meaningless small talk with Henry, and he had an uncanny knack for knowing when she was out on the deck. When she entered the house, she pushed down the lock button on the screen door. At least it prevented Henry's coming in and making himself at home, which seemed to be too much of a habit with him. No more, she told herself. No more.

In Portland, Amy sat at her small kitchen table with a Coke. A new project at work would keep her busy, and that was good. She wanted to stay too busy to think, to feel anything except fatigue at the end of the day. Was it time to move back to Portland? She kept asking herself and so far had not answered.

Her mother was not likely to change her mind, she told herself. At times, if she worked at it, she could almost see Lucy's refusal as reasonable. Then it slipped away. What harm could come to Robert now? Beyond redemption, beyond reproof. What difference could it make if the police suspected him of anything at all? Dig him up and hang him? She shuddered and took another drink from the can.

Decide what to do about the damn pictures! she told herself sharply. That was what she had to do this trip. Decide. Would they be enough to get David out of trouble? Why would they? If only she could see a clear way they could be used, there wouldn't be a question what to do with them. Hand them over. But they had nothing to do with Jill's death so many years ago.

She was still trying to untangle a swirl of conflicting and confusing thoughts when her cell phone chimed. To her surprise Chloe was calling.

"Amy, can we meet somewhere and talk? I have to talk to you."

"I'm in Portland," Amy said.

"I know. So am I. There's a coffee shop a few blocks from your apartment. Will you meet me there? Please."

Doubly surprised, since Chloe was not in the habit of saying please to anyone, Amy said, "Where?"

She knew the small coffee shop/bakery combination, and fifteen minutes later she walked inside. Chloe was already in a booth with a cup of coffee.

"Thanks for coming," Chloe said huskily when Amy slid into the seat opposite her.

The waitress came, Amy ordered coffee, and both she and Chloe remained silent until her coffee was served and the waitress gone again.

"This is hard," Chloe said, her eyes downcast as she toyed with a spoon. "I realized an hour or so ago that what I had come up for was simply to get you alone and tell you something. At the house, you never know when Lucy or Henry will be around, or someone else, or the phone, or something will interrupt." She glanced at Amy, then went back to examining her spoon.

"When we were in the town house, and Robert was a prosecutor, oh, ten or twelve years ago, I really wanted a divorce. But of course, I had to think of Travis and what it would do to him, and I held my peace. But the marriage, such as it was, had been over for years. Then Robert was elected and began to spend more and more time in Salem, traveling around the state. It was a relief, but it meant a lonesome life. I mean, in spite of whatever problems there are in a marriage, there's still a home, things you do together and all that. About four years ago, I was up here in Portland, and decided to drop in on Robert's apartment on the way back down, have dinner, whatever. I thought that maybe a new place, his apartment, would rekindle something, make it exciting for both of us."

Amy felt transfixed as Chloe talked, apparently to her spoon.

Now and again her attention flashed to Amy, then away so quickly it was little more than a blink. Her voice was low, nearly inaudible.

"So I went to his apartment, and I discovered a woman was either living with him or was a very frequent visitor. I know this is hard for you. I'm talking about your brother. Anyway, that day I waited, and when Robert got there, I told him I wanted a divorce. He begged me not to do it. He actually begged me and he talked about the career he saw looming for him, and for me he said. Big things in store for us, but not if there was a divorce. I was outraged and humiliated and I left. But that weekend, when he came home, he started again. There was a party that we had to attend, and he encouraged me to talk to Nick Aaronson. Threw me at him, is more like what he did, and Nick was everything that Robert wasn't. Warm, attentive, sympathetic, and he made it clear that he was attracted to me, had been since our college days."

Another quick glance at Amy, a sip of coffee, playing with her spoon again. It seemed she needed a pause, a small time-out, a moment to moisten her lips.

"We had an affair," she said then, in a near whisper. "Several months. Then I broke it off, ashamed, mortified at my own behavior."

When she stopped again the silence extended until Amy broke it. "Why are you telling me this?" Her voice was as low as Chloe's had been.

"I have to," Chloe said. "I decided I didn't care if it hurt Robert's career, I wanted a divorce." Her words were coming so fast they were hard to follow, hard to separate out as individual words. "I told him so, and he showed me a picture of Nick and me in bed. He'd had us followed, had pictures. He said I'd ruin his career and he'd ruin me by publishing the pictures. I'd lose Travis, lose everything. He wanted to keep up the pretense of a good marriage. It was good for his image, he said."

Chloe looked directly at Amy then for the first time. "I don't know where the pictures are," she said. "And I don't want Lucy to find them. If she decides to sell the house, she'll clean out and pack up everything, and she'll come across them eventually. I can't bear to think what it would do to her to find out that Robert was blackmailing me into remaining in the marriage for his public image, nothing else."

Amy drew back from her unwavering regard.

"If you find them," Chloe said, "please give them to me so I can burn them. That's all I'm asking. I just want to burn them."

Swiftly she picked up both their checks and slid from the booth, went to the cashier, paid and walked out.

Amy sat in her corner of the booth for several minutes without moving or touching her coffee. She had not even tasted it. She pushed it back and slid out of the booth.

How much of it was true? she asked herself, walking back to her apartment. And why had Chloe told her? Had she simply wanted an admission that Amy had them? An effort to gain Amy's sympathy? She remembered her own decision earlier, that if she had found no use for the pictures, eventually she would give them to Chloe and be done with them and with Chloe. The truth was, she thought with surprise, she really did have some sympathy for Chloe, who had spent half her life in a loveless marriage. Meanwhile, she still had to decide what to do with the damn pictures. Nothing for now, she finally told herself. Leave them in the safe-deposit box for now, and think about it.

Chloe was rigid with fury as she drove away. Amy had the pictures, she knew. The way Amy avoided looking at her, her general attitude since before Chloe had left the house. She had them. She would hand them over, Chloe told herself, as she had been doing all week. Amy wasn't like Robert, a blackmailer. She was like Lucy, soft and forgiving, understanding. She would hand them over.

And then, Chloe thought grimly, watch out, Nick. He had stopped calling, didn't return her calls, didn't answer his doorbell the times she had gone to the condo. He was cutting her out. She had steeled herself to one more act of debasement, but it would be worth it when Amy gave her the pictures. Her years of sacrifice, of living a lie, today, it would all be worth it, once she had the pictures. She would make Nick get it that she had nothing to lose by using the pictures. Nothing at all.

Barbara leaned back in her chair and rubbed her eyes. She had been reading one report after another for several hours and had made scant notes. Her phone buzzed and Maria said Bailey was on the line.

"I have something," he said without preliminaries.

"Tell me."

"I'll show you. Forty-five minutes? An hour? Office, home, your dad's place. Where?"

She glanced at her watch. It was four-fifteen. "Dad's place. We'll wait for you there."

He hung up with as little ceremony as his greeting. Cell phone, she guessed. He hated and feared them for the danger, he claimed, of brain cancer that they posed. He spent as little time as possible using his. That he had used it probably meant he was on the road. She called Frank to make sure he'd be there.

"That's all he said," she told him half an hour later. "He'll show us. David went to the clinic at two today. Out a little after three and Bailey called an hour and a few minutes later. If he let someone follow them to Shelley's house, I'll strangle him."

Frank waved that away. "You know better. Anything in discovery yet?"

"No. Nothing to take to the bank. Nothing new."

Bailey arrived half an hour later. "Traffic," he said with a grumpy expression. "Friday get-out-and-drive traffic." He was hot and more rumpled looking than usual. He had been driving his old Dodge that was without air-conditioning. Barbara waited impatiently as Frank played host and offered Bailey a cold beer. He accepted with a sigh and they went out to the back porch to sit at a table in the shade. Bailey pulled a gadget from his pocket and placed it in the center of the table. It was the size of a half-dollar coin, shiny and metallic, without any visible moving parts. Just a shiny case of some sort.

"That's it. Show-and-tell," he said.

"What is it?" Barbara demanded. "Stop playing games. What's up?"

"Okay. Okay," he said after taking a long drink. "You know how David and I work it. I drive up to the back gate, someone unlocks it to let him in and I leave. Pick him up the same way. They call, I go to the gate, he gets in and off we go. Today, a block or two away, he's fussing with that seat belt. You know, the belts in the Dodge, a little hard to get right sometimes. So he's having trouble with it, moving around some, and he feels something in his pocket. I stop to let him fish it out, and it's that." He pointed to the object on the table.

"So what is it?" Barbara snapped. "Get to the point."

"A GPS signaling device." He looked at it admiringly. "A beauty, isn't it? Two hundred bucks."

"You brought it here? For God's sake!"

"It's disabled," Bailey said. "I called Hal Jarvis to meet us at a bar I know on 99, and drove around a little and ended up there and pretty soon Hal and another guy showed up."

Hal Jarvis was his electronics expert, one he turned to often. Barbara believed Hal could wire the wind and make it tell tales.

"See, what we decided we'd do was have Hal and his buddy keep driving while Hal worked on it and eventually figured out how to disable it. I took David on out to Shelley's house, and drove back to the bar and waited for Hal and friend to come back. I guess the guys tracking them were pretty confused before it was all over."

"How do they track it without being noticed?" Frank asked, picking up the device and studying it curiously.

"Not hard. It's sending a signal to a satellite that traces it on a computer map. You could stay half a mile away and know exactly where that baby is at all times. Until it stops sending, at least. Like I said, it's a beauty."

"How did it get in his pocket?" Barbara asked. "Does David know?"

"Sure. The receptionist let him in, and just inside the clinic a guy bumped into him a little and put his hand out to steady David, and must have dropped that in his pocket at the same time. With his right hand messed up like it is, David isn't using that right pocket and he didn't notice a thing at the time, not until he was trying to get his belt fixed."

"Did he get a name, description?"

"No name. The guy had a name tag, but David didn't get to see the name. Stocky guy, five-nine, one seventy-five, sandy hair, light blue eyes, florid complexion. Good description."

Barbara drew in a breath. One of the staff. A physical therapist or one of the interns. A staff member who had known when to expect David. Their plan to change his appointment time from week to week to keep a routine from being noticeable to an outsider had been futile. The enemy was within.

"Darren will put a name on him," Frank said. "Good work, Bailey. Another beer?" He didn't wait for an answer. Bailey was not known to turn down anything potable. On his way to the refrigerator, Frank said, "They'll know you found it and disabled it, I guess."

"Maybe not," Bailey said. "Sometimes they malfunction, or the signal gets lost for some reason. Hal said he thought they'd probably start getting a little garbage before it stopped altogether. They were heading toward Fox Hollow Road when that happened."

When Frank returned, he had a tray with cheese and crackers, wine for Barbara and another beer for Bailey. "I thought we might call Darren and have him bring Todd over here, order in something. What time has he been getting off these days?"

"Not before seven. I'll call him." Barbara went in to make the call.

Frank poured himself a bit of wine and sipped it. "The GPS didn't work. He'll try something different, I imagine."

Bailey's gloom deepened. "As long as David has to keep coming to town once a week, it's going to be tricky. Depends on how bad someone wants to find out where the hideout is, how much he's willing to spend to get it done. So far it's probably been under a grand, maybe a little more, but not much more."

Barbara rejoined them and nodded to Frank. "They'll be along at about seven-thirty."

"Our next step is the question," Frank said.

"My question is this," Barbara said. "What's in it for someone to track down David?"

It was no longer a question of a hate crime, she knew. Someone was spending money to find David. Why?

"That's the question, all right," Frank commented.

"He wants to stop the trial, put an end to it immediately, not risk further questions," Barbara said. "David convicted by death, case closed."

After a moment, Frank nodded. Case closed by another murder.

22

Ribs had been delivered and consumed, leftovers packed up for another meal for the noncooks, and now Todd was in the living room watching television and the others were in Frank's study. Darren was examining the GPS with as much curiosity as Frank had shown earlier.

"One of my staff?" he said quietly. "I'll serve his head on a platter."

"That's the last thing we want you to do," Frank said. "You had to be alerted, however. Describe him for Darren," he said to Bailey.

He repeated the description and Darren nodded. "One of the new interns, Erik Strohman. Now what?"

"We're trying to decide," Frank said. "But we don't want him to know we're on to him. Meanwhile David is still safely out of sight and reach. Is it imperative for his therapy to have him check in weekly at the clinic?"

"He's coming along, working at it on his own. Weekly? Maybe not. But I have to see him often, change his regimen. As he continues to make progress, we alter treatments."

"Is there any possibility of your going out to Shelley's to treat him?" Frank asked.

"Another possibility," Barbara said, before Darren had a chance to respond. "I could pick David up on Sunday afternoons and bring him here. We're always over for dinner anyway, and you and David could go up to the guest room and put him through his paces. After dinner I could take him back to Shelley's house."

Frank nodded. It would do, he thought, and he did like the idea. He wanted to get to know David better and there had been little opportunity to do so. But what really pleased him was the way Barbara was protecting Darren. Eventually a wedding would come along, he hoped, but it was not pressing. It was enough for now that it was working for them.

"And meanwhile those other guys will be scouring the Fox Hollow Road area, looking for a possible hideout," Bailey said, grinning. "It's a long road."

"I'm okay with either plan," Darren said. "When David's ready for some equipment, weights, something like that, I can get it over here."

"Okay, then," Barbara said, satisfied. "You might want to keep an eye on Erik Strohman. He could be into lifting the silverware, and meanwhile as far as he's concerned, his mission was a success."

Bailey left soon after that and Darren and Todd didn't stay much longer. Darren had to go to the clinic in the morning, and Todd was eager to get back to his science project. The new school season was starting the following week, and he kept finding material to add, determined to have his project finished by then.

"I won't be long," Barbara told Darren at the door as he was leaving. "I need to tidy up a few loose ends."

Back in the study, she said, "I'm looking through discovery for the first sign that McNulty is referring to anything from that old police file, and as soon as I find it, I'll demand the right to use the same material. I'm making a list of names for Bailey to check out. Is the landlady the same one from that long ago, same neighbors? Things like that. So far, McNulty's suggesting it's all current but I suspect he's fudging it more than a little bit."

Because officially she had no right to that old police file, she could not use it to impeach any new testimony that differed from what had been said before. The relevant information in that file had to be added to discovery, and it had not been done yet, except for the autopsy report.

"McNulty won't make it easy," Frank said. "You'll probably have to file a motion."

"I know. I've been drafting it, getting it ready." She pointed to her bulging briefcase. "That's how I'll spend the weekend, reading. Maybe by next week I'll have a few answers. It's Labor Day on Monday, no office hours. By Tuesday I hope to know more than I do now."

On Saturday afternoon Lou Granville called. A new art show was on display, she said, and she was certain Barbara would be interested in seeing it. Barbara arrived in the shop at two.

"You promise not to out her," Lou said grimly.

"Yes. I told you I wouldn't."

"I know. Just a reminder for both of us. Once a month Maas puts her daughter on a bus to Spokane to spend time with her father, and she goes to a friend's apartment in Richland, where she stays until Sunday night. It's a couple of weeks during the summer, same kind of arrangement." Lou was clearly troubled as she continued. "Her pal is as deep in her own closet as Maas is. Works in a bank, middle-management job, no kids."

"Name?" Barbara asked.

Lou hesitated. "You really need it?"

"I don't know. I might. Same promise regarding her, Lou. She's safe with me."

Lou nodded. "Gwendolyn Trilby. Forty-six, never married, never outed."

"Thanks, Lou. I owe you a big one."

As Barbara walked to the door, Lou said, "It's a hell of a life, Barbara. A real hell of a life."

Barbara turned, went to Lou and embraced her. "I know it is, my friend. I know it is. Thank you."

When her team gathered on Tuesday morning, Barbara was grim. "We have three different stories to check out," she said. "Nick Aaronson's current statement is that he saw Robert stagger into the house, with a bloody hand pressed against his face, and hurry upstairs with Chloe at his heels. He found Mrs. McCrutchen in the living room, thanked her and took off with his date, Belinda Hulse. He also said that David and Jill came in soon after Robert did, that David was holding Jill's arm, and hustled her out. Find Hulse, Bailey. I want to hear her version of what happened. No one else has mentioned that either Aaronson or Hulse were among the lingerers at the party. Not a mention of any of that in the old police file."

Bailey made a note of the name to add to the others she already had given him.

"Next, Chloe's story has changed. Now she says she saw that Robert's face was bloody and she rushed upstairs after him to make sure he was all right. He had a bloody nose. She washed off the blood, put a washcloth on his nose and so on. Again, a different story. And now, after all these years, Dr. Elders recalls perfectly how possessive David was toward Jill, how he hovered over her, tried to monopolize her all that evening."

Frank nodded. "That's what he told me the first time we talked."

"In the police file there's no mention of him beyond the fact that he'd been there early in the evening." She frowned. "Why the changes now? From all three of them. What do they have in common, if anything? Beyond the obvious fact that they all want to see David convicted. But why?"

"Elders could be jealous," Frank said. "Upstart of a student making a big splash, getting a prestigious appointment at Oxford, national recognition for his books, while he's fading away in obscurity. It could be made even worse because David voices opinions that he finds odious and wrong. He could simply want to take him down in flames. It could even be unconscious on his part."

"And likely Aaronson doesn't want investigations launched into the deals he and Robert McCrutchen hatched between them. Keep the focus on what happened twenty-two years ago," Barbara said. "It could be time to look into some of those deals. Who would be good at that?"

"Let me think about it a bit," Frank said. "It takes a certain kind of skill and training, and a good deal of time to unravel dubious zoning deals, land deals, as well as possibly dubious charities. Not my cup of tea, and not yours, either."

Barbara shuddered. "You know it. And both those explanations might account for the desire to see a conviction, but neither one addresses the murder of Jill or Robert, or the attack on David. Separate issues? There are too damn many strings in this bow. It still leaves Chloe's new story and I don't have a clue about why she changed it."

Shelley said, "You know who might have kept notes, papers, everything, including a journal, a diary or something with an account of the party? A business student. Aren't they trained to keep all documents? I knew one or two, and they did. The yearbook might tell the majors of the graduating students."

"Good thinking," Barbara said. "I bet you're right. David told me Jill kept a diary as a kid. Maybe Jill's notes and papers were preserved. And she might have mentioned names of classmates, even friends who knew her and suspected that she was in a lesbian relationship. I can't believe no one suspected. If anyone kept Jill's papers, it was probably Olga Maas. She named her daughter Gillian. I'll give her a call, and I'll have another look at that yearbook."

"When you go to the McCrutchen house, I'll tag along," Frank said. He was curious about Lucy's attitude the last time he'd talked to her. Of course, he had told himself, she might have just had a bad time with the plumbing or something, but he didn't think so. It had something to do with him, or with the case they were working on. He trusted intuition to a point, but he liked to back it up with reason, and he had not come up with a satisfactory one yet.

Alone a few minutes later, Barbara thought about Olga Maas. She would be at school, no doubt until close to five, an awkward time to call, since she might be preparing dinner. It couldn't be helped, she decided—she would call at five. She then called Amy, whose only real question about a visit concerned David.

"Is there any chance of my visiting him anytime at all?" she asked after Barbara assured her that he was making good progress.

"I'll find out," Barbara said. "Meanwhile, would it be a terrible imposition for us to come over and have another look at that yearbook?"

"Not at all. When?"

"I'd like to ask your mother something at the same time. Do you know if she'll be there?"

"She'll be home from about three on, and I'll be here all day, so just come on over when you're ready."

That afternoon when Amy opened the door for them, she was dressed in jeans and a T-shirt with dancing flamingoes. She looked much younger than her thirty-six years. Lucy joined them in the hall, and she was wearing a very handsome beige silk pantsuit. She greeted Barbara and Frank pleasantly and motioned for them to come into the living room.

"I'm resuming some of the things I used to do," she said, as if explaining her clothing. "We're starting up the literacy project that tutors English as a second language. Meetings, always meetings before anything else happens." She smiled ruefully, but she was distant and polite, not the open friendly woman she had been on previous visits. "Amy tells me you have a question?" She looked at Barbara, not quite ignoring Frank, but close enough, he thought. Close enough.

"Yes. Did you know Nick Aaronson before the night of the party here?"

Amy stiffened and a wary look crossed her face. She glanced toward her mother, then swiftly looked away.

"I knew him only as a regular at the seminars Henry held here. Why?"

"Do you recall if he came to thank you and tell you he was leaving on the night of the party?"

Lucy frowned and shook her head. "I don't really remember, but I imagine he did. He always thanked me after the seminars. It was as if his mother had drilled it into him, to thank the hostess before leaving. I should think he did the same thing that night."

"Thanks," Barbara said. "One more question. Who did the laundry following the party?"

Lucy looked bewildered. "Laundry?"

"I assume you didn't do it," Barbara said. "I'd just like to speak to whoever did. Again, just trying to settle a few little things about the night of the party."

"That would have been Alice Jost. I can give you the last address I had for her. I haven't seen her in years."

"I'd appreciate that," Barbara said. "Thanks. Amy, let's have a look at the yearbook."

Amy jumped up and after she and Barbara left, Frank leaned forward and said, "Lucy, have I offended you in some way?"

She looked stricken for a moment, then shook her head. "No. Of course not. It's just... Oh, the situation. I thought it might not be appropriate for me to be seen having dinner with anyone who is connected with the trial. Let's have a glass of wine. I'll get that address, and then I have a question of my own to ask."

He went with her to the kitchen where she consulted a phone book, jotted down the number and handed it to him. She took a bottle of Fumé Blanc from the refrigerator, poured into two glasses and held out one for him.

"My autumn crocuses are already starting to bloom," she said, walking to the door where she stood gazing out. "It's weeks too early for them."

"It's been a strange summer," he said. "Many things seem out of season. Your question?"

She turned, glanced past him toward the study, then opened the screen door. "Let's sit out there until they finish."

Seated on the deck, she asked, "Is David in danger of being convicted of Jill Storey's murder?"

"There's always that danger when someone is accused," he said. "Juries are unpredictable. We will do everything in our power to prevent a conviction, but the danger persists until there's a verdict."

Lucy looked toward the other end of the deck. "It's time to move the plants indoors," she said faintly.

Frank took a sip of wine, watching her. "Why are you so troubled, Lucy? Why are you convinced that David is not a murderer? You really don't know him very well, do you?"

She shook her head. "Hardly at all. Amy told me about the incident she witnessed. I had no idea she saw anything like that. Will she have to testify?"

"I don't know," Frank said. "She was so young, and she obviously cares very much for him. It could be very difficult for her to testify."

"You mean, they'll savage her, don't you?"

"It's possible."

Lucy closed her eyes. "Please don't put her through that."

Frank did not respond. There was no response to such a plea. "You haven't answered my question," he said gently. "Why do you believe he's innocent?"

Lucy looked at him, picked up her wine and sipped it before answering. "I believe, the same as Amy does, that Jill was a lesbian, and he had no romantic interest in her, no reason to murder her."

"But you thought he was innocent before you knew what Amy saw that night," he said, still speaking softly.

"Just a feeling," she said. She smiled a patently false smile. "The nights are getting so cool, aren't they? I should find a woolly bear, see what kind of winter to expect."

"Cold, wet and dark," Frank said. "As usual."

Her smile at his words was genuine this time. "You already found your woolly bear."

Frank laughed. But he regretted that the window had closed on any real conversation. She had told him nothing yet, and had no intention of telling him anything, but it was there, whatever it was, simmering in the background.

"I have some irises to divide," Frank said. "A beautiful pink

with a red fall, a faithful rebloomer. Would you like a start or
two?"

"I'd love them. Rebloomers are scarce, mislabeled so at times."

They chatted until Barbara and Amy rejoined them. Frank was
satisfied. He would be back.

Driving toward Frank's house minutes later, Barbara asked,
"Anything?"

"She doesn't want Amy to testify. She knows a little about how
it will go."

"And Amy would claw her way through Sleeping Beauty's
thicket to get to the stand," Barbara commented. "There are too
many damn agendas playing out. Everyone's hiding something,
every last one of them."

Frank nodded. Every single one of them.

At five Barbara called Olga Maas.

"I'm sorry," Olga said. "I really have nothing else to tell you."

"It's been suggested," Barbara said quickly, "that you have Jill
Storey's school papers, notebooks and such. I'd like very much
to have a look at them whenever it's convenient for you."

"It would never be convenient," Olga said shortly. "Goodbye,
Ms. Holloway."

"Either in your home or perhaps at Ms. Trilby's home,"
Barbara said.

She heard a faint gasp, followed by a lengthy silence. She
waited.

"How dare you threaten me? What gives you the right to intrude in my private life?" Olga's voice was little more than a
whisper.

"Ms. Maas, please believe me. I intend no harm to either you
or Ms. Trilby, but I have to have information. I have a client
whose life is at risk, one you know as well as I do is innocent. I

need more information, and you can provide some of it by letting me see those school papers. Wherever you say, but soon."

There was another long pause. "Check into a motel in Richland on Saturday. I'll bring them Saturday afternoon. Call my
cell to tell me which motel and where."

Again, she spoke in a near whisper. Barbara could imagine a
white-knuckled grip on a phone, a face drained of color, the
pallor of fear. "Thank you," she said. "I'll call you on Saturday."
She hung up, hating what she had just done, especially hating
the need to do it.

23

Barbara arrived at a Holiday Inn in Richland by two-thirty on Saturday. As Olga had said in Eugene, it was a long drive, and a bright hot one that day. She tossed her things down, sat at a round table and called Olga, who said she would be there by three.

While she waited, using the supply she had brought with her, she started a pot of coffee, then washed her face and hands, wishing she had plenty of time for a long shower.

Olga was prompt, and she was carrying a cardboard carton that appeared heavy. Barbara took it and placed it on the table.

"Please, sit down. I made coffee. Join me?"

"No. That's all," she said pointing to the box. "I removed a few things and burned them. You're free to look through the rest." The hostility in her glance at Barbara was chilling.

"Ms. Maas, I told you I intend no harm to you or your friend. I sincerely mean that. I won't ask you to testify, and if your name comes up in the trial, it will be only as Olga Trenval, Jill Storey's roommate who verified the details of the key to David's apartment. That's already on record, your statement from twenty-two years ago. No one is likely to connect you to that name after so many years. I'm sorry to cause you such distress, but I have to think of my client's best interests and do what I can to protect him. You know the situation between him and Jill in their troubled adolescence, but the facts have been twisted to make it appear that they were childhood sweethearts, inseparable as a couple from their earliest days, and that he was possessive and jealous, to the point of murder."

Olga's eyes widened in disbelief. "That's crazy!"

"I know and you know, but they have statements from some people attesting to it," Barbara explained.

Olga shook her head. "He was her best friend. He practically saved her life in those days."

"Please sit down and talk to me," Barbara said.

Although Olga sat down, she was rigid, remote and wary.

Barbara poured coffee for them both.

"First," Olga said, "you tell me something. How did you find out? Who told you?"

"A good friend in Eugene. She knows everyone in the northwest, and she trusts me. She isn't hiding, but she protects those who are. You're still safe. Would it be a disaster if you were discovered?"

Olga said bitterly, "My ex would go to court to get custody of our daughter, and my parents would help him. Is that disaster enough? I'd lose my job and I have few resources to engage in a custody fight. I'd lose her."

"Does she know, or suspect?"

"No. When she's eighteen, she'll go to the university, probably in Seattle, and I'll tell her then. She'll be beyond anyone's reach as far as custody is concerned. We'll move to Seattle in five years."

"Does your ex suspect?"

"No. He decided I was frigid. He's remarried, three more children." She smiled a bitter, crooked smile. "After Jill... afterward, I went home, as I told you. They thought I was just afraid, but I was devastated. I tried hard to find religion again. I really tried to be straight. I went to church and prayed. Got my degree, got a master's, met Duane. I thought maybe being married, having a child would cure me." She laughed without humor. "There's no *cure*, Ms. Holloway. I'm what I am."

"Ms. Maas," Barbara said slowly when Olga became silent, "I'll have to make a case that David and Jill were not romantically involved, and the only way to do that may be to reveal her homosexuality. Was there anyone else who knew at the time?"

Olga's rigidity visibly increased. She shook her head. "I don't think anyone even suspected. Women can be seen as just friends as long as they behave in public, and we did. My name is going to come up after all, isn't it?"

"Not as Olga Maas. I doubt that this community pays any attention to what goes on in Eugene, and I feel certain that no one is going to care enough to put the two names together. One more question," she said. "Did you mention David's key to anyone? Can anyone else testify about it?"

"No. I went to work. No one there was interested in our living arrangement. I didn't tell anyone."

Barbara nodded and glanced at the box. "I'd better start looking through that material. It could take a while."

Olga rose from the table. She had not touched her coffee. "I was going to take it all home and burn it in the grill. That's where I burned the few things I removed. It's time to put it behind me. Long past time. Keep it, Ms. Holloway."

Barbara went to the door with her. Olga paused, looked directly at her and said, "I know I should do the noble thing and agree to come down and testify, save David if that's what it will take, but I can't. I won't. I'm not noble. I'm afraid. I may be ashamed of it for the rest of my life, but I'm afraid. I want to believe you won't bring harm to us, but I don't dare trust you. If you compel me to testify, I'll deny it all."

"Ms. Maas, I can't compel your testimony. No one can force you to cross state lines to testify in Eugene. All anyone can do is seek your cooperation, and I'm grateful for that box of material, for your agreeing to see me again. Thank you."

Olga studied her for a long moment, then turned and walked away without speaking again.

Barbara sat down and finished her coffee, thinking how it would have been to have lived in fear for years. Lou had it right, she thought—it was a hell of a life.

Shower, she told herself and went to do it. It was close to five before she checked her cell phone. She had had it turned off for Olga's visit. There was a message from Bailey, as brief as he was in person. "Belinda Hulse, married to Joseph Cernick, Eugene resident, died of cancer 1994."

Dead end, she thought, frustrated, grimacing at the unintentional pun. She had brought a bottle of wine along, and got it out, uncorked it, and poured wine into a tumbler and sat at the table again, eyeing the box of papers. Not now, she decided irritably.

She took a sip of wine. Lucky Mr. Aaronson. How convenient for him to have no one to refute or confirm his altered story. She took another sip, longer. He would have known Belinda Hulse Cernick was dead; you don't lose track of classmates a dozen years from your graduation, not if you both live in the same town. He would have known.

Aaronson, mystery man, she thought. What was it that made Amy stiffen at the mention of his name? What did she know about him, and how could she be induced to tell what it was?

Belatedly she remembered she was supposed to call Darren, and had meant to call him as soon as she checked in. And she had to go out and eat before she got light-headed. She had not stopped for lunch along the way.

She made her call, resolutely denied herself another glass of wine and went out to find a restaurant. The papers could wait until she got home and had space to spread them out to sort and look through them. No hurry about them, she suspected, since Olga, no doubt, had burned every scrap that had anything personal on it, the kind of material Barbara had hoped to find.

Soon after dawn on Sunday Barbara was on the road again, and by early afternoon, she pulled into her own driveway, almost miraculously without a speeding ticket.

Darren met her, followed her to the bedroom, and stood by the door of the bathroom when she went in to wash her face and hands.

"I imagined you tangling it up with a semi, or in a ditch, kidnapped by headhunters, fighting off Sasquatch, running away with a pirate with a patch over one eye, trying to outrun state police."

She laughed. "That last bit wouldn't be too far from the mark. I missed you, too."

"Let's go to bed," he said.

"I thought you'd never ask."

That afternoon Bailey had picked up David and dropped him off at Frank's house, and now Frank and David were sitting on the back porch watching the cats watch birds splashing in the birdbath.

"Do they ever make a run for them?" David asked.

"Rarely. They're too lazy, and too smart. They tried early on, learned it was futile, and now, as you see, they pretend to have no interest. Casual observers, that's all."

David took a drink from a can of beer, smiling as Thing One decided he had seen enough of the show, stretched out belly up and sunned his underside.

"David," Frank asked, "how did you get started asking the hard questions? You must have been pretty young. You're still young to have found so many answers."

"Vietnam," David said after a moment, no longer smiling. "There were casualties from Gresham, of course. My folks took me to the funeral service for the son of one of their friends. The preacher went on and on about the sacrifice he had made for his country, in the service of God, now safe in the arms of Jesus. I had a lot of trouble digesting that, I guess. I asked my father later why we were fighting Vietnam, and he said he didn't know. My mother defended the war, fighting godless communists, and so on. She had bought into the whole argument and I couldn't understand why. I asked her if she believed that kid was in the arms of Jesus, and she waffled. Finally all she could tell me was to believe. Because it might be right. No one knew why. I was seven."

Frank nodded. "Seven, and a lifetime of questioning arose from that question and answer. No one knew. Were you aware that you had started a journey of your own?"

"Not right away. It took a couple more years and several more questions with answers that seemed to miss the mark. I really had trouble with the idea that everyone in Vietnam was doomed to burn in hell because they didn't believe what they should. And why people thought it was good for them to burn in hell forever. I turned to books instead of asking people I knew."

"Saved, or damned by reading. Depends on who's voicing that opinion, doesn't it?"

"Does it matter?" David asked after a moment. "Sometimes in a woods or out on the desert, somewhere alone, a place that hasn't been overrun by traffic or fast food joints, a place without cans on the ground, I've felt a peace that can't be described, only experienced. That's the god I believe in, transcendent, found in the creation of the universe itself, in the infinity of space and the mystery of time, the immediacy of sand and trees, the wonder of it, the miracle of it, the blessing to have the gift to experience it. That's god enough for me."

"Amen," Frank said softly.

"You know the Chinese curse, may you live in interesting times? Those are our times, Mr. Holloway. We live in an interesting time when several different tipping points are converging. Political, climatic, dogmatic religiosity. The next dozen years will determine our future, I feel certain. Another dozen years."

"I may miss the show," Frank said drily. "I can't say I regret that."

"And I may be in prison, and I confess I do regret that."

David lifted his beer, and Frank drank his iced tea.

"You know what I like about Barbara, among other things," David said. "She doesn't do a con job, but tells it like it is. A rare trait. I don't see it often, but I've been surrounded by too many academics, and kept my eye on too many politicians and their spinmeisters. I see where she got that trait. I appreciate it from both of you."

"Speaking of her, I think they've arrived," Frank said. He had heard the car, then the front door closing. They both stood to greet Barbara and Darren. Todd and Darren were carrying bags, Darren's clear plastic with what looked like colored balls, and Todd's day pack slung over his arm.

Barbara introduced Todd, and he held up his hand in a high-five greeting that David met with his own high five. Darren must have told Todd that David had little function in his right hand, and the gesture was exactly right, Frank thought.

"I read your book, Mr. Etheridge," Todd said. "I brought it over, and if you feel like it, I hoped you'd be able to autograph it for me. Maybe with a big X or something. I thought it was super."

David laughed. "I'll demonstrate my real talent," he said. "I'll sign it with my left hand, a clear case of forgery, of course, but you'll know and you have witnesses to make your case."

Todd put his pack on a chair and took out the book and a pen, then watched as David signed his name with his left hand. The signature looked childish, but both he and Todd were pleased.

"After your dad fixes me, I'll sign it again," David said. "Make it a collector's item someday." He nodded toward a CD that had come out with the book. "What's that?"

Todd looked embarrassed. "My video for a science project. I forgot it was in there."

"Aren't we allowed to see it?" David asked. "I'd like to very much."

Todd glanced at Darren, then at Frank. "Is that okay?"

"We all want to see it," Frank assured him.

He grinned, and nodded to David. "Showtime after dinner."

"And now it's time to play ball," Darren said. "Let's go upstairs and see how things are going." He and David walked into the house together.

"I'll go make sure this works with your DVD player," Todd said, and followed them inside.

Frank looked at Barbara enquiringly, and she said, "Not much. Olga Maas is scared to death and will deny everything if pressed, but she gave me a box of stuff to bring home. She had a go at the material first and burned some things. So not much of interest may be left. Right back." She went inside, helped herself to a glass of wine, returned and took the chair David had left. She told him about Bailey's call. "I'll have Shelley go down that list of party attendees and check each one for dope on who Aaronson really left with that night. Maybe Hulse-Cernick, maybe not. I want to know for sure." She scowled. "This whole case is one god-awful mess. I keep reaching for things that turn into smoke in my hands."

"It's early," Frank said, but he shared her frustration. They had not been able to settle on a good place to dig in.

"I have to find the right approach to get Amy to tell what she knows about Aaronson. Maybe he sneaked in a squeeze, and it's no more than that, but maybe it's something else," Barbara said.

And he had to find a way to get Lucy to tell him what was on her mind, Frank thought.

"Thumbscrews," Barbara muttered. "The president would probably okay that."

Interesting times, Frank thought, echoing David's words silently. He rose. "Time to get busy in the kitchen. We'll have dinner in the dining room. It's getting too cool these evenings for the porch."

The days were shrinking, Barbara thought, alone on the porch, with November coming too quickly, and there was nowhere to start. *Remember,* she told herself sternly, *you don't have to do anything except instill a reasonable doubt.* Wise words, she knew, and insufficient words to still the doubt in her mind that she had enough ammunition to do even that much.

Darren and David returned, with David carrying the bag of balls, which he placed on the table. Darren went inside and returned with a tray holding two more cans of beer and the bottle of wine. "Todd's in there helping your dad," he said. "Frank's teaching him to cook," he told David.

"I wish someone had taught me," David said. "I'm one of those open-a-can, or thaw-a-frozen-something kind of cooks."

Barbara laughed. "I'm into thawing entrées and tossing a salad. You want more, you go fix it." She eyed David closely and asked, "How is it working out at Shelley's house? I hope you're not getting bored."

"No way. In fact, Alex and I are going to write a book, a graphic novel. His illustrations, my text."

"Good God!" Barbara said. "Pure subversion, no doubt."

David glanced at Darren. "Alex is a good artist," he said.

Quickly Barbara said, "He knows who Alex is, but Todd doesn't. Not yet, anyway."

"Subversive as hell," David said with a grin. "Alex talked to his agent about it, and I talked to mine. They'll get together this coming week to work out the details of who gets to handle it. They both love the idea. I may be able to pay my debts, if they're anywhere near the mark on this one."

"I don't suppose we get a clue about the subject," Barbara said.

"You're right. Not a clue."

"Oh, well. I'll buy the damn book. David, change of subject. Amy asks about you all the time, and she would really like to visit. Would you agree to that?"

He regarded her for a moment. "I don't want to put her at risk," he said soberly. "I know someone's out to kill me and who-ever it is might go after her if he thinks that's the next best thing."

"Your reluctance is only because of a possible danger to her, not personal?"

"Exactly." He looked out over the garden, the two lazy cats, the birdbath now abandoned by the birds and, as if addressing the vista, he said in a low voice, "I'm no good for her. She isn't a child, but she's very innocent in many ways, trusting, too trusting perhaps, and too transparent. She hasn't learned how to hide. I'm probably a polar opposite, too cynical, too pessimistic. It's infectious, that kind of pessimism. It would be criminal to see someone like her contaminated by it. It tends to change your outlook on life, on other people."

"Maybe she's the one to decide such things," Barbara said. "If I arrange something I think is safe, is it okay with you?"

His nod was a long time in coming.

Frank's dinner was pork tenderloin in crust, redolent with herbs and garlic, smooth mashed sweet potatoes, grilled zucchini and sweet red peppers, tomatoes with basil. He and Todd exchanged looks of satisfaction at the praise dinner received.

Todd's video was a smashing success, they all agreed after viewing it. He had measured the salinity of the water before and after the melting occurred, listed the species that would be affected, showed diagrams of how the Gulf Stream could be diverted and what it would mean to northern Europe, with coastal flooding.

"I'm very impressed," David said sincerely. "First-class work. Congratulations."

Later, in the car with Frank taking him back to Shelley's house, David said, "Now and then kids like Todd pop up here and there, and I feel some of my pessimism fading a little bit. Maybe there's still hope."

"I know," Frank said. "He gives us hope."

24

On Friday Shelley said with evident relief, "I found her. The woman who can refute Aaronson's testimony."

"Wonderful," Barbara said, putting aside the new batch of discovery that had been delivered that day. "Tell me."

"Her name is Christa Roznick Warner. Lives in Santa Barbara. The night of the party her date was asleep on the sofa and she got a ride to her apartment with Aaronson and a woman named Tiffany something. She doesn't know her last name. They left the party at midnight or a few minutes after."

"Good girl! Will she give us a deposition?"

"Yes. I'll go down next Wednesday, be back late Thursday. Made my reservations, all set."

"One down, or at least slowed down," Barbara said. "That's the day I'm due to argue for the release of the police file. Lucky Wednesday. Let's hope. How's it going at your place?"

"Great. Those two guys are like a couple of little boys with a dirty secret. You should hear them laughing. Or one of them vanishes up in the woods or someplace, or just gets as still as a stone for a time. Then there's a flurry of talking or laughing. They won't tell me anything about it. Oh, and we're all set for tomorrow. Good weather, late-summer cookout time. David's been on the phone with Amy this week, by the way."

"She must be floating," Barbara commented. "If he brings her back down to earth, I hope it's not with a thud."

"He's not easy to get to know," Shelley said. "I mean, he can be really funny, but I always feel as if there's something else lurking behind the humor, something dark."

After Shelley left, Barbara mulled over her comment, something dark lurking behind David's humor. That sarcastic streak, cynicism, pessimism, whatever it was, almost everyone seemed to sense it. He was a multilayered man who revealed no more than the surface, and that surface was what the jury would see. Would they react with the same unease that many others did, sense something dark lurking? She was very much afraid that regardless of any pretrial coaching, David, like Olga, would be what he was. It was too late to send him to charm school.

It was clear, however, that Alex trusted him, or he would not have revealed his own secret identity as the mysterious X whose cartoons skewered powerful people with deadly accuracy.

Barbara had given Amy directions to the house, and she arrived promptly at one o'clock, carrying two bottles of wine. "You told me to bring nothing, but that doesn't seem quite fair," Amy said. Darren came from the bedroom, hair still moist from his shower, and after introductions, they were ready to go.

It was a good day, she thought later, perfect weather, a hike in the woods, during which she had noticed that Darren kept a close eye on David for a while, then stopped being a therapist, satisfied apparently. He and David had vanished for a short time for the weekly evaluation, and had reappeared looking pleased. Good omens, she kept thinking. After a quick intake of breath, Amy had accepted Alex's grotesque appearance exactly the same way the others did. Barbara had told her about his birth defect, but no one was ever truly prepared. And if Alex or Dr. Minnick thought it strange that the sister of a murder victim was joining a group that included the accused killer, that had not been apparent.

Sitting on the back terrace after their hike, Amy talked about the new project her company had undertaken—a green complex with a medical center, some retail shops, a grocery store and a cluster of houses. She and a partner were in charge of designing the individual houses, to be as energy efficient as modern technology could provide. She appeared excited by the new task.

As they chatted, David was holding one of the balls Darren had given him the previous week. Suddenly the ball made a squeaking noise. David looked startled and Darren smiled broadly.

"I'll be damned," David said. "It worked!"

"You worked," Darren said. "Good job. Stick with that one for a while before you move on to the next. Make sure it works every time."

The squeak punctuated the conversation for the next few minutes until they were all laughing. Then David put the yellow ball aside, went into the house and came back with a blue one. It didn't make a sound.

Amy picked up the yellow ball and asked David, "May I keep this? A memento of today."

That afternoon Frank took a plastic bag with iris rhizomes and his cooler out to the car and drove to Lucy McCrutchen's house. She met him at the door with a smile.

"What is all that?" she said, pointing to the cooler.

"A surprise for later. Now it's planting time."

She had the spot picked out, and stood aside as he dug the rich soil and planted the irises, then watered them in.

"They should do well in that spot," he said. "What color are those?" He pointed to adjacent irises.

"A lovely monochrome periwinkle-blue. That will make a nice combination."

He nodded. It would. As he started to move away from the flowers, he happened to glance at the hedge and saw Henry Elders. He quickly vanished.

Lucy evidently had not seen him, and Frank made no mention of it as they walked back to the house and he went in to wash his hands. Lucy had prepared another tray with wine and snacks. He carried it out to the deck.

"The weather will change so soon," she said with regret. "We always liked sitting out here at this time of day. I miss it when the rains start."

"We always liked this time, too," Frank said.

"It doesn't go away, does it?" she said softly. "You still miss her."

"For some of us, I don't think it goes away," he said after a moment.

They were both silent for a time, then she said in the same low voice, "Frank, I think we could be friends, and I'd like that, but you should know I'm not looking for someone else."

"Neither am I," he said, just as softly. "Friendship is a precious gift, one to be treasured."

They both lifted their wineglasses, and while they didn't touch them together, they signaled a message given and accepted.

"When the sun dips behind that golden chain tree," Lucy said, motioning toward the western sky, "it gets chilly out here this time of year. Time to go inside. And then you have to tell me what's in that mysterious cooler."

"Deal," he said, eyeing the tree. "Ten minutes? Not much longer than that."

She looked at her watch. "I'll time it." She glanced at him. "Barbara asked if Nick Aaronson spoke to me before he left the party that night, or if David did. I've been thinking back to it, and I'm sure Nick did. I just thought it likely before, but I'm sure. I was in the living room, and I remembered that Nick hadn't been drenched in sweat from dancing like the rest of the kids. I'm certain that David didn't come in."

"Did you notice the time?" Frank asked.

"Not particularly, but they were still dancing, the stereo was still loud. Henry came in when they turned off the stereo, and Nick had already gone. I remembered noticing the difference, how cool Nick had seemed, and how hot Henry was."

"Good," Frank said. "Thanks. If it becomes important, will you testify to it?"

She nodded. "If it's important."

"Thinking about that night, can you recall the early events, when people arrived, who was opening the door, things like that?"

"Some of it," she said. "They started arriving at about six-thirty. Robert agreed to be the doorman and I didn't pay much attention to who was coming or when. I had put food out on the dining-room table, and most of them began to help themselves. There were hamburgers and sausages to grill, and we left it up to them to tend to the grill if that's what they wanted. Mac, Henry and I made up our plates and came out here, out of the way, to eat our dinners. A lot of the young people were on the deck, milling about, finding chairs and so on. At some point Henry fixed a plate to take home to Harriet. His wife. He came back when they turned on the stereo and started to dance. At about eight, I think."

"Tell me something about Mrs. Elders," Frank said. "How ill was she?"

"It was bad. When we first came, she seemed relatively well with mild symptoms of ichthyosis, not disabling or disfiguring, but it progressed year by year, until she never left the house except for medical appointments. Other things were wrong with her— diabetes, hypertension, a glandular problem. She had gained a great deal of weight and she had no tolerance for heat and couldn't expose herself to sunshine. Her skin itched unbearably and movement had become painful. She often used a walker, she was so unsteady in her gait. Eventually she needed a wheelchair. They had to have central air-conditioning installed, and afterward she kept the house extremely cool, too cool for anyone else, I suspect."

"That poor woman," Frank said. "Her life must have been a torment for her."

"It was. I felt so sorry for them both. I think everyone was relieved when she had a stroke and died within a day."

They both became silent for a time and watched as the sun dropped below the tree. "Eight minutes," she said, and they went inside.

He opened the cooler and began emptying it. "A few tomatoes," he said. "A cold roasted chicken, potato salad, green salad, tomatoes stuffed with shrimp and mushrooms that I'd like to pop in the microwave for a minute. I can't entice you to go out to dinner with me, so dinner has come to you."

She laughed. "A picnic! I was planning to eat leftovers. This looks a lot better. Thank you."

Frank had been gone only a few minutes when Amy got home that night. She looked in at Lucy in the family room, said good-night and went upstairs. Sitting at her desk, she took the yellow ball from her bag and held it. Foam, as soft as a marshmallow, her slightest pressure caused it to make the squeaking noise. A small child could have done it. She felt tears well in her eyes and closed them. She wanted to find whoever had done that to David and kill him.

There had to be something she could do. She knew her testimony about what she had overheard was not enough. Jill's words had been too ambiguous and she had been so young, who would believe her? Remembering what her mother had said, that it would not be hard to prove that Jill had been gay, she was afraid that her own statement, believed or not, would be irrelevant.

There had to be a way the pictures could help. She saw again her mother's anguish and her fear that Robert had gone out after Jill. And maybe he had. He had been a blackmailer. Where would he have drawn the line? A feeling of dread verging on horror accompanied the thought that she didn't know if her brother could have committed murder.

She wanted more than anything to talk it over with her mother, to confide in her, get her opinion, her advice. For the first time in her life she couldn't do that.

"The only thing I've found that's even mildly interesting is the fact that no one seems to know who tipped off the police that David had given his key to Jill Storey," Barbara told Frank on Sunday. Darren had gone to pick up Todd at his mother's house, and afterward they had some more school shopping to do. They would be along later. She and Frank were on his back porch.

He told her about his visit with Lucy. "She's prepared to say that Aaronson left while there was still dancing going on."

"And McNulty will tear into her," Barbara said. "Why would she remember the order of guests leaving after so many years? On the other hand Nick Aaronson had an excellent reason to recall a bloody hand, a bloody face. He was alarmed enough to collect his date and another woman and get out of there. That, backed by Chloe's version, and Elders's claim that David was possessive and had monopolized Jill all evening will seem conclusive even without several people who remember that David and Jill had been inseparable during high school."

They were both silent until Barbara said, "I have a bad feeling about this, Dad. I know, I always get anxious before a trial, but this is different. McNulty can make a case and I can't refute it. I have Amy's story, a kid who had a crush on David, and still does. He'll back it, of course, but that means very little. And Lucy's testimony will be easy to discredit as a faulty memory of an insignificant event from twenty-two years ago. The same goes for the woman Aaronson gave a ride to that night along with Tiffany someone. Did they leave before or after the fight on the deck? Who can say? As for Belinda Hulse, now deceased, Aaronson was thinking of a different party, different night. Or he can simply stick to the story that he took Hulse home. He said/she said. I can muddy the water a little, but that's all I can do. Also, I'm worried about David's taking the stand. I'm afraid of how the jury will react to him. One or two get turned-off, there it all goes."

Although Frank had his own dark misgivings about how the case was shaping up, he did not voice them, not with Barbara as gloomy as she was. He told her instead what he had learned about Henry Elders's dead wife. "Now he keeps an eye on Lucy like a lovesick boy."

"Amy said he's courting her," Barbara commented. "From what little I've seen of Lucy McCrutchen, I think she might take a flyswatter to him if he becomes too much of a nuisance."

Frank chuckled. Then he told her about the two men he had talked to about Nick Aaronson's various dealings with Robert McCrutchen. "Rick Salazar and Boyd Chasten."

Barbara didn't know them, but was familiar with their reputations as investigative reporters, with a penchant for ferreting out government secrets. Recently, they had published articles concerning some contracts for a Umatilla toxic site cleanup that was underway, with huge cost overruns and missed deadlines.

"Wow, they're big-time," she said.

He nodded. "They are particularly interested in a pending deal on the coast, something to do with a liquid gas facility. Mc-Crutchen was instrumental in some hearings regarding zone changes. This could be bigger than we imagined when we first heard Nick Aaronson's name."

She thought about it, then shrugged. "Hard to connect it to a murder from twenty-two years ago, and that's my immediate concern."

They were silent again for several minutes. The cats joined them on the porch, stood up at the table to look over the plate of cheese and Frank told them to beat it.

Barbara drained her wineglass and rose to go refill it. At the door she said, "If nothing breaks in the next few weeks, I may have to decide if David's best bet is a plea bargain."

Startled, Frank swiveled around to look at her, but she was already entering the house. He knew how much she detested plea bargains if she was convinced her client was innocent. For her to be considering it was more ominous than any of her other words had been.

On Tuesday of the following week Barbara and Frank drove out to Shelley's house to talk with David. Both Alex and Dr.

Minnick said they had things to do and vanished, leaving the three of them alone in the living room.

"It's the problem of the key we're trying to pin down," Barbara said.

"Why is it a problem?" David was wearing jeans and a T-shirt, and he was holding the blue ball, which remained silent.

"Who tipped off the cops about the key?" Barbara said. "I think it was what set Robert off, and he apparently thought he was onto something. What I'd like you to do is try to recreate as clearly as you can exactly what happened when you got to the house the night of the party until after you passed the key to Jill."

He shrugged. "I walked over, as I told you. She was already there, a lot of people were already there." Barbara held up her hand, but before she spoke he said, "Okay, step by step. I rang the bell. Robert opened the door. Jill was with several people toward the end of the hall near the kitchen door." He was speaking in a noninflected voice, the reading of a boring Dick and Jane story. "She saw me and walked back to where I was. I handed her the key. She kissed my cheek and put the key in her pocket. Robert was by the door, and obviously he saw that, but no one else was close. No one else was paying any attention. They were facing away from us. Jill said to come on and eat something, and she went back to the group, and they all went outside. I followed them out."

His expression was unreadable, his face so masklike that he could have been talking in his sleep.

Barbara wanted to slap some sense of his own danger into him. Her impatience was reflected in her voice when she asked brusquely, "Were most people outside by then?"

"Dr. and Mrs. McCrutchen were out there with Elders. Others were hanging out around the grill, or getting beer. From fifteen to twenty people. If the next question is did Jill mention the key to anyone, the answer has to be no. She was getting a hamburger, adding tomatoes and onions, ketchup. After that, the stereo was turned on and they started dancing. I can't believe she mentioned that key to anyone."

"Later, when you left, did you tell anyone that you were leaving?"

"No."

"Not even Mrs. McCrutchen?"

"I said no. I looked in the living room but she wasn't there, and I left."

"Apparently no one mentioned the key, and no one knows when you left the party," Barbara said. "But someone tipped off the police, and Aaronson says you left with Jill. That's where it stands."

"Aaronson's lying."

She ignored that and asked, "When did the police first interview you?"

"What difference—?" He drew in a breath. "Sunday. They got a statement about the party."

"No mention of the key?"

"No."

"Did they tell you not to leave town at that interview?"

"No. I couldn't leave. I had to see Olga. She was in bad shape. We both were. I spent most of the day and night with her and I felt I couldn't leave until…" He stopped and shook his head, and finally he began to show something other than boredom or indifference as he spoke. "I don't know now what I was thinking, but I stayed with Olga. We didn't know what to do with Jill's things. Then Jill's sister came and took most of them. Olga kept a couple of boxes. I had to sell some textbooks and that took another day, to unpack them, take them over to the university bookstore. When I got back, a detective was there looking for me. He showed me the key and asked if it was for the apartment, asked why Jill had had it."

"You went out to sell books? Why?" Barbara asked.

"The guy I was going to ride home with went on without me. I didn't have enough money for bus fare." His voice was again nearly toneless, the words clipped.

"What day was that?"

"I don't know. I wasn't checking the calendar. Maybe Wednesday, maybe later. I helped Olga pack up and load her car. She went home late that week, and I left by bus the next day."

"So on Sunday evening or Monday they got the tip," Barbara said. "Anonymous phone call. The newspaper accounts didn't mention a thing about the situation concerning it, only that it was to your apartment, but the police knew the truth. And it was left like that. By that weekend the theory was that a transient, someone on drugs, probably killed her, and finally it was filed as an unsolved murder."

"They were incompetent then, and they are incompetent today," David said flatly.

"They'll go to court with a vengeance," she said, regarding him steadily, struggling to keep her anger at a distance. "No one mentioned that little confrontation on the deck at the time, and now four different witnesses have emerged concerning it, three with damning statements, three respected citizens with no discernible motive for doing you harm. The prosecutor is the one who will be sore, and with cause. And if you take the stand with the attitude you've shown today, the prosecutor will chip away at you for however long it takes to get you to lose your temper. And you will lose it. This isn't a contest of who's smarter, it's his ball, his game, his playing field. And he's going to be out to get you."

"You came here today to ask the same things we've already gone over. A few insignificant details missing, nothing that adds or takes away from the facts you already knew. Jesus Christ, what do you expect of me? Just tell me what you expect of me? Why did you come here today?"

"Today is nothing compared to what's coming your way. There's going to be pretrial publicity, letters to the editor, radical radio broadcasts bringing up every negative they can think of. Those agitators, the demonstrators who rioted following your lectures are certain to demonstrate again, maybe every day of the trial. It's going to be nearly impossible to put together an impartial jury. Today we were less than an hour. McNulty will take hours, days. He'll go over your statement word by word, make you repeat the same things a dozen times with various connotations. I can't stop him. Just in case some of the jurors have missed the pretrial smears, he'll see to it that it's brought out that you profess atheism, that you have no higher authority, no god, no moral compass guiding you, no conscience. I can object, but no one can unsay words. And you'll show anger, coldness, indifference, boredom, contempt, whatever the hell it is driving you. You'll lose the jury and he'll have won. That's what I came to tell you today. To demonstrate to you that you're in a hellish position. They won't go for the death penalty this time, but a conviction, another trial for Robert McCrutchen's murder, another conviction, and you'll be in prison fighting for your life for as long as you have life. That's what I came to tell you."

David had grown rigid with her words, her fury. He stood up as stiff and cold as an ice sculpture. "Message delivered," he said. "Are you done?"

"David, sit down!" Frank said in a tone that Barbara had rarely heard—commanding, hard, authoritative.

David looked startled, but resumed his chair.

"Today is just a taste of what lies ahead for you," Frank said crisply. "In two weeks here or at the office Barbara is going to take you through your testimony step by step, after which I will take McNulty's role and tear that testimony to shreds if you show any sign of weakness. Do you understand what I'm saying? We intend to fight for your life, and I intend for you to assist us, not hinder that fight. You have two weeks to consider your tone and your attitude. *Now* we're done."

Frank rose and said to Barbara, "Let's go."

Without another word David jumped up. He looked at the blue ball he was holding, threw it against the wall and walked out. The ball didn't bounce when it hit. It squeaked loudly, like a scream of protest, and dropped to the floor.

Driving a few minutes later, Barbara said, "I'm sorry I lost it like that, Dad."

"Don't be. He needed to see your frustration, and understand the cause. Perhaps he does now."

"I think he's furious, but also desperately hurt and even frightened. His star was rising, pretty successful books, a plum of an appointment, recognition, then a vicious attack that damaged him, makes him accept therapy that must be humiliating, and the last straw, the charge of murder, knowing he'll have to submit to people he considers little more than idiots. So he builds that wall to protect himself, make himself untouchable, unreachable."

"And we have to make him dismantle it and show the side that stayed with Olga until she left town. I imagine they clung to each other and wept for a good deal of the time they were together those last days."

"The question is, can he do that? Reveal himself like that?" Barbara wondered.

Frank nodded. That was the question. In two weeks they might know the answer. Depending on that answer, both he and

Barbara could be compelled to urge David to take a plea bargain, with every expectation of a lesser sentence if he did so and admitted contrition and remorse. Grimly he followed the thought to the next step. David's pride would not allow him to go that route, and he most likely would be convicted of first-degree murder if his response to the reprieve of two weeks was the wrong one.

25

Barbara argued on Wednesday that since the prosecutor was using material from the old police file on Jill Storey's murder, she had every right to examine the same material. It had to be included in discovery. The judge agreed.

"For all the good it does," Barbara said to Shelley, back in the office. "I'm going home to change clothes."

"Barbara, something's happening out at the house," Shelley said. "I don't think David said a word all day after you and your father were out there. Alex told me that David went off into the woods and stayed until nearly dark. He was just about to go look for him when he came back."

"He's got things to think about," Barbara said. "I hope to God we put a scare in him."

"I'll keep you posted," Shelley promised. "I was afraid he'd pack his things and take off."

"If he does, I'll personally kill him dead. I don't think he will, but keep me posted."

Damn that man, she thought savagely after Shelley left. He was perfectly capable of deciding to go somewhere else and thumb his nose at them all. She remembered when she said to Frank that she hoped never to see David again. "If wishes were horses," she muttered, and left to change her clothes.

She planned to spend the next day or two sorting, then examining Jill's old papers from four years of college. After glancing at them quickly, she had closed the box again. When Olga had finished looking for whatever she had removed, she had simply dumped the rest back into the box in no order whatsoever. Papers, term papers, tests, charts that were incomprehensible, essays, some dated, many not. Some weren't even paper-clipped, if they had been clipped together in the first place. It added nothing to Barbara's mood to contemplate tackling them, just in case there might be something. Such a remote possibility, it was almost one to be dismissed.

After Amy left on Friday Lucy brought in the mail and sat at the small kitchen desk looking through it. Two letters were for Chloe. It was annoying that some of her mail was still being delivered at the house, but a letter or two each week appeared in the mailbox. Lucy wrote the forwarding address on the envelopes and put them aside, then opened her own mail.

She looked up when there was a tap on the screen door and Henry said good morning. The screen door was locked. She got up to admit him.

"Good morning, Henry. Another perfect day, isn't it?"

"Very nice. I see that you're busy, and I won't keep you. I just wanted to invite you to dinner tonight. I know Amy's always gone on Fridays. I thought it might be a good night to get out."

She shook her head. "Thanks, Henry, it's a kind thought, but I have plans already."

"Oh, I'm sorry," he said. He turned as if to leave, but then faced her again. "Lucy, there's something I have to say. For your own good, a warning. Don't get too comfortable with Holloway. You know he's a criminal attorney, defending the man who killed that unfortunate young woman years ago, and more than likely killed your son. Attorneys like that will use you, twist your words, get you to say things you don't mean, even things that aren't true. They're slick and cunning, and you just haven't been subjected to that kind of manipulation before."

Lucy took a step backward. "Henry, you know perfectly well that he's a *defense* attorney, and he is most certainly not trying to manipulate me in any way. As for David having killed that girl, I don't believe for a minute that he did, or that he murdered Robert."

"That evening after Chloe left," Henry said with an intensity that was startling, "on the night Robert was shot, he told me about a fight they had over the girl. On the night of the party he walked out on the deck for a breath of fresh air. He had no idea she was already out there. He went to speak to her. David followed him and made crazy accusations, then attacked him and knocked him down, off the deck. David learned that night that his girlfriend was a prostitute, Lucy, and he killed her. That's what Robert was looking into. That's why he was killed. David's the man Holloway's defending, and he's a killer. And Holloway will use you. Believe me, he'll use you. I urge you, please, just keep away from him."

"Henry, I don't think I need protection. As you saw, I am quite busy. If you'll excuse me." Lucy went to the screen door and pulled it open, stood by it until he walked out, then closed and locked it again. She knew he was aware of what she was doing as she returned to the desk, took her chair, put her glasses on and picked up another piece of mail.

Why had Robert told such a monstrous, vicious lie? Why had he done that? Of course, Henry would have repeated it to the police, and they would have believed it. He had no reason to make up such a story. David would deny it, and his denial would be dismissed. She bit her lip and closed her eyes thinking of Amy on the witness stand, the scathing questions, disbelief, mockery, suggestions of adolescent fantasy.

Her thoughts kept returning to Robert, the son she had loved in spite of his failings. Why had he done it? She found herself looking toward the door again and again and abruptly rose and walked from the room. For the first time ever she felt exposed in the kitchen and family room. She hadn't curtained the windows or put up drapes in either room—the backyard was too private to close off the view and the light. Now she felt as if eyes were following her every motion.

That night when Amy arrived home, Lucy met her in the front hall. "I'd like to talk to you," she said, "if you're not too tired."

Amy felt falling-down tired, but she nodded and to her surprise her mother motioned toward the living room. She obviously had been sitting in there for a time; her coffee cup was on the table, a book on the sofa. Amy couldn't remember the last time she'd sat with her mother in the living room.

She put her purse and a portfolio case down and sank into a chair. Lucy sat at the end of the sofa.

"I made coffee," Lucy said. "In the carafe, still hot."

Amy shook her head. "Is something wrong?"

"Amy, please tell me something. I know you care about David, but can you explain it? I mean, you were so young when he came for the seminars, and I can't believe you and he ever did more than make polite noises to each other."

"What difference does it make?" Amy asked, and felt ashamed of the tone she had used. Quickly she said, "You'll laugh and tell me to stop being ridiculous. It's what I would say in your place."

"I won't laugh," Lucy said.

Looking at her more closely, Amy knew she would not laugh. She appeared to be closer to tears than to laughter. "It sounds so silly now," she said, "but it wasn't when it happened. That night, the night of the party…" She told Lucy about the beer, Robert's and Dr. Elders's reactions, and then David's. "He knew it was okay," she said. "We weren't evil or wicked. We were four-teen, trying out things. He understood. He rolled his eyes, shrugged his shoulders and winked. End of story, but I've never forgotten. I've never forgotten him. I bought his books when they were published, and collected reviews and every other scrap of publicity I could find. There's been a lot, first because of the demonstrations and then after his arrest." She looked at her hands, unaware until then that they had been clenched. She flexed her fingers and turned her palms up, then dropped both hands to her lap. In a lower voice she continued. "I thought I'd never see him again and I never would have made any attempt to see him, and I guess I was willing to think it was a case of puppy love, a kid's first real crush, my first rock star or some-thing. But when he reappeared, it all came back as strong as it was that night."

"Oh, my dear," Lucy said softly. "Thank you for telling me."

"Now you tell me what's happened, what's wrong," Amy said.

Lucy nodded. "This morning Henry came over." She told it all, including the warning about Frank Holloway. "You, David and I are the only ones who know what happened out there, but if the police believed Henry, it could be the reason they arrested David. I can't find a reason for them to disbelieve that story. But why would Robert have done it, lied like that?"

Amy felt cold all over and shook her head. If Dr. Elders testified to that story, who would believe her? No one. Her lips felt too stiff for words to form and escape. She moistened them. "Mother, will you tell them?"

Lucy nodded. "I have to, don't I?" The tears she had held off all day suddenly flowed in spite of her effort not to let go. In an instant Amy was at her side, and they held each other and rocked back and forth, both weeping.

After several minutes Amy pulled away and, choking, said, "I need a Kleenex." She hurried from the room to find a box of tissues, blew her nose and took the box to her mother. "I'll bring in the coffee," she said, and left again.

Then, sitting on the floor by the low table, she poured coffee for them both. "I think Robert said that because he was afraid someone would find out David was staying here, in his house, that his name and David's would be linked. It could have been damaging to his political career. Those demonstrators might even have come here, brought a lot of bad publicity."

Lucy did not protest the possible explanation. It was plausible. If Robert had brought charges of murder against David, told that story to back up the charges, it probably would have been accepted, especially since Robert had been a prosecutor. He would have known how much evidence was necessary to make such charges. Believing and still disbelieving that line of reasoning, she had to admit to herself that she didn't know if Robert could have done that, lied to involve David. If he would have done that. She didn't know if he had followed Jill that night. She ducked her head and reached for another tissue.

Amy took her hand and held it. "Is it all right with you if I stay here for the next few months? Until after the trial is over?"

"God, yes! I want you to. We'll redecorate the study, however you want it. Then you make it yours for as long as you want. And I'll put drapes on the kitchen and family-room windows. We live in a fishbowl."

"And keep doors locked at all times," Amy added. She pressed Lucy's hand. "Did Dr. Elders really say it was for your own good?"

Lucy nodded.

"He's such a creep. You know the two things that kids hate more than almost anything else? It's when adults tell them it's for their own good. Or even worse, this hurts me more than it hurts you. Followed by a whap alongside the head."

They both laughed.

They talked more that night, then went through the house together turning off lights and making sure doors were locked. In bed afterward, Amy lay awake for a long time. Barbara would get David off, she told herself. Her mother's account of the scene on the deck and her own would be more than enough to counter Dr. Elders. There was no way to check his story. It could all be a lie, an elaboration on a chance remark, his own revised history. Barbara would find others to verify that Jill had been a lesbian, that David was never her boyfriend the way Elders made it sound.

Then, free again, he would leave.

She turned over and closed her eyes. *Sleep,* she told herself. *Stop thinking about it.* But the order was ignored and soon she was again lying with her eyes open in the dark. She had not mentioned the pictures, that Robert had been a blackmailer on top of whatever else he had been. It was too much. It had nothing to do with the distant past. And those pictures had nothing to do with Jill Storey or David.

That night at the same time that Amy was twisting and turning, unable to keep her eyes closed long enough for sleep to come, Barbara was in her downtown office glaring at the stacks of papers on her coffee table. They pretty much covered it.

She had placed back in the box everything that appeared to be earlier than Jill Storey's senior year of college. Then she had started doing the same thing with all papers before January of that final year, and still, there were stacks of papers, notebooks, typed papers, handwritten notes. All those about statistics had been next to go back to the box after a cursory glance through them. Although nothing of a personal nature had turned up, she had been able to see a distinct pattern in Jill's working methods.

First the class syllabus, so many quizzes, grade percentage assigned to each, papers with grade percentages, tests, final term paper, followed by a list of reading materials. As Jill finished each task, she had checked it off, sometimes dating her check mark. All neat and concise, checked off before the deadline, until the middle of March, when her illness hit. Apparently from then until early May she had not been able to keep up with reading, or the papers when due, and there were missed tests. In May, in shaky handwriting, she had penciled in new dates, apparently the dates various instructors had allowed for her to finish the work.

It was little more than a synopsis of an illness and the toll it exacted, Barbara thought in disgust. Nothing personal, nothing to indicate her feelings, reveal friendships. Nothing. Period.

She had to admire Jill's industry, though. She had crammed six or seven weeks of work into little more than two weeks. The early handwritten papers were all neat, highly legible. Later, the evidence of illness was betrayed by shaky, spidery writing, like that of an old person. She suspected that the final typed papers had been copied by Olga from Jill's drafts.

Barbara rose and stretched, walked to the outer office, back, did it again, and made herself stop. She was too tired to keep walking. She eyed the sofa, shook her head. She would be too stiff to move on Saturday if she fell asleep there. Earlier she had tried to work at home, but had given up. Todd had a friend over, and the two boys were in and out of the den again and again, making sandwiches, tiptoing around, just there. Darren had been in the living room. He was simply reading, but just being there, she had decided, was too much, and she had packed up everything and returned to the office. She needed space to spread out papers, and space to walk without bumping into anyone or hearing anyone whispering, talking, breathing.

She was missing something. She could feel it all through her bones, her skin, her hair. She was missing something.

Wearily, she returned to the table to put away everything. Tomorrow, she told herself. There was still a tomorrow.

Six weeks of tomorrows. The thought filled her with alarm and despair. Only six more weeks.

26

Darren always woke early, six or six-thirty, and that Saturday was no different. Although he was quiet, no door slamming or singing in the shower, Barbara woke up also. She rolled over and pulled the lightweight blanket over her face, but for the next two hours her sleep was broken again and again by what she had come to recognize as anxiety dreams. Lost in a strange city where she could not read the street signs and no one would speak to her. Lost in a hotel with endless corridors lined with closed doors without numbers. Lost keys, several variations of lost keys, the key to her house, key to the office, to the car. She came wide-awake and gave up trying to return to sleep.

When Todd and his friend emerged from the den to get their breakfasts, she escaped to her office over the garage, but she felt confined, caged in the small space, and remained there only a few minutes. She needed to walk.

She drove to the foot of Skinner's Butte, parked and went to the bike trail by the river and started what was to be a very long walk, trying to sort out what she knew about her case. So little, she thought, sorting would not take long. The dreams had been disturbing, and she hated it when her anxiety about a case haunted her sleep, as well as her waking hours. Lost. Wandering endlessly and not getting anywhere. Lost car keys, office keys, lost house keys. Locked out. That summed it up. She was locked out and could not find the wedge to force a single door to open and let her in. Lost car keys. Going nowhere, getting nowhere.

When her thighs began to throb and burn, she sat down to rest, then walked some more. The morning had been pleasantly cool, but the sun was bright and minute by minute the day became warmer, then hot. Everything was parched, brittle and dulled by summer dust. Dried-up blackberries clung to stems, so desiccated that not even the wasps were tempted by them.

If only they had found a bitter enemy, she thought morosely, but to all appearances Robert McCrutchen had not made enemies. And that was part of her problem, she realized. She could not keep the two deaths separated in her mind; they kept merging, one getting in the way of the other one. She started to walk again, but the trail was getting more crowded. Earlier there had been few others, a jogger or cyclist now and then, but now it seemed to be a thoroughfare, a public highway, with half the Eugene population intent on using the one trail. And the park was getting filled with family picnics, kids tossing Frisbees, babies in strollers and playpens. It seemed to her that everyone in the park was making noise.

She returned to her car, sat for a minute or two, then headed for her downtown office. She was as parched as the grass and the bushes, and she knew she was as ready to flare up as the dry trees with the least provocation.

In a week, after hours of insufferable questions, David would either prove himself capable of facing a hostile prosecutor and keeping his cool, or she would have to decide if his only chance was a plea bargain. Life without parole, possibly a death sentence, or a plea bargain. But it wouldn't stop there. If a jury found him guilty, or if he took a plea bargain, there would be another trial, with the same forlorn prospects. He would be found guilty a second time, or take another plea bargain, with one sentence to follow the other, and he would spend the rest of his life in prison. She saw no way out of that.

She did not have enough to put forward an effective defense and had no real hope for an acquittal.

Her hands tightened on the steering wheel as she remembered Shelley's expressed alarm, her fear that David might pack his things and take off. If he saw no hope in the outcome of a trial, it was almost a certainty that he would do just that, Barbara thought. She also believed that David would die before facing a lifetime in prison.

In her office she drank a glass of water, put on coffee and took a second glass of water to her desk. She was missing something, and she had dreamed of lost keys. The key. Something she kept overlooking. She began to sift through the burgeoning file, and finally pulled out the page of *x*'s with the word *Key* scrawled on it. Something about the key had made Robert McCrutchen draw the *x*'s, write that word. Who had tipped off the police? And when had the newspapers printed that tip? Why had the police informed the media and then left it unexplained after they knew how it had come about?

She found the folder of news clippings that Shelley had assembled and started rereading them. On Monday following Jill Storey's murder there was an account of it, including the item about the key to David's apartment. She read it carefully. No attribution, just the bare account and the sentence, "It has been learned that in Jill Storey's possession was the key to an apartment rented by David Etheridge, another senior from the Gresham community."

She leaned back in her chair, thinking. The investigators asked David about it on Tuesday. They must not have known on Sunday when they got his first statement about the party, but by Tuesday they had been tipped. The newspaper had it first? She reread the police report. An anonymous tip on Monday, followed up on Tuesday. The explanation of the circumstances followed along with verification by both roommates and the shop where David had the key made. There was no mention of sharing the tip with the media. They hadn't shared it. There was no mention of it in any of the statements the police issued concerning the murder. The newspaper had it first.

She smelled coffee and went to pour herself a cup, thinking. Had the killer been disappointed that no arrest had followed the newspaper account? Had he then made certain the police knew about the key by calling and leaving them the same tip? The police never explained it, since they had not issued a statement concerning it in the first place, but whoever had tipped them off might not have known the circumstances, might have been bitterly disappointed that no arrest had been made.

She looked again at Robert McCrutchen's page of x's. He must not have known why Jill had that key until he read the police file. He had believed Jill was moving in with David, that they were lovers, that she had used him for twenty-five dollars. He had been taken. From his words and his actions, as described by Amy, he had not interpreted what Jill said to mean she was a lesbian.

Chloe's revised story about the bloody nose was a lie. Her original statement was that she had gone upstairs with Robert, helped him off with his shoes and stayed with him for a while.

No one had questioned that. Two contradictory stories made both of them suspect.

Aaronson's statement about a bloody hand and face was another lie. He wasn't even there at the right time. Why lie about it now? To forestall an investigation into the possibility that Robert had killed Jill Storey? Fear that such an investigation would uncover illegalities concerning Robert's questionable deals with Nick Aaronson? Some other reason she couldn't even guess at? It didn't matter, she decided, why they lied. She just had to demonstrate that they had.

She had blindsided herself by connecting Robert's murder with Jill Storey's, she thought then. Thinking the same person had killed them both had kept her in a cage without a door. So much for intuition and hunches. Her father had it right, trust intuition only if it could be verified by facts and evidence. She had to start over, rethink everything, starting with the confrontation on the deck that night.

Jill had gone back in the house first, David had followed, and then Robert, and no one had seen him again that night. He had been furious with Jill and David and knew Jill had used him, had prostituted herself for twenty-five dollars, and that she despised him. Frat boy, fun loving, flirting with all the women, impregnating one while sleeping with another one, or possibly more than one other. He might well have followed Jill, followed her home, taken out his rage, his humiliation by strangling her and trying to frame David for the death.

Why hadn't Robert followed through, accused David at the time? She was gazing again at his page of x's. And why do that, place an x where he knew or believed the other party attendees had been? She couldn't even be certain that was what the x's represented. She found Amy's representation of the deck, the placement of the attendees, and laid the two side by side. The only real difference was in the spacing, and the outline of the house that Amy had included. She had started higher on the paper, providing space for the dogwood tree and her position under it. Her view was from that spot, with space on the left for the rest of the house that she had not drawn. Robert had started farther down, with little space for anything past the deck, and positioned on the sheet of paper in such a way that the right side was blank. Had he been interrupted before he completed it, or had that been enough to satisfy his own purposes?

Perhaps it was as simple as wanting to make sure that no one could contradict the lie he told about the incident on the deck, at least no one except David and, as the accused, his version could be dismissed as self-serving. Elders, another lifelong resident who was well respected, had dutifully reported the lie to the police, as a good citizen should.

It would do, she told herself irritably. She didn't have to know why Robert hadn't made the accusation at the time, or why he had not completed his schematic. She didn't have to prove anything, just make it as plausible as possible in order to bring a reasonable doubt to bear on the jury's verdict. It was nearly impossible to accuse a dead person of a crime unless there was overwhelming evidence to back up the accusation. She would be unable to accuse Robert, she well knew, but she might be able to instill a doubt. Just instill a doubt. That was the first glimmer of hope she had found to date.

It was five o'clock and she knew she should go home. She hadn't left a note, and had not called during the day. Of course, Darren knew she was working on a difficult case but, even so, she owed him some explanation. Still, she hesitated. Todd and his pal were probably still there. Chatter, music, something would be going on, something that demanded at the very least politeness, and she was in no mood to be polite. She called the house and left a message on the answering machine, not giving anyone time to pick up the phone before she hung up. Her message was brief, and no doubt rude, she thought, but to the point. "I've been delayed, so don't wait for me. I'll have something to eat before I come home."

She sat without moving for a minute, then called Frank's number. He would be home or not. If not, she would get a sandwich or something.

Fifteen minutes later, in his kitchen she told him that she had opted out of going home for dinner, then outlined the only case she could make.

"All right," Frank said. "What's wrong with it, besides not having a shred of proof?"

"I don't know," she said. "I just feel as if the shoes don't quite fit." She had asked him what was wrong with a case he had been struggling with and that had been his answer, years earlier. She was surprised to hear the same words now, this time coming from her. "I'll have to find out where Robert was parked. I guess Lucy McCrutchen might know." She drank a little wine, bit into a piece of cheese, then said, "If it's shot down, I don't have anything else to offer."

Frank nodded. He knew that. "But the shoes don't quite fit," he said. He knew the feeling, a deep gut feeling that something was wrong. "Let's order in something to eat and go over it all step by step, find the weak spots and see if we can plug them."

"I have a list," she said. "A problems list."

"Dinner order first. What kind of food do you want?"

"I couldn't care less. Whatever is put down in front of me."

He called Martin and ordered whatever the special was, and they sat in his study and began to consider her list of problems.

"We can't demonstrate that Jill Storey was a lesbian. Olga Maas absolutely will not cooperate, and I haven't found anyone else who suspected much less knew except David." She went on down her list. Amy was too young then to make a credible witness today. Robert had not followed through with an accusation, if he had been the tipster. No one had talked about the incident on the deck then, and now it was just David's word, backed by Amy. Both easily dismissed. Elders's statement about Robert's version of it on the last day of his life, plus his statements about how possessive and jealous David had appeared on the night of the party.

"I know how it will appear," she said. "I'll be more or less accusing a dead man who was highly regarded and very well liked, solid family man, church member in good standing, not even a hint of scandal attached to him. Who's going to believe he'd proposition a prostitute and want to take her to his room with his fiancé in the house, on the same night he announced his engagement? Damn few. The most I'll be able to do is bring in some testimony that shows he played around with women in Salem. And even that could backfire, be seen as besmirching the reputation of a fine man who can no longer defend himself. And David is going to be depicted as evil incarnate—antireligion, anti-American, anti-everything decent people hold dear. Depending on his attitude on the stand, he could reinforce that image."

Frank could not find a single problem on her list that he would have omitted or altered.

The dinners of veal marsala with linguine were delivered. After a mostly silent meal, Barbara outlined in some detail the only case she could see to make. Use a snapshot or two of David as an underdeveloped adolescent, one the prettiest girl in school would not have chosen with romance on her mind. Shoot down Aaronson's testimony and Chloe's, as well, or at the very least make them suspect. The housekeeper at that time would testify that she had found no blood on Robert's clothes, a towel or washcloth following the party, but she was shaky, easily confused. There was little she could do about Elders's testimony as to what he said about David's possessiveness, but she could raise objections to anything Robert had told him as hearsay.

Frank shook his head. "Depends on the judge," he said. "If McNulty claims it has the moral imperative of a deathbed statement, it could stand. You can argue the point, but it's a coin toss as to the outcome."

"A deathbed statement is valid only if the person is aware of imminent death," she said. "Presumably Robert had no idea that he would be dead in the next couple of hours."

"Again, it depends on the judge," Frank said soberly. "Keep in mind that judges can be as firm in their faith as anyone else, and can feel as threatened by anyone who challenges that faith."

"If he comes down on the wrong side, that will be grounds for an appeal."

"You don't want to go there," Frank said. "That's anticipating a guilty verdict, and you can't accept that prematurely. It colors everything you think and do once you accept that. Give it more time. We may still come up with something to substantiate the possibility that Robert followed Jill home that night."

"It isn't enough to suggest it, is it?" Barbara asked.

"It's loose. But as you said, all you have to do is establish a reasonable doubt." He eyed her closely. "You didn't sleep much last night, did you? Put all this aside for now, get a good night's sleep and do something relaxing tomorrow. Sometimes the best thing to do is nothing, at least for a short time. On Monday I'd like to come over to your office and read through discovery and that police file, if you don't object."

"God, no! Maybe you'll find things I missed and that would be a blessing."

"I don't expect that," he said. "But sometimes it's good to get a feel for the folks making statements through their words. Now, Aaronson and Chloe are little more than names, and I haven't decided what I think of Elders. Just the nosy neighbor Amy thinks is a creep, or the sorry object Lucy sees that makes her preface most of her comments about him by calling him 'poor Henry.' Or a vindictive son of a bitch. I think he spies on Lucy a lot of the time. Courting her? Just nosy? What?"

"A pitiful, nosy, old vindictive creep," Barbara said. "All of the above. You know the possibility that no one has really addressed is that someone could have been waiting for Jill to come home that night. Someone we know nothing about and, at this late date, won't be able to find in any event. Someone with gloves, prepared to do murder. And he, if he is out there, got a free pass for it. That could have been what the police were inclined to believe at the time, but it got them nowhere. They interviewed neighbors, other residents of the apartment building, and so on, and found nothing. After so many years, I'd get even less."

27

To Barbara's surprise Darren had Sunday planned. He announced it while they were having breakfast.

"I told David we'd be there around one-thirty," he said. "The boys will take off on a hike of their own, and after I have ten or fifteen minutes with David, we'll take a more leisurely stroll in the woods, or hike a mountain, whichever seems more appealing."

She looked at her briefcase involuntarily, and he laughed in his low-key way, took her hand, and said, "That's why. If you stay home, within an hour you'll be at work, and you need a day off as much I do."

She smiled ruefully. "I know. It's just—"

"Forget it," he said. "Also, David asked Amy to come along today. Not much I could do about that. So she'll come over here at twelve-thirty. For today, you let your body take over, no thinking, no planning, no scheming, just physical activity. That's the therapist talking."

She laughed this time, put her hand to her temple and made a key-turning motion. "Gotcha," she said.

It was a perfect day, Barbara thought. The boys had orders to return by four-thirty, and the others had followed Alex up a steep new trail he had cleared just enough to be navigated to a high-level plateau where ferns and huckleberries competed for sun and space. The head-high ferns stirred sinuously in a breeze almost too faint to be felt. David and Amy had lagged behind the others going up and again descending, apparently talking constantly. Her cheeks were high pink, not altogether from the sun and heat, and her curly hair was clinging damply to her moist forehead. She looked happy and beautiful.

Barbara was content to let the conversation ebb and flow around her. She was turned off, she reminded herself lazily. She was not really aware of what had started the exchange concerning who was good at the job.

"We grant intelligence and training or education," David said. "Persistence is high on the list of necessary qualities, but flexibility tops it. I knew a smithy back in Gresham who said every horse is different, every foot different. He had to be ready to change his approach each and every time. I remember how that surprised me. I'd thought a horse is a horse is a horse."

"There are people with slightly different sized feet," Darren said. "Poor souls sometimes go through life with one shoe too tight or too loose."

Barbara felt a mild shock, as if coming awake from near sleep. Synchronicity, she thought, to have shoes that didn't fit come up again, in an altogether different context.

"They haven't found the right shoe salesman," David said. "But it applies up and down the line. Every occupation and profession requires flexibility or the ability to adapt, however you phrase it. The best surgeons, the best engineers, politicians, bricklayers, name it, they share that quality."

Amy laughed. "I had to prove my geometry problem solutions again and again on the blackboard because I used a different route, a different set of theorems to get there than the teacher expected. She pursed her lips a lot."

"David," Barbara asked, "how was Elders as a teacher?"

"Steel rod," he said. "He didn't know how to bend or adapt to different students and their different approaches and needs."

She suspected that Elders and David had clashed more than usually happened with students and teachers. One couldn't bend and the other was too independent to accept without proof any conventional wisdom.

"I heard a talk-show guest say that the perfect school system would mean that no matter where in the country you were, if you walked in on a fourth-grade math class at any given hour, they would all be on the same page, doing the same problems," Alex said. "Idiot."

The conversation drifted on to the new rules in place for schools, and Barbara turned off again until Shelley said, "I wish it would rain." She was sniffing, looking toward the southwest. The wind had shifted, not bringing in the smell of marine air as it usually did, but the smell of woods aflame to the south and west. Sooner or later everyone who lived near woods learned to dread that smell.

"After two good rains," Alex said to Amy, "we'll go collect chanterelles. I know where they are."

Soon after that, the boys got back from their hike with pockets full of agates and it was time to leave. On the way back to town Barbara thought how good the day had been. Not a word about the coming trial, the trouble David was in. His brief session with Darren was left unremarked, and the coolness that had arisen the last time she had seen him was not in evidence. He had held the blue ball throughout the conversation on the patio, and although it had remained silent, it had not been thrown.

In the backseat the boys showed Amy their find, and she proved to be a good audience, and was properly impressed. They dropped off Todd's friend before going on to the house. There, Amy thanked Barbara profusely for allowing another visit. Almost shyly, she said, "We want to meet somewhere for lunch now and then. I said only if you agreed. After all this time I'm sure no one's paying any attention to me, where I go, or anything else, but if you think I'd put him in danger, that's that."

Barbara glanced at Darren, who nodded. "I don't think you're being followed, either," she said. "If you meet at a café or someplace, it probably is fine."

"That's what we'd like to do," Amy said. "Thanks. Just now and then, not every day."

After she left, Darren said, "He was as tense and tight as a strung violin when we got there. He's too intelligent not to know the danger he faces, and he feels helpless. For a lot of people, that's the worst possible state to be in. Anyway, your domain, not mine. Mine is his physical recovery, and it will go much better if he can relax. After the hike, and having a friend show up, he was more relaxed."

"The humanizing effect of having a woman around," Barbara said drily. "Every guy needs a gal."

"You better believe it," Darren said, grinning. "Let's go to your dad's house. He probably has beer and cheese, and I'm starved and thirsty."

On Monday after Frank settled down to start reading the thick files of discovery and the police reports, Barbara called the McCrutchen house. Amy answered the phone.

"I'd like to speak to your mother," Barbara said.

Amy asked her to hold for a minute, and when she came back, she said, "Barbara, we were going to call you this morning. Mother has something to tell you."

"We'll come over. When's a good time?"

"Now? As good a time as any."

"Half an hour," Barbara said. She disconnected and told Frank. "Whatever it is Lucy McCrutchen has been holding back might be ready to toss into the pot. Half an hour, at the house. I said *we*. Okay?"

More than okay, Frank thought, closing the file. About time was more like it.

Amy met them at the door and whatever happiness had colored her cheeks the day before was gone, replaced by a tightness, a look of worry and anxiety. She led them to the living room, where Lucy was already seated, with an equally strained expression.

"Please," she said, "make yourselves comfortable. Would you like coffee?" Coffee service and cups were on the low table.

"Thanks, but no," Barbara said, sitting in a damask-covered chair opposite Lucy. Frank sat down and leaned forward slightly, a listening attitude. "Amy said you have something to tell us," Barbara said.

"Yes." Lucy nodded. Then, in a calm, overly controlled manner, she told them about Henry's visit on Friday. She did not repeat his warning concerning defense attorneys. "It was a lie," she said. "A fabrication. I know that Henry repeated that story to the police. Why wouldn't he? David's nothing to him and he was very fond of Robert and trusted him. I realized I had to tell what I knew was the truth about it. I had convinced myself that since no one but Amy, David and I knew about it, there was no reason to refer to it. None of us would have volunteered anything about it. I was wrong.

"That night, the night of the party, after Henry left, I decided that since the dance music had stopped, the party should have been over. I wanted the few who lingered to leave, I have to admit. I left the living room, turned off the dining-room lights and put the kitchen lights on dim, and went out to the deck to sit and wait for the rest of them to leave. I couldn't go to bed until they left, of course. The house was hot and stuffy, and the air felt good." Her voice was even, almost without inflection. She kept gazing at a point in the corner of the room as she spoke.

"I saw what happened on the deck that night. I heard what Robert said, what Jill said. David didn't attack Robert. He warded off a punch and Robert lost his balance and fell. That was the extent of an attack. Jill ran back inside and after Robert got back on the deck, David went in. I didn't see Amy and had no idea she was out there. I waited for a time and went in, and by then everyone had left except for one boy sleeping on the sofa."

Finally she looked at Barbara, then at Frank, and her voice dropped to nearly a whisper. "I'm sorry I never said anything about it until now. I should have told, but— I should have told. Then the news accounts seemed to indicate that a transient had done it and I thought it was over." She looked away, back at the corner of the room. "I thought that no one would ever mention that incident. I couldn't believe Robert would bring up anything that reflected so poorly on him, and David was too decent to talk about it. I convinced myself that it had nothing to do with Jill's death."

Barbara regarded her, trying to control her anger. "How far away from the group were you? Why didn't any of them see you?"

"It would be easier to show you than try to tell you," Amy said. She got to her feet, and the others also stood, then followed her out to the deck.

"That night the grill was here," Amy said, pointing to a spot near the kitchen door. "We had a picnic table here, within easy reach, for the condiments, buns, things like that. Over here—" she moved past the places she was indicating, stopped "—one of the outdoor tables and chairs, pretty close to the house. And several more feet, and closer to the lawn, the other table and chairs. Mother was there, at the table farthest from the door. With the lights so dim, and the rest of the house dark, the dining room, bedroom, then the apartment all dark, she was deep in shadows. The disco lights in the family room were off and just one lamp at the far end, near the piano, was still on."

Barbara eyed the distance. "From that far away you could hear them clearly?"

Lucy nodded. "Yes. It was very quiet out here, and Robert was loud, then Jill raised her voice, too. I could hear them."

Her voice was losing that calm control, as if being out on the deck, remembering that scene, was cracking the protective shell she had been hiding behind.

"Maybe we could have some of that coffee you offered," Frank said. "It's getting cooler day by day, isn't it? Sweater weather already."

The sun was quite warm, but Lucy looked chilled and walked ahead back into the house and to the living room. She busied herself with the coffee, and by the time she passed cups around, she was under complete control again.

"Will you require a signed statement?" she asked Barbara.

"Yes. It can wait. I have a question, one that I called about, in fact. Do you know where various people parked that night? You, your husband, Robert, Jill, anyone else you can think of."

"Some," Lucy said. "Mac parked out on the street. In case of an emergency and he had to leave during the night, he had to have access to his car, of course. I parked in the garage and

Robert did, too." She stopped, and her hands were shaking as she said, in a hushed voice, "Robert parked in the garage!" She looked at Amy and color flushed her face. "He couldn't have gotten his car out! Not from in the garage."

With that tremulous voice, and her transparent relief, she signaled exactly what she had been going through, Frank realized. She had believed, or feared, that her son had gone after Jill, that he had killed her.

Lucy shook herself and in a more lively voice than she had yet used, she said, "Cars lined the driveway from the street all the way around, and people had to park out at the curb, of course. I imagine that Jill had to park down the street by the curb, since so many had already arrived before she got here."

Barbara asked her to repeat what she had heard that night, and either she was parroting what Amy had said, or she had heard the same words.

"How did you interpret what Jill was saying?" Barbara asked.

"I thought it meant she was a lesbian, that men disgusted her. Barbara, I have to say that I don't believe that girl was really a prostitute. Not in the sense people generally mean. She was ill and desperate, facing a possible eviction, and she did what she had to do to save herself. I think the disgust she expressed was directed inwardly as much as toward men."

"Had you met her earlier, before she became ill?"

"Yes. She was here several times early in the school term, a lively, vivacious young woman who appeared happy. She was absent for a number of weeks, and when she came back, she was almost skeletal, pale, desperate. She was slender to begin with, and probably had lost ten or fifteen pounds and had become ethereal looking. The night of the party, as I told you, she seemed almost manic, no doubt with relief that the school year was over, she had her grades and was recovering her health."

Barbara turned to Amy. "Will you make a drawing to scale of the whole area again, this time including your mother's position."

Amy said of course she would. "Today. I'll drop it off at your office."

Neither Barbara nor Frank had any more questions, and minutes later they walked out, got in Barbara's car, and she said, "Shit!"

Not only had Lucy McCrutchen just blown her only defense case out of the water if Robert had not been able to get his car out that night, but Lucy and Amy might add fuel to the case for McNulty if he accepted Elders's statement that David had learned on the night of the party that his lover was a prostitute.

28

Thank God for routine, Barbara thought more than once that week as she sifted through the mass of papers, sorting, designating statements to the different facets of the coming trial. Opening statement. Stipulations. Chloe statements, Aaronson statements. Medical examiner's original report and autopsy. Statements from old schoolmates. On and on and on.

When she got tired of the chore, she walked around her office. When the office proved too confining, she walked along the river bike trail.

On Friday afternoon, a brisk wind was rippling the flashing water, as if trying to impede the flow, even reverse it, creating turbulence that caught the sunlight in bright splashes of silver, like jewelry being tried on and whisked away, discarded.

She was sitting on a bench in sunlight, but the wind was cold, and she pulled her jacket closer around her and thrust her hands into her pockets. She kept thinking of the dreams that were continuing. She couldn't remember the last time she had lost her house keys or car keys, or lost herself in a city, but night after night in her dreams she relived the same wrenching anxiety of lost items or self. She scowled at the river. "I know," she said under her breath, as if the rushing water were responsible. "I admit it," she said, not quite out loud. "I'm losing this case and there's not a thing I can do about it."

The water rushed on, messenger from land to sea, from high mountains to deep water, sharing the secrets of time, creation, volcanoes, forests, particle by particle.

She was getting too chilled and finally started back to her car, back to the office, back to routine. She had to reread David's book with a highlighter in hand. McNulty would read from it, make David answer with a yes/no response if those were his words, and there was enough ammunition in those words to fell an army. Taken out of context, read in a harsh voice, incredulity and contempt voiced in equal amounts, David's words alone could be enough to condemn him. Somewhere in that book, he had written that such words would have guaranteed his being burned at the stake just a few hundred years ago. Nothing changed, she thought, nothing changed ultimately. Mere words could still bring about his damnation. She recalled Frank's remark made months before—half the world is trying to kill the other half over ideas.

On Sunday night, after Barbara, Darren and Todd left, Frank sat in his study. He was concerned about Barbara. She was too detached, too remote, withdrawn. It was a bad sign. She was looking at defeat, losing a capital case for the first time, and was in despair with helplessness. He knew exactly how that affected a defense attorney and it worried him.

Barbara had done a good job with discovery and the police file, leaving nothing for him to come across that she had not already considered, and he knew as well as she did that there was virtually no defense to be made from what scant testimony they had in their favor. The ambiguity of Jill's words made interpretation very dependent on the mind-set of those who heard them.

He made a note. They should go back to Lucy's house and do a little playlet out on the deck, make certain that words spoken at the end could be heard from where Lucy had been. He suspected that McNulty would argue that they could not have been heard clearly from such a distance. It could come down to having the jury hear words on the deck.

He was making a list of questions for David's ordeal on Tuesday, and he realized he was dreading it as much as Barbara.

Barbara arrived at Frank's office at eight-thirty on Tuesday. Shelley would come with David at nine, and they would begin. It would be a long day, with breaks every hour or so, a lunch break, and time afterward to discuss anything that might prove to be a problem.

"Two pretrial meetings in chambers next week," Barbara said, taking off her sweater. "We're to have our witness list ready and pass it over by the end of next week. Right on schedule."

She sounded and looked tired. "There's something interesting I wanted to show you," she said, pulling papers from her briefcase. "This is the schematic Amy drew with her computer program. Really professional." She had redone her original drawing, this time labeling the rooms being shown, and the position of both Lucy on the deck and herself under the dogwood tree. She had used small circles to represent the people shown both inside the family room, and those outside. Now, with all the lines in place, the whole drawing was centered. "She left all that out before," Barbara said, indicating the side of the deck, "but she left space for her mother's position. I guess it was totally unconscious on her part."

She put that drawing on the table, and next to it, she placed the sheet with the *x*'s that Robert had drawn. She shifted it so that the three *x*'s were lined up with Amy's three circles.

"Same thing without walls," Barbara said. "Apparently he had the same kind of gift for spatial relationships. I don't think there's a doubt what he was doing. Either he didn't need the walls to visualize it all, or else he hadn't finished it when he was shot."

Frank agreed. "He didn't know Lucy and Amy had witnessed that scene and he left no space for them." The word *Key* was scrawled on the top of the paper. He had that exactly right, Frank thought. The incident on the deck was the key.

Barbara returned both papers to her briefcase and brought out her yellow legal notepad, and another one for David to use, along with a pen. Frank's identical notepad was on his desk, ready.

Shelley and David arrived a few minutes later and Barbara said, "Briefly, this is how we'll be handling it. First I'll outline the case the prosecution is going to make, based on what I know now. We'll talk after I summarize it. When we're through with that, I'll do the same thing with the case I'll make for the defense. Then, you'll take the stand, and I'll ask questions. You have to answer truthfully, of course, and I'll allow you to expand on your answers. If you're too succinct, I'll ask you to elaborate. It's going to be a drag, but it's important. We'll discuss that part, and then Dad will become prosecutor. You should answer his questions as briefly as possible, volunteer nothing and stay calm and alert to possible traps. We believe the prosecutor will read selections from your book and demand yes or no answers when he asks if those are your words. When we get to my redirect examination, we will return to those sections and put the words in context, and let you explain what you meant, or address them in any way that seems necessary. We don't know which selections he might choose to attack, but the book is jammed full of possibilities."

David smiled a tight, mirthless smile. "He'll find possibilities," he said.

"Just one more thing," Barbara said. "Every charge he makes will be presented in sworn testimony. Ready?"

He shrugged. "Ready or not, fire away."

Barbara outlined the case for the prosecution. Childhood sweethearts, inseparable, David jealous and possessive, suspicious at the party, saw Jill go out, followed by Robert, and went after them. Learned that Jill was prostituting herself. Attacked Robert. Took Jill by the arm and left with her. Chloe went upstairs with Robert who had a bloody nose. Aaronson saw Robert's bloody hand, blood on his face, collected his date and left the party. Jill was living with, or planned to live with David, had a key to his apartment. Robert told Elders about the unwarranted attack the night he was shot.

As she outlined the case, David's expression went from incredulity to disbelief, and finally to a cool remoteness that was impossible to read.

"A prosecution that's one lie after another from start to finish," he said when she was done.

"We know that. But, David, always assume the prosecutor believes the case he's making, and will work his ass off to convince a jury that he's right," Barbara said.

"In other words, you're telling me that I'm screwed," David said.

"I didn't say that. I'm saying that he's going to make a case that will be hard to refute. I can't do anything about what Chloe says. The housekeeper who did the laundry will testify that there was no blood on a washcloth, clothing or towels, but under cross-examination, intimidated, she could admit that it was a long time ago and it's possible that she can't remember exactly. We have a statement from the woman who got a ride with Aaronson that night along with his date—someone named Tiffany. No last name. He will swear he took Belinda Hulse home, and admit that it's possible that they gave someone else a ride, that he forgot about her. A he said/she said situation, coin flip which is right. Belinda Hulse died some years ago. We haven't been able to find anyone else who arrived or left with her. Lucy McCrutchen will testify that Aaronson thanked her while dancing was still going on. If they were still dancing, the incident on the deck was yet to play itself out, and she was in the shadows watching when it did."

For the first time David registered surprise. "I didn't realize we were playing to a full house that night," he said.

Suppressing her annoyance at his sardonic tone, Barbara told him about it, then continued.

"Olga refuses to testify and would deny everything anyway. I haven't found anyone else to testify that Jill was a lesbian. Amy will be ridiculed as a romantic girl, or it might even be suggested that she and Lucy McCrutchen discussed their testimony and made sure there was no contradiction. Elders is like Chloe, no way I can prove him wrong. Either Robert told him what he claims, or he didn't. In the end, you and Lucy McCrutchen will be the most important witnesses we present."

"But I'm not screwed," David said.

Before Barbara could respond, Frank said it was time for a break.

It was just as well, Barbara knew. The retort she might have made would have added nothing but a release of some of her pent-up frustration.

Patsy brought in coffee, and Barbara and Shelley went out to the hallway where Shelley said, "Oh, dear."

"Yep," Barbara agreed. "Oh, dear." That summed it up, she thought. It was enough. She composed herself and returned to the office.

Sipping coffee, David asked, almost lazily, "Did Robert follow Jill that night? Did he murder her?"

"We don't think so," Frank said when Barbara remained quiet. "For a time we thought that was the case, but his car was in the garage, hemmed in."

"Too bad," David said, as if talking about a minor difficulty with a missing button. "It could have explained why both Chloe and Aaronson are going to perjure themselves, to protect him for whatever reason."

"We're guessing it's to prevent an investigation into him and his deals with Aaronson," Barbara said. "Now they're stuck with those stories."

"Oh," David said with a nod of understanding. "I wonder what Elders's motive is."

"I wish I knew," Barbara said. "Either Robert lied, or Elders did. No way to prove either. Dad has a theory."

"He may resent your success," Frank said. "Consciously or unconsciously, he may harbor hostility that his upstart student made it big while he continued to plod along."

David laughed. "That fits him. He goes by the rules, and hates it when anyone who doesn't gets rewarded. Like me. One more question before we start again. What's the prosecutor's name? What do you know about him?"

Barbara recited what they knew. "Roy McNulty, fourteen years in the D.A.'s office, said to be a good prosecutor, with a lot of wins under his belt. Family man, four kids, active in civic affairs, avid fan of the U of O teams."

David nodded with mock gravity. "Good devout Catholic Irishman who agrees with the Vatican that South American liberation theology is heresy. Wanna bet?"

"It's irrelevant," Barbara said. "Fifteen minutes are up. Let's get back to the job at hand."

"Irrelevant? I don't think so," David said. "Depends on which side of that ongoing debate he would take. Blind, unquestioning, absolute obedience to authority without regard for personal morality or principles, or not."

"This isn't the time or place for philosophical discussions," Barbara snapped.

She started the questions again, beginning with David's earliest memories of Jill.

When they broke for lunch, she didn't know which of them was more exasperated, she or David. They both remained silent over sandwiches and salads.

Before she resumed, Barbara said, "David, you have to stop acting as if you're defending a dissertation. You'll be defending your life, as I'll be trying to do also."

He nodded without comment, and it began again.

His answers were so brief they sounded truculent, brusque, and again and again she asked him to elaborate, to explain, to furnish more detail. What had he thought, felt?

When she finished, she spread her hands, then stood. "Let's have a break."

"I flunked, didn't I?" David said, and again the mockery was heavy in his voice, whether directed at her or himself was impossible to tell.

"David," Frank said quietly, "we want you to reveal the man who wept over the Trail of Tears, when Indians were driven from their homes, their farms, their lands and made the forced march to Oklahoma, and died along the way. The man who wept when the same thing happened to the Northwest Indians, defeated, rounded up, herded like cattle to barren reservations. The man who held Olga in his arms and wept with her over the death of her lover and his best friend. That man is all through your book, revealed in your indignation, your pain, your fury, and you're keeping him buried so deep now that you're like a robot, when it's your own life at stake."

David turned away. "You want too much," he said.

"We want to save your life," Frank said.

"I'll get some coffee," Barbara said. Shelley hurried out after her when she left the office. Neither spoke until Barbara asked Patsy if coffee was made.

"Coming right up," Patsy said. "I thought it was about time." She looked closely at Barbara, then at Shelley, and a worried expression crossed her face.

When she brought in coffee, she had added a plate of cookies. And where she had them stashed away God alone knew, Frank thought, thanking her.

After the break Frank assumed his prosecutor's role. He asked the same kinds of questions he knew McNulty would ask, insinuating, insulting, disbelieving questions. "When you played with Jill Storey, did you play doctor? Did you play house? Did you skinny-dip?"

David's annoyance and impatience grew more and more evident. He looked at his watch often, shifted in his chair, snapped answers.

After an hour Frank stopped. "That's enough," he said. "Just a taste of what to expect."

"Am I excused?" David was dripping sarcasm with the words.

"Not yet," Frank said. He stood, crossed the office and opened the bar concealed behind a book case, brought out a bottle and glasses, then resumed his chair. He took his time uncorking the bottle, pouring. To his surprise Shelley accepted a glass of wine, something he had never seen her do except with meals. David shook his head.

"Did you have questions about what we've just done?" Frank asked after he and Barbara both had a glass of wine.

"No. This whole thing is a crock. No point in questioning it. The verdict is already in."

"Not yet," Frank said equably. "If you take that attitude to the witness stand, however, it won't take long to reach that verdict. You have four weeks to think about it. Meanwhile, something else we have to bring up is a plea bargain."

"Next page," David said sharply. "You know I won't go that route."

"Nevertheless, it's our duty to inform you of your rights," Frank said. He held up his wineglass to the light. "This is very nice. Shiraz. Are you sure you don't want a little?"

Abruptly David laughed, this time with apparent amusement. "I've met my match, Mr. Holloway. You'd make a dandy prosecutor, and I suspect you're just as good a defense attorney."

Frank nodded toward Barbara. "She's better. Anyway, about a plea bargain. It's on the table right up until the trial begins. If remorse is expressed with sufficient humility, the sentence is reduced. That takes care of that particular duty." He eyed David shrewdly. "I wonder if you know the most important sentence in your book. Not that McNulty will ask that particular question. I'm just curious."

"Tell me," David said.

"Do unto others as you would have others do unto you. A good thought, good sentence. One I believe you subscribe to wholeheartedly."

David nodded. "Yes. I do." He motioned toward the bottle of wine. "Maybe I'll have just a little."

"Help yourself," Frank said. He turned to Shelley and asked about the forest fires in the Coast Range.

"Too close for comfort," she said. "I don't want to be able to smell smoke from them, but we do. Alex ordered a pump for the swimming pool and what looks like an industrial hose to keep the house soaked down if the fires come over the top of the hill. If the weather forecast is reliable, there will be no rain for several more weeks. That's a long time for fires to rage."

They talked for a few more minutes, and then Shelley and David left to drive back to her house.

As soon as they were out of the office, Barbara poured another glass of wine. "I don't know how you can do it," she said. "Keep your patience with him the way you do. I was ready to send him packing a long time ago."

Earlier, watching and listening as she went over the case details, Frank had come to a startling realization, one that he knew he could never share with her. The new insight explained why she and David clashed the way they did. David was behaving in exactly the same way she would, if she were the accused. She was as impatient with him as she was with herself so often, and David reacted predictably, exactly the way she would have, ready to leap up and storm out, scornful of the system, sarcastic, mocking. Neither one of them could see it, he had thought in wonder.

29

On Thursday Frank picked half-a-dozen ripe tomatoes, regretful that their season was coming to an end. He put four of them in a bag to take to Lucy, and he and Barbara returned to the McCrutchen house.

They wanted to test the acoustics on the deck, to be prepared if it became an issue, Frank had told Lucy on the phone. She dreaded it more than she could say, reliving that night, revisiting that ugly scene. It was a clear, cool day with a slight breeze, and Lucy shivered as the group went out to the deck. Amy positioned her and Barbara, and Lucy and Frank went to the end of the deck.

"This is about where they stood," Amy said in a subdued voice. They were close to the end of the deck, several feet from the wall of the house. "There were plants out here then," she said.

Frank nodded and handed her a printout. "Your part," he said. "I'll begin." Then in his lawyerly voice, he recited,

"'The time has come,' the Walrus said,
'to talk of many things:
Of shoes—and ships—and sealing wax—
Of cabbages—and kings—
And why the sea is boiling hot—
And whether pigs have wings.'"

Across the deck both Barbara and Lucy were smiling. Lucy's dread had vanished.

"What a ham!" Barbara said.

Frank bowed to Amy and she, smiling, read her lines.

"'Will you walk a little faster?' said a whiting to a snail,
'There's a porpoise close behind us, and he's treading on my tail.
See how eagerly the lobsters and the turtles all advance!
They are waiting on the shingle—will you come and join the dance?'"

"And she's another one," Lucy said.

"Enough?" Frank asked.

"Loud and clear," Barbara said.

Frank and Amy rejoined them. "I don't think we were overly loud," he said.

"Definitely not," Amy agreed.

"If you'd like another chance, with our voices lower, or raised, we could oblige," Frank said. "I'm ready for another go-around." He cleared his throat.

All three audience members were laughing and groaning too much for him to be heard. He stopped, looking mildly hurt.

"Don't encourage him," Barbara warned. "And for God's sake, don't let him start on Kipling!"

"I think we deserve a cup of coffee," Lucy said.

Then Amy said in a low voice, "For heaven's sake! Here he comes."

Dr. Elders appeared at the side of the house, carrying a few pink roses. "I thought I heard sounds of laughter," he said. "A party? I brought a table decoration."

"Barbara, do you want to see how we've redone the studio?" Amy asked. She tilted her head toward the kitchen door.

"Of course," Barbara said. "Hello, Dr. Elders. Excuse us, please." She followed Amy inside and to the study. It had been painted a creamy white, with light blue drapes and a russet-colored carpet. "Very handsome," Barbara said. "You really dislike Elders, don't you?"

"He's a total creep. He spies on us, or on Mother, anyway. Creepy. I wish she'd just tell him to buzz off, but she won't. It would be unneighborly," Amy said.

"Did he ever do or say anything to make you feel uncomfortable with him, besides that incident with the beer?" Barbara asked curiously. Amy's reaction to him seemed a little too strong for just disapproval of a nosy old man.

"Not really. I used to have to take stuff over for them, you know, when his wife was sick and he was teaching full-time. A cake or pie, sometimes a casserole. After that nonsense with the beer, I always felt that he was watching to catch me doing something else evil. I hated going over there. I'd stop at the end of the walk from the front, and peek around to see if he was out on the patio. It comes right up to the walk, and he'd often be at a table outside the kitchen, reading or grading papers or something, right there. I'd wait and wait for him to go inside so I could just put something down on the table and take off. But it hardly ever happened. I hated going inside his house, too. Like a refrigerator, and it smelled funny. Medicinal probably, but then it just smelled funny and I hated it." She shrugged. "The kind of stuff kids hate and never really forget, I guess."

"Did he have a walk put in just to be able to pop in over here easily?"

Amy shook her head. "No, of course not. The gas meter is outside the kitchen, at this end of the house, and I guess the builder added the walk so the meter reader could get to it."

"I'd better go back and see how Dad's doing," Barbara said.

"I'll get back to work," Amy said. Her computer and books were on the desk. She hesitated, then said, "Barbara, how's David? Is anything wrong? He hasn't called, and I thought he would. I hate to be the one to make calls. In case he's busy or something."

And that was the reason to inspect the study, Barbara understood. "He's got a lot on his mind," she said. "Nothing's changed, as far as I know."

Amy looked as if she wanted to ask questions, to talk, say something, but she remained silent, then took a step toward the desk. "I'd better get back to work." She sounded woebegone.

Barbara found Frank, Lucy and Dr. Elders in the family room. Seeing her, Frank put down a coffee cup and got to his feet. "We'll be going," he said. "Thank you for the coffee."

"I should thank you for the tomatoes. Two gifts in one day. I feel as if it's a birthday," Lucy said.

"Unbirthday gift," Frank said.

A smile crossed Lucy's face. "The best kind," she said. "Three hundred sixty-four times a year to give or receive gifts. Thank you. And you, Henry, for the flowers."

Elders looked blank, then said hurriedly, "My pleasure. You're welcome."

In the car, minutes later, Frank chuckled. Barbara looked at him with raised eyebrows. "Elders," he said. "He doesn't know Alice at all, and I think he believed Lucy and I were talking in code."

And he, Barbara knew, could probably recite every nonsense rhyme and song in *Alice in Wonderland*.

Barbara worked through Saturday and into the night, going over the witness list McNulty had provided, practically memorizing the statements he would be using in court. Afterward, sitting in her downtown office, she thought about the meeting they'd had on Friday, how many statements or witnesses either she or McNulty had argued for or against admitting. Cool arguments, rarely reaching a point of high passion or even indignation. Businesslike, efficient, they could have been talking about playground rules. In the end both lawyers and the judge had agreed that it appeared that the trial would be over within a week.

She knew she should wrap things up and go home, sleep, but she continued to sit at her desk, sometimes blank, other times with furious thoughts racing through her mind, struggling against accepting that she could find nothing in any of the statements that offered hope.

She kept missing something, she knew, and began her search again, then again. It was very late when she finally gave it up and went home. Darren was asleep, and she assumed Todd was. She was glad since she didn't want to talk, or to listen to anything they might say. Glad, but also faintly resentful that Darren could sleep when she was so awake. After turning and twisting in bed for what seemed a very long time, she gave up and went to the living room where she sat in the dark and struggled anew, this time against what she had come to accept as true.

Sunday night at dinner with Frank, in answer to his question, Darren outlined his plan for the two interns forced upon him. "I'm giving them the standard test they use at the college in the nursing program," he said. "Physiology, anatomy, nervous system, cardiovascular, and so on. And I've culled a dozen physicians' prescriptions for their patients for rehabilitation. Some are simple instructions, some are pretty complex and all of them are actual cases from my files—stroke victims, head injuries, other traumas, spinal problems, amputations, a mixed bag. The guys are to describe exactly how they would proceed with therapy. And they're both going to fail."

Barbara listened as if from a great distance. She tried to concentrate on what Darren was saying, what her father was saying, but their words kept sliding away, out of focus as instantly as she heard them. She was failing him, she knew, as she had known she would. She had warned him, and herself, that it could come to this, and here it was happening, and she seemed powerless to put her own problems aside even temporarily to offer him the kind of support he deserved and needed.

Frank had asked something else, or commented, and Darren said, "We'll have a special board meeting after I have test results, and we'll discuss it. They know I won't certify them unless I'm satisfied. I think they'll be prepared for whatever course of action they decide is necessary." In his soft, musical way, he said, as if it meant little to him, "I won't challenge or question whatever action they take, of course."

She had come to realize what it was she had lost, she thought, as Darren's words, then Frank's, drifted past her. Whatever edge she had once had was gone, whether intuition, a gift for hunches that turned out to be right, some insight into those she interviewed, a knack for spotting the incongruity in testimony, whatever it was, it was gone. She was left with words on paper that revealed only their dictionary meaning. Nothing more than that. And that was not enough.

Short of a confession, the words alone were not enough and

never had been. Without that special something that had not just guided her for years but had, at times, controlled her, dominated her, she had nothing. She felt empty, hollow.

She found herself studying her father and wondering, was that what happened to him? Had he lost that *something?* He had given up taking capital cases, no more life-and-death issues, except as her colleague at times, but never taking the lead, never litigating. She wished he would tell her why, but she could not ask any more than she could ever reveal her own self-discovery.

The one thing she knew with certainty was that she, too, would have to give up capital cases. She could never again risk another person's life knowing what she knew about herself.

30

The days galloped or stalled, sometimes the same day did both. From nine until three gone in a flash, and then the clock became stuck and the hands were mired as minutes were like hours.

Barbara gazed at her blank screen, tentatively keyed in the word *The*. Nothing followed. She deleted the word and started over. Her opening statement was a blank screen, continued to be a blank screen. She tried a different first word—*This*. She stared at the word. Nothing. She hit Delete. She got up and paced. She was getting nowhere.

All right, she told herself, *I'm blocked. Why?* The answer was not long in coming. She no longer believed in her case, what pitiful defense she had to mount. It was meaningless.

At three-thirty Maria buzzed her to say David was on the phone. She was not surprised when he got straight to the point without any small talk.

"I want to talk to you," he said. "Is this a good time?"

"Sure. Do you want me to come out to the house, or meet somewhere?"

"Alex loaned me his car. I'm on my way over. Ten minutes." He disconnected.

He had decided it was time to fire her, she thought distantly. She wouldn't blame him. She never had been fired before, another first. She realized that she was keeping his curt announcement at a distance, the way she was keeping everything else as far removed as she possibly could. She was adding another layer to the protective shell that she was pulling tighter and tighter about herself. In the end it might suffocate her.

David was prompt. He had on a Windbreaker, hiking boots, jeans. During the past months, he had become tanned, and he looked fit, healthy now. When he took off his Windbreaker, he pulled a red ball from the pocket.

"Congratulations," Barbara said. "Another rung up the ladder for you." She didn't bother to ask how long he had been borrowing a car, leaving his sanctuary. He would stay or not out there.

"Thanks. Here?" He motioned toward the easy chairs by the inlaid table.

"Sure. Comfort of home, all that."

He nodded and sat down. "The first time I came in here, what I saw was a lot of money tied up in a fancy office, and I thought another attorney making it big off the misery of others. Wrong. Alex told me your dad and Shelley ponied up for all the trimmings. Proud of their kids, something like that. Rightfully so. After I looked you up, tried to estimate how much pro bono time you and Shelley put in, I wondered if you made a cent as an attorney. But it was working both ways back there in the beginning. My hunch was that you were okay, the backdrop suggested otherwise. I'm very glad I listened to the hunch. Sometimes it pays to put reason aside."

Taken aback, more surprised by his words than she wanted to acknowledge, Barbara could only nod. Her first hunch about him had been to tell him to get lost. To give herself something to do instead of speaking, she poured coffee for them both, passed a cup across the table to him and picked up her own to take a sip. He ignored his.

"What's the opposite of a den of thieves?" he asked in a musing sort of way.

"Cloisters?"

He smiled. "I don't think so. But whatever it is, I've found myself in the middle of it. You're surrounded by some good people, Barbara, and Amy and her mother are also good people. It seems a strange place to find myself, so completely surrounded by good people. Nothing I've known before quite prepared me for it. At times it's been a bit bewildering, in fact, and I haven't known how to react. I've been rude and sarcastic, testing, always testing others, watchful for a sign of perfidy or hypocrisy. It doesn't take long generally to come across one or the other, or most often both." He laughed. "I can't think I've quite come around yet to humility, but in time even that could come to me, possibly."

"David, where are you leading with this?"

"To the edge of the cliff maybe," he said lightly. "I had lunch with Amy today. Does she understand what they're going to do to her on the witness stand?"

Barbara nodded. "I think she's prepared."

"She can't be. You know how rapists and serial killers in prison sometimes get letters from adoring women? Some kind of perversion, I imagine, but she'll be painted as one of them, ridiculed, mocked, scorned, vilified. And her mother? What will it do to her to denigrate her son in favor of a killer? Her son's killer. How is she going to live with that?"

"They both believe you're innocent. As I do, and Dad does," Barbara stated.

"I know and, in case I forget to say this, I'm very grateful. But that's not the question. What will testifying to what she witnessed that night do to Lucy McCrutchen?"

There was no way to answer that, and Barbara remained silent.

"Exactly. A part of her will die on that stand. Death is final, absolute. That part will be irrecoverable. Olga Maas will live in fear that she will be exposed as a lesbian, lose her daughter. And it could happen. People, good people, are going to be hurt, Barbara, desperately hurt, if this debacle goes to trial."

"You know what will happen if you run," she said in a low voice. "A fugitive, admitting your guilt by fleeing, you would be captured and taken directly to prison, or else shot down resisting arrest."

"Or something," he said. He lifted his coffee cup for the first time, took a sip and put it down. He leaned forward and watched her intently as he said, "Barbara, I've come to have a great deal of respect for you and your father because you play it straight with me. Play it straight now. If our positions were reversed, what would you do?"

She rose, walked to her desk and ran her fingers across it, then went on to the window and moved the blind aside, looked out, seeing nothing. He was waiting, watching her. She returned to her chair and sat down again.

"I don't know," she said.

David nodded. "Thank you," he said. "I'll be on my way. Thanks for seeing me on such short notice. You might tell Darren I'm working on the red ball these days. He'll be pleased, I think."

She remained seated as he put on his jacket and went to the door, where he turned to look at her again. "I won't be deciding immediately. I want to finish a draft for the book Alex and I are working on. I owe him big. I'll be seeing you." He let himself out.

She should have offered him words of encouragement. Told him all she had to do was raise a reasonable doubt. She didn't have to prove anything. A reasonable doubt was not an impossible bar.

She thought of something they had chanted back in high school—shoulda, woulda, coulda, didn't, won't. Rebellious bravado. Meaningless. She repeated it under her breath and this time added a word—can't. With that she stood and went back to her desk where she stared at her blank screen.

Maria tapped at her door, entered the office and asked if Barbara wanted her to do anything. She said no. Told her to go home. Shelley looked in and said she'd be leaving and Barbara waved goodbye and absently gazed at her blank screen.

David's words came to mind—*Sometimes it pays to put reason aside.* He had too many faces. She never knew which one she would see next. He was like some curious dice Todd and his friends used for a game, ten sided, twelve sided? Too many possible faces, and unpredictable as to which face would be revealed next. That was David. Her first encounter with him had made her not want to see him again. He had been arrogant, impatient, angry, sarcastic to the extreme. Lucy said he was too decent to have talked about the scene on the deck. Amy knew him as an understanding adult at the time she was suffering through adolescence. Frank wanted him to reveal the man who had held Olga and wept with her over the loss of a friend. And now he was concerned that good people were going to be desperately hurt. She remembered the line in his book that Frank had called the most important one. *Do unto others as you would have others do unto you.* That was David, too.

It hadn't been just a hunch that first day, she thought then. That had been a very conscious thought. She had not wanted to deal with a man who made such harsh judgments about people. He had been right, though. Robert McCrutchen had been a two-bit, small-town politician who had meant nothing to David.

But she had put a hunch aside later, she realized, and she had followed reason instead. Her first intuition, her hunch, had been that both murders and the attack on David had been committed by the same person. Reason had prevailed, and left her staring at a blank screen.

Start over, she told herself, and remembered that she had done that before, but each time the new start had been based on a false premise. Start over, this time with the assumption that there was only one killer, she thought clearly. It was time to put reason aside.

Later she was startled to hear a tap on her door. It opened and Frank walked in. She looked at him blankly, then shook herself. "What's wrong? What are you doing here?"

"I brought you something to eat," he said brusquely. "Darren said he had orders never to bring any food here, but, by God, I don't have such orders. Do you have any idea what time it is? Have you had a bite all day?"

She looked at her watch. Twenty minutes before ten! Instantly she felt light-headed from hunger or fatigue, possibly both. She shook her head. "I don't know. I don't remember. Dad, there's something we have to talk about."

"After you eat," he said. He was carrying a basket. Her round table was covered with papers, as was her desk. There were papers on her sofa. "Out here," he said, backing out, holding the door open with his foot. Maria's desk was spotless. He put the basket down on the desk and pulled a second chair close to it.

"Darren called you?" she asked, taking the other chair, behind Maria's desk.

"No. I called. Conyers brought over a five-pound chunk of halibut this evening, caught this morning. I called to invite you all over to help eat it tomorrow. Darren said you were still working." He pointed to the basket and took off a cover. "Leftovers. They'll do."

The smell of chicken and spaghetti with pesto made her mouth water instantly and she picked up a piece of chicken before she had a plate in place.

Frank sat and watched her for a moment, shook his head and got up again to make coffee.

Besides the chicken and pasta, he had included salad with snap beans vinaigrette. His leftovers were better than any restaurant food she could remember. She ate greedily.

"Why do you do that to Darren?" he asked after a moment. "He'd like nothing better than to pamper you just a little bit. If you'd get off your high horse and let him."

"I'd feel too guilty. This is wonderful."

He realized that she had given him an honest answer and did not press the point.

Neither spoke again until she sighed deeply and leaned back in her chair. "I was pretty hungry," she said.

"I noticed." He poured coffee and sat down again. "What have you been up to?"

"I'll tell you a story," she said, "and then show you some things. First the narrative. And understand this is bare bones, few if any details. To be filled in later, if we're lucky." At his nod, she started.

"Jill was desperate to make her grades and get enough money

together with Olga to avoid eviction. She talked to instructors and got an extension for class work and tests, and she got money from Robert in return for a tumble in bed. She wasn't interested in history, just needed the credits to graduate, and she put off the history until she finished the other class work, but then she found she couldn't complete Elders's assignments. He had loaded her with a dozen books to read, a long report to write, and she had to defend a character from history to his satisfaction. Impossible tasks for the shape she was in and too little time. She went to his office to plead her case, but he was a strict master, one who set rules and followed them. Probably she was crying, possibly he ended up holding her, and no doubt they wound up on his couch. She got a high B from his class, in spite of missing half the seminars. She was young, beautiful, vulnerable, and he was fifty-one years old with a very ill wife who smelled bad and kept the house like a tomb. He was equally vulnerable, no doubt."

Frank was shaking his head, but she ignored that and continued. "So that night, the dancing stopped. No pun intended. Elders told Lucy good-night and left. Aaronson and his date and the other woman had left earlier and Lucy went out to the deck to get some fresh air. Amy had already gone out to the grass under the tree. And Elders, at home, not wanting to go inside that medicinal-smelling crypt, sat on his own patio and fantasized about the beautiful Jill, vivacious and manic that night, and all his. Then he overheard the incident on the deck with Robert and David, and Elders knew that he had been taken as much as Robert. Whether he took the gloves or they were in his car doesn't really matter—he had them. Either he beat Jill to her apartment and waited, or he followed her. If he tried to talk to her, no doubt, she would have been as harsh with him as she had been with Robert, and he killed her."

When Frank looked as if he wanted to interrupt, she held up

her hand. "Wait. No one else knew about the key, and that's what Robert was interested in finally. Who tipped off the police about the key? Only another observer of that scene on the deck could have known. That's what he learned from the old police file. He wrote *Key* on the sheet of paper and filled in where he knew people had been, and he left room for the patio in Elders's yard. He had not yet filled in the lines and walls, or the patio with Elders on it when he was interrupted. It's eight feet from the end of the deck to the hedge, another two or three feet, and the patio begins, with a table and chairs right there. He'd have been about as close as Amy was, and closer than Lucy. He could have heard it all."

"Christ on a mountain, Bobby! You can't accuse a man based on nothing!"

"Fast forward," she said, again ignoring his protest. "He didn't know Robert had that old file until that Sunday night when he ate with Chloe and Robert. Chloe left while they were still eating, and something was said that made Elders realize that Robert was going to pursue it, find out who had tipped off the police about the key, and that Robert would decide it had to have been him. The grade, the way Elders watched Jill the night of the party, a lot of little things that he had seen and paid no attention to would have coalesced, and then the business of the key and the tip. He said Robert was a good prosecutor, remember. But even more than that rationale, David had come back. All the old hurt and feeling of betrayal, or whatever Elders felt about it, was surfacing again, and here was Robert, the man who had slept with the woman he had thought was his, had paid to sleep with her. Elders could have gotten the gun that evening without any trouble. He had the run of the house, and knew about it. He did get it, and he used it. And again tried to frame David, by telling the police the story he made up."

Frank had subsided, and was leaning back in his chair simply watching and listening, with such a look of skepticism that it was almost withering.

"I know," she said. "Not an iota of proof. But there could be damning evidence, Dad. He ambushed David, tried to kill him, assuming his death would finish the cycle, wipe the slate, close the case with David the accepted killer, and all three of them dead and gone. The three who had made a fool of him."

"What evidence?" Frank got in when she paused this time.

"Mrs. Elders ended up in a wheelchair, but she had used a walker, and before that, had she used a heavy walking stick? It seems a reasonable assumption, with that kind of progression. If she used a stick, it would have been a heavy one. She was very heavy, overweight. Is that walking stick still in the house? If it is, there could be traces of hair and blood. And will his shoes still have traces of David's blood? He might have thought he cleaned them, but you know how hard it is to really clean it off all the way. And shoes, all the seams in the upper parts, the shoelaces? If those shoes are still there, they'll have traces of blood. He's so sure of himself, I doubt he gave a thought to getting rid of the shoes or the walking stick. I doubt that he ever gets rid of anything."

She drank her coffee while Frank thought about it, and she fully understood his doubts, and knew how difficult it would be to convince anyone of the truth of her theory. But there had to be a way to demonstrate that truth.

"I keep remembering how many times you said Elders was jealous of David, and I think he was for the reason you thought, but also because he still must believe that David and Jill were lovers. The real story about the key was never made public, and who would have told him? So, unless Robert did, he probably still thinks it. And I also remember how many times you've said in the past that once a person has killed someone, it seems easier to do it again." She sighed deeply.

Very quietly she then said, "Dad, I believe he's insanely jealous of David and always was. But now, if he's fixed his sights on Lucy McCrutchen, and if he thinks you're competing, and if he thinks that her eventual brush-off is because of you, I think she could be in danger. And so could you—the final solution. Murder gets easier."

31

"Exhibit one," Barbara said, back in her own office. She had cleared the table, stacked papers in a precarious pile and kept the few that had been on the sofa. She pointed to the topmost one as she spoke. "A syllabus from her statistics class, dates when various assignments were due, papers, quizzes, whatever. She was checking them off as she did them, and it was okay until March, then nothing, until new dates were penciled in and eventually checked off. March thirteenth, extended to May first. It's like that for all of her other classes. All checked off eventually except history. Elders's class, same thing until March, new dates penciled in, but only two check marks. Look at the list of books he assigned her, eleven in all, with papers due in two weeks. And a character out of history to defend. She couldn't do it."

Frank studied the papers, put them down silently and waited.

"Exhibit two," she said. "Robert McCrutchen's curious drawing." This time she put the sheet of paper with x's on the table, and beside it another sheet with the same x's, but with some additions. "I finished it the way Amy finished hers, filling in the blank spaces, the end of the deck, yard, and so on. Amy allowed for her mother and her own positions, and Robert allowed for the eight-foot space from the end of the deck to the hedge, and beyond to the table and chairs, and another x." With the new additions, the whole was neatly centered, exactly as Amy's had been centered when finished.

"He allowed space to finish it," Barbara said, "but he didn't get a chance. He knew, Dad. That's what that means. He knew Elders heard it all."

She watched Frank study the new drawing for a long time, put it down and stare into space for what seemed another long time.

"No one knew the truth about the key except the ones involved in the apartment business," she said when he turned his gaze back to her, "and Jill didn't even have it until she got to the party and David gave it to her. Robert saw that, and Elders heard about it when they had the confrontation on the deck. Robert would have reasoned that Elders was the one who tipped off the police. Robert had experience as a prosecutor. He knew to what lengths Jill had gone to make twenty-five dollars, and I have no doubt he would have guessed how far she had gone to make her grades. She said he disgusted her, they all disgusted her. Probably neither he nor Elders took that to mean she was a lesbian, any more than Bailey did, but rather that she had used other men either for money or for grades. He would have put the pieces together. He knew she missed half the seminars, but she graduated and kept her scholarship. He had known Elders all his life and knew he was strict, one who set the rules and followed them."

"You can't make the case," Frank said quietly. "All he has to do is deny that he sat on the patio that night, and claim that Jill

Storey made her oral report to his satisfaction and handed in the various papers. It isn't up to him to explain why she didn't keep the notes or copies with her other papers. She could have lost them, or tossed them. He'll be seen as a gentleman in his seventies, a respectable, retired professor without a blemish on his reputation, and you'll be defending a man seen as godless and perhaps anti-American. It won't even be a contest."

"I know. That's why I want to start with the shoes and the walking stick."

"Have you figured out your next step?"

She nodded. "I intend to serve him with a subpoena to appear as a defense witness. I expect him to protest, since he's already on the D.A.'s list as a prosecution witness. I'll explain to him that as a hostile defense witness he'll have to answer questions that haven't come up in his previous testimony."

Baiting the tiger, Frank thought, always a dangerous game to play. He said, "No judge is going to permit a fishing expedition in order for you to investigate a possible alternative explanation in the course of a trial. An accusation against Elders in public without a shred of corroboration will be considered no more than a smear, a desperate ploy to save your client. The judge will toss it and most likely admonish you."

She nodded. "I know. A subpoena is my opening gambit. We'll go on from there."

She stood and stretched. "You should go on home. It's late. I'm going to put my things away here and head out. Thanks for dinner."

He got up and they went to the outer office where he gathered his basket and the dishes. "Remember, dinner tomorrow night. Fresh halibut." At the outer door, he paused and said, "When you figure out your next move, let me in on it."

After she closed and locked the door behind him, she smiled

ruefully. Canny old man, he knew she was groping in the dark and had no next move planned yet. But, she also thought in satisfaction, for the first time this case felt right. It felt exactly right. The shoes fit.

On Friday Barbara told Maria that if Elders called, to tell him she was tied up and would call back when she had time. "Let me know if he does, and when," she added. She looked in on Shelley, who was on the phone. "When you're done, come on back," she said, waved and went on to her own office.

At her desk she placed a call to Bailey. "Something for you," she said. "When you have a few minutes, no rush, but today sometime." He said half an hour. Next she called Frank. "Want to drop in? Bailey's coming in half an hour." He said he would be there. Satisfied, she considered the next day or two. With the trial scheduled for two weeks from Tuesday, it would be tight, but not impossible. She crossed her fingers. Not impossible.

Shelley tapped on her door, then entered. "Something for me to do?" she asked hopefully.

"Yes, indeed. Might not be possible, but go through the motions at least." She gave her the list of books Elders had assigned to Jill Storey. "As I said, it might be an impossible task, but I'd like to know how many of these are available in the U of O library or the public library, if they were available twenty-two years ago, how many would be interlibrary loans, and to make a miracle complete, how many of them Jill Storey actually checked out."

Shelley glanced over the list and nodded, but she looked doubtful. "If they even have that on record, it might be hard to get very soon."

"I know, and it might not be possible at all, but I want to be able to say we're checking. Don't ask to borrow any of them, just find out if they're available. How many copies they have might be good to know, also." She motioned toward the easy chairs. "Have a seat. I'll bring you up-to-date while I'm waiting for Bailey and Dad."

Shelley's eyes shone with excitement. "You have something!"

"Maybe," Barbara said.

Although Bailey looked like a bum who had long since pawned his watch, he managed always to be on time, and he always delivered. His two saving graces, Barbara thought as she greeted him that day. Frank had already arrived.

They arranged themselves around the low table, helped themselves to coffee, and she began by filling in her conclusions about Elders. Bailey raised his eyebrows but offered no comment.

"Tomorrow afternoon," Barbara said, "I want you to get inside his house and make a search for a heavy walking stick or something of the sort. Don't take it, just get pictures, measurements, location. And see how many hard-soled leather shoes he has and pictures of them."

"You want me to break and enter," he said. "And get shot."

"He won't be there," she said. "And he'll leave through the back door. I can't believe he'd lock it behind him just to go next door. But if he does, well, your call."

"Break and enter," he said lugubriously.

"Don't get caught," she said. "This is what I'm planning. I want to take Dad over to the McCrutchen house tomorrow. Elders is sure to pop in. He's jealous of Dad, thinks he's horning in on his territory, and he always shows up when we do. Be where you can see him go around the hedge from his place. I'll be sure to keep him for at least fifteen minutes, and I'll signal when you have to skedaddle. If you find the stick and get out before I call, you call me."

Bailey looked decidedly unhappy. "Broad daylight, neighbors out and about. Illegal entry. Does he have a dog?"

"No dog. No cat. If he has goldfish, they're not likely to yell for help. Take a clipboard and a flashlight. They'll get you entry anywhere without a question."

He scowled at her. "Barbara, don't tell me how to run my business. Okay?"

She grinned. "Right."

They discussed it for several more minutes, and after Bailey and Shelley left, Frank said, "Then what?"

"If Bailey finds what I think he will, I want to get Elders here in the office on Monday, and have Dressler in Shelley's office listening to us. That attack on David was Dressler's assault case. I think I can interest him in resolving it." She eyed him speculatively. "Any idea what kind of excuse we can come up with to go back to the house?"

"I'll think of something," Frank said, but it was quite apparent that he was as unhappy as Bailey about the day shaping up.

Elders called at two and again at a few minutes past four. Each time Maria gave him the same message that Barbara was tied up and would return his calls as soon as possible.

"At five put on the voice mail," Barbara said when Maria told her about the second call. The recording stated that the office was closed for the weekend and office hours would resume on Monday at eight in the morning. "Please call back," Barbara said mockingly. "Your call is very important to us." Maria giggled.

Shelley came in at four-thirty. "A few things," she said, sitting on the sofa. "One of the books is up at Oregon State, one is in Princeton and one in the University of Pennsylvania. It would take three weeks to get the out-of-state books, if you're lucky. Longer than that twenty-two years ago. Two copies of two of them, one of each of the others at the U of O, one at the public library. If someone else had checked out a book or two, it could have been weeks before it was returned. If there's a record of who checked out what that long ago, no one today seems to know where it would be. They doubt it exists at all. I made a copy of that list and put down where each one of the books is." She put the list on the table.

"Good girl," Barbara said. "That son of a bitch assigned those books knowing Jill couldn't get them in time to make a report in a couple of weeks. Sadistic bastard."

"You think he did it deliberately, don't you?"

Barbara nodded. "I do. Are you going to be home on Sunday?"

"Sure. Why?"

"Darren's really pleased that David's started working with the red ball, some kind of milestone. He wants to see him, and give him a new set of exercises, and depending on what Bailey finds, I'll want to talk things over with you. I thought Sunday might be a good time for both, if it's convenient for you and Alex."

"You know it is. Now my news. Alex and David sent in a proposal a few weeks ago and the agents seem to think they have a very good offer coming in the next few days. They're both being so closemouthed about what they're up to, I can't stand it, but Alex is pretty happy with what his agent told him."

"I guess you're getting a touch of what Alex goes through when you're hot on a case and he's clueless about what's up. I'm amazed at how well Darren is accepting it. I think he's taking his cues from Alex. Everyone is someone's mentor these days."

"I think we both latched on to some pretty good guys," Shelley said with a soft smile.

After Shelley left, Barbara told Maria to go home. "I don't want anyone on hand in case Elders decides to come calling. I'll leave as soon as I clear my desk."

Then, straightening up in her office, thinking of Shelley's words, she thought that there were times when she envied Shelley. It didn't bother her at all that she did little or nothing about being a conventional good wife, one who planned the meals, did the shopping, the many things that girls were taught came with their role in life. And Alex was one of the happiest men Barbara knew.

She stopped shuffling papers to put away and said under her breath, "I'll make it up to Darren later." She couldn't have said exactly what she would make up since he was to all appearances also a very happy man. But he deserved more from her, she felt, and there it was again, a wave of guilt that she seemed unable to shed.

Briskly, she finished putting things away. Halibut at her father's house, leftovers for home, no doubt. Sunday dinner with him, and more leftovers. Four very good meals in the offing to counter the sketchy meals they had been having, with Darren working late most days, Todd with a heavy load of homework, and Barbara a kitchen klutz.

"I'll learn to cook more dishes," she said vehemently. "After this case is over and done with."

If she couldn't be guilt-free, then she had to learn to cook at the very least. Even as she mouthed the words, she suspected she was either kidding herself or lying.

32

On Saturday morning Barbara called David. "You said Darren would be pleased with your progress, and were you ever right! He wants to see you tomorrow. Game?"

"Okay," he said. "I'll be here."

"Good. Also, is it okay if we bring Amy with us? I haven't asked her yet, so it's up to you."

There was a long pause. "Barbara, why are you doing this? Pushing her on me, like this. You know as well as I do that it's no good, and I suspect you could come up with the same reasons I have."

"Maybe she'll reach that same decision in time, but I can't make it for her. Is it okay?"

After another pause he said, "Sure, why not," and hung up.

Good old David, she thought, disconnecting. Nothing more to say, hang up.

She picked up Frank at twenty minutes before two, and was

surprised when he appeared with three pieces of dowel in his hand. "Your version of a heavy walking stick?" she asked.

He frowned. "My reason for going over there today."

She shrugged and they went out to her car. As she drove she said, "Dad, is there something out in the back of her yard that you simply have to look at? Her petunias or something?"

His frown deepened. "I'll bait him," he said. "Or whistle for him, or stand on my head and get his attention."

She grinned. "You and Lucy could dance a polka out there."

"As Bailey said, don't tell me how to run my business," he said, not quite snapping at her, but close.

She drove the rest of the way silently, and he did not say another word.

Amy opened the door for them and examined Barbara's face anxiously. "Anything new?"

"Maybe," Barbara said. "Working on it."

"Mother's in the family room. Come on back," Amy said.

Although Lucy appeared pleased to see them, there was also an underlying strain on her face, and shadows beneath her eyes. She looked at the dowel lengths curiously.

"This is what I mentioned on the phone," Frank said. "Something that's been bothering me. You have too little security here, and this is the least you can do. What I'd really recommend is for you to bring in a security firm and let them install a complete system, but this is a start. One for each of the sliding doors."

The outside door was closed that day, and he put one of the dowels in the track and demonstrated that the door could not be opened with it in place. She had hung drapes, he noticed, and that was a good move, if she remembered to close them in the evening when an outsider would be invisible, and everyone inside more or less under a spotlight.

"We've never felt unsafe here," Lucy said in a low voice.

"Times change," Frank said. "Is the apartment open? I'll put one in there, and the last one's for the kitchen door."

"I'll open it for you," Lucy said, and they walked out.

As soon as they left the room, Amy said, "Barbara, what's going on with David? He seemed different when we had lunch the other day."

"You can ask him tomorrow," Barbara said. "Darren wants to see him, and we'll go out again. You're invited. Another hike in the woods, a little time for a private talk, whatever. One o'clock? Are you up for it?"

"God, yes! If he'll talk about whatever it is. Probably he won't though." She looked and sounded dismal. "Is there anything I can do to help? Anything?"

"If I think of anything, I'll certainly let you know," Barbara said. "Promise." She looked past Amy, out the glass door, and nodded toward it. "Look at them." Lucy and Frank had left by the kitchen door, and were walking toward the flower border. "Get two gardeners together and that's what happens, out to inspect the petunias or something."

"She's showing off her chrysanthemums," Amy said, clearly not interested in what they were doing. "Barbara, is Nick Aaronson involved in some way?"

Barbara looked at her curiously. "Why do you ask?"

Amy began to study her hands, as if they were foreign to her. "First, tell me. Is he?"

"I don't think so, except for the fact that he lied in his statement to the police. I don't know why he did that." She saw Elders join Frank and Lucy, and said, "You were right about Dr. Elders, I guess. He's ever alert, isn't he? Must have had Boy Scout training." She glanced at her watch, twenty minutes past two. Elders was walking toward the house.

Amy said, "Let's go to the study for a minute."

"In a second. I think he wants to come in." Barbara went to remove the dowel as Dr. Elders tried to open the door. "Good afternoon," she said as he entered.

He smiled and said good-afternoon, then asked, "Did you receive my messages yesterday? You didn't return my calls."

"I know. My apologies, it was a very busy day for me."

"I'd like a word with you," he said with a significant glance at Amy.

"Oh? We were in the middle of something. I don't think it will be long. We can probably finish in a minute or two. In the study?" she said to Amy. To Elders she added, "I'll be right back."

She followed Amy to the study and closed the door after them. "Now, what's on your mind?"

Amy looked miserable. "I guess it wouldn't explain why Nick Aaronson lied about the night of the party," she said hesitantly. "I think he and Chloe had an affair, recently, not back then. I guess that wouldn't make any difference, would it?"

"You think so, or you know so?" Barbara asked.

"I know," she said stiffly.

"Did you ever work jigsaw puzzles?" Barbara asked after a moment. At Amy's nod, she said, "You know how it stays just a thousand pieces scattered on a table for a long time, then piece by piece it begins to represent something. That's another piece, and I don't know what it means, or if it makes a difference or even if it belongs in this puzzle. But it's another piece and until you have them all, and they're all in place, the puzzle is just a bunch of disconnected bits and pieces. Thanks for telling me. I'll have to give it some thought."

"If it doesn't fit anywhere," Amy said in a low voice, "can you put it out of mind? You know, keep it confidential?"

Barbara nodded. "It isn't my secret to tell. There's no reason for me to divulge it if it doesn't belong in the puzzle I'm working with."

"Thanks," Amy said. "I guess Dr. Elders is expecting you back in the family room. I'll just hang out in here."

Barbara walked through the hall back toward the family room and paused there in the doorway. At the far end, Elders was standing at the sliding door, hands clasped behind his back, gazing out. She had no doubt that he was watching Frank and Lucy. She took a few steps into the room and said, "I'm very sorry to keep you waiting. Shall we sit in here and talk?"

Elders spun around as if startled. "Oh, good. No problem at all waiting for a minute or two. In here is fine. You see, I think there's been a mistake. I was served with a subpoena for some mysterious reason."

Barbara sat on the sofa and he took a chair near her. He was smiling genially.

"It wasn't a mistake," she said. "Have you ever participated in a criminal trial?"

"Not exactly my field," he said. He sounded as though the very idea was distasteful.

"Of course not. Few people have, and fewer know how the process works, I imagine. Let me explain. As a prosecution witness you will be asked questions that deal with the statements you already made to the investigators. Then, after Mr. McNulty is finished, the defense will be allowed to examine those same statements, ask for more explanation, for more in-depth answers, whatever seems appropriate. At that time the defense attorney is not allowed to introduce any material not already testified to. And that sometimes can present a problem if the defense has reason to ask questions the prosecution has not already referred to. Do you follow that?"

"But it seems the prosecutor will know what must be revealed."

"To his satisfaction," Barbara said agreeably. "But that might not be to the satisfaction of the defense attorney. Anyway, that part is called the cross-examination, simply referring to what's gone before. Then the prosecution can have a redirect examination to bring out the points he wants to make once more, after which the witness is dismissed. That's where the subpoena comes in. It allows the defense attorney to recall the witness when the defense is presenting its case. As a defense witness, especially one designated as a hostile defense witness, you may be asked questions not already referred to in order to reveal to the jury new facts that are sometimes contradictory to what has already been stated."

"Hostile defense witness? I have no hostility toward you or the defense team."

"But you may have information that you would prefer not to discuss, Dr. Elders." Her cell phone rang and she glanced at her watch again. Two-forty. "Excuse me," she said, and answered the call.

"Done," Bailey said. "See you at the old man's house."

"Thank you very much," she said. "Of course, I'll get to it immediately." She stood. "I'm terribly sorry," she said to Elders. "That's how it's been the past few days, one thing after another."

"Ms. Holloway, I deserve a better answer than you've given me. What kinds of questions do you propose to ask? What's on your mind? Why do you think I may have more information than my statements indicate?"

"Dr. Elders, if it would be possible for you to come to the office on Monday, I'll make certain to leave time open for you. Let's say at two in the afternoon? I'll answer your questions then, but I really must leave now."

His lips were a tight line as he regarded her. He nodded. "I'll be there at two, and I certainly do expect some real answers. This is outrageous. To label me a hostile witness, when I'm doing all I can to cooperate with all concerned in this unfortunate business."

Barbara nodded and went to the door. Frank and Lucy were not in sight. She walked out to the deck and back inside through the kitchen door to find her father and Lucy at a small table looking at a catalog.

"Dad, I'm sorry to interrupt, but I have to leave now. The call I was expecting just came through."

Frank looked genuinely regretful as he stood and apologized to Lucy. "And I'm sorry," he said. "You're right, that is a wonderful catalog. Thanks for showing it to me. I'll order a copy right away. Things in there I never saw for sale before. I may end up redoing a whole section of my own garden. Ah, well, a garden is never done."

In the car a minute later Barbara said, "Bailey has something. He'll be at the house."

Frank told her to slow down, and they both remained silent until she pulled into his driveway. Bailey was sitting in his old Dodge in the driveway. Barbara groaned. A car like that parked on the McCrutchens' street in a nice residential section?

"Why not go with a marching band?" she grumbled as they entered Frank's house.

"Barbara, don't give me a hard time. Okay? I parked down near Franklin and walked in by way of the alley, lined with garbage cans, naturally, and wide-open."

"Did you find it?" she asked.

"Sure. That place gave me the creeps. It looked as if the woman kicked, and he closed her door and never once opened it again. Her clothes in the closet, stuff in drawers, even a bad smell, all right there. Creepy."

"And?"

"There's a double garage, half-used for storage, and in it a walking stick, a walker, and a wheelchair all lined up, ready to go. He has two pairs of leather shoes."

"And a pair on his feet," she said. "Good job. Pictures?"

Bailey scowled. "Pictures, measurements, the works. They're on the digital. Want to see them, or wait for prints?"

"As long as you have them, that's good enough. I'll want prints. Tell me about the cane."

"Heavy oak, not a regular cane, no crook, or anything like it. A straight stick, like an English walking stick or something. It would do the job."

"Great. Tell me something. How do I fix a phone to be a speaker phone and at the same time not allow any noticeable sound to come back through it?"

"Where?" Bailey asked.

"My office. I'll want it Monday afternoon."

He nodded. "Monday morning I'll have a look."

"Good enough," she said. "And that was good work today. You didn't get caught, or shot at or anything. It must have been boring."

He gave her a murderous look.

33

The day was brisk and sunny, but there was a smell of marine air blowing in. Rain had moved in at the coast, damping the forest fires that had ravaged the Coast Range for the past three or four weeks. Not yet, Barbara thought, sniffing the cool air, but soon. A front would come through, bring rain, and the long wet season would begin. She looked forward to it.

"For our hike," she said to Alex, "let's go back to the surprise you led us to last year. You know the one I mean?"

He nodded but looked dubious. "Not much to see right now."

"That's why I'd like to go," she said.

The woods were so dry the ferns rustled like paper in the breeze blowing through them, and the lichen looked faded and dusty. Ground that had been spongy earlier in the season crunched underfoot and Barbara felt almost as if she could hear whispers in the rustling fern fronds, that if her hearing were more acute, she might hear the words, *Soon. Soon the rain will come. Soon.*

Alex led the way to where a waterfall had appeared the year before, but that day, at the end of the dry summer and fall, there was no water, not even a trace, only an outcropping of rocks, a ledge, a dry streambed with a rocky bottom, obviously a water channel cut into the mountainside, fringed by dispirited brambles and salmonberries with dried fruits that looked like fired stones.

"We'll come back after a few good rains," Barbara said when David looked at her in puzzlement. "When we come back, you'll see one of nature's gifts." She looked at the others. "I'd like a word with David. We'll catch up in a minute." They moved out of earshot, and she said, "You asked what I'd decide in a reversal of positions. I have an answer today that I couldn't give you before—I'd hang in there and wait."

"Now you'll tell me there's light at the end of the tunnel," he said.

"Two weeks ago, even last week I couldn't *find* the tunnel. Now I have it fixed in my sight. Don't press for more, please. And I won't say trust me. I'm too suspicious to ever trust anyone who feels the need to say that. I suspect you are also."

He studied her face. "For now. But, Barbara, time is closing in. I have a calendar, you know."

She nodded. "That's all I'm asking. For now. And when we all come back to this spot, you'll see what I think of as a miracle. You'll see. Let's catch up to the others."

When they returned to town later, Darren drove to the house for Amy to get her car. They didn't go in, since he had to go to Springfield to collect Todd, who was at his mother's house for the weekend.

Amy hesitated at the car door. "I'm grateful, Barbara. Whatever you said to David must have been something good. He was so down last week, but I think you gave him hope. Thanks."

They watched her get in her car and leave. Then Darren shifted gears to back out of the driveway.

"On to Dad's house," Barbara said. "Are you okay?"

"Fine," Darren said, but he looked tired. "The two geniuses both flunked, by the way. Just as I thought they would. We'll go on from there."

He would write his letter to the major, with threats, reprisals, repercussions to follow, no doubt swiftly. She put her hand on his thigh as he drove to Frank's house. He covered her hand with his.

Darren dropped her off at Frank's house and left. In the kitchen, while Frank did whatever he was doing at the counter, she said, "David has no intention of being on hand for a trial. He's aware of the odds, and he's concerned that too many people will be hurt badly if they have to testify. Lucy and Amy, both directly, and Olga, although absent, will also suffer as will her daughter. He knows that, and he isn't willing to let it happen for what he sees as a lost cause."

Frank nodded, his face grim as he turned toward her. "I know," he said. "Do you have a time line on him?"

"No. And he isn't likely to tell us. But, Dad, I don't see any way out of this unless I take a chance. I know it's a gamble. Elders has had since Friday to worry about what I'm up to and how much incriminating evidence I might have found. I want to push him to the limit, and I don't know how he'll spring if he thinks it's over. He could try to bluff it out."

"Or do something else," Frank said, finishing her thought.

"It's what that something else could be that worries me," she said. "He's an unknown factor."

Monday morning Bailey arrived with two telephones in his old duffel bag. "Easier to do it this way," he said, bringing them out. "They're fixed and ready to go. We'll put your phone and Shelley's in the closet for now and I'll show you how to use these. Kid stuff."

As it turned out, it *was* kid stuff. When he told her to try it, she asked Maria to buzz her. "Thanks," she said when she answered. "Please hold the calls for now." She pushed a button when she hung up. "Testing, just testing," Barbara said. "Come to the door and wave if you're receiving." A moment later Shelley waved to her at the doorway, and she pushed the same button again, restoring the phone to normal usage. They put the other phones in her closet and she was ready for Elders.

"Bailey, will you be around, in reach later today?" she asked.

"I can be. To do what? More breaking and entering?"

"I don't know. Not yet. Just be around, in case. Okay?"

He shrugged. "Here?"

"Maybe in Danny's Juice Bar. I may want you to tag along behind Elders when he leaves, not sure yet."

Bailey nodded, as morose as usual, but he would be there and be ready. She murmured her thanks and watched him amble out.

As soon as he was gone she called Lieutenant Dressler. "I have a lead for you in the David Etheridge assault," she said. "It's a big one, good as gold."

"Come on over," he said. "I'm in the office."

"I can't. Too many people dropping in today. Can you make it over here around two, a few minutes later? I won't take much of your time."

He grumbled but said he'd be there, and she leaned back in her chair. Stage set for Act One, she thought, and hoped this would turn out to be a one-act play.

Elders was prompt, and he was not a happy man, frowning and thin lipped. He also looked tired, as if he needed a bit more sleep. When Barbara admitted him to her own office, both Frank and Shelley were out of sight, Shelley's door closed.

"Please," she said, indicating one of the clients' chairs. She went behind her desk to take her own chair, ignoring his glance toward the comfortable seating arrangement on the other side of the room. Her desk was covered with papers. She shuffled a few of them together and put them inside a folder, then looked across at him.

"I told you what to expect as a defense witness," she said. "You'll have to hold yourself in readiness to be recalled to the stand and I'll do the direct examination this time."

"Yes, yes," he said sharply. "I find this totally outrageous and demand to know what you think you can gain, since I'll already have testified to what little I know of this business."

"There will be areas that have not yet been touched on," she said. "Of course, my function is totally different from that of the prosecution. As in most trials each side has a strong belief in the rightness of the side being represented. I know David Etheridge did not murder Jill Storey, Robert McCrutchen or anyone else, and I'll be working to convince a jury of my conviction. I don't have to prove anything, but simply to give them a plausible alternative explanation as to what happened, one that they find as acceptable as the case the prosecution presents. A reasonable doubt is all that's required."

"Just get on with it," he snapped. "What areas are you talking about?"

Her phone buzzed and she lifted the receiver to hear Maria say her party had arrived. "Thank you," she said. "I'll get to it right away. Please hold all calls for now." She replaced the receiver and pushed the button.

"Sorry," she said. "There won't be any more interruptions. One of the areas I'll explore is the matter of Jill Storey's final grades. She was quite ill that spring, and she met with her instructors to get an extension of time to complete her classes. In every case such an extension was granted, and she completed the assignments satisfactorily, except for yours. There is no indication that she completed her work for your seminars. Missing a seminar was an automatic reduction of a grade by fifteen percent, and she missed four. Automatic failure. Also, for her extension you assigned her a number of books to read, and several of them were not available locally, and would have arrived weeks too late for her to read and have enough time to write a comprehensive report. Another failure. A large part of the grade, according to your syllabus, was to assume the role of a historical figure and defend whatever position that character took in the late eighteenth or early nineteenth century. She never did that, apparently. Yet she was given a grade B for the class, ensuring that she would graduate and maintain a high enough grade average to keep a valuable scholarship." She looked at him and waited for a response.

"An instructor has a great deal of discretion," he said icily. "The syllabus is a general outline of what to expect. No one is forced to stick to it in extenuating circumstances."

"I see," Barbara said. "So you can explain exactly what she did to receive that grade. Very well. Another area I'll explore is your statement, repeated several times, that she was both promiscuous and a prostitute. I have not been able to verify that or find another person who can offer any substantiation whatsoever."

"It was common knowledge," he snapped.

"So you claimed. But if it was common knowledge surely there is someone who can verify it. Not her classmates, her roommate, coworkers, friends, no one except you has made such a statement. Can you provide any corroboration?"

"Robert told me," he said.

"But since he's dead, I'm afraid that still won't satisfy the need for substantiation. It's simply hearsay." She opened the file on her desk and drew out the sheet of paper Robert had drawn. "Do you recognize this? It was under Robert McCrutchen's hand when he was found dead."

Elders glanced at it, shook his head. "He played tic-tac-toe or something." He was watchful, and at the same time looked disdainful and impatient.

"I don't think so. See, we came across this one, also." It was the schematic she had filled in, including an *x* on Elders's patio. "Quite apparently Robert McCrutchen was trying to determine who made anonymous calls first to the press, then to the police, to say that Jill Storey had the key to David's apartment."

Elders stared at it without moving for several seconds, then said, "That doesn't mean a thing." His expression did not change, and if he was alarmed, nothing he did revealed it.

"I think it does. You were so hot from all that dancing. You were very fond of dancing in those days, I understand, and you were very actively dancing the night of the party. Jill was vivacious and beautiful, wasn't she, Dr. Elders? A pleasure to dance with, a pleasure to watch. When the music stopped, you went home, but you didn't go inside your refrigerated house. You lingered on the patio to cool down. No doubt, you were nearly as hyper as the young people, invigorated, stimulated, too keyed up to go inside, go to bed. You needed a little time first. And you heard what happened on the deck. That's when you heard about the key to David's apartment, isn't it? Why didn't you admit it then? Why the anonymous calls instead of simply telling what you had heard?"

"I don't know what you're talking about," he said. "The newspaper had an article that said she had his key. Obviously she was sleeping with him, living with him."

Barbara shook her head. "That didn't come from the police, the official source. It was a rumor, a tip from an anonymous caller. The police satisfied themselves about the key and never made such a claim, because it was a lie, easily proved as such. But anyone who simply heard what was said on the deck might well have believed it. You believed it."

"I tell you, Robert was my source. He told me what happened out there. David was insanely jealous, and thought Robert was flirting with Jill. He attacked Robert because Jill Storey was his lover. That's why she had his key."

"Strange that Robert would lie about it," she said. "You see, there were two other eyewitnesses to that scene, both as reputable as you are, and they know exactly what was said, what happened. And it was not that."

"That's a damn lie! No witnesses were out there!"

"What they will testify to is that Jill did sleep with Robert, and he gave her money. She was desperate for her rent. And she was equally desperate to make her grades. I ask you again, how will you account for the B grade you gave her for a course she did not complete?"

"You're accusing me of sleeping with her!"

"Of course, I am. She was desperate, beautiful, no doubt weeping, and you were also desperate, weren't you? A wife incurably ill, and a beautiful young woman willing to do anything to stay in school. Did she promise more than she gave you? Were you expecting repeat visits? Then you found out you were not the only one, and that she had David's key. You knew you had been made a fool of, used, and that you and Robert both disgusted her. That's the gist of my direct examination, Dr. Elders."

"You can't prove a word of this," he said tightly. "It's all a fabrication."

"As I said before, I don't have to prove it, merely to give the jury an alternative explanation as to what happened to Jill Storey. And I will do that, with the implication that you either followed her that night, or perhaps you got there first and waited for her, and she gave you the same curt dismissal she had given Robert. She didn't need either of you anymore."

"It will be seen as nothing but a filthy insinuation without merit." He had become pale as she spoke, and his voice was almost tremulous. He was leaning forward, both hands clutching the armrests of his chair.

"Perhaps. But understand, I won't stop there. I'll also imply that you murdered Robert McCrutchen because he realized that you had witnessed that confrontation on the deck and knew about the key. With his background experience as a prosecutor, he would have put the pieces together. He would have known that all the attitudes you attributed to David were simple projections of your own jealousy, possessiveness, suspicion, watchfulness. He would have recalled how you watched her the night of the party, how you hovered over her, and he would have guessed how she got that B grade. It may be even more telling that they were both here again, Robert and David, one who had slept with her, and the other who you thought was her lover, both back there, in that house. Your humiliation and pain surfaced again. They had to be punished, didn't they? You shot Robert and you attacked David and tried to kill him. The three who had made your life a torment, the woman who had betrayed and used you, the two men she had slept with. All punished. That's the extent of the implications that will certainly be clear to everyone by the time I finish my examination of you under oath, Dr. Elders."

He jumped up, ashen faced, a tic in his jaw working, hands clenched. "Yes! I heard them on the deck! She was a filthy whore! Using men! Throwing them aside like dirt when she was finished with them. But you can't prove a thing. There's no proof."

"Possibly the police will want a search warrant to look for

evidence. Perhaps the weapon used to attack David. Possibly they will want to interview other former students, find out if you ever showed leniency to anyone besides Jill. I understand that your reputation was that of a strict instructor who paid close attention to the syllabus and was unyielding when students broke any rules. Dr. Elders, the jury will find the implications compelling. And very likely the police will want to ask you some of those same questions in a more private setting, not in open court."

"I'm going to talk to my lawyer. We'll sue you, destroy you and everyone associated with you! You're not going to get away with this!" he shouted.

"I suggest you make it a defense attorney, Dr. Elders," Barbara said.

He wheeled about and hurried to the door in a stiff and lurching gait. As soon as he was out of the office, Barbara pushed the button on her phone, then hit her cell-phone speed dial for Bailey.

"He's leaving. Keep on him, and don't let him toss a stick into the river. Or set it on fire."

"Jeez," Bailey said, and disconnected.

Her door flew open and Frank and Lt. Dressler stormed in with Shelley close behind. "He called for backup," Frank said, motioning toward the lieutenant, "but they could be too late."

"Bailey's on it," she said. "You heard it all?"

"We heard enough," Dressler said angrily. "You have some explaining to do. You practically told him to get out of here and destroy incriminating evidence, if there is any!"

"Get your guys to his house before he gets there," she said. "He wasn't giving an inch until the very end. He needed a stronger shove."

Dressler already had his cell phone in his hand. "I'll be back," he said, and stepped out of the office.

Frank, equally angry, snapped, "I'm going to Lucy's house."
He pushed past Dressler and out.

Barbara stood, ready to follow him, and Dressler stepped into
the doorway, blocking it. "You stay right where you are!" he
ordered.

34

Frank arrived at Lucy's driveway in time to see Bailey pulling in behind Elders's car next door. Bailey stopped inches away from Elders's rear bumper. Frank stopped his own car, got out, and hurried across the lawn just as the garage door opened and Elders emerged, carrying a heavy walking stick.

"Get that car out of my way," he yelled at Bailey, brandishing the stick.

"Drop it, Elders," Frank said as he drew near. "It's over. Put the stick down." He motioned Bailey to stay back, and saw that Bailey had his handgun out, not pointed, but hanging down toward the ground.

"You!" Elders cried, looking at Frank. "You turned her against me! It's your fault!" He took a step toward Frank.

"Put the stick down!" Bailey said, and he raised the gun. "Just put it down on the driveway and move back from it."

Frank shook his head at Bailey and said in a quiet voice,

"Elders, we know all about it. It's really over. Give me the stick and let's talk." He moved forward a step, another, and Elders stood fixed in place. "We know you were swept away by that beautiful girl weeping in your office. A sick wife at home, a man in his prime, you lost control. It happens to men in their prime, doesn't it?" His voice was low, even soothing, as he continued to move toward Elders with a slow, measured pace. "You need to talk about it," he said, "explain how it happened, how you couldn't help yourself."

"She was so soft and small, so sweet," Elders said in a distant, hollow voice. "She smelled like flowers, leaning against me, crying. So tired of struggling, leaning against my shoulder, letting me support her, letting me help her. I just wanted to help her."

Another car pulled in behind Bailey's, and two men got out. Elders shook himself, his gaze flickered from Frank to the men and back.

"They're detectives," Frank said. "They want to talk to you."

With a cry Elders threw the stick at Frank and ran back inside the garage. The door crashed down. Frank took a deep breath, to still the curses forming.

"You might want to get inside," he said to the detectives. "He could decide to do something drastic." One of the men pulled out a cell phone as they walked toward the house. Bailey's gun was out of sight and he was leaning against his car nonchalantly.

Frank turned to go to Lucy's house, and in the yard near the hedge both Lucy and Amy were standing with shocked, disbelieving expressions.

"Do you have a key to his house?" Frank asked Lucy. "They might need it."

Lucy nodded, and all three went back to her house. When Frank came out again with the key to Elders's front door, one of the detectives was gone, he assumed, around the house to keep a watch on the back door. He handed the key to the remaining detective, who had his cell phone against his ear, and accepted the key with a nod.

"Unless you arrest me and put me in jail, I'm going after my father," Barbara said to Dressler. "He could be in danger and so could Lucy McCrutchen."

His look was bitter. "We'll both go. My car. Come on."

Neither one spoke as he drove, then pulled in at the driveway. When Barbara got out, she saw Bailey standing by his car. He jerked his thumb toward Lucy's house and she nodded.

"I'll be next door," she said to Dressler. She hurried across the lawn and by the time she reached the front door, Bailey was at her side.

"Not a peep from Elders," he said. "One guy at the back, one out here, waiting for more guys, someone in charge. Elders was moving fast. He could have had time to go straight through and out the back. You want me here, or over there?"

She bit her lip. "You'd better come on in. Are you carrying?"

He nodded and they entered together through the unlocked door. Inside, she heard voices in the family room and she and Bailey went there and stopped at the door. Lucy and Amy were side by side on the sofa, Frank in a chair close to them. "Dad, I need a word with you," Barbara said from the hall door.

He came quickly. "What's going on?"

Bailey repeated what he had told Barbara and Frank's expression turned grimmer than it had been. "Christ on a mountain," he said softly, with a swift glance at the family room. The drapes were open, the door closed but likely not locked.

"Keep an eye out back here," he said, "and we'll go out the front door. Bring up the rear."

Bailey stepped into the family room and Frank called to Lucy and Amy, "Come on, we're leaving by the front door."

They both jumped up and hurried to join him and Barbara. "What's happening?" Lucy asked. "Where's Henry?"

"I'll explain," Frank said. "Let's get out of here first."

He ushered them on ahead and they had all started down the hall toward the front door when Bailey yelled, "Behind you!" His shout was followed immediately by the sound of a shot, shockingly loud in the enclosed space. Barbara and Frank both spun around to see Bailey stagger and fall, and Elders standing in the open door to the powder room with a handgun pointed at them. Lucy screamed.

"Get in the living room," Elders rasped. "All of you, the living room." He was as pale as death and the hand holding the gun was shaking. He was holding on to the wall with his other hand.

Very quietly Frank said, "Do exactly what he says. Let's go to the living room."

Elders followed them, and inside he said, "Sit on the sofa. Not you," he said to Barbara. "Lucy, Amy, Holloway, on the sofa." They sat down, Lucy and Amy clutching each other. Elders pointed the gun at Barbara. "Go to the door and tell them to stay back. Tell them I have a gun. Then come back here. Or I'll shoot your father."

She edged past him and went to the front door and delivered his message. She saw Dressler, what looked like an army of officers, flashing red lights. It was a scene from a movie, she thought distantly.

"Tell him I'm calling your cell phone," Dressler yelled back to her. "Tell him I want to talk to him."

Behind her Elders told her to get away from the door and close it. She did as he ordered, and when she turned back toward the living room, at the far end of the hall, she saw Bailey leaning against the wall. He shook his head and she stepped into the living room.

"He's going to call my cell phone and wants to talk to you," she told Elders, back in the living room.

"We'll make a deal," he said. "Lucy, we'll make a deal. You and I will leave. They'll let us. We'll go away, just the two of us."

"If you had your own gun, why did you use Robert's?" Frank asked in an easy, conversational voice.

"I just wanted to show him what I meant. It wasn't safe to leave it in an unlocked drawer. Someone like David could walk in and pick it up. I was making a point, and I brought it back later, just to show him what I meant. He was acting crazy, making crazy accusations, abusive, threatening. Yelling about the moths. I would have closed the screen door. I forgot, but I would have closed it."

Barbara's phone chimed. "It's in my purse," she said, and Elders nodded, keeping his focus on Frank. Moving slowly and carefully, she pulled the phone from her purse and answered the call. "Dressler," she said to Elders. "The lieutenant who wants to talk to you."

His gaze was fixed on Frank unblinkingly. "You turned him against me, didn't you? The way you turned Lucy against me. She never used to lock me out. She used to smile at me and make me welcome. You turned her against me."

"Dr. Elders," Barbara said. "Lieutenant Dressler says he's willing to make a deal. He knows you care about Lucy, that you want to leave with her. He wants to talk about it."

"I warned her about you," Elders said, staring at Frank with that same, nearly hypnotic fixity.

Barbara moved closer to him, to the side away from the gun, away from the door. He didn't seem to notice until she said, "He thinks it's a good idea to let you and Lucy go away together. He'll help you." She held out the phone toward him. "He won't talk about it to me. It has to be your deal."

Finally he glanced at her. "He'll make a deal?"

"That's what he said. But only with you, not through me." She held the phone out and he reached for it. Beyond him, leaning against the door frame she could see Bailey. He was dripping blood, one arm hanging limply at his side, but he was holding his own gun. As soon as Elders reached for the phone, grasped it, she moved quickly back and away, and Bailey fired a shot. Lucy and Amy both screamed, and Frank jumped to his feet as Elders dropped his gun and fell to his knees. Barbara lunged forward to grab the gun before he could and, with it in her hand, she rolled away as Elders fell the rest of the way to the floor. He was sobbing, mixed with gasping, choking, incoherent words.

Frank reached the doorway just as Bailey slumped, and began sliding down. Frank caught him and lowered him to the floor.

An ambulance had come and gone with two patients and police officers in attendance. Frank had followed in his car to see to Bailey.

Dressler had taken statements from Lucy, Amy and Barbara, and had spoken briefly to the media horde that had appeared in record time. A shooting had occurred, an investigation was underway and no further details were yet available had been the gist of his statement. Now they were all gone.

It seemed that every working phone was chiming, buzzing, ringing, playing music. Amy disconnected hers while Barbara was still talking to Darren, reassuring him that everything was okay, she was fine, details later.

"David heard something about a shooting on the news, and he's on his way here," Amy said. She was still pale and shaken, but recovering faster than Lucy. "Is this the end of it?" Amy asked Barbara. "David's out of it?"

Barbara nodded. "There will be some formalities, but it's really over for him." Except, she added to herself, for a lawsuit against Elders for assault with intent to kill.

Amy closed her eyes hard and took several deep breaths, and Barbara's phone chimed again.

It was Frank this time. "He's all right, mad as hell and filled with dope, with a bullet in his shoulder that they'll dig out a little later. Hannah's with him. I'll come back and bring his keys for you to drive his car to the house."

Lucy sat huddled on the sofa with her arms tight about her body, very pale and pinched looking. Barbara went to sit by her. "You need something. Strong hot coffee, or a good stiff drink?"

"He must be crazy," Lucy said in a low voice.

"He flipped out, but he isn't crazy," Barbara said. "At least not in the general sense. He knew what he was doing all along and covered his tracks all the way. He was determined to frame David for both deaths, driven by jealousy and resentment, and it almost worked. Keep that in mind, it almost worked."

Amy said, "I'll make coffee. Can you tell us about it, how you knew?"

"Let's do coffee first, and wait for David. He deserves to know the truth. Dad will be back soon and we'll all talk."

They went to the kitchen, where Amy started a pot of coffee, then drew Barbara aside to ask, "Will you have to use that information I gave you? About Chloe?"

"No. I should tell you this, however. An investigation has begun to look into Nick Aaronson's deals with your brother. That could get ugly in days to come."

Amy shrugged. "After these past few months, I think we can deal with it. Thanks." She already knew exactly what she would do with the damn pictures, she thought then. Burn them and send the ashes to Chloe.

When the coffee was ready, they went out to the deck and back inside through the family-room door.

Frank arrived, followed minutes later by David. In the family room, Barbara explained what she had pieced together from statements and observation. "Those *x*'s were the solution finally," she said. "Robert wrote the word *Key* on the paper and we kept trying to make it mean key to the mystery, key to what happened, when he really meant key, a material, physical key."

"Sometimes a cigar is just a cigar," David commented.

Barbara knew her smile was little more than halfhearted, but she gave him one anyway. "I think they'll find DNA evidence on the walking stick, and on a pair of shoes, and that will really wrap it up."

Frank had been gazing at the window filled with plants. It was dark outside, making a fine black backdrop for the greenery. "Elders will talk," he said. "They'll have someone ask in a civilized way, and he'll tell everything. He really wants to talk about it."

"How serious is his wound?" Lucy asked.

"Not bad. Bailey's a good shot. He aimed for the arm and got it. If he had wanted to shoot him dead, he could have done that."

"Thank God he was here," Lucy said with a shudder.

Curious, Barbara thought, how no one voiced what they all knew was true—Elders had been building up to killing Frank.

She turned to David, who had remained silent for the most part. "We'll have to talk, and I'll have some things to attend to, but the charges will be dismissed. I doubt that your presence will be required. You'll be free to go anywhere you want, get on with your life."

"I'm rather committed to finishing a book with Alex," David

said, "and there's unfinished business with Darren. No Oxford this year or maybe ever, my apartment's sublet for the year, and I'm on sabbatical. Seems I'm not going anywhere soon, but I don't have to keep imposing on Shelley and Alex. I'll get out of their hair."

"David, we have a perfectly good apartment," Lucy said. "I want someone to be here in the house. I would welcome you as a tenant."

Amy flushed a deep red, and David appeared startled.

Before he could respond Barbara stood and said, "Dad, maybe it's time to head for home, don't you think?"

He stood. "I do. I'll give you a call in a few days," he said to Lucy.

Barbara hesitated, then said, "Lucy and Amy, I'm very sorry to have caused this terrible situation today. I deliberately pushed Elders without taking into account possible unintended consequences. I apologize."

David walked to the door with Barbara and Frank, where he embraced her, kissed her cheek, and said, "Thank you. Not only for this outcome, but a lot of things along the way. Thank you." He opened the door and they walked out.

Frank went across the lawn with her to Bailey's car still parked in Elders's driveway. Other cars were still there, as detectives were making a thorough search of the property.

"Come on to the house," Frank said, opening the car door. "We'll haul Darren and Todd over and order in some dinner. I think you and I deserve it."

"Will you forgive me?" she asked. "I put you at risk, and caused Bailey to get hurt. I'm so sorry."

He drew her to him and held her close for a moment. "Ah, Bobby, Bobby. Let's go home and drink some wine and talk about lettuces and things."

She had tears in her eyes when she got behind the wheel. Go home, she thought. There would be the trouble at the clinic, Darren's position there, new tensions, new problems. She started to drive. But they'd deal with them. They would deal with them.

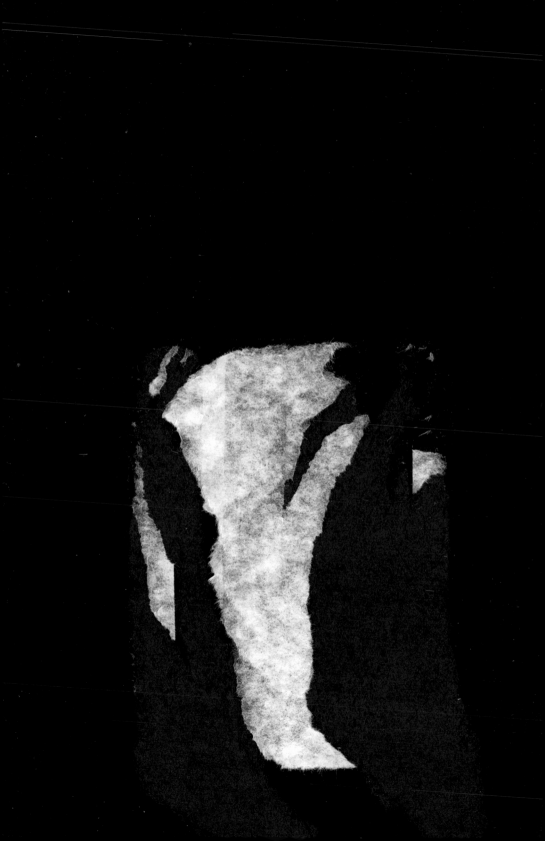